IN THE BEGINNING...

FIRST VOYAGES takes the reader on an exciting journey back to the early days of science fiction. In these first stories written by science fiction's most masterful writers is found the groundwork for modern SF. Here are the technical genius and the dramatic gifts of Heinlein, the wry wit of deCamp, Sturgeon's pyrotechnic inventiveness, the nightmare world of van Vogt, del Rey's pathos, the human insights of Budrys, Anderson's hypnotic style, Clarke's intellect, Aldiss' grotesquerie—and more.

FIRST VOYAGES

EDITED BY DAMON KNIGHT, MARTIN H. GREENBERG &
JOSEPH D. OLANDER

AVON
PUBLISHERS OF BARD, CAMELOT AND DISCUS BOOKS

FIRST VOYAGES is an original publication of Avon Books. This work has never before appeared in book form.

"The Isolinguals," "The Faithful," "Black Destroyer," "Life-Line," "Ether Breather," "Loophole," "Tomorrow's Children," and "That Only a Mother" were originally published in *Astounding Science Fiction,* Copyright 1937, 1938, 1939, 1946, 1947, 1948 by Street & Smith Publications, Inc.

"Walk to the World" was originally published in *Space Science Fiction,* Copyright 1952 by Space Publications, Inc.

"T" was originally published in *Nebula Science Fiction,* Copyright © 1956 by Peter Hamilton.

The above titles were first collected in *Now Begins Tomorrow,* edited by Damon Knight, Copyright © 1963 by Damon Knight.

AVON BOOKS
A division of
The Hearst Corporation
959 Eighth Avenue
New York, New York 10019

Copyright ©1981 by Martin Greenberg, Damon Knight and Joseph Olander
Published by arrangement with the authors
Library of Congress Catalog Card Number: 80-69937
ISBN: 0-380-77586-7

First Avon Printing, May, 1981

Printed in the U.S.A.

ACKNOWLEDGMENTS

"The Isolinguals," by L. Sprague de Camp. Copyright © 1937 by Street & Smith Publications, Inc.; Copyright renewed. Reprinted by permission of the author.

"The Faithful," by Lester del Rey. Copyright © 1938 by Street & Smith Publications, Inc.; Copyright renewed. Reprinted by permission of the Scott Meredith Literary Agency, Inc., 845 Third Avenue, New York, New York 10022.

"Black Destroyer," by A. E. van Vogt. Copyright © 1939 by Street & Smith Publications, Inc.; Copyright renewed. Reprinted by permission of Forrest J Ackerman, Ackerman Sci-Fi Agency, 2495 Glendower Ave., Hollywood, California 90067.

"Life-Line," by Robert A. Heinlein. Copyright © 1939 by Street & Smith Publications, Inc.; Copyright renewed. Reprinted by permission of the author.

"Ether Breather," by Theodore Sturgeon. Copyright © 1939 by Street & Smith Publications, Inc.; Copyright renewed. Reprinted by permission of the author.

"Proof," by Hal Clement. Copyright © 1942 by Street & Smith Publications, Inc.; Copyright renewed. Reprinted by permission of the author.

"Loophole," by Arthur C. Clarke. Copyright © 1946 by Street & Smith Publications, Inc.; Copyright renewed. Reprinted by permission of the Scott Meredith Literary Agency, Inc., 845 Third Ave., New York, New York 10022.

"Tomorrow's Children," by Poul Anderson. Copyright © 1947 by Street & Smith Publications, Inc.; Copyright renewed. Reprinted by permission of the author.

"That Only a Mother," by Judith Merril. Copyright © 1948 by Street & Smith Publications, Inc.; Copyright renewed. Reprinted by permission of the author and the author's agent, Virginia Kidd, 538 E. Hartford St., Milford, Pennsylvania 18337. Introduction adapted by permission of the author and her agent, Virginia Kidd, from *The Best of Judith Merril*, copyright © 1976 by Judith Merril.

CONTENTS

INTRODUCTION

In an earlier version of this book I pointed out a curious fact about famous science fiction writers: rather than trudging slowly through the apprentice and journeyman stages, they emerge with instant and explosive brilliance.

There are exceptions, of course; Ray Bradbury, Frederik Pohl, and Isaac Asimov were published for years before anybody realized how good they were. Who remembers Gardner Dozois's first story? Who remembers *mine*? (Nobody, I hope. I did allow it to be resurrected briefly by the appropriately named *UnEarth* magazine, but only to demonstrate that there is hope for any young writer, no matter how rotten.)

It is possible (I tell myself) that the superstars began by writing junk, but that it was so awful it never got published; or, alternatively, that they didn't begin to write until they were past thirty and had all their brain cells. Either or both of these explanations may be true. But I like to think that the writers I admire really did step full-grown out of the egg, like the offspring of Dejah Thoris and John Carter in the Mars books of Edgar Rice Burroughs. The record tells us nothing to the contrary.

My collaborators, Martin H. Greenberg and Joseph D. Olander, suggested the new version of this book and did much more than their part of the work. To the original list of ten authors—de Camp, del Rey, van Vogt, Heinlein, Sturgeon, Clarke, Anderson, Merril, Budrys, and Aldiss—we have added ten more: Hal Clement, Cordwainer Smith, Charles L. Harness, Katherine MacLean, Zenna Henderson, Philip K. Dick, Edgar Pangborn, Avram Davidson, J. G. Ballard, and Ursula K. Le Guin.

To paraphrase something I said in the introduction to the earlier version, there would be a hell of a hole in science fiction if these twenty writers had never been born. Without them, the sf magazines might still be lumbering along in the old girl-vs.-bug-eyed-monster pattern, or, more likely, be as extinct as Big Little Books. Reading their stories as a group, and realizing that each one was the first bright glimpse of an enduring talent, I think you will find them as fascinating as I do.

DAMON KNIGHT

THE ISOLINGUALS

by L. Sprague de Camp

Thirty years ago I heard the editor of the Ladies' Home
Journal *say in a speech that fiction writing is the only
craft that gets harder with practice. He meant that when
a writer has once used a story idea, the next time he must
dig deeper into his unconscious for another. I have found
it true. Forty-odd years ago there seemed to be plenty of
theretofore unused ideas of the "what if?" kind floating
around, waiting to be captured in print.*

*When I re-read my early works I wince at the crudity
of the writing; but I suppose that's life. To be accurate,
"The Isolinguals" is No. 3 in my opus-card file. No. 1 is
Schuyler Miller's and my novel* Genus Homo, *completed
later, and No. 2 a little caveman tale, "The Hairless Ones
Come." Since both were published well after "The Isolinguals," the latter will serve very well as a "first voyage."*

Nick looked at the cop, and the cop looked at Nick. The
fruit vendor's friendly smile suddenly froze. The cop didn't
know it, but something had gone *ping* inside Nick's head.
He wasn't Niccolo Franchetti any longer. He was Decimus
Agricola, engineering officer of the good old XXXIInd
Legion. He had been standing behind his ballista, laying it
for the Parthians' next charge. Of the crew, only he and
two privates had not been struck down by the Asiatics'
terrible arrows.

Then something awful had happened: the vast red rock

1

desert of Mesopotamia had vanished, and with it the swirling masses of hostile cavalry, the heaps of dead and
wounded, and everything else. One of the ballista crew
was gone likewise; the other had metamorphosed into this
fat fellow in the tight clothes. His catapult had, in the
same twinkling, become a little two-wheeled wagon piled
with fruit. He was standing on a paved street, lined with
buildings of fantastic height.

Decimus blinked incredulously. Sorcery! Those Parthians were said to be good at it. The man looking at him
must be Cartoricus, the Gaulish replacement. *"Onere!"* he
shouted. "Load!"

The man in dark blue just stared. Decimus lost his
temper. "What's the matter, don't you understand good
Latin? They'll be at us again in a minute!" The man did
nothing. Decimus felt for his sword. It wasn't there. He
was wearing queer, uncomfortable clothes like the other.
He snatched an apple; at the touch of it his mind reeled.
It felt like a real apple, not a sorcerer's illusion. He bit into
it. Then stark terror seized him. He threw the apple at the
fat man and started to run.

Arthur Lindsley picked up the hand set. "Hello? . . .
Oh, it's you, Pierre. How's the esteemed son-in-law this
morning?"

"Fairish," replied the instrument. "I'm up at Rockefeller
Med. Bill Jenkins has a case that might interest you. None
of their high-powered psychiatrists have been able to do
a thing with it. Want to come up?"

Lindsley looked at his watch. "Let's see—my elementary biology class lets out at two thirty. I can come up
then."

"Fine. And could you round up a couple of good
linguists and bring 'em along?"

"Huh? What for?"

"Take too long to explain over the 'phone. Can you
bring them?"

"Well, there's Van Wyck over at Barnard, and Squier's
office is down the hall. Say, are you and Elsa going to have
Christmas dinner with us?"

"Sorry, but we promised my folks to have it with them
this year. Yeah, we're taking the train for Quebec next
Thursday. Thanks anyway. Now please bring some really
good language sharks. It might be important."

Professor Lindsley sighed as he hung up. He didn't look forward with much pleasure to the undiluted company of his two sons all day Christmas. Hugh would talk interminably about the vacuum-cleaner business. Malcolm would drape himself over the furniture and make languid remarks in his newly acquired college voice about how art is all. What did Pierre mean by dragging Elsa off to spend Christmas with his Canuck parents? They were the only intelligent members of the family, besides himself—

Lindsley took the new Tenth Avenue Subway up to the Medical Center, with his two linguists in tow. Squier had been in, but not Van Wyck. A search of the language department had unearthed a Dr. Fedor Jevsky, who said he'd be ver-r-ry glad to come. Lindsley was a smallish man, very erect, with snapping eyes and a diminutive white beard. He looked odd, leading the rangy Squier and the obese Jevsky like a couple of puppies.

Dr. Jenkins' office was jammed. The thickset, shabby man was speaking: "It's just like I told the guys down at the hospital, doc; Mrs. Garfinkle and I been married ten years, and she never showed no symptoms or nothin'. We're just poor woiking people—"

Jenkins' bedside voice suddenly recovered its normal snap. "Come in, Arthur; I take it these are your linguists. I've got a queer job for them."

Pierre Lamarque's broad, coppery face grinned at his father-in-law from across the room. Jenkins was explaining: "—and all at once her normal personality went out like a light. She began talking this gibberish, and didn't know her husband or the city or anything else. That's just the trouble; we can't locate a single physical paranoiac symptom, and aphasia won't work either. Split personality, yes, but it doesn't explain her making up what seems to be a whole new language of her own. But that's not all. She's the third of these cases the hospital has received in twenty-four hours. Sure, naturally we gave 'em all the routine tests."

The telephone rang. "Yes? Oh, Lord! . . . Yes. . . . No. . . . Glad you let me know." Jenkins hung up. "Twelve more cases. Seems to be an epidemic."

"Jevsky had inclined his globular form—it was impossible for him to bend—in front of the plain-looking woman on the chair. She seemed to be so earnestly trying to tell him something with that rush of strange syllables. He suddenly seemed to catch something, for he barked at her what sounded like "Haybye-ded-yow?"

The rush of sound stopped, and the woman's face broke into a grateful smile. Then the torrent began again.

Jevsky wasn't listening. He spoke to Jenkins. "What foreign languages has Meesez Garfinkle studied?"

"None at all; she was born in New York City; both parents spoke English, at least of a sort; she left school at the end of the eighth grade. What do you think you've got, Dr. Jevsky?"

"I'm not sure, but it might be Gothic."

"What!"

The vast shoulders shrugged. "I know it sounds crazy, but *habai-dêdjau* means "if I had' in Gothic. I don't really know the language, except for a few fragments like that; nor, I theenk, will many of my colleagues. You, Dr. Squier?"

The other linguist shook his head. "The Celtic languages are my specialty. But I suppose there's at least one Gothic scholar in New York City. There's at least one of everything else."

Jenkins shook *his* head. "No, gentlemen, it's hardly worth trying to dig one up on such a fantastic hypothesis. Guess we have a new form of dementia here. Sorry I hauled you up; she acted so rational that I thought you might find something. By the way, what *is* Gothic?"

Squier answered: "The language of the ancient Goths; it's more or less the common ancestor of English, Dutch, and German. A complicated affair with about nine thousand useless inflections. We have only a partial knowledge of it."

The telephone rang again. When Jenkins had hung up, he swore. "More cases. They're coming in regularly now. They've got one who seems to be talking some kind of English dialect, and they're bringing him up here. Suppose you all stick around for a while."

They stood or sat on the floor. Lindsley argued with one of the Rockefeller psychiatrists about politics. The biologist thought Slidell and his so-called Union Party were a real menace, that they were aiming for a dictatorship and were pretty good shots. The psychiatrist didn't; he admitted that Slidell was a fanatical demagogue and all that, but said that if the other parties would stop trying to cut each other's throats they could squash the would-be dictator overnight.

At last the hospital men brought in a slim, blond youth with a harassed expression. Jenkins rose. "I understand you're—"

The young man interrupted. He spoke a peculiar English, rather like a strong Irish brogue. "If thou're going to ask me who I be, like the rest of these knaves, my name is Sergeant Ronald Blake, of the theerd company of Noll Croomle's foot, and a mor-r-tal enemy of ahl Papists! Now are ye satisfied?"

Squier said, "Whose foot? I mean, how do you spell him?"

The youth frowned. "I'm no clerk, but I bethink me 'tis C-r-o-m-w-e-l-l, Croomle."

Lindsley spoke up, "What year is it?"

"Certainly, 'tis the year of our Lord sixteen forty-eight."

The scientists looked at one another.

Jenkins said, "We seem to be getting somewhere, but I'm not sure just where. Young man, suppose you tell us just what happened."

"Well, I had gone home on leave, and my wife asked me to go down to the butcher's, and I had just toorned on the main street o' the village when I spied my old friend Hawks. 'Hoy, Ronald,' he says, 'how's the brave soldyer lad? And is't true thou wert at Naseby?' So I began to tell him ahl about the great battle, and how at the end the Cavaliers fled like rabbits, with their long hair streamin' out behind—" The voice from the past, if such it was, rolled on and on. Sergeant Blake was evidently a man who believed in getting in all the details.

Later, Lindsley and his son-in-law sat in the former's office. Tobacco smoke crawled bluely up through the rays of the desk lamp.

"Something's gone haywire," said the professor. "I can't believe this is an ordinary form of insanity, or any extraordinary form, either. How can you explain how Mike Watrous, package dispatcher at a department store, a young man of little learning and few talents, not only gets the idea that he's a sergeant in the Parliamentary army in the English Civil War, but also acquires a complete biography, personality, and accent to go with it?

How many literate people, let alone those of Mike's background and tastes, know that Oliver Cromwell pronounced his name 'Croomle'? In most cases of this kind the victim thinks he's Napoleon or Julius Caesar, but after the delusion has come on he doesn't know any more about Napoleon or Caesar, really, than he did before."

Lamarque shrugged. "Any other hypothesis I can think of seems equally crazy, unless you're going to admit the transmigration of souls, or some such nonsense. Suppose I caught this disease, or whatever it is, and thought I was the first Lamarque, who came over to Canada in 1746, or thereabouts. I wouldn't have the vaguest idea of how to go about talking eighteenth-century French."

Lindsley sighed. "And now they want us to drop everything we're doing and try to help them out. I wish they made these psychiatrists—and that includes our friend Jenkins—learn enough advanced biology so they wouldn't come running to us when they get stumped. But I suppose we'll have to go through the motions, anyway. The worst of it is that I haven't the foggiest notion of where to start—"

Hans Rumpel was making a speech. He was in fine form. His Yorktown audience drank in his flood of words, his piercing yells, his windmill gestures. "Red plot. . . . Jewish assassins. . . . Destruction of civilization—" he screeched.

Hans faltered; his oratory died away to a mumble. His audience was mildly surprised to see him going through the motions of stroking an imaginary beard. Then his voice rose again, this time not in English, but in mournful Hebrew. He was, in fact, reciting a Hebrew service, just as he—not Hans Rumpel, but Levi ben Eliezar, a respected rabbi of the Hasidim—had been reciting it in a Krakow synagogue in the year 1784. The would-be saviors of civilization from the horrors of democratic government looked at one another. Was he another of those cases they had been reading about? Hans stopped his chant, gaped at his audience, and fell on his knees. He was praying with mountain-moving fervor—

Professor Lindsley emerged from behind the tarn of books and papers and threw his eye shade in the corner. "Pierre! Let's cut this damn nonsense and get some breakfast. It's seven o'clock."

Lamarque appeared. "Any luck? None here, either. Can't find anything definite, although Minakuchi's paper on ancestral memory in rats might be worth following up."

Lindsley frowned. "Something you said the day before yesterday gave me an idea, but it popped out of my mind like a watermelon seed, before I could grab it. I've been trying to think of it ever since. Must be getting old."

Later, Lamarque made a face. "With all the advances in our modern civilization, nobody has yet found how to make a drug store serve good coffee. Oh, remind me to wire Quebec and tell the folks the Christmas dinner is off. What's the latest from Jenkins?"

"More of the same. At the present rate every hospital in New York will be full in a couple of days, and all the medicos in town are running around in circles, and the psychiatrists are just dithering. Bill says they're fairly sure it isn't infectious, from what case histories they've been able to trace. And *we* aren't any further than when we started—"

Sunday, in the new church on Tremont Avenue, the Bronx, H. Perkins rolled his eyes around so that he could see the congregation. Pretty miserable showing. Why had the vestry wanted to build this church, anyway? He'd heard a lot about the "return to religion" since 1950, but they didn't seem to be returning to *his* denomination. Such a worried-looking lot, too! Between the threat of a dictatorship by that bellowing mounteback, Slidell, and the strange plague of insanity, he didn't wonder. What would happen if Slidell got in?

H. Perkins passed down the aisle with his most seraphic expression. The "plate"—a most unplatelike object, when you thought of it—was coming toward him again, giving forth a pleasant clink as each coin went into it. He reached over and took it from Mrs. Dinwiddie—and it was as though meek H. Perkins had never been. He, Joshua Hardy, had been standing on a heaving deck yelling to the verminous crew the commands from "Old Pegleg." They'd just sighted a Spaniard, and were cracking on sail to have a closer look. Might be the monthly treasure ship from Colon. And here he was, in the aisle of a church, surrounded by people in strange clothes, and holding a little velvet bag with two dark wood handles.

Josh was too impulsive to make a really top-notch

pirate. He shook the bag; to his ears came that sweetest of sounds, the clink of coin. Better grab the loot and run, boys. "Avast, ye lubbers," he roared. "*Give* me that!" He snatched the other little bag. "Ho, you over there, stand and deliver! *Where* in fifteen thousand bloody hells is my cutlass?" He raced down the aisle to cut off the fellow with the remaining bag. Too late! The chase pounded out into the street—

Professor Lindsley slammed down his brief case. "I'm about ready to give up and go in for the transmigration of souls after all," he said wrathfully to Lamarque, who was peering into a microscope. On the microscope slide was a bit of nerve tissue of one of the cases who had gotten himself killed by an automobile.

Lindsley continued: "They're going to start a concentration camp for new cases, as every institution for miles around is full. The roads leading out of New York are jammed; people are leaving. Glad we sent our women-folks off to Quebec while you could still buy transportation. A driver of a Madison Avenue bus had a seizure and ran his bus into a hydrant between Fifty-third and Fifty-fourth Streets. What's new around here?"

"If you mean research, nothing. But the first case in the university faculty has happened."

"Huh? Tell me about it, quick!"

"It was in the lunch room. You know Calderwood, the mathematician? As sane and sober a man as you'll find. Well, at lunch to-day he jumped up with a howl and began throwing things. Then he got into the kitchen and chased everybody out with a carving knife.

"But the best part happened next. Some of them watched him around a corner. He marched into the dining room, took off his pants, pulled a tablecloth off one of the tables, and wound it around his waist like a skirt. Then he stuck the knife through one of his garters.

"He must have been a sketch. Wish I'd been there to see. He strutted up and down for a while, apparently challenging the people, in his own lingo, to come back and fight.

"Well, our friend Squier heard the fuss and came up. Squier had a bright idea. He talked Gaelic to Calderwood, and he calmed down right away. Seems he wasn't Graham Calderwood any more, but the terrible Gavin MacTaggart, a wild Highlander looking for a MacDonald throat to cut. If he couldn't have a MacDonald, a Gordon would do. They got him rounded up eventually."

Lindsley took off his glasses and rubbed his red-rimmed eyes. "You're an unfeeling young devil. How'd you like to be a member of poor Graham's family? Did you see about my classes?"

"Yeah. One of your students in advanced biology is down too! Arne Holmgren. Know him? He thinks he's a Viking. When they took him away he was roaring some early Scandinavian battle-song; at least, that's what I suppose it was. Say, hadn't you better get some sleep? You can't work efficiently if you don't, you know."

Lindsley started to snap back an irritated reply, but checked himself. "Maybe you're right, Pierre. When my normally saintly disposition starts to go sour there's something wrong. If anybody 'phones, tell 'em you don't know when I'll be back."

Chase Burge lay on his back with his eyes closed, enjoying the last moment of his doze. His conscience, which woke up a little more slowly than the rest of him, showed signs of stirring. He shouldn't have lost his temper yesterday in that argument. But, damn it, Hobart was so rabid on the subject.

Then he sat up suddenly, the last vapors of sleep gone from his brain. How had he gotten into this strange room? He'd gone to bed perfectly sober. He'd been snatched! He sprang from the bed.

The door opened and a man in a dressing gown walked into the room. Chase tensed himself to spring; but, no, the man might have a gun. Better find out what it was all about.

"Morning, son," said the kidnaper. "I think one of my shirts strayed into your bureau—"

"Where am I?" snarled Chase.

"Where— Oh, my Lord—" The gray-haired man looked at him with a horrified expression. "You've got it, too!"

"Got what? What did you kidnap me for? My folks haven't any dough to speak of!"

The other man composed himself with an effort. "Who do you think you are? No, I mean that as a serious question."

"I'm Chase Burge, of 351 West 55th Street, and I demonstrate automobiles for a living. Who are *you?*"

"I'm Chase Burge. Senior, that is. You're Chase Burge, Junior, and I'm your father."

"No, you're not. My father's dead, and he didn't look like you anyway. Is this a funny way of adopting me, or what?"

Chase Burge, Senior, sat down with a perplexed expression. "Let me explain. You just think you're me. But you're really me—no, I mean you're you. You're your own son, really; that is, you're the son of the man you think you are, but who is really me. Oh dear, I wish I could explain! It's this way: you're suffering a delusion that you're your own father—"

Chase interrupted. "You sound like something out of Gilbert and Sullivan. If anybody has delusions around here it's —uk!" His hand had touched his chin. In a flash he was at the mirror.

"Holy Moses, where did I get this D'Artagnan effect? Have I been unconscious long?"

"Why, you've been wearing that goatee for five years. Lots of the young men wear them."

Chase Burge, Junior, began to laugh hysterically. "Oh, Lord, I guess I am crazy! I know, this is a loony bin that I've been shut up in. I'm crazy, and so are you, unless you're one of the keepers."

Pierre Lamarque threw down *his* brief case. "I think I have something, but I'm not sure."

"Let's have it, quick!" barked Lindsley.

"Let me begin at the beginning. I was down at the hospital looking over the new cases. They had one who they said was an Englishman of about 1300. I couldn't understand him at all, never realized how fast the language changes. He told us we were a 'pock of foals,' which didn't make much sense, until a professor told me it meant 'pack of fools.'

"But the prize exhibit was one of the new cases from out of town—a Mrs. Rhodes of White Plains. They told me she was—or had been—one of the outstanding uplifters of her community; during the revival of prohibition agitation twelve years ago she was one of the leading lights in the movement.

"Well, you ought to see her now! She chatters in Renaissance Italian, and slinks around with a snaky glide you wouldn't believe possible for a lady prohibitionist in her forties. She'd made a dead set for all the doctors in the place, until they're scared to be alone with her. Says she's Elena della Colleoni.

"That gave me an idea, so I stopped in at the library, and found that there really was such a person as Elena della Colleoni." Lamarque grinned wickedly. "She was a notorious strumpet at the court of Cesare Borgia."

Lindsley polished his glasses slowly. Lamarque knew that meant an idea coming, and kept still.

"I—think—I—begin—to see," said the older biologist. "First, the cases, when we catch them, all act scared to death, but otherwise perfectly sane, except that they've acquired the personality of some one, real or imaginary, who lived before them.

"Secondly, the pseudopsyche is always an individual who might conceivably have been the case's direct ancestor, as in the case of the redcap over in the Jersey Heights Terminal who thought he was a Zulu warrior and tried to use a traveler's umbrella as an assagai. Sometimes the descent would be difficult to trace, as in the case of Mrs. Rhodes-Colleoni, but you go back enough generations and you could be almost anybody's descendant. In one case—that of the young man who thought he was his own father—we know the phylogenic relationship of the case and its pseudopsyche for a fact.

"Thirdly, in at least some cases, and conceivably in all, the pseudopsyche corresponds to a person who really lived."

"But," objected Lamarque, "if they are real, how come the fact hasn't been noted before this?"

"Hm-m-m. Well, consider the ratio between the total number of people who've lived in the last couple of millennia and the number who were prominent enough to leave a historical record of their doings. You'll see how small the chances are of turning up any big shots.

"Fourthly, the average age of the pseudopsyche is around thirty. That doesn't prove anything by itself. Jerry Plotnik's revising the average to include the latest data now. But the age figures are much too closely grouped for a random distribution: no children, and hardly any elderly people.

"Now suppose—just suppose—that the pseudopsyche is a piece of ancestral memory that's gotten carried along in the germ cells, like a piece of ultra-microscopic motion-picture film, and suppose that something happens to substitute this carried-over memory for the case's real one. You'd think you're the ancestor whose memory you've been carrying around. For obvious reasons. It would end at a point before the time when the said ancestor's child from whom you're descended was conceived. Suppose we call the phenomenon genotropism. That's not a very good name, but it'll do until I think of a better one."

Lamarque whistled. "I hope if it happens to me that I'll be one of my French ancestors and not one of my oboriginal ones. I might be sort of unmanageable as an Ojibway Indian. But say, won't this knock Weismann's theory into a cocked hat?"

"If it's correct, it'll do worse than that. I'll have to eat what I've been saying for thirty years about Lamarkism's being a zombie among evolutionary theories. But remember, this idea of ours is still just an idea, and we haven't any *positive* evidence whatever yet. More than one scientist has been caught because he assumed that because a theory of his *might* account for certain facts, it therefore *was* the explanation."

"Uh-huh, I get you. But now that we have your theory, what are we going to do with it?"

"Damned if I know," said Lindsley, reaching for his pipe.

The manager of the "Venus" looked gloomily at his audience, if you could call it that. Everybody who could scrape up the price of a fare was trying to get out of town, and the rest weren't spending much on entertainment. You didn't feel safe on the streets any more. Still, burlesque was holding up better than any other form of entertainment: a lot of the movie places had closed. Then, too, a merciful providence had decreed that two of the "Venus'" biggest creditors should come down with the plague.

Betty Fiorelli was working up to the climax of her strip tease. A few more grinds and bumps, and more clothing had gone into the wings. He'd told her to give 'em the works. The cops weren't likely to send an inspector around at a time like this. A faint "Ah-h-h!" from the audience. But what was the girl up to? Instead of sidling coyly into the wings, she was standing squarely facing the audience, and her rich voice rolled out in verse after sonorous verse of classic Greek, which was just that to her hearers.

Three minutes later the few strollers on 42nd Street gaped incredulously at the sight of a tall and well-made young woman, clad—precisely in a pair of high-heeled shoes, speeding like an arrow along the sidewalk, while after her panted the manager of the "Venus" and three stage hands. They knew not that they pursued, not Betty Fiorelli, but Thea Tisimicles, the great poetess of Lemnos, whose contemporaries (of the Fifth Century B.C.) thought she surpassed even Sappho.

The fishy-eyed man was talking earnestly to Professor Lindsley: "O.K., but I think you scientific guys are nuts for not getting out while the getting's good. You can stay until we pull out the inner police cordon, and then out you go. There's no use keeping the cordon there when the gangs of iso—isolinguals have begun turning up all over New Joisey and Westchester. What does 'isolingual' mean, anyway?"

"It means they speak the same language. You can see how it is. A case speaks Anglo-Saxon, say. He wanders around until he runs into somebody else who speaks Anglo-Saxon, and they join up for purposes of offense and defense. Pretty soon you have a gang. Come in, Jerry. Dr. Plotnik, Detective Inspector Monahan. Dr. Plotnik's been helping us with the mathematical side of our research."

"You mean he's one of these lightning calculators?"

"Whoop! You'll insult him. He's a mathematical genius, which is something else."

The detective applied another match to his cigar. "Something's fishy about this whole business."

Plotnik gave a sort of gurgle. "You're telling us?"

"No, sonny, I didn't just mean the disease. The National Patriots have been showing all kinds of activity. We've been getting reports from the police all over the country. A lot of them have been filtering into New York, when everybody else is trying to get out. We've caught a few trying to get through the cordons. And the big bug who owns 'em, Slidell, has disappeared."

"What!" exclaimed Lindsley.

"Yeah. You ain't read about it in the papers, because they all been too busy with the plague. But it looks to me

—it almost looks—as if there might be a human origin to it."

"But how?" Plotnik stopped.

"I dunno. Maybe they poisoned the water. Thought I'd take a little run down below the cordon and see if we couldn't catch one of these tough babies that Slidell's been sending around to beat up people he don't like. Maybe we could find out why they ain't afraid of the plague. Like to come along?"

Plotnik stood up, almost upsetting his chair. "You get Pierre Lamarque to go instead of me; I just had an idea that'll take a little time to work out."

Snowflakes glided slantwise out of a gray January sky. "Better park here," said the detective, as Lindsley swung his car off Broadway at 72nd Street. "Won't do to go too far downtown. Look, there's another!"

Lindsley and Lamarque peered through the windows, and saw a hurrying figure slip into a doorway. There was something odd about the figure.

Lamarque spoke: "He's wearing a football helmet!"

"Huh?" said the detective, blinking. "Well, anyways, we're gonna take a closer look at his fancy headpiece. Got your guns, you two?" He slid out of the car, skidded a little on the snow, and steadied himself.

"Town's sure gonna get buried in snow, with nobody to remove it. Keep your eyes peeled for the isos."

The three marched abreast along the deserted street. Professor Lindsley almost stumbled over a body, half buried in the snow. He recognized a State trooper's uniform. He looked about, squinting against the snowflakes, and realized that the half dozen other darkish humps in the snow were also corpses. "Say, Monahan—"

"Sh-h! Want our friend to hear you? Now, Professor Lamarque, you stand on this side of the doorway and tackle him in the legs when he comes out. I'll do the rest."

Lamarque had given up trying to explain that he wasn't a full professor. Moreover, unless something was done about the plague soon, it looked as though he never *would* be a full professor. The university buildings were deserted save for a few dauntless scientists still trying to get at the cause and cure of the affliction.

"Remember," Monahan was whispering, "the foist guy that shows a sign of going nutty, one of the others taps him on the head, but gentlelike, see? We don't want no fractured skulls." He flipped his blackjack up and down to illustrate "gentlelike."

The black outline of a man, weaving slowly along the sidewalk, materialized out of the snowflakes. He came up to the ambuscade, saying something in a pleading whine.

"Naw, scram you!" hissed the detective, flipping his blackjack suggestively.

The man scrammed.

Lindsley looked nervously up and down the street, and at the two younger men beside the doorway, Damn it, he'd been a fool to come! Guerrilla warfare was no occupation for a sixty-year-old biology professor. He'd partly brought it on himself, by being the only man to present a plausible theory to the authorities—well, at least as plausible as any others. With New York City practically lost to civilized control they'd have listened to anybody. At the present rate, in another month New England and the Middle Atlantic States would be a wilderness, inhabited solely by roving bands of isolinguals who battled each other with clubs, rocks, and the loot of hardware stores.

Suppose some of them came along now? Thinking that they had been translated by magic into a strange and terrifying world, they were as dangerous as wild beasts. Lindsley wondered what it was like to shoot a man. And then the door opened and the man in the football helmet came out.

Lamarque tackled the fellow neatly below the knees. He got out one yell before the detective was all over him, kneeling on his ribs and stuffing snow in his mouth. Then Monahan yanked off the helmet and slapped the man's skull with his blackjack.

"Come on!" he snapped, getting up and dragging the body by the coat collar toward the car.

A cluster of figures loomed out of the semidarkness. Lindsley counted six—no, seven, and felt in his pocket for the pistol. The seven just stared. Monahan brought out *his* pistol. The seven gave back apprehensively. Evidently they'd had painful experience—perhaps in the Battle of Herald Square, when a National Guard detachment and a troop of State police had scattered a horde of embattled isolinguals, only to be seized themselves, many of them, and start killing each other.

One of the seven spoke up in what sounded like a Slavonic tongue. The detective tried to smile sweetly. "Can't understand you," he said, wagging his head. The leader's sign was audible above the hiss of the falling flakes, and the seven trudged off.

The detectives stuffed their captive into the car. Lindsley let in the clutch slowly; the right rear wheel spun a few revolutions and then gripped the snow.

Monahan yelled in his ear, "Step on it, doc!"

Lindsley jumped and tried to comply. In the mirror he had a glimpse of people swarming out of the doorway. A submachine gun crackled; a hole the diameter of a finger appeared in the windshield, surrounded by a spider web of cracks. Lindsley heard a gasp from the captive, and a stream of profanity from Monahan. "They got our prisoner, the—"

The car slithered around the corner of West End and 72nd. "Damn good thing this wasn't an old front-engined car," the rasping voice continued. "They'd have let daylight into us sure. Bet the rear end looks like a gravel sizer. Take it easy, doc; they can't see to shoot more'n a block or two."

Later Monahan said, "Nope, the stiff didn't have no papers on him, but I still think he's a National Patriot. How you coming along with those helmets?"

"All finished," replied Lindsley. "I've been standing over the analysts with a club for twenty-four hours. The shielding inside the helmet was a lead-bismuth-antimony alloy, with traces of platinum and two of the rare metals. My son-in-law's gone out to wire the specifications to Albany and Washington."

"Hope it ain't too late. We better clear out to-night, before any more of us come down with the plague."

"There's still one telephone wire open," continued Lindsley. "And the man I was talking to told me the first case has been reported from San Francisco. A scrub lady started doing a hula. Must be a Polynesian sailor in her family tree somewhere. I—ah—" The voice trailed off. Professor Arthur Lindsley was asleep.

A lurch and the clash of metal on metal awoke him. "Hey, what—"

The detective's heroic cursing left off. "You hurt? Guess we're all right. Hey, Joe, where the hell are we? Poughkeepsie? We're on our way to Albany, professor, or rather we *was* on our way before the truck pushed us into this here lamppost. Guess it was a case driving, from the way he weaved. Maybe I should 'a' tried to hunt up a 'plane."

Lamarque's voice came out of the dark: "Looks as if there's been another battle, from the corpses scattered around. Will that left door still open? Say, Monahan, don't you ever sleep?"

"Yeah, I grab a little now and then. Come on."

The drug store's shattered front gaped at them with a defeated air. Inside, the detective's flashlight dug a pallid clerk out from behind the soda fountain. "Don't shoot, please!" he quavered. "You're not isolinguals? A gang of 'em took over the town yesterday, and then this evening a bigger gang came along and drove 'em out. I thought they'd all gone and came down to open up shop, but some more came along just now. Look, quick, there they are again!"

"Stand back there!" roared Monahan. The figure in the doorway shouted something back, and the detective's pistol went off.

"Quick, you guys, pile the——" But the two scientists and the other cop were already furiously building a barricade of chairs and tables. A few stones sailed past their heads and made beautiful crashes among the glassware.

Lindsley peered over the top of the upturned table. A figure, wild in the moonlight, rose from the sidewalk and raised a length of pipe or something. Lindsley fumbled for his pistol. Where the devil was the safety catch on the thing? He pulled the trigger. As his senses cleared after the flash and report, he saw that the figure was still there. He gripped the gun in both hands and tried again. The figure doubled over and went *fthup!* in the slush.

Hours later Lamarque wiped his mouth on his sleeve. "If I drink another malted milk I'll get indigestion. What else have you, Mr. Bloom?"

"Sorry, sir, but the isos cleaned out all the pies and bread and things. And the gas is shut off, so I can't make any coffee. It'll have to be sodas or nothing, unless you want to try some cough drops."

"Ugh! Any luck on the 'phone, Joe?"

"Nope. Unless somebody finds us by dark it'll be just tough. They're waiting for that to rush us."

Unless somebody found them— There wouldn't be any street lights to shoot by. And four pistols wouldn't stop the horde of isolinguals waiting out of sight around the corners.

Darkness—no moon this time. The voices of the isos wafted into the drug store. The leaders were evidently haranguing their men. Then there was a full-throated yell, and the slopping of many feet in the slush. Bloom, the clerk, was carefully setting a row of bottles on the floor to use as missiles. If you didn't have a gun you had to use something.

Lamarque's pistol cracked. "Got one!"

Then the fusillade. But they came on in a solid mass. Lindsley thought, "These are really good, honest citizens I'm shooting, except for their malady." He realized that he had been squeezing the trigger of an empty gun. How the devil did you load the things? He'd never get it figured out before they swarmed in and finished them off. They were almost in the drug store now—

Monahan stopped his target practice to say, "Now why the hell are they all running one way? What's that noise? If it's a machine gun, boy, we're saved!"

Lindsley never imagined he'd find that implacable hammering the sweetest of sounds. The armored car skidded to a stop, and two football-helmeted soldiers jumped out.

Monahan turned to Lamarque. "What's that? Sorry, but I didn't get you. What? *Hey!*" He flung his arms around the young biologist in a bearlike hug. "Soldier! You got any more helmets?"

Lamarque's muttering rose to a frenzied shriek.

"Yeah, they're in the truck."

"*What* truck?"

"They were right behind us; ought to be along any— Yeah, here they come."

"Well, get one, quick! This guy's gone screwy like the others!"

When the helmet had been forced on Lamarque's unwilling head, Monahan rubbed his shins. "Lord, professor, I didn't know you was that strong. I guess the guy you toined into never loined no Queensbury rules or nothing. But you shouldn't have tried to bite me."

Lamarque was acutely embarrased. "I—I'm sorry. You

know I haven't any recollection of the past few minutes at all, up to the time you put the helmet on me——"

" 'S all right; it wasn't your fault. Now let's find some of the isos we winged and put helmets on them. . . ."

Forty-eight hours later, Lindsley rubbed his eyes. "What do you mean by waking me up at this time of day, you young scoundrel? Oh, the paper. What's the news, quick?"

Lamarque seated himself on the bed with his slightly satanic grin. "You guessed right. They sent the army down to surround the area we figured the radiations were coming from, or rather that Plotnik figured they were coming from by finding the mass center of the locations of the cases reported. They were all wearing our cute little helmets, so the radiations didn't affect them.

"When they closed in and started searching houses they rounded up several thousand National Patriots. There was a little shooting, but most of the N.P.'s surrendered quietly enough when they saw what they were up against.

"The military located the cause of the whole works in an old house on Christopher Street. The place was full of radio apparatus from cellar to roof. They found Slidell himself, and his master mind, a Dr. Falk, whom nobody ever heard of, but who modestly describes himself as the greatest scientist of the age. Maybe he's right.

"This Falk got scared when he saw bayonets pointed at his stomach, and let out the whole story. Seems he found a complicated combination of harmonics on a long radio wave that would work this ancestral-memory switch, and he and Slidell figured to disorganize the whole country with it. And when his broadcasting set was turned off and everybody became himself again, we'd find Slidell installed as dictator and the N.P.'s running everything. Of course, in the meantime they'd be wearing the helmets and would be shielded from the radiations.

"The army turned the thing off right away, and all our medieval knights and yeomen are now ordinary citizens, and busy picking up the pieces. Slidell, of course, made a speech. Too bad there wasn't a stenographer there to record it. I suppose he and Falk will be shot for murder, treason, and every other crime on the books, though I think they could plead insanity with some justice.

"Oh, yes, you're now the head of the department, and

I'm a full professor. Also, we're famous, and are about to be intensively photographed and interviewed."

Lindsley scratched his diminutive beard. "Seems to me, Pierre, that we're getting away with murder. Plotnik really figured out the source of those radiations, and Monahan had the idea of suspecting the N.P.'s and setting out to catch one."

"Don't worry about them. They're getting their share of the glory."

"I suppose so. But right now what I want is a vacation from all scientific thought."

THE FAITHFUL

by Lester del Rey

Lester del Rey is a member of the distinguished club of fans-turned-writers—he first achieved recognition in the science fiction community as a frequent contributor to the letter columns of sf magazines. All the while, he was hard at work on his own stories and verse. Finally, "The Faithful" was accepted by Astounding Science Fiction *and published in the April, 1938 issue.*

"The Faithful" is typical of several stories that Lester del Rey wrote for John W. Campbell, Jr.—including his famous "Helen O'Loy" (December, 1938), "The Day Is Done" (May, 1939), and "Kindness" (October, 1944)—in that it radiates feeling and pathos. It is also notable for being one of those relatively rare first stories that was purportedly written on a dare.

—THE EDITORS

Today, in a green and lovely world, here in the mightiest of human cities, the last of the human race is dying. And we of Man's creation are left to mourn his passing, and to worship the memory of Man, who controlled all that he knew save only himself.

I am old, as my people go, yet my blood is still young and my life may go on for untold ages yet, if what this last of Men has told is true. And that also is Man's work, even as we and the Ape-People are his work in the last analysis. We of the Dog-People are old, and have lived a

21

long time with Man. And yet, but for Roger Stren, we might still be baying at the moon and scratching the fleas from our hides, or lying at the ruins of Man's empire in dull wonder at his passing.

There are earlier records of dogs who mouthed clumsily a few Man words, but Hungor was the pet of Roger Stren, and in the labored efforts at speech, he saw an ideal and a life work. The operation on Hungor's throat and mouth, which made Man-speech more nearly possible was comparatively simple. The search for other "talking" dogs was harder.

But he found five besides Hungor, and with this small start he began. Selection and breeding, surgery and training, gland implantation and X-ray mutation were his methods, and he made steady progress. At first money was a problem, but his pets soon drew attention and commanded high prices.

When he died, the original six had become thousands, and he had watched over the raising of twenty generations of dogs. A generation of my kind then took only three years. He had seen his small back-yard pen develop into a huge institution, with a hundred followers and students, and had found the world eager for his success. Above all, he had seen tail-wagging give place to limited speech in that short time.

The movement he had started continued. At the end of two thousand years, we had a place beside Man in his work that would have been inconceivable to Roger Stren himself. We had our schools, our houses, our work with Man, and a society of our own. Even our independence, when we wanted it. And our life span was not fourteen, but fifty or more years.

Man, too, had traveled a long way. The stars were almost within his grasp. The barren moon had been his for centuries. Mars and Venus lay beckoning, and he had reached them twice, but not to return. That lay close at hand. Almost, Man had conquered the universe.

But he had not conquered himself. There had been many setbacks to his progress because he had to go out and kill the others of his kind. And now, the memory from his past called again, and he went out in battle against himself. Cities crumbled to dust, the plains to the south became barren deserts again, Chicago lay covered in a green mist. That death killed slowly, so that Man fled from the city and died, leaving it an empty place. The mist hung there, clinging days, months, years—after Man had ceased to be.

I, too, went out to war, driving a plane built for my people, over the cities of the Rising Sun Empire. The tiny atomic bombs fell from my ship on houses, on farms, on all that was Man's, who had made my race what it was. For my Men told me I must fight.

Somehow, I was not killed. And after the last Great Drive, when half of Man was already dead, I gathered my people about me and we followed to the north, where some of my Men had turned to find a sanctuary from the war. Of Man's work, three cities still stood—wrapped in the green mist, and useless. And Man huddled around little fires and hid himself in the forest, hunting his food in small clans. Yet hardly a year of the war had passed.

For a time, the Men and my people lived in peace, planning to rebuild what had been, once the war finally ceased. Then came the Plague. The anti-toxin which had been developed was ineffective as the Plague increased in its virulency. It spread over land and sea, gripped Man who had invented it, and killed him. It was like a strong dose of strychnine, leaving Man to die in violent cramps and retchings.

For a brief time, Man united against it, but there was no control. Remorselessly it spread, even into the little settlement they had founded in the north. And I watched in sorrow as my Men around me were seized with its agony. Then we of the Dog-People were left alone in a shattered world from whence Man had vanished. For weeks we labored at the little radio we could operate, but there was no answer; and we knew that Man was dead.

There was little we could do. We had to forage our food as of old, and cultivate our crops in such small way as our somewhat modified forepaws permitted. And the barren north country was not suited to us.

I gathered my scattered tribes about me, and we began the long trek south. We moved from season to season, stopping to plant our food in the spring, hunting in the fall. As our sleds grew old and broke down, we could not replace them, and our travel became even slower. Sometimes we came upon our kind in smaller packs. Most of them had gone back to savagery, and these we had to mold to us by force. But little by little, growing in size, we drew south. We sought Men; for two hundred thousand years we of the Dog-People had lived with and for Man.

In the wilds of what had once been Washington State we came upon another group who had not fallen back to the law of tooth and fang. They had horses to work for them, even crude harnesses and machines which they could operate. There we stayed for some ten years, setting up a government and building ourselves a crude city. Where Man had his hands, we had to invent what could be used with our poor feet and our teeth. But we had found a sort of security, and had even acquired some of Man's books by which we could teach our young.

Then into our valley came a clan of our people, moving west, who told us they had heard that one of our tribes sought refuge and provender in a mighty city of great houses lying by a lake in the east. I could only guess that it was Chicago. Of the green mist they had not heard—only that life was possible there.

Around our fires that night we decided that if the city were habitable, there would be homes and machines designed for us. And it might be there were Men, and the chance to bring up our young in the heritage which was their birth-right. For weeks we labored in preparing ourselves for the long march to Chicago. We loaded our supplies in our crude carts, hitched our animals to them, and began the eastward trip.

It was nearing winter when we camped outside the city, still mighty and imposing. In the sixty years of its desertion, nothing had perished that we could see; the fountains to the west were still playing, run by automatic engines.

We advanced upon the others in the dark, quietly. They were living in a great square, littered with filth, and we noted that they had not even fire left from civilization. It was a savage fight, while it lasted, with no quarter given nor asked. But they had sunk too far, in the lazy shelter of Man's city, and the clan was not as large as we had heard. By the time the sun rose there was not one of them but had been killed or imprisoned until we could train them to our ways. The ancient city was ours, the green mist gone after all those years.

Around us were abundant provisions, the food factories which I knew how to run, the machines that Man had made to fit our needs, the houses in which we could dwell, power drawn from the bursting core of the atom which needed only the flick of a switch to start. Even without hands, we could live here in peace and security for ages. Perhaps here my dreams of adapting our feet to handle Man's tools and doing his work were possible, even if no Men were found.

We cleared the muck from the city and moved into Greater South Chicago, where our people had had their section of the city. I, and a few of the elders who had been taught by their fathers in the ways of Man, set up the old regime, and started the great water and light machines. We had returned to a life of certainty.

And four weeks later, one of my lieutenants brought Paul Kenyon before me. Man! Real and alive, after all this time! He smiled, and I motioned my eager people away.

"I saw your lights," he smiled. "I thought at first some men had come back, but that is not to be; but civilization still has its followers, evidently, so I asked one of you to take me to the leader. Greetings from all that is left of Man!"

"Greetings," I gasped. It was like seeing the return of the gods. My breath was choked; a great peace and fufillment surged over me. "Greetings, and the blessings of your God. I had no hope of seeing Man again."

He shook his head. "I am the last. For fifty years I have been searching for men—but there are none. Well, you have done well. I should like to live among you, work with you—when I can. I survived the Plague somehow, but it comes on me yet, more often now, and I can't move nor care for myself then. That is why I have come to you.

"Funny." He paused. "I seem to recognize you. Hungor Beowulf, XIV? I am Paul Kenyon. Perhaps you remember me? No? Well, it was a long time, and you were young. But that white streak under the eye still shows." A greater satisfaction came to me that he remembered me.

Now one had come among us with hands, and he was of great help. But most of all, he was of the old Men, and gave point to our working. But often, as he had said, the old sickness came over him, and he lay in violent convulsions, from which he was weak for days. We learned to care for him, when he needed it, even as we learned to fit our society to his presence. And at last, he came to me with a suggestion.

"Hungor," he said, "if you had one wish, what would it be?"

"The return of Man. The old order, where we could work together. You know as well as I how much we need Man."

He grinned crookedly. "Now, it seems, Man needs you more. But if that were denied, what next?

"Hands," I said. "I dream of them at night and plan for them by day, but I will never see them."

"Maybe you will, Hungor. Haven't you ever wondered why you go on living, twice normal age, in the prime of your life? Have you never wondered how I have withstood the Plague which still runs in my blood, and how I still seem only in my thirties, though nearly seventy years have passed since a man has been born?"

"Sometimes." I answered. "I have no time for wonder, now, and when I do— Man is the only answer I have."

"A good answer," he said. "Yes, Hungor, Man is the answer. That is why I remember you. Three years before the war, when you were just reaching maturity, you came into my laboratory. Do you remember?"

"The experiment," I said. "That is why you remember me?"

"Yes, the experiment. I altered your glands somewhat, implanted certain tissues into your body, as I had done to myself. I was seeking the secret of immortality. Though there was no reaction at the time, it worked, and I don't know how much longer we may live—or you may; it helped me resist the Plague, but did not overcome it."

So that was the answer. He stood staring at me a long time. "Yes, unknowingly, I saved you to carry on Man's future for him. But we were talking of hands.

"As you know, there is a great continent to the east of the Americas, called Africa. But did you know Man was working there on the great apes, as he was working here on your people? We never made as much progress with them as with you. We started too late. Yet they spoke a simple language and served for common work. And we changed their hands so the thumb and fingers opposed, as do mine. There, Hungor, are your hands."

Now Paul Kenyon and I laid plans carefully. Out in the hangars of the city there were aircraft designed for my people's use; heretofore I had seen no need of using them. The planes were in good condition, we found on examination, and my early training came back to me as I took the first ship up. They carried fuel to circle the globe ten times, and out in the lake the big fuel tanks could be drawn on when needed.

Together, though he did most of the mechanical work between spells of sickness, we stripped the planes of all their war equipment. Of the six hundred planes, only two were useless, and the rest would serve to carry some two thousand passengers in addition to the pilots. If the apes had reverted to complete savagery, we were equipped with tanks of anaesthetic gas by which we could overcome them and strap them in the planes for the return. In the houses around us, we built accommodations for them strong enough to hold them by force, but designed for their comfort if they were peaceable.

At first, I had planned to lead the expedition. But Paul Kenyon pointed out that they would be less likely to respond to us than to him. "After all," he said, "men educated them and cared for them, and they probably remember us dimly. But your people they know only as the wild dogs who are their enemies. I can go out and contact their leaders, guarded of course by your people. But otherwise, it might mean battle."

Each day I took up a few of our younger ones in the planes and taught them to handle the controls. As they were taught, they began the instruction of others. It was a task which took months to finish, but my people knew the need of hands as well as I; any faint hope was well worth trying.

It was late spring when the expedition set out. I could follow their progress by means of television, but could work the controls only with difficulty. Kenyon, of course, was working the controls at the other end, when he was able.

They met with a storm over the Atlantic Ocean, and three of the ships went down. But under the direction of my lieutenant and Kenyon the rest weathered the storm. They landed near the ruins of Capetown, but found no trace of the Ape-People. Then began weeks of scouting over the jungles and plains. They saw apes, but on capturing a few they found them only the primitive creatures which nature had developed.

It was by accident they finally met with success. Camp had been made near a waterfall for the night, and fires had been lit to guard against the savage beasts which roamed the land. Kenyon was in one of his rare moments of good health. The telecaster had been set up in a tent near the outskirts of the camp, and he was broadcasting a complete account of the day. Then, abruptly, over the head of the Man was raised a rough and shaggy face.

He must have seen the shadow, for he started to turn sharply, then caught himself and moved slowly around. Facing him was one of the apes. He stood there silently, watching the ape, not knowing whether it was savage or well-disposed. It, too, hesitated; then it advanced.

"Man—Man," it mouthed. "You came back. Where were you? I am Tolemy, and I saw you, and I came."

"Tolemy," said Kenyon, smiling. "It is good to see you, Tolemy. Sit down; let us talk. I am glad to see you. Ah, Tolemy, you look old; were your father and mother raised by Man?"

"I am eighty years, I think. It is hard to know. I was raised by Man long ago. And now I am old; my people say I grow too old to lead. They do not want me to come to you, but I know Man. He was good to me. And he had coffee and cigarettes."

"I have coffee and cigarettes, Tolemy." Kenyon smiled. "Wait, I will get them. And your people, is not life hard among them in the jungle? Would you like to go back with me?"

"Yes, hard among us. I want to go back with you. Are you many here?"

"No, Tolemy." He set the coffee and cigarettes before the ape, who drank eagerly and lit the smoke gingerly from a fire. "No, but I have friends with me. You must bring your people here, and let us get to be friends. Are there many of you?"

"Yes. Ten times we make ten tens—a thousand of us,

almost. We are all that was left in the city of Man after the great fight. A Man freed us, and I led my people away, and we lived here in the jungle. They wanted to be in small tribes, but I made them one, and we are safe. Food is hard to find."

"We have much food in a big city, Tolemy, and friends who will help you, if you work for them. You remember the Dog-People, don't you? And you would work with them as with Man if they treated you as Man treated you, and fed you, and taught your people?"

"Dogs? I remember the Man-dogs. They were good. But here the dogs are bad. I smelled dog here; it was not like the dog we smell each day, and my nose was not sure. I will work with Man-dogs, but my people will be slow to learn them."

Later telecasts showed rapid progress. I saw the apes come in by twos and threes and meet Paul Kenyon, who gave them food, and introduced my people to them. This was slow, but as some began to lose their fear of us, others were easier to train. Only a few broke away and would not come.

Cigarettes that Man was fond of—but which my people never used—were a help, since they learned to smoke with great readiness.

It was months before they returned. When they came there were over nine hundred of the Ape-People with them, and Paul and Tolemy had begun their education. Our first job was a careful medical examination of Tolemy, but it showed him in good health, and with much of the vigor of a younger ape. Man had been lengthening the ages of his kind, as it had ours, and he was evidently a complete success.

Now they have been among us three years, and during that time we have taught them to use their hands at our instructions. Overhead the great monorail cars are running, and the factories have started to work again. They are quick to learn, with a curiosity that makes them eager for new knowledge. And they are thriving and multiplying here. We need no longer bewail the lack of hands; perhaps, in time to come, with their help, we can change our forepaws further, and learn to walk on two legs, as did Man.

Today I have come back from the bed of Paul Kenyon.

We are often together now—perhaps I should include the faithful Tolemy—when he can talk, and among us there has grown a great friendship. I laid certain plans before him today for adapting the apes mentally and physically until they are men. Nature did it with an ape-like brute once; why can we not do it with the Ape-People now? The Earth would be peopled again, science would rediscover the stars, and Man would have a foster child in his own likeness.

And—we of the Dog-People have followed Man for two hundred thousand years. That is too long to change. Of all Earth's creatures, the Dog-People alone have followed Man thus. My people cannot lead now. No dog was ever complete without the companionship of Man. The Ape-People will be Men.

It is a pleasant dream, surely not an impossible one.

Kenyon smiled as I spoke to him, and cautioned me in the jesting way he uses when most serious, not to make them too much like Man, lest another Plague destroy them. Well, we can guard against that. I think he, too, had a dream of Man reborn, for there was a hint of tears in his eyes, and he seemed pleased with me.

There is but little to please him now, alone among us, wracked by pain, waiting the slow death he knows must come. The old trouble has grown worse, and the Plague has settled harder on him.

All we can do is give him sedatives to ease the pain now, though Tolemy and I have isolated the Plague we found in his blood. It seems a form of cholera, and with that information, we have done some work. The old Plague serum offers a clue, too. Some of our serums have seemed to ease the spells a little, but they have not stopped them.

It is a faint chance. I have not told him of our work, for only a stroke of luck will give us success before he dies.

Man is dying. Here in our laboratory, Tolemy keeps repeating something; a prayer, I think it is. Well, maybe the God whom he has learned from Man will be merciful, and grant us success.

Paul Kenyon is all that is left of the old world which Tolemy and I loved. He lies in the ward, moaning in agony, and dying. Sometimes he looks from his windows and sees the birds flying south; he gazes at them as if he would never see them again. Well, will he? Something he muttered once comes back to me:

"For no man knoweth—"

BLACK DESTROYER

by A. E. van Vogt

"Black Destroyer" was for me writing by system about a system. I have discussed in other publications my 800-word scene with its five steps. So here I shall dwell on the sentences and the words in them.

Notice the sentences at the beginning of BD: "On and on Coeurl prowled. The black, moonless, almost starless night yielded reluctantly . . ." etc. Each word was chosen for the sound of the letters in it—I had my own theory, gleaned from various sources, of what those sounds evoked from a reader, even though they were merely read and not spoken aloud.

What we have here is the evocation of mood, atmosphere and—at the end of paragraph two—purpose: the alien being is looking for food on an almost foodless planet.

So that when the human-manned spaceship lands, Coeurl is right there, cunning, merciless, desperate for their flesh. But, of course, as author I had read Oswald Spengler's "Decline of the West," with its theory of cyclic history. And so the human scientists aboard that marvelous spaceship represent the peak of earth culture. They analyze that here is a being at the final cycle of the historical development of his race.

Accordingly, despite Coeurl's super ability to use energy, they defeat him with their system understanding.

Use of mood words, and action verbs (avoidance of the verb "to be" as much as possible), and presentation of unusual concepts, these were my early interests in writing *science fiction. "Black Destroyer" was one of four (out of five) of my earliest stories in the genre in which I utilized what turned out to be a dynamic combination.*

The story idea itself, as with most of my stories, came to me in a dream.

On and on Coeurl prowled! The black, moonless, almost starless night yielded reluctantly before a grim reddish dawn that crept up from his left. A vague, dull light, it was, that gave no sense of approaching warmth, no comfort, nothing but a cold, diffuse lightness, slowly revealing a nightmare landscape.

Black, jagged rock, and black, unliving plain took form around him, as a pale-red sun peered at last above the grotesque horizon. It was then Coeurl recognized suddenly that he was on familiar ground.

He stopped short. Tenseness flamed along his nerves. His muscles pressed with sudden, unrelenting strength against his bones. His great forelegs—twice as long as his hindlegs—twitched with a shuddering movement that arched every razor-sharp claw. The thick tentacles that sprouted from his shoulders ceased their weaving undulation, and grew taut with anxious alertness.

Utterly appalled, he twisted his great cat head from side to side, while the little hairlike tendrils that formed each ear vibrated frantically, testing every vagrant breeze, every throb in the ether.

But there was no response, no swift tingling along his intricate nervous system, not the faintest suggestion anywhere of the presence of the all-necessary id. Hopelessly, Coeurl crouched, an enormous catlike figure silhouetted against the dim reddish skyline, like a distorted etching of a black tiger resting on a black rock in a shadow world.

He had known this day would come. Through all the centuries of restless search, this day had loomed ever nearer, blacker, more frightening—this inevitable hour when he must return to the point where he began his systematic hunt in a world almost depleted of id-creatures.

The truth struck in waves like an endless, rhythmic ache at the seat of his ego. When he had started, there had been a few id-creatures in every hundred square miles, to be

mercilessly rooted out. Only too well Coeurl knew in this
ultimate hour that he had missed none. There were no id-
creatures left to eat. In all the hundreds of thousands of
square miles that he had made his own by right of ruthless
conquest—until no neighboring coeurl dared to question
his sovereignty—there was no id to feed the otherwise
immortal engine that was his body.

Square foot by square foot he had gone over it. And
now—he recognized the knoll of rock just ahead, and the
black rock bridge that forced a queer, curling tunnel to his
right. It was in that tunnel he had lain for days, waiting
for the simple-minded, snakelike id-creature to come forth
from its hole in the rock to bask in the sun—his first kill
after he had realized the absolute necessity of organized
extermination.

He licked his lips in brief gloating memory of the moment his slavering jaws tore the victim into precious tooth-
some bits. But the dark fear of an idless universe swept
the sweet remembrance from his consciousness, leaving
only certainty of death.

He snarled audibly, a defiant, devilish sound that quavered on the air, echoed and re-echoed among the rocks,
and shuddered back along his nerves—instinctive and hellish expression of his will to live.

And then—abruptly—it came.

He saw it emerge out of the distance on a long downward slant, a tiny glowing spot that grew enormously into
a metal ball. The great shining globe hissed by above
Coeurl, slowing visibly in quick deceleration. It sped over
a black line of hills to the right, hovered almost motionless
for a second, then sank down out of sight.

Coeurl exploded from his startled immobility. With tiger
speed, he flowed down among the rocks. His round, black
eyes burned with the horrible desire that was an agony
within him. His ear tendrils vibrated a message of id in
such tremendous quantities that his body felt sick with the
pangs of his abnormal hunger.

The little red sun was a crimson ball in the purple-black
heavens when he crept up from behind a mass of rock and
gazed from its shadows at the crumbling, gigantic ruins of
the city that sprawled below him. The silvery globe, in
spite of its great size, looked strangely inconspicuous
against that vast, fairylike reach of ruins. Yet about it was

a leashed aliveness, a dynamic quiescence that, after a moment, made it stand out, dominating the foreground. A massive, rock-crushing thing of metal, it rested on a cradle made by its own weight in the harsh, resisting plain which began abruptly at the outskirts of the dead metropolis.

Coeurl gazed at the strange, two-legged creatures who stood in little groups near the brilliantly lighted opening that yawned at the base of the ship. His throat thickened with the immediacy of his need; and his brain grew dark with the first wild impulse to burst forth in furious charge and smash these flimsy, helpless-looking creatures whose bodies emitted the id-vibrations.

Mists of memory stopped that mad rush when it was still only electricity surging through his muscles. Memory that brought fear in an acid stream of weakness, pouring along his nerves, poisoning the reservoirs of his strength. He had time to see that the creatures wore things over their real bodies, shimmering transparent material that glittered in strange, burning flashes in the rays of the sun.

Other memories came suddenly. Of dim days when the city that spread below was the living, breathing heart of an age of glory that dissolved in a single century before flaming guns whose wielders knew only that for the survivors there would be an ever-narrowing supply of id.

It was the remembrance of those guns that held him there, cringing in a wave of terror that blurred his reason. He saw himself smashed by balls of metal and burned by searing flame.

Came cunning—understanding of the presence of these creatures. This, Coeurl reasoned for the first time, was a scientific expedition from another star. In the older days, the coeurls had thought of space travel, but disaster came too swiftly for it ever to be more than a thought.

Scientist meant investigation, not destruction. Scientists in their way were fools. Bold with his knowledge, he emerged into the open. He saw the creatures become aware of him. They turned and stared. One, the smallest of the group, detached a shining metal rod from a sheath, and held it casually in one hand. Coeurl loped on, shaken to his core by the action; but it was too late to turn back.

Commander Hal Morton heard little Gregory Kent, the chemist, laugh with the embarrassed half gurgle with

which he invariably announced inner uncertainty. He saw
Kent fingering the spindly metalite weapon.

Kent said: "I'll take no chances with anything as big as
that."

Commander Morton allowed his own deep chuckle to
echo along the communicators. "That," he grunted finally,
"is one of the reasons why you're on this expedition, Kent—
because you never leave anything to chance."

His chuckle trailed off into silence. Instinctively, as he
watched the monster approach them across that black rock
plain, he moved forward until he stood a little in advance
of the others, his huge form bulking the transparent metalite suit. The comments of the men pattered through the
radio communicator into his ears:

"I'd hate to meet that baby on a dark night in an alley."

"Don't be silly. This is obviously an intelligent creature.
Probably a member of the ruling race."

"It looks like nothing else than a big cat, if you forget
those tentacles sticking out from its shoulders, and make
allowances for those monster forelegs."

"Its physical development," said a voice, which Morton
recognized as that of Siedel, the psychologist, "presupposes
an animal-like adaptation to surroundings, not an intellectual one. On the other hand, its coming to us like this is
not the act of an animal but of a creature possessing a
mental awareness of our possible identity. You will notice
that its movements are stiff, denoting caution, which suggests fear and consciousness of our weapons. I'd like to get
a good look at the end of its tentacles. If they taper into
handlike appendages that can really grip objects, then the
conclusion would be inescapable that it is a descendant of
the inhabitants of this city. It would be a great help if we
could establish communication with it, even though appearances indicate that it has degenerated into a historyless
primitive."

Coeurl stopped when he was still ten feet from the fore-
most creature. The sense of id was so overwhelming that
his brain drifted to the ultimate verge of chaos. He felt as
if his limbs were bathed in molten liquid; his very vision
was not quite clear, as the sheer sensuality of his desire
thundered through his being.

The men—all except the little one with the shining metal
rod in his fingers—came closer. Coeurl saw that they were

frankly and curiously examining him. Their lips were moving, and their voices beat in a monotonous, meaningless rhythm on his ear tendrils. At the same time he had the sense of waves of a much higher frequency—his own communication level—only it was a machinelike clicking that jarred his brain. With a distinct effort to appear friendly, he broadcast his name from his ear tendrils, at the same time pointing at himself with one curving tentacle.

Gourlay, chief of communications, drawled: "I got a sort of static in my radio when he wiggled those hairs, Morton. Do you think—

"Looks very much like it," the leader answered the unfinished question. "That means a job for you, Gourlay. If it speaks by means of radio waves, it might not be altogether impossible that you can create some sort of television picture of its vibrations, or teach him the Morse code."

"Ah," said Siedel. "I was right. The tentacles each develop into seven strong fingers. Provided the nervous system is complicated enough, those fingers could, with training, operate any machine."

Morton said: "I think we'd better go in and have some lunch. Afterward, we've got to get busy. The material men can set up their machines and start gathering data on the planet's metal possibilities, and so on. The others can do a little careful exploring. I'd like some notes on architecture and on the scientific development of this race, and particularly what happened to wreck the civilization. On earth civilization after civilization crumbled, but always a new one sprang up in its dust. Why didn't that happen here? Any questions?"

"Yes. What about pussy? Look, he wants to come in with us."

Commander Morton frowned, an action that emphasized the deep-space pallor of his face. "I wish there was some way we could take it in with us, without forcibly capturing it. Kent, what do you think?"

"I think we should first decide whether it's an it or a him, and call it one or the other. I'm in favor of him. As for taking him in with us—" The little chemist shook his head decisively. "Impossible. This atmosphere is twenty-eight percent chlorine. Our oxygen would be pure dynamite to his lungs."

The commander chuckled. "He doesn't believe that, apparently." He watched the catlike monster follow the first two men through the great door. The men kept an anxious distance from him, then glanced at Morton questioningly. Morton waved his hand. "O.K. Open the second lock and let him get a whiff of the oxygen. That'll cure him."

A moment later, he cursed his amazement. "By Heaven, he doesn't even notice the difference! That means he hasn't any lungs, or else the chlorine is not what his lungs use. Let him in! You bet he can go in! Smith, here's a treasure house for a biologist—harmless enough if we're careful. We can always handle him. But what a metabolism!"

Smith, a tall, thin, bony chap with a long, mournful face, said in an oddly forceful voice: "In all our travels, we've found only two higher forms of life. Those dependent on chlorine, and those who need oxygen—the two elements that support combustion. I'm prepared to stake my reputation that no complicated organism could ever adapt itself to both gases in a natural way. At first thought I should say here is an extremely advanced form of life. This race long ago discovered truths of biology that we are just beginning to suspect. Morton, we mustn't let this creature get away if we can help it."

"If his anxiety to get inside is any criterion," Commander Morton laughed, "then our difficulty will be to get rid of him."

He moved into the lock with Coeurl and the two men. The automatic machinery hummed; and in a few minutes they were standing at the bottom of a series of elevators that led up to the living quarters.

"Does that go up?" One of the men flicked a thumb in the direction of the monster.

"Better send him up alone, if he'll go in."

Coeurl offered no objections until he heard the door slam behind him, and the closed cage shot upward. He whirled with a savage snarl, his reason swirling into chaos. With one leap, he pounced at the door. The metal bent under his plunge, and the desperate pain maddened him. Now, he was all trapped animal. He smashed at the metal with his paws, bending it like so much tin. He tore great bars loose with his thick tentacles. The machinery screeched; there were horrible jerks as the limitless power pulled the cage along in spite of projecting pieces of metal that scraped the outside walls. And then the cage stopped, and he snatched off the rest of the door and hurtled into the corridor.

He waited there until Morton and the men came up with drawn weapons. "We're fools," Morton said. "We should have shown him how it works. He thought we'd double-crossed him."

He motioned to the monster, and saw the savage glow fade from the coal-black eyes as he opened and closed the door with elaborate gestures to show the operation.

Coeurl ended the lesson by trotting into the large room to his right. He lay down on the rugged floor, and fought down the electric tautness of his nerves and muscles. A very fury of rage against himself for his fright consumed him. It seemed to his burning brain that he had lost the advantage of appearing a mild and harmless creature. His strength must have startled and dismayed them.

It meant greater danger in the task which he now knew he must accomplish: To kill everything in the ship, and take the machine back to their world in search of unlimited id.

With unwinking eyes, Coeurl lay and watched the two men clearing away the loose rubble from the metal doorway of the huge old building. His whole body ached with the hunger of his cells for id. The craving tore through his palpitant muscles, and throbbed like a living thing in his brain. His every nerve quivered to be off after the men who had wandered into the city. One of them, he knew, had gone—alone.

The dragging minutes fled; and still he restrained himself, still he lay there watching, aware that the men knew he watched. They floated a metal machine from the ship to the rock mass that blocked the great half-open door, under the direction of a third man. No flicker of their fingers escaped his fierce stare, and slowly, as the simplicity of the machinery became apparent to him, contempt grew upon him.

He knew what to expect finally, when the flame flared in incandescent violence and ate ravenously at the hard rock beneath. But in spite of his preknowledge, he deliberately jumped and snarled as if in fear, as that white heat burst forth. His ear tendrils caught the laughter of the men, their curious pleasure at his simulated dismay.

The door was released, and Morton came over and went inside with the third man. The latter shook his head.

"It's a shambles. You can catch the drift of the stuff. Obviously, they used atomic energy, but . . . but it's in wheel form. That's a peculiar development. In our science, atomic energy brought in the nonwheel machine. It's possible that here they've progressed—*further* to a new type of wheel mechanics. I hope their libraries are better preserved than this, or we'll never know. What could have happened to a civilization to make it vanish like this?"

A third voice broke through the communicators: "This is Siedel. I heard your question, Pennons. Psychologically and sociologically speaking, the only reason why a territory becomes uninhabited is lack of food."

"But they're so advanced scientifically, why didn't they develop space flying and go elsewhere for their food?"

"Ask Gunlie Lester," interjected Morton. "I heard him expounding some theory even before we landed."

The astronomer answered the first call. "I've still got to verify all my facts, but this desolate world is the only planet revolving around that miserable red sun. There's nothing else. No moon, not even a planetoid. And the nearest star system is *nine hundred light-years* away.

"So tremendous would have been the problem of the ruling race of this world, that in one jump they would not only have had to solve interplanetary but interstellar space traveling. When you consider how slow our own development was—first the moon, then Venus—each success leading to the next, and after centuries to the nearest stars; and last of all to the anti-accelerators that permitted galactic travel. Considering all this, I maintain it would be impossible for any race to create such machines without practical experience. And, with the nearest star so far away, they had no incentive for the space adventuring that makes for experience."

Coeurl was trotting briskly over to another group. But now, in the driving appetite that consumed him, and in the frenzy of his high scorn, he paid no attention to what they were doing. Memories of past knowledge, jarred into activity by what he had seen, flowed into his consciousness in an ever developing and more vivid stream.

From group to group he sped, a nervous dynamo—
jumpy, sick with his awful hunger. A little car rolled up,
stopping in front of him, and a formidable camera whirred
as it took a picture of him. Over on a mound of rock, a
gigantic telescope was rearing up toward the sky. Nearby,
a disintegrating machine drilled its searing fire into an
ever-deepening hole, down and down, straight down.

Coeurl's mind became a blur of things he watched with
half attention. And ever more imminent grew the moment
when he knew he could no longer carry on the torture of
acting. His brain strained with an irresistible impatience;
his body burned with the fury of his eagerness to be off
after the man who had gone alone into the city.

He could stand it no longer. A green foam misted his
mouth, maddening him, he saw that, for the bare moment,
nobody was looking.

Like a shot from a gun, he was off. He floated along in
great, gliding leaps, a shadow among the shadows of the
rocks. In a minute, the harsh terrain hid the spaceship and
the two-legged beings.

Coeurl forgot the ship, forgot everything but his purpose, as if his brain had been wiped clear by a magic,
memory-erasing brush. He circled widely, then raced into
the city, along deserted streets, taking short cuts with the
ease of familiarity, through gaping holes in time-weakened
walls, through long corridors of moldering buildings. He
slowed to a crouching lope as his ear tendrils caught the id
vibrations.

Suddenly, he stopped and peered from a scatter of fallen rock. The man was standing at what must once have
been a window, sending the glaring rays of his flashlight
into the gloomy interior. The flashlight clicked off. The
man, a heavy-set, powerful fellow, walked off with quick,
alert steps. Coeurl didn't like that alertness. It presaged
trouble; it meant lightning reaction to danger.

Coeurl waited till the human being had vanished around
a corner, then he padded into the open. He was running
now, tremendously faster than a man could walk, because
his plan was clear in his brain. Like a wraith, he slipped
down the next street, past a long block of buildings. He
turned the first corner at top speed; and then, with dragging belly, crept into the half-darkness between the building and a huge chunk of débris. The street ahead was

barred by a solid line of loose rubble that made it like a valley, ending in a narrow, bottlelike neck. The neck had its outlet just below Coeurl.

His ear tendrils caught the log-frequency waves of whistling. The sound throbbed through his being; and suddenly terror caught with icy fingers at his brain. The man would have a gun. Suppose he leveled one burst of atomic energy—*one burst*—before his own muscles could whip out in murder fury.

A little shower of rocks streamed past. And then the man was beneath him. Coeurl reached out and struck a single crushing blow at the shimmering transparent headpiece of the spacesuit. There was a tearing sound of metal and a gushing of blood. The man doubled up as if part of him had been telescoped. For a moment, his bones and legs and muscles combined miraculously to keep him standing. Then he crumpled with a metallic clank of his space armor.

Fear completely evaporated, Coeurl leaped out of hiding. With ravenous speed, he smashed the metal and the body within it to bits. Great chunks of metal, torn piecemeal from the suit, sprayed the ground. Bones cracked. Flesh crunched.

It was simple to tune in on the vibrations of the id, and to create the violent chemical disorganization that freed it from the crushed bone. The id was, Coeurl discovered, mostly in the bone.

He felt revived, almost reborn. Here was more food than he had had in the whole past year.

Three minutes, and it was over, and Coeurl was off like a thing fleeing dire danger. Cautiously, he approached the glistening globe from the opposite side to that by which he had left. The men were all busy at their tasks. Gliding noiselessly, Coeurl slipped unnoticed up to a group of men.

Morton stared down at the horror of tattered flesh, metal and blood on the rock at his feet, and felt a tightening in his throat that prevented speech. He heard Kent say:

"He *would* go alone, damn him!" The little chemist's voice held a sob imprisoned; and Morton remembered that

Kent and Jarvey had chummed together for years in the way only two men can.

"The worst part of it is," shuddered one of the men, "it looks like a senseless murder. His body is spread out like little lumps of flattened jelly, but it seems to be all there. I'd almost wager that if we weighed everything here, there'd still be one hundred and seventy-five pounds by earth gravity. That'd be about one hundred and seventy pounds here."

Smith broke in, his mournful face lined with gloom: "The killer attacked Jarvey, and then discovered his flesh was alien—uneatable. Just like our big cat. Wouldn't eat anything we set before him—" His words died out in sudden, queer silence. Then he said slowly: "Say, what about that creature? He's big enough and strong enough to have done this with his own little paws."

Morton frowned. "It's a thought. After all, he's the only living thing we've seen. We can't just execute him on suspicion, of course—"

"Besides," said one of the men, "he was never out of my sight."

Before Morton could speak, Siedel, the psychologist, snapped, "Positive about that?"

The man hesitated. "Maybe he was for a few minutes. He was wandering around so much, looking at everything."

"Exactly," said Siedel with satisfaction. He turned to Morton. "You see, commander, I, too, had the impression that he was always around; and yet, thinking back over it, I find gaps. There were moments—probably long minutes —when he was completely out of sight."

Morton's face was dark with thought, as Kent broke in fiercely: "I say, take no chances. Kill the brute on suspicion before he does any more damage."

Morton said slowly: "Korita, you've been wandering around with Cranessy and Van Horne. Do you think pussy is a descendant of the ruling class of this planet?"

The tall Japanese archeologist stared at the sky as if collecting his mind. "Commander Morton," he said finally, respectfully, "there is a mystery here. Take a look, all of you, at that majestic skyline. Notice the almost Gothic outline of the architecture. In spite of the megalopolis which they created, these people were close to the soil. The buildings are not simply ornamented. They are ornamental in themselves. Here is the equivalent of the Doric column, the Egyptian pyramid, the Gothic cathedral, growing out of the ground, earnest, big with destiny. If this lonely, desolate world can be regarded as a mother earth, then the land had a warm, a spiritual place in the hearts of the race.

"The effect is emphasized by the winding streets. Their machines prove they were mathematicians, but they were artists first; and so they did not create the geometrically designed cities of the ultra-sophisticated world metropolis. There is a genuine artistic abandon, a deep joyous emotion written in the curving and unmathematical arrangements of houses, buildings and avenues; a sense of intensity, of divine belief in an inner certainty. This is not a decadent, hoary-with-age civilization, but a young and vigorous culture, confident, strong with purpose.

"There it ended. Abruptly, as if at this point culture had its Battle of Tours, and began to collapse like the ancient Mohammedan civilization. Or as if in one leap it spanned the centuries and entered the period of contending states. In the Chinese civilization that period occupied 480–230 B.C., at the end of which the State of Tsin saw the beginning of the Chinese Empire. This phase Egypt experienced between 1780–1580 B.C., of which the last century was the 'Hyksos'—unmentionable—time. The classical experienced it from Chæronea—338—and, at the pitch of horror, from the Gracchi—133—to Actium—31 B.C. The West European Americans were devastated by it in the nineteenth and twentieth centuries, and modern historians agree that, nominally, we entered the same phase fifty years ago; though, of course, we have solved the problem.

"You may ask, commander, what has all this to do with your question? My answer is: there is no record of a culture entering abruptly into the period of contending states. It is always a slow development; and the first step is a merciless questioning of all that was once held sacred. Inner certainties cease to exist, are dissolved before the ruthless probings of scientific and analytic minds. The skeptic becomes the highest type of being.

"I say that this culture ended abruptly in its most flourishing age. The sociological effects of such a catastrophe would be a sudden vanishing of morals, a reversion to almost bestial criminality, unleavened by any sense of ideal, a callous indifference to death. If this . . . this pussy is a descendant of such a race, then he will be a cunning creature, a thief in the night, a cold-blooded murderer, who would cut his own brother's throat for gain."

"That's enough!" It was Kent's clipped voice. "Commander, I'm willing to act the rôle of executioner."

Smith interrupted sharply: "Listen, Morton, you're not going to kill that cat yet, even if he is guilty. He's a biological treasure house."

Kent and Smith were glaring angrily at each other. Morton frowned at them thoughtfully, then said: "Korita, I'm inclined to accept your theory as a working basis. But one question: Pussy comes from a period earlier than our own? That is, we are entering the highly civilized era of our culture, while he became suddenly historyless in the most vigorous period of his. *But* is it possible that his culture is a later one on this planet than ours is in the galactic-wide system we have civilized?"

"Exactly. His may be the middle of the tenth civilization of his world; while ours is the end of the eighth sprung from earth, each of the ten, of course, having been builded on the ruins of the one before it."

"In that case, pussy would not know anything about the skepticism that made it possible for us to find him out so positively as a criminal and murderer?"

"No; it would be literally magic to him."

Morton was smiling grimly. "Then I think you'll get your wish, Smith. We'll let pussy live; and if there are any fatalities, now that we know him, it will be due to rank carelessness. There's just the chance, of course, that we're wrong. Like Siedel, I also have the impression that he was always around. But now—we can't leave poor Jarvey here like this. We'll put him in a coffin and bury him."

"No, we won't!" Kent barked. He flushed. "I beg your pardon, commander. I didn't mean it that way. I maintain pussy wanted something from that body. It looks to be all there, but something must be missing. I'm going to find out what, and pin this murder on him so that you'll have to believe it beyond the shadow of a doubt."

*   *   *

It was late night when Morton looked up from a book and saw Kent emerge through the door that led from the laboratories below.

Kent carried a large, flat bowl in his hands; his tired eyes flashed across at Morton, and he said in a weary, yet harsh, voice: "Now watch!"

He started toward Coeurl, who lay sprawled on the great rug, pretending to be asleep.

Morton stopped him. "Wait a minute, Kent. Any other time, I wouldn't question your actions, but you look ill; you're overwrought. What have you got there?"

Kent turned, and Morton saw that his first impression had been but a flashing glimpse of the truth. There were dark pouches under the little chemist's gray eyes—eyes that gazed feverishly from sunken cheeks in an ascetic face.

"I've found the missing element," Kent said. "It's phosphorus. There wasn't so much as a square millimeter of phosphorus left in Jarvey's bones. Every bit of it had been drained out—by what superchemistry I don't know. There are ways of getting phosphorus out of the human body. For instance, a quick way was what happened to the workman who helped build this ship. Remember, he fell into fifteen tons of molten metalite—at least, so his relatives claimed—but the company wouldn't pay compensation until the metalite, on analysis, was found to contain a high percentage of phosphorus—"

"What about the bowl of food?" somebody interrupted. Men were putting away magazines and books, looking up with interest.

"It's got organic phosphorus in it. He'll get the scent, or whatever it is that he uses instead of scent—"

"I think he gets the vibrations of things," Gourlay interjected lazily. "Sometimes, when he wiggles those tendrils, I get a distinct static on the radio. And then, again, there's no reaction, just as if he's moved higher or lower on the wave scale. He seems to control the vibrations at will."

Kent waited with obvious impatience until Gourlay's last word, then abruptly went on: "All right, then, when he gets the vibration of the phosphorus and reacts to it like an animal, then—well, we can decide what we've proved by his reaction. Can I go ahead, Morton?"

"There are three things wrong with your plan," Morton

said. "In the first place, you seem to assume that he is only animal; you seem to have forgotten he may not be hungry after Jarvey; you seem to think that he will not be suspicious. But set the bowl down. His reaction may tell us something."

Coeurl stared with unblinking black eyes as the man set the bowl before him. His ear tendrils instantly caught the id-vibrations from the contents of the bowl—and he gave it not even a second glance.

He recognized this two-legged being as the one who had held the weapon that morning. Danger! With a snarl, he floated to his feet. He caught the bowl with the fingerlike appendages at the end of one looping tentacle, and emptied its contents into the face of Kent, who shrank back with a yell.

Explosively, Coeurl flung the bowl aside and snapped a hawser-thick tentacle around the cursing man's waist. He didn't bother with the gun that hung from Kent's belt. It was only a vibration gun, he sensed—atomic powered, but not an atomic disintegrator. He tossed the kicking Kent onto the nearest couch—and realized with a hiss of dismay that he should have disarmed the man.

Not that the gun was dangerous—but, as the man furiously wiped the gruel from his face with one hand, he reached with the other for his weapon. Coeurl crouched back as the gun was raised slowly and a white beam of flame was discharged at his massive head.

His ear tendrils hummed as they canceled the efforts of the vibration gun. His round, black eyes narrowed as he caught the movement of men reaching for their metalite guns. Morton's voice lashed across the silence.

"Stop!"

Kent clicked off his weapon; and Coeurl crouched down, quivering with fury at this man who had forced him to reveal something of his power.

"Kent," said Morton coldly, "you're not the type to lose your head. You deliberately tried to kill pussy, knowing that the majority of us are in favor of keeping him alive. You know what our rule is: If anyone objects to my decisions, he must say so *at the time*. If the majority object, my decisions are overruled. In this case, no one but you objected, and, therefore, your action in taking the law into your own hands is most reprehensible, and automatically debars you from voting for a year."

Kent stared grimly at the circle of faces. "Korita was right when he said ours was a highly civilized age. It's decadent." Passion flamed harshly in his voice. "My God, isn't there a man here who can see the horror of the situation? Jarvey dead only a few hours, and this creature, whom we all know to be guilty, lying there unchained, planning his next murder; and the victim is right here in this room. What kind of men are we—fools, cynics, ghouls —or is it that our civilization is so steeped in reason that we can contemplate a murderer sympathetically?"

He fixed brooding eyes on Coeurl. "You were right, Morton, that's no animal. That's a devil from the deepest hell of this forgotten planet, whirling its solitary way around a dying sun."

"Don't go melodramatic on us," Morton said. "Your analysis is all wrong, so far as I am concerned. We're not ghouls or cynics; we're simply scientists, and pussy here is going to be studied. Now that we suspect him, we doubt his ability to trap any of us. One against a hundred hasn't a chance." He glanced around. "Do I speak for all of us?"

"Not for me, commander!" It was Smith who spoke, and, as Morton stared in amazement, he continued: "In the excitement and momentary confusion, no one seems to have noticed that when Kent fired his vibration gun, the beam hit this creature squarely on his cat head—and didn't hurt him."

Morton's amazed glance went from Smith to Coeurl, and back to Smith again. "Are you certain it hit him? As you say, it all happened so swiftly—when pussy wasn't hurt I simply assumed that Kent had missed him."

"He hit him in the face," Smith said positively. "A vibration gun, of course, can't even kill a man right away —but it can injure him. There's no sign of injury on pussy, though, not even a singed hair."

"Perhaps his skin is a good insulation against heat of any kind."

"Perhaps. But in view of our uncertainty, I think we should lock him up in the cage."

While Morton frowned darkly in thought, Kent spoke up. "Now you're talking sense, Smith."

Morton asked: "Then you would be satisfied, Kent, if we put him in the cage?"

Kent considered, finally: "Yes. If four inches of micro-steel can't hold him, we'd better give him the ship."

Coeurl followed the men as they went out into the corridor. He trotted docilely along as Morton unmistakably motioned him through a door he had not hitherto seen. He found himself in a square, solid metal room. The door clanged metallically behind him; he felt the flow of power as the electric lock clicked home.

His lips parted in a grimace of hate, as he realized the trap, but he gave no other outward reaction. It occurred to him that he had progressed a long way from the sunk-into-primitiveness creature who, a few hours before, had gone incoherent with fear in an elevator cage. Now, a thousand memories of his powers were reawakened in his brain; ten thousand cunnings were, after ages of disuse, once again part of his very being.

He sat quite still for a moment on the short, heavy haunches into which his body tapered, his ear tendrils examining his surroundings. Finally, he lay down, his eyes glowing with contemptuous fire. The fools! The poor fools!

It was about an hour later when he heard the man—Smith—fumbling overhead. Vibrations poured upon him, and for just an instant he was startled. He leaped to his feet in pure terror—and then realized that the vibrations *were* vibrations, not atomic explosions. Somebody was taking pictures of the inside of his body.

He crouched down again, but his ear tendrils vibrated, and he thought contemptuously: the silly fool would be surprised when he tried to develop those pictures.

After a while the man went away, and for a long time there were noises of men doing things far away. That, too, died away slowly.

Coeurl lay waiting, as he felt the silence creep over the ship. In the long ago, before the dawn of immortality, the coeurls, too, had slept at night; and the memory of it had been revived the day before when he saw some of the men dozing. At last, the vibration of two pairs of feet, pacing, pacing endlessly, was the only human-made frequency that throbbed on his ear tendrils.

Tensely, he listened to the two watchmen. The first one walked slowly past the cage door. Then about thirty feet behind him came the second. Coeurl sensed the alertness of these men; knew that he could never surprise either while they walked separately. It meant—he must be doubly careful!

Fifteen minutes, and they came again. The moment they were past, he switched his senses from their vibrations to a vastly higher range. The pulsating violence of the atomic engines stammered its soft story to his brain. The electric dynamos hummed their muffled song of pure power. He felt the whisper of that flow through the wires in the walls of his cage, and through the electric lock of his door. He forced his quivering body into straining immobility, his senses seeking, searching to tune in on that sibilant tempest of energy. Suddenly, his ear tendrils vibrated in harmony—he caught the surging change into shrillness of that rippling force wave.

There was a sharp click of metal on metal. With a gentle touch of one tentacle, Coeurl pushed open the door, and glided out into the dully gleaming corridor. For just a moment, he felt contempt, a glow of superiority, as he thought of the stupid creatures who dared to match their wit against a coeurl. And in that moment, he suddenly thought of other coeurls. A queer, exultant sense of race pounded through his being; the driving hate of centuries of ruthless competition yielded reluctantly before pride of kinship with the future rulers of all space.

Suddenly, he felt weighed down by his limitations, his need for other coeurls, his aloneness—one against a hundred, with the stake all eternity; the starry universe itself beckoned his rapacious, vaulting ambition. If he failed, there would never be a second chance—no time to revive long-rotted machinery, and attempt to solve the secret of space travel.

He padded along on tensed paws—through the salon—into the next corridor—and came to the first bedroom door. It stood half open. One swift flow of synchronized muscles, one swiftly lashing tentacle that caught the unresisting throat of the sleeping man, crushing it; and the lifeless head rolled crazily, the body twitched once.

Seven bedrooms; seven dead men. It was the seventh taste of murder that brought a sudden return of lust, a pure, unbounded desire to kill, return of a millennium-old habit of destroying everything containing the precious id.

As the twelfth man slipped convulsively into death, Coeurl emerged abruptly from the sensuous joy of the kill to the sound of footsteps.

They were not near—that was what brought wave after wave of fright swirling into the chaos that suddenly became his brain.

The watchmen were coming slowly along the corridor toward the door of the cage where he had been imprisoned. In a moment, the first man would see the open door —and sound the alarm.

Coeurl caught at the vanishing remnants of his reason. With frantic speed, careless now of accidental sounds, he raced—along the corridor with its bedroom doors— through the salon. He emerged into the next corridor, cringing in awful anticipation of the atomic flame he expected would stab into his face.

The two men were together, standing side by side. For one single instant, Coeurl could scarcely believe his tremendous good luck. Like a fool the second had come running when he saw the other stop before the open door. They looked up, paralyzed, before the nightmare of claws and tentacles, the ferocious cat head and hate-filled eyes.

The first man went for his gun, but the second, physically frozen before the doom he saw, uttered a shriek, a shrill cry of horror that floated along the corridors—and ended in a curious gurgle, as Coeurl flung the two corpses with one irresistible motion the full length of the corridor. He didn't want the dead bodies found near the cage. That was his one hope.

Shaking in every nerve and muscle, conscious of the terrible error he had made, unable to think coherently, he plunged into the cage. The door clicked softly shut behind him. Power flowed once more through the electric lock.

He crouched tensely, simulating sleep, as he heard the rush of many feet, caught the vibration of excited voices. He knew when somebody actuated the cage audioscope and looked in. A few moments now, and the other bodies would be discovered.

"Siedel gone!" Morton said numbly. "What are we going to do without Siedel? And Breckenridge! And Coulter and— Horrible!"

He covered his face with his hands, but only for an

instant. He looked up grimly, his heavy chin outthrust as he stared into the stern faces that surrounded him. "If anybody's got so much as a germ of an idea, bring it out."

"Space madness!"

"I've thought of that. But there hasn't been a case of a man going mad for fifty years. Dr. Eggert will test everybody, of course, and right now he's looking at the bodies with that possibility in mind."

As he finished, he saw the doctor coming through the door. Men crowded aside to make way for him.

"I heard you, commander," Dr. Eggert said, "and I think I can say right now that the space-madness theory is out. The throats of these men have been squeezed to a jelly. No human being could have exerted such enormous strength without using a machine."

Morton saw that the doctor's eyes kept looking down the corridor, and he shook his head and groaned:

"It's no use suspecting pussy, doctor. He's in his cage, pacing up and down. Obviously heard the racket and— Man alive! You can't suspect him. That cage was built to hold literally *anything*—four inches of micro-steel—and there's not a scratch on the door. Kent, even you won't say, 'Kill him on suspicion,' because there can't be any suspicion, unless there's a new science here. Beyond anything we can imagine—"

"On the contrary," said Smith flatly, "we have all the evidence we need. I used the telefluor on him—you know the arrangement we have on top of the cage—and tried to take some pictures. They just blurred. Pussy jumped when the telefluor was turned on, as if he felt the vibrations.

"You all know what Gourlay said before? This beast can apparently receive and send vibrations of any lengths. The way he dominated the power of Kent's gun is final proof of his special ability to interfere with energy."

"What in the name of all the hells have we got here?" One of the men groaned. "Why, if he can control that power, and send it out in any vibrations, there's nothing to stop him killing all of us."

"Which proves," snapped Morton, "that he isn't invincible, or he would have done it long ago."

Very deliberately, he walked over to the mechanism that controlled the prison cage.

"You're not going to open the door!" Kent gasped, reaching for his gun.

"No, but if I pull this switch, electricity will flow through the floor, and electrocute whatever's inside. We've never had to use this before, so you had probably forgotten about it."

He jerked the switch hard over. Blue fire flashed from the metal, and a bank of fuses above his head exploded with a single bang.

Morton frowned. "That's funny. Those fuses shouldn't have blown! Well, we can't even look in, now. That wrecked the audios, too."

Smith said: "If he could interfere with the electric lock, enough to open the door, then he probably probed every possible danger and was ready to interfere when you threw that switch."

"At least, it proves he's vulnerable to our energies!" Morton smiled grimly. "Because he rendered them harmless. The important thing is, we've got him behind four inches of the toughest of metal. At the worst we can open the door and ray him to death. But first, I think we'll try to use the telefluor power cable—"

A commotion from inside the cage interrupted his words. A heavy body crushed against a wall, followed by a dull thump.

"He knows what we were trying to do!" Smith grunted to Morton. "And I'll bet it's a very sick pussy in there. What a fool he was to go back into that cage and does he realize it!"

The tension was relaxing; men were smiling nervously, and there was even a ripple of humorless laughter at the picture Smith drew of the monster's discomfiture.

"What I'd like to know," said Pennons, the engineer, "is, why did the telefluor meter dial jump and waver at full power when pussy made that noise? It's right under my nose here, and the dial jumped like a house afire!"

There was silence both without and within the cage, then Morton said: "It may mean he's coming out. Back, everybody, and keep your guns ready. Pussy was a fool to think he could conquer a hundred men, but he's by far the most formidable creature in the galactic system. He may come out of that door, rather than die like a rat in a trap. And he's just tough enough to take some of us with him—if we're not careful."

The men backed slowly in a sólid body; and somebody said: "That's funny. I thought I heard the elevator."

"Elevator!" Morton echoed. "Are you sure, man?"

"Just for a moment I was!" The man, a member of the crew, hesitated. "We were all shuffling our feet—"

"Take somebody with you, and go look. Bring whoever dared to run off back here—"

There was a jar, a horrible jerk, as the whole gigantic body of the ship careened under them. Morton was flung to the floor with a violence that stunned him. He fought back to consciousness, aware of the other men lying all around him. He shouted: "Who the devil started those engines!"

The agonizing acceleration continued; his feet dragged with awful exertion, as he fumbled with the nearest audioscope, and punched the engine-room number. The picture that flooded onto the screen brought a deep bellow to his lips:

"It's pussy! He's in the engine room—and we're heading straight out into space."

The screen went black even as he spoke, and he could see no more.

It was Morton who first staggered across the salon floor to the supply room where the spacesuits were kept. After fumbling almost blindly into his own suit, he cut the effects of the body-torturing acceleration, and brought suits to the semiconscious men on the floor. In a few moments, other men were assisting him; and then it was only a matter of minutes before everybody was clad in metalite, with antiacceleration motors running at half power.

It was Morton then who, after first looking into the cage, opened the door and stood, silent as the others crowded about him, to stare at the gaping hole in the rear wall. The hold was a frightful thing of jagged edges and horribly bent metal, and it opened upon another corridor.

"I'll swear," whispered Pennons, "that it's impossible. The ten-ton hammer in the machine shops couldn't more than dent four inches of micro with one blow—and we only heard one. It would take at least a minute for an atomic disintegrator to do the job. Morton, this is a super-being."

Morton saw that Smith was examining the break in the wall. The biologist looked up. "If only Breckenridge weren't dead! We need a metallurgist to explain this. Look!"

He touched the broken edge of the metal. A piece crumbled in his fingers and slithered away in a fine shower of dust to the floor. Morton noticed for the first time that there was a little pile of metallic débris and dust.

"You've hit it." Morton nodded. "No miracle of strength here. The monster merely used his special powers to interfere with the electronic tensions holding the metal together. That would account, too, for the drain on the telefluor power cable that Pennons noticed. The thing used the power with his body as a transforming medium, smashed through the wall, ran down the corridor to the elevator shaft, and so down to the engine room."

"In the meantime, commander," Kent said quietly, "we are faced with a super-being in control of the ship, completely dominating the engine room, and its almost unlimited power, and in possession of the best part of the machine shops."

Morton felt the silence, while the men pondered the chemist's words. Their anxiety was a tangible thing that lay heavily upon their faces, in every expression was the growing realization that here was the ultimate situation in their lives; their very existence was at stake, and perhaps much more. Morton voiced the thought in everybody's mind:

"Suppose he wins. He's utterly ruthless, and he probably sees galactic power within his grasp."

"Kent is wrong," barked the chief navigator. "The thing doesn't dominate the engine room. We've still got the control room, and that gives us *first* control of all the machines. You fellows may not know the mechanical set-up we have; but, though he can eventually disconnect us, we can cut off all the switches in the engine room *now*. Commander, why didn't you just shut off the power instead of putting us into spacesuits? At the very least you could have adjusted the ship to the acceleration."

"For two reasons," Morton answered. "Individually, we're safer within the force fields of our spacesuits. And we can't afford to give up our advantages in panicky moves."

"Advantages. What other advantages have we got?"

"We know things about him," Morton replied. "And right now, we're going to make a test. Pennons, detail five men to each of the four approaches to the engine room. Take atomic disintegrators to blast through the big doors. They're all shut, I noticed. He's locked himself in.

"Selenski, you go up to the control room and shut off everything except the drive engines. Gear them to the master switch, and shut them off all at once. One thing though—leave the acceleration on full blast. No anti-acceleration must be applied to the ship. Understand?"

"Aye, sir!" The pilot saluted.

"And report to me through the communicators if any of the machines start to run again." He faced the men. "I'm going to lead the main approach. Kent, you take No. 2; Smith, No. 3, and Pennons, No. 4. We're going to find out right now if we're dealing with unlimited science, or a creature limited like the rest of us. I'll bet on the last possibility."

Morton had an empty sense of walking endlessly, as he moved, a giant of a man in his transparent space armor, along the glistening metal tube that was the main corridor of the engine-room floor. Reason told him the creature had already shown feet of clay, yet the feeling that here was an invincible being persisted.

He spoke into the communicator: "It's no use trying to sneak up on him. He can probably hear a pin drop. So just wheel up your units. He hasn't been in that engine room long enough to do anything.

"As I've said, this is largely a test attack. In the first place, we could never forgive ourselves if we didn't try to conquer him now, before he's had time to prepare against us. But, aside from the possibility that we can destroy him immediately, I have a theory.

"The idea goes something like this: Those doors are built to withstand accidental atomic explosions, and it will take fifteen minutes for the atomic disintegrators to smash them. During that period the monster will have no power. True, the drive will be on, but that's straight atomic explosion. My theory is, he can't touch stuff like that; and in a few minutes you'll see what I mean—I hope."

His voice was suddenly crisp: "Ready, Selenski?"

"Aye, ready."

"Then cut the master switch."

The corridor—the whole ship, Morton knew—was abruptly plunged into darkness. Morton clicked on the dazzling light of his spacesuit; the other men did the same, their faces pale and drawn.

"Blast!" Morton barked into his communicator.

The mobile units throbbed; and then pure atomic flame ravened out and poured upon the hard metal of the door. The first molten droplet rolled reluctantly, not down, but up the door. The second was more normal. It followed a shaky downward course. The third rolled sideways—for this was pure force, not subject to gravitation. Other drops followed until a dozen streams trickled sedately yet unevenly in every direction—streams of hellish, sparkling fire, bright as fairy gems, alive with the coruscating fury of atoms suddenly tortured, and running blindly, crazy with pain.

The minutes ate at time like a slow acid. At last Morton asked huskily:

"Selenski?"

"Nothing yet, commander."

Morton half whispered: "But he must be doing something. He can't be just waiting in there like a cornered rat. Selenski?"

"Nothing, commander."

Seven minutes, eight minutes, then twelve.

"Commander!" It was Selenski's voice, taut. "He's got the electric dynamo running."

Morton drew a deep breath, and heard one of his men say:

"That's funny. We can't get any deeper. Boss, take a look at this."

Morton looked. The little scintillating streams had frozen rigid. The ferocity of the disintegrators vented in vain against metal grown suddenly invulnerable.

Morton sighed. "Our test is over. Leave two men guarding every corridor. The others come up to the control room."

He seated himself a few minutes later before the massive control keyboard. "So far as I'm concerned the test was a success. We know that of all the machines in the engine room, the most important to the monster was the electric dynamo. He must have worked in a frenzy of terror while we were at the doors."

"Of course, it's easy to see what he did," Pennons said. "Once he had the power he increased the electronic tensions of the door to their ultimate."

"The main thing is this," Smith chimed in. "He works with vibrations only so far as his special powers are concerned, and the energy must come from outside himself. Atomic energy in its pure form, not being vibration, he can't handle any differently than we can."

Kent said glumly: "The main point in my opinion is that he stopped us cold. What's the good of knowing that his control over vibrations did it? If we can't break through those doors with our atomic disintegrators, we're finished."

Morton shook his head. "Not finished—but we'll have to do some planning. First, though, I'll start these engines. It'll be harder for him to get control of them when they're running."

He pulled the master switch back into place with a jerk. There was a hum, as scores of machines leaped into violent life in the engine room a hundred feet below. The noises sank to a steady vibration of throbbing power.

Three hours later, Morton paced up and down before the men gathered in the salon. His dark hair was uncombed; the space pallor of his strong face emphasized rather than detracted from the outthrust aggressiveness of his jaw. When he spoke, his deep voice was crisp to the point of sharpness:

"To make sure that our plans are fully co-ordinated, I'm going to ask each expert in turn to outline his part in the overpowering of this creature. Pennons first!"

Pennons stood up briskly. He was not a big man, Morton thought, yet he looked big, perhaps because of his air of authority. This man knew engines, and the history of engines. Morton had heard him trace a machine through its evolution from a simple toy to the highly complicated modern instrument. He had studied machine development on a hundred planets; and there was literally nothing fundamental that he didn't know about mechanics. It was almost weird to hear Pennons, who could have spoken for a thousand hours and still only have touched upon his subject, say with absurd brevity:

"We've set up a relay in the control room to start and stop every engine rhythmically. The trip lever will work a hundred times a second, and the effect will be to create vibrations of every description. There is just a possibility that one or more of the machines will burst, on the principle of soldiers crossing a bridge in step—you've heard that old story, no doubt—but in my opinion there is no real danger of a break of that tough metal. The main purpose is simply to interfere with the interference of the creature, and smash through the doors."

"Gourlay next!" barked Morton.

Gourlay climbed lazily to his feet. He looked sleepy, as if he was somewhat bored by the whole proceeding, yet Morton knew he loved people to think him lazy, a good-for-nothing slouch, who spent his days in slumber and his nights catching forty winks. His title was chief communication engineer, but his knowledge extended to every vibration field; and he was probably, with the possible exception of Kent, the fastest thinker on the ship. His voice drawled out, and—Morton noted—the very deliberate assurance of it had a soothing effect on the men—anxious faces relaxed, bodies leaned back more restfully:

"Once inside," Gourlay said, "we've rigged up vibration screens of pure force that should stop nearly everything he's got on the ball. They work on the principle of reflection, so that everything he sends will be reflected back to him. In addition, we've got plenty of spare electric energy that we'll just feed him from mobile copper cups. There must be a limit to his capacity for handling power with those insulated nerves of his."

"Selenski!" called Morton.

The chief pilot was already standing, as he had anticipated Morton's call. And that, Morton reflected, was the man. His nerves had that rocklike steadiness which is the first requirement of the master controller of a great ship's movements; yet that very steadiness seemed to rest on dynamite ready to explode at its owner's volition. He was not a man of great learning, but he "reacted" to stimuli so fast that he always seemed to be anticipating.

"The impression I've received of the plan is that it must be cumulative. Just when the creature thinks that he can't stand any more, another thing happens to add to his trouble and confusion. When the uproar's at its height, I'm supposed to cut in the anti-accelerators. The commander thinks with Gunlie Lester that these creatures will know nothing about anti-acceleration. It's a development, pure and simple, of the science of interstellar flight, and couldn't have been developed in any other way. We think when the creature feels the first effects of the anti-acceleration—you all remember the caved-in feeling you had the first month—it won't know what to think or do."

"Korita next."

"I can only offer you encouragement," said the archeologist, "on the basis of my theory that the monster has all the characteristics of a criminal of the early ages of any civilization, complicated by an apparent reversion to primitiveness. The suggestion has been made by Smith that his knowledge of science is puzzling, and could only mean that we are dealing with an actual inhabitant, not a descendant of the inhabitants of the dead city we visited. This would ascribe a virtual immortality to our enemy, a possibility which is borne out by his ability to breathe both oxygen and chlorine—or neither—but even that makes no difference. He comes from a certain age in his civilization; and he has sunk so low that his ideas are mostly memories of that age.

"In spite of all the powers of his body, he lost his head in the elevator the first morning, until he remembered. He placed himself in such a position that he was forced to reveal his special powers against vibrations. He bungled the mass murders a few hours ago. In fact, his whole record is one of the low cunning of the primitive, egotistical mind which has little or no conception of the vast organization with which it is confronted.

"He is like the ancient German soldier who felt superior to the elderly Roman scholar, yet the latter was part of a mighty civilization of which the Germans of that day stood in awe.

"You may suggest that the sack of Rome by the Germans in later years defeats my argument; however, modern historians agree that the 'sack' was an historical accident, and not history in the true sense of the word. The movement of the 'Sea-peoples' which set in against the Egyptian civilization from 1400 B.C. succeeded only as regards the Cretan island-realm—their mighty expeditions against the Libyan and Phœnician coasts, with the accompaniment of Viking fleets, failed as those of the Huns failed against the Chinese Empire. Rome would have been abandoned in any event. Ancient, glorious Samarra was desolate by the tenth century; Pataliputra, Asoka's great capital, was an immense and completely uninhabited waste of houses when the Chinese traveler Hsinan-tang visited it about A.D. 635.

"We have, then, a primitive, and that primitive is now far out in space, completely outside of his natural habitat. I say, let's go in and win."

One of the men grumbled, as Korita finished: "You can talk about the sack of Rome being an accident, and about this fellow being a primitive, but the facts are facts. It looks to me as if Rome is about to fall again; and it won't be no primitive that did it, either. This guy's got plenty of what it takes."

Morton smiled grimly at the man, a member of the crew. "We'll see about that—right now!"

In the blazing brilliance of the gigantic machine shop, Coeurl slaved. The forty-foot, cigar-shaped spaceship was nearly finished. With a grunt of effort, he completed the laborious installation of the drive engines, and paused to survey his craft.

Its interior, visible through the one aperture in the outer wall, was pitifully small. There was literally room for nothing but the engines—and a narrow space for himself.

He plunged frantically back to work as he heard the approach of the men, and the sudden change in the tempest-like thunder of the engines—a rhythmical off-and-on hum, shriller in tone, sharper, more nerve-racking than the deep-throated, steady throb that had preceded it. Suddenly, there were the atomic disintegrators again at the massive outer doors.

He fought them off, but never wavered from his task. Every mighty muscle of his powerful body strained as he carried great loads of tools, machines and instruments, and dumped them into the bottom of his makeshift ship. There was no time to fit anything into place, no time for anything —no time—no time.

The thought pounded at his reason. He felt strangely

weary for the first time in his long and vigorous existence. With a last, tortured heave, he jerked the gigantic sheet of metal into the gaping aperture of the ship—and stood there for a terrible minute, balancing it precariously.

He knew the doors were going down. Half a dozen disintegrators concentrating on one point were irresistibly, though slowly, eating away the remaining inches. With a gasp, he released his mind from the doors and concentrated every ounce of his mind on the yard-thick outer wall, toward which the blunt nose of his ship was pointing.

His body cringed from the surging power that flowed from the electric dynamo through his ear tendrils into that resisting wall. The whole inside of him felt on fire, and he knew that he was dangerously close to carrying his ultimate load.

And still he stood there, shuddering with the awful pain, holding the unfastened metal plate with hard-clenched tentacles. His massive head pointed as in dread fascination at that bitterly hard wall.

He heard one of the engine-room doors crash inward. Men shouted; disintegrators rolled forward, their raging power unchecked. Coeurl heard the floor of the engine room hiss in protest, as those beams of atomic energy tore everything in their path to bits. The machines rolled closer; cautious footsteps sounded behind them. In a minute they would be at the flimsy doors separating the engine room from the machine shop.

Suddenly, Coeurl was satisfied. With a snarl of hate, a vindictive glow of feral eyes, he ducked into his little craft, and pulled the metal plate down into place as if it were a hatchway.

His ear tendrils hummed, as he softened the edges of the surrounding metal. In an instant, the plate was more than welded—it was part of his ship, a seamless, rivetless part of a whole that was solid opaque metal except for two transparent areas, one in the front, one in the rear.

His tentacle embraced the power drive with almost sensuous tenderness. There was a forward surge of his fragile machine, straight at the great outer wall of the machine shops. The nose of the forty-foot craft touched— and the wall dissolved in a glittering shower of dust.

Coeurl felt the barest retarding movement; and then he kicked the nose of the machine out into the cold of space, twisted it about, and headed back in the direction from which the big ship had been coming all these hours.

Men in space armor stood in the jagged hold that yawned in the lower reaches of the gigantic globe. The men and the great ship grew smaller. Then the men were gone; and there was only the ship with its blaze of a thousand blurring portholes. The ball shrank incredibly, too small now for individual portholes to be visible.

Almost straight ahead, Coeurl saw a tiny, dim, reddish ball—his own sun, he realized. He headed toward it at full speed. There were caves where he could hide and with other coeurls build secretly a spaceship in which they could reach other planets safely—now that he knew how.

His body ached from the agony of acceleration, yet he dared not let up for a single instant. He glanced back, half in terror. The globe was still there, a tiny dot of light in the immense blackness of space. Suddenly it twinkled and was gone.

For a brief moment, he had the empty, frightened impression that just before it disappeared, it moved. But he could see nothing. He could not escape the belief that they had shut off all their lights, and were sneaking up on him in the darkness. Worried and uncertain, he looked through the forward transparent plate.

A tremor of dismay shot through him. The dim red sun toward which he was heading was not growing larger. *It was becoming smaller* by the instant, and it grew visibly tinier during the next five minutes, became a pale-red dot in the sky—and vanished like the ship.

Fear came then, a blinding surge of it, that swept through his being and left him chilled with the sense of the unknown. For minutes, he stared frantically into the space ahead, searching for some landmark. But only the remote stars glimmered there, unwinking points against a velvet background of unfathomable distance.

Wait! One of the points was growing larger. With every muscle and nerve tense, Coeurl watched the point becoming a dot, a round ball of light—red light. Bigger, bigger, it grew. Suddenly, the red light shimmered and turned white—and there, before him, was the great globe of the spaceship, lights glaring from every porthole, the very ship which a few minutes before he had watched vanish behind him.

Something happened to Coeurl in that moment. His brain was spinning like a flywheel, faster, faster, more incoherently. Suddenly, the wheel flew apart into a million aching fragments. His eyes almost started from their sockets as, like a maddened animal, he raged in his small quarters.

His tentacles clutched at precious instruments and flung them insensately; his paws smashed in fury at the very walls of his ship. Finally, in a brief flash of sanity, he knew that he couldn't face the inevitable fire of atomic disintegrators.

It was a simple thing to create the violent disorganization that freed every drop of id from his vital organs.

They found him lying dead in a little pool of phosphorus.

"Poor pussy," said Morton. "I wonder what he thought when he saw us appear ahead of him, after his own sun disappeared. Knowing nothing of anti-accelerators, he couldn't know that we could stop short in space, whereas it would take him more than three hours to decelerate; and in the meantime he'd be drawing farther and farther away from where he wanted to go. He couldn't know that by stopping, we flashed past him at millions of miles a second. Of course, he didn't have a chance once he left our ship. The whole world must have seemed topsy-turvy."

"Never mind the sympathy," he heard Kent say behind him. "We've got a job—to kill every cat in that miserable world."

Korita murmured softly: "That should be simple. They are but primitives; and we have merely to sit down, and they will come to us, cunningly expecting to delude us."

Smith snapped: "You fellows make me sick! Pussy was the toughest nut we ever had to crack. He had everything he needed to defeat us—"

Morton smiled as Korita interrupted blandly: "Exactly, my dear Smith, except that he reacted according to the biological impulses of his type. His defeat was already foreshadowed when we unerringly analyzed him as a criminal from a certain era of his civilization.

"It was history, honorable Mr. Smith, our knowledge of history that defeated him," said the Japanese archeologist, reverting to the ancient politeness of his race.

LIFE-LINE

by Robert A. Heinlein

Robert A. Heinlein was thirty-two when "Life-Line" appeared in the August, 1939 issue of Astounding Science Fiction, *certainly not an old man, but nevertheless ancient by the standards of science fiction, since so many of its leading practitioners first published in their teens. (Isaac Asimov, whose first sale was also in 1939, was nineteen at the time.)*

Heinlein had graduated from the United States Naval Academy in 1929 and served in the Navy until illness forced him to retire in 1934. He then held the now-standard variety of jobs by which so many budding writers support themselves, but unlike most others, he did not accumulate a long list of rejection slips before his maiden sale. This fine story was, it is true, bounced by Collier's before being submitted to John W. Campbell, Jr. But Robert A. Heinlein would later have the sweet revenge of making history as one of the first sf writers to break into the "slick" magazines.

"Life-Line" contains all of the technical genius and dramatic gifts that would make its author one of the leading writers in the history of modern science fiction.

THE EDITORS

The chairman rapped loudly for order. Gradually the catcalls and boos died away as several self-appointed sergeant-at-arms persuaded a few hot-headed individuals to sit down. The speaker on the rostrum by the chairman seemed unaware of the disturbance. His bland, faintly insolent face was impassive. The chairman turned to the speaker and addressed him in a voice in which anger and annoyance were barely restrained.

"Dr. Pinero"—the "Doctor" was faintly stressed—"I must apologize to you for the unseemly outburst during your remarks. I am surprised that my colleagues should so far forget the dignity proper to men of science as to interrupt a speaker, no matter"—he paused and set his mouth —"no matter how great the provocation." Pinero smiled in his face, a smile that was in some way an open insult. The chairman visibly controlled his temper and continued: "I am anxious that the program be concluded decently and in order. I want you to finish your remarks. Nevertheless, I must ask you to refrain from affronting our intelligence with ideas that any educated man knows to be fallacious. Please confine yourself to your discovery—if you have made one."

Pinero spread his fat, white hands, palms down. "How can I possibly put a new idea into your heads, if I do not first remove your delusions?"

The audience stirred and muttered. Someone shouted from the rear of the hall: "Throw the charlatan out! We've had enough."

The chairman pounded his gavel.

"Gentlemen! Please!"

Then to Pinero, "Must I remind you that you are not a member of this body, and that we did not invite you?"

Pinero's eyebrows lifted. "So? I seem to remember an invitation on the letterhead of the Academy."

The chairman chewed his lower lip before replying. "True. I wrote that invitation myself. But it was at the request of one of the trustees—a fine, public-spirited gentleman, but not a scientist, not a member of the Academy."

Pinero smiled his irritating smile. "So? I should have guessed. Old Bidwell, not so, of Amalgamated Life Insurance? And he wanted his trained seals to expose me as a fraud, yes? For if I can tell a man the day of his own death, no one will buy his pretty policies. But how can you expose me, if you will not listen to me first? Even supposing you had the wit to understand me? Bah! He has sent jackals to tear down a lion." He deliberately turned his back on them.

The muttering of the crowd swelled and took on a vicious tone. The chairman cried vainly for order. There arose a figure in the front row.

"Mr. Chairman!"

The chairman grasped the opening and shouted: "Gentlemen! Dr. van Rhein Smitt has the floor." The commotion died away.

The doctor cleared his throat, smoothed the forelock of his beautiful white hair, and thrust one hand into a side pocket of his smartly tailored trousers. He assumed his women's-club manner.

"Mr. Chairman, fellow members of the Academy of Science, let us have tolerance. Even a murderer has the right to say his say before the State exacts its tribute. Shall we do less? Even though one may be intellectually certain of the verdict? I grant Dr. Pinero every consideration that should be given by this august body to any unaffiliated colleague, even though"—he bowed slightly in Pinero's direction—"we may not be familiar with the university which bestowed his degree. If what he has to say is false, it cannot harm us. If what he has to say is true, we should know it." His mellow, cultivated voice rolled on, soothing and calming. "If the eminent doctor's manner appears a trifle inurbane to our tastes, we must bear in mind that the doctor may be from a place, or a stratum, not so meticulous in these matters. Now our good friend and benefactor has asked us to hear this person and carefully assess the merit of his claims. Let us do so with dignity and decorum."

He sat down to a rumble of applause, comfortably aware that he had enhanced his reputation as an intellectual leader. Tomorrow the papers would again mention the good sense and persuasive personality of "America's Handsomest University President." Who knows; maybe now old Bidwell would come through with that swimming-pool donation.

When the applause had ceased, the chairman turned to where the center of the disturbance sat, hands folded over his little round belly, face serene.

"Will you continue, Dr. Pinero?"

"Why should I?"

The chairman shrugged his shoulders. "You came for that purpose."

Pinero arose. "So true. So very true. But was I wise to come? Is there anyone here who has an open mind, who can stare a bare fact in the face without blushing? I think not. Even that so-beautiful gentleman who asked you to hear me out has already judged me and condemned me. He seeks order, not truth. Suppose truth defies order, will he accept it? Will you? I think not. Still, if I do not speak, you will win your point by default. The little man in the street will think that you little men have exposed me, Pinero, as a hoaxer, a pretender.

"I will repeat my discovery. In simple language, I have invented a technique to tell how long a man will live. I can give you advance billing of the Angel of Death. I can tell you when the Black Camel will kneel at your door. In five minutes' time, with my apparatus, I can tell any of you how many grains of sand are still left in your hourglass." He paused and folded his arms across his chest. For a moment no one spoke. The audience grew restless.

Finally the chairman intervened, "You aren't finished, Dr. Pinero?"

"What more is there to say?"

"You haven't told us how your discovery works."

Pinero's eyebrows shot up. "You suggest that I should turn over the fruits of my work for children to play with? This is dangerous knowledge, my friend. I keep it for the man who understands it, myself." He tapped his chest.

"How are we to know that you have anything back of your wild claims?"

"So simple. You send a committee to watch me demonstrate. If it works, fine. You admit it and tell the world so. If it does not work, I am discredited, and will apologize. Even I, Pinero, will apologize."

A slender, stoop-shouldered man stood up in the back of the hall. The chair recognized him and he spoke.

"Mr. Chairman, how can the eminent doctor seriously propose such a course? Does he expect us to wait around for twenty or thirty years for someone to die and prove his claims?"

Pinero ignored the chair and answered directly.

"*Pfui!* Such nonsense! Are you so ignorant of statistics that you do not know that in any large group there is at

least one who will die in the immediate future? I make you
a proposition. Let me test each one of you in this room,
and I will name the man who will die within the fortnight,
yes, and the day and hour of his death." He glanced
fiercely around the room. "Do you accept?"

Another figure got to his feet, a portly man who spoke
in measured syllables. "I, for one, cannot countenance
such an experiment. As a medical man, I have noted with
sorrow the plain marks of serious heart trouble in many of
our elder colleagues. If Dr. Pinero knows those symptoms,
as he may, and were he to select as his victim one of their
number, the man so selected would be likely to die on
schedule, whether the distinguished speaker's mechanical
egg timer works or not."

Another speaker backed him up at once. "Dr. Shepard
is right. Why should we waste time on voodoo tricks? It
is my belief that this person who calls himself *Dr*. Pinero
wants to use this body to give his statements authority. If
we participate in this farce, we play into his hands. I
don't know what his racket is, but you can bet that he has
figured out someway to use us for advertising his schemes.
I move, Mr. Chairman, that we proceed with our regular
business."

The motion carried by acclamation, but Pinero did not
sit down. Amidst cries of "Order! Order!" he shook his
untidy head at them, and had his say.

"Barbarians! Imbeciles! Stupid dolts! Your kind have
blocked the recognition of every great discovery since
time began. Such ignorant canaille are enough to start
Galileo spinning in his grave. That fat fool down there
twiddling his elk's tooth calls himself a medical man. Witch
doctor would be a better term! That little bald-headed runt
over there— You! You style yourself a philosopher, and
prate about life and time in your neat categories. What
do you know of either one? How can you ever learn when
you won't examine the truth when you have a chance? Bah!"
He spat upon the stage. "You call this an Academy of
Science. I call it an undertakers' convention, interested
only in embalming the ideas of your red-blooded predecessors."

He paused for breath and was grasped on each side by
two members of the platform committee and rushed out
the wings. Several reporters arose hastily from the press

table and followed him. The chairman declared the meeting adjourned.

The newspapermen caught up with Pinero as he was going out by the stage door. He walked with a light, springy step, and whistled a little tune. There was no trace of the belligerence he had shown a moment before. They crowded about him. "How about an interview, doc?" "What d'yuh think of modern education?" "You certainly told 'em. What are your views on life after death?" "Take off your hat, doc, and look at the birdie."

He grinned at them all. "One at a time, boys, and not so fast. I used to be a newspaperman myself. How about coming up to my place?"

A few minutes later they were trying to find places to sit down in Pinero's messy bed-living room, and lighting his cigars. Pinero looked around and beamed. "What'll it be, boys? Scotch or Bourbon?" When that was taken care of he got down to business. "Now, boys, what do you want to know?"

"Lay it on the line, doc. Have you got something, or haven't you?"

"Most assuredly I have something, my young friend."

"Then tell us how it works. That guff you handed the profs won't get you anywhere now."

"Please, my dear fellow. It is my invention. I expect to make some money with it. Would you have me give it away to the first person who asks for it?"

"See here, doc, you've got to give us something if you expect to get a break in the morning papers. What do you use? A crystal ball?"

"No, not quite. Would you like to see my apparatus?"

"Sure. Now we're getting somewhere."

He ushered them into an adjoining room, and waved his hand. "There it is, boys." The mass of equipment that met their eyes vaguely resembled a medico's office X-ray gear. Beyond the obvious fact that it used electrical power, and that some of the dials were calibrated in familiar terms, a casual inspection gave no clue to its actual use.

"What's the principle, doc?"

Pinero pursed his lips and considered. "No doubt you are all familiar with the truism that life is electrical in nature. Well, that truism isn't worth a damn, but it will help to give you an idea of the principle. You have also been told that time is a fourth dimension. Maybe you believe it, perhaps not. It has been said so many times that it has ceased to have any meaning. It is simply a cliché that windbags use to impress fools. But I want you to try to visualize it now, and try to feel it emotionally."

He stepped up to one of the reporters. "Suppose we take you as an example. Your name is Rogers, is it not? Very well, Rogers, you are a space-time event having duration four ways. You are not quite six feet tall, you are about twenty inches wide and perhaps ten inches thick. In time, there stretches behind you more of this space-time event, reaching to, perhaps, 1905, of which we see a cross section here at right angles to the time axis, and as thick as the present. At the far end is a baby, smelling of sour milk and drooling its breakfast on its bib. At the other end lies, perhaps, an old man some place in the 1980s. Imagine this space-time event, which we call Rogers, as a long pink worm, continuous through the years. It stretches past us here in 1939, and the cross section we see appears as a single, discreet body. But that is illusion. There is physical continuity to this pink worm, enduring through the years. As a matter of fact, there is physical continuity in this concept to the entire race, for these pink worms branch off from other pink worms. In this fashion the race is like a vine whose branches intertwine and send out shoots. Only by taking a cross section of the vine would we fall into the error of believing that the shootlets were discreet individuals."

He paused and looked around at their faces. One of them, a dour, hard-bitten chap, put in a word.

"That's all very pretty, Pinero, if true, but where does that get you?"

Pinero favored him with an unresentful smile. "Patience, my friend. I asked you to think of life as electrical. Now think of our long, pink worm as a conductor of electricity. You have heard, perhaps, of the fact that electrical engineers can, by certain measurements, predict the exact location of a break in a transatlantic cable without ever leaving the shore. I do the same with our pink worms. By applying my instruments to the cross section here in this room I can tell where the break occurs; that is to say, where death takes place. Or, if you like, I can reverse the connections and tell you the date of your birth. But that is uninteresting; you already know it."

The dour individual sneered. "I've caught you, doc. If what you say about the race being like a vine of pink worms is true, you can't tell birthdays, because the connection with the race is continuous at birth. Your electrical conductor reaches on back through the mother into a man's remotest ancestors."

Pinero beamed. "True, and clever, my friend. But you have pushed the analogy too far. It is not done in the precise manner in which one measures the length of an electrical conductor. In some ways it is more like measuring the length of a long corridor by bouncing an echo off the far end. At birth there is a sort of twist in the corridor, and, by proper calibration, I can detect the echo from that twist."

"Let's see you prove it."

"Certainly, my dear friend. Will you be a subject?"

One of the others spoke up. "He's called your bluff, Luke. Put up or shut up."

"I'm game. What do I do?"

"First write the date of your birth on a sheet of paper, and hand it to one of your colleagues."

Luke complied. "Now what?"

"Remove your outer clothing and step upon these scales. Now tell me, were you ever very much thinner, or very much fatter, than you are now? No? What did you weigh at birth? Ten pounds? A fine bouncing baby boy. They don't come so big any more."

"What is all this flubdubbery?"

"I am trying to approximate the average cross section of our long pink conductor, my dear Luke. Now will you seat yourself here? Then place this electrode in your mouth. No, it will not hurt you; the voltage is quite low, less than one micro-volt, but I must have a good connection." The doctor left him and went behind his apparatus, where he lowered a hood over his head before touching his controls. Some of the exposed dials came to life and a low humming came from the machine. It stopped and the doctor popped out of his little hide-away.

"I get sometime in February, 1902. Who has the piece of paper with the date?"

It was produced and unfolded. The custodian read, "February 22, 1902."

The stillness that followed was broken by a voice from the edge of the little group. "Doc, can I have another drink?"

The tension relaxed, and several spoke at once: "Try it on me, doc." "Me first, doc; I'm an orphan and really want to know." "How about it, doc? Give us all a little loose play."

He smilingly complied, ducking in and out of the hood like a gopher from its hole. When they all had twin slips of paper to prove the doctor's skill, Luke broke a long silence.

"How about showing how you predict death, Pinero?"

"If you wish. Who will try it?"

No one answered. Several of them nudged Luke forward. "Go ahead, smart guy. You asked for it." He allowed himself to be seated in the chair. Pinero changed some of the switches, then entered the hood. When the humming ceased he came out, rubbing his hands briskly together.

"Well, that's all there is to see, boys. Got enough for a story?"

"Hey, what about the prediction? When does Luke get his 'thirty'?"

Luke faced him. "Yes, how about it?"

Pinero looked pained. "Gentlemen, I am surprised at you. I give that information for a fee. Besides, it is a professional confidence. I never tell anyone but the client who consults me."

"I don't mind. Go ahead and tell them."

"I am very sorry, I really must refuse. I only agreed to show you how; not to give the results."

Luke ground the butt of his cigarette into the floor. "It's a hoax, boys. He probably looked up the age of every reporter in town just to be ready to pull this. It won't wash, Pinero."

Pinero gazed at him sadly. "Are you married, my friend?"

"No."

"Do you have anyone dependent on you? Any close relatives?"

"No. Why? Do you want to adopt me?"

Pinero shook his head. "I am very sorry for you, my dear Luke. You will die before tomorrow."

DEATH PUNCHES TIME CLOCK

. . . within twenty minutes of Pinero's strange prediction, Timons was struck by a falling sign while walking down Broadway toward the offices of the *Daily Herald* where he was employed.

Dr. Pinero declined to comment but confirmed the story that he had predicted Timons' death by means of his so-called chronovitameter. Chief of Police Roy. . . .

Legal Notice

To whom it may concern, greetings; I, John Cabot Winthrop III, of the firm of Winthrop, Winthrop, Ditmars and Winthrop, Attorneys-at-law, do affirm that Hugo Pinero of this city did hand to me ten thousand dollars in lawful money of the United States, and did instruct me to place it in escrow with a chartered bank of my selection with escrow instructions as follows:

The entire bond shall be forfeit, and shall forthwith be paid to the first client of Hugo Pinero and/or Sands of Time, Inc. who shall exceed his life tenure as predicted by Hugo Pinero by one per centum, or to the estate of the first client who shall fail of such predicted tenure in a like amount, whichever occurs first in point of time.

Subscribed and sworn,
John Cabot Winthrop III.

Subscribed and sworn to before
me this 2nd day of April, 1939.
Albert M. Swanson
Notary Public in and for this
county and State. My commission
expires June 17, 1939.

"Good evening, Mr. and Mrs. Radio Audience, let's go to press! Flash! Hugo Pinero, the Miracle Man from Nowhere, has made his thousandth death prediction without anyone claiming the reward he offered to the first person who catches him failing to call the turn. With thirteen of his clients already dead, it is mathematically certain that he has a private line to the main office of the Old Man with the Scythe. That is one piece of news I don't want to know about before it happens. Your coast-to-coast correspondent will *not* be a client of Prophet Pinero—"

The judge's watery baritone cut through the stale air of the courtroom. "Please, Mr. Weems, let us return to our subject. This court granted your prayer for a temporary restraining order, and now you ask that it be made permanent. In rebuttal, Dr. Pinero claims that you have presented no cause and asks that the injunction be lifted, and that I order your client to cease from attempts to interfere with what Pinero describes as a simple, lawful business. As you are not addressing a jury, please omit the rhetoric and tell me in plain language why I should not grant his prayer."

Mr. Weems jerked his chin nervously, making his flabby gray dewlap drag across his high stiff collar, and resumed:

"May it please the honorable court, I represent the public—"

"Just a moment. I thought you were appearing for Amalgamated Life Insurance."

"I am, your honor, in a formal sense. In a wider sense I represent several other of the major assurance, fiduciary

and financial institutions, their stockholders and policy
holders, who constitute a majority of the citizenry. In
addition we feel that we protect the interests of the entire
population, unorganized, inarticulate, and otherwise un-
protected."

"I thought that I represented the public," observed the
judge dryly. "I am afraid I must regard you as appearing
for your client of record. But continue. What is your
thesis?"

The elderly barrister attempted to swallow his Adam's
apple, then began again: "Your honor, we contend that
there are two separate reasons why this injunction should
be made permanent, and, further, that each reason is sufficient alone.

"In the first place, this person is engaged in the practice
of soothsaying, an occupation proscribed both in common
law and statute. He is a common fortuneteller, a vagabond
charlatan who preys on the gullibility of the public. He is
cleverer than the ordinary gypsy palm reader, astrologer
or table tipper, and to the same extent more dangerous. He
makes false claims of modern scientific methods to give a
spurious dignity to the thaumaturgy. We have here in
court leading representatives of the Academy of Science to
give expert witness as to the absurdity of his claims.

"In the second place, even if this person's claims were
true—granting for the sake of argument such an absurdity"—Mr. Weems permitted himself a thin-lipped smile—
"we contend that his activities are contrary to the public
interest in general, and unlawfully injurious to the interests of my client in particular. We are prepared to produce numerous exhibits with the legal custodians to prove
that this person did publish, or cause to have published,
utterances urging the public to dispense with the priceless
boon of life insurance to the great detriment of their welfare and to the financial damage of my client."

Pinero arose in his place. "Your honor, may I say a few
words?"

"What is it?"

"I believe I can simplify the situation if permitted to
make a brief analysis."

"Your honor," put in Weems, "this is most irregular."

"Patience, Mr. Weems. Your interests will be protected.
It seems to me that we need more light and less noise in

LIFE-LINE

this matter. If Dr. Pinero can shorten the proceedings by speaking at this time, I am inclined to let him. Proceed, Dr. Pinero."

"Thank you, your honor. Taking the last of Mr. Weems' points first, I am prepared to stipulate that I published the utterances he speaks of—"

"One moment, doctor. You have chosen to act as your own attorney. Are you sure you are competent to protect your own interests?"

"I am prepared to chance it, your honor. Our friends here can easily prove what I stipulate."

"Very well. You may proceed."

"I will stipulate that many persons have canceled life-insurance policies as a result thereof, but I challenge them to show that anyone so doing has suffered any loss or damage therefrom. It is true that the Amalgamated has lost business through my activities, but that is the natural result of my discovery, which has made their policies as obsolete as the bow and arrow. If an injunction is granted on that ground, I shall set up a coal-oil-lamp factory, and then ask for an injunction against the Edison and General Electric companies to forbid them to manufacture incandescent bulbs.

"I will stipulate that I am engaged in the business of making predictions of death, but I deny that I am practicing magic, black, white or rainbow-colored. If to make predictions by methods of scientific accuracy is illegal, then the actuaries of the Amalgamated have been guilty for years, in that they predict the exact percentage that will die each year in any given large group. I predict death retail; the Amalgamated predicts it wholesale. If their actions are legal, how can mine be illegal?

"I admit that it makes a difference whether I can do what I claim, or not; and I will stipulate that the so-called expert witnesses from the Academy of Science will testify that I cannot. But they know nothing of my method and cannot give truly expert testimony on it—"

"Just a moment, doctor. Mr. Weems, is it true that your expert witnesses are not conversant with Dr. Pinero's theory and methods?"

Mr. Weems looked worried. He drummed on the table top, then answered, "Will the court grant me a few moments' indulgence?"

"Certainly."

Mr. Weems held a hurried whispered consultation with his cohorts, then faced the bench. "We have a procedure to suggest, your honor. If Dr. Pinero will take the stand and explain the theory and practice of his alleged method, then these distinguished scientists will be able to advise the court as to the validity of his claims."

The Judge looked inquiringly at Pinero, who responded: "I will not willingly agree to that. Whether my process is true or false, it would be dangerous to let it fall into the hands of fools and quacks"—he waved his hand at the group of professors seated in the front row, paused and smiled maliciously—"as these gentlemen know quite well. Furthermore, it is not necessary to know the process in order to prove that it will work. Is it necessary to understand the complex miracle of biological reproduction in order to observe that a hen lays eggs? Is it necessary for me to re-educate this entire body of self-appointed custodians of wisdom—cure them of their ingrown superstitions—in order to prove that my predictions are correct?

"There are but two ways of forming an opinion in science. One is the scientific method; the other, the scholastic. One can judge from experiment, or one can blindly accept authority. To the scientific mind, experimental proof is all-important, and theory is merely a convenience in description, to be junked when it no longer fits. To the academic mind, authority is everything, and facts are junked when they do not fit theory laid down by authority.

"It is this point of view—academic minds clinging like oysters to disproved theories—that has blocked every advance of knowledge in history. I am prepared to prove my method by experiment, and, like Galileo in another court, I insist, 'It still moves!'

"Once before I offered such proof to this same body of self-styled experts, and they rejected it. I renew my offer; let me measure the life length of the members of the Academy of Science. Let them appoint a committee to judge the results. I will seal my findings in two sets of envelopes; on the outside of each envelope in one set will appear the name of a member; on the inside, the date of his death. In the other envelopes I will place names; on the outside I will place dates. Let the committee place the envelopes in a vault, then meet from time to time to open the appro-

priate envelopes. In such a large body of men some deaths
may be expected, if Amalgamated actuaries can be trusted,
every week or two. In such a fashion they will accumulate
data very rapidly to prove that Pinero is a liar, or no."

He stopped, and thrust out his chest until it almost
caught up with his little round belly. He glared at the
sweating savants. "Well?"

The judge raised his eyebrows, and caught Mr. Weems'
eye. "Do you accept?"

"Your honor, I think the proposal highly improper—"

The judge cut him short. "I warn you that I shall rule
against you if you do not accept, or propose an equally
reasonable method of arriving at the truth."

Weems opened his mouth, changed his mind, looked up
and down the faces of the learned witnesses, and faced the
bench. "We accept, your honor."

"Very well. Arrange the details between you. The temporary injunction is lifted, and Dr. Pinero must not be
molested in the pursuit of his business. Decision on the
petition for permanent injunction is reserved without
prejudice pending the accumulation of evidence. Before
we leave this matter I wish to comment on the theory
implied by you, Mr. Weems, when you claimed damage to
your client. There has grown up in the minds of certain
groups in this country the notion that because a man or
corporation has made a profit out of the public for a number of years, the government and the courts are charged
with the duty of guaranteeing such profit in the future,
even in the face of changing circumstances and contrary to
public interest. This strange doctrine is not supported by
statute nor common law. Neither individuals nor corporations have any right to come into court and ask that the
clock of history be stopped, or turned back."

Bidwell grunted in annoyance. "Weems, if you can't
think up anything better than that, Amalgamated is going
to need a new chief attorney. It's been ten weeks since you
lost the injunction, and that little wart is coining money
hand over fist. Meantime, every insurance firm in the
country's going broke. Hoskins, what's our loss ratio?"

"It's hard to say, Mr. Bidwell. It gets worse every day.
We've paid off thirteen big policies this week; all of them
taken out since Pinero started operations."

A spare little man spoke up. "I say, Bidwell, we aren't accepting any new applicants for United, until we have time to check and be sure that they have not consulted Pinero. Can't we afford to wait until the scientists show him up?"

Bidwell snorted. "You blasted optimist! They won't show him up. Aldrich, can't you face a fact? The fat little pest has something; how, I don't know. This is a fight to the finish. If we wait, we're licked." He threw his cigar into a cuspidor, and bit savagely into a fresh one. "Clear out of here, all of you! I'll handle this my own way. You, too, Aldrich. United may wait, but Amalgamated won't."

Weems cleared his throat apprehensively. "Mr. Bidwell, I trust you will consult me before embarking on any major change in policy?"

Bidwell grunted. They filed out. When they were all gone and the door closed, Bidwell snapped the switch of the inter-office announcer. "O.K.; send him in."

The outer door opened. A slight, dapper figure stood for a moment at the threshold. His small, dark eyes glanced quickly about the room before he entered, then he moved up to Bidwell with a quick, soft tread. He spoke to Bidwell in a flat, emotionless voice. His face remained impassive except for the live, animal eyes. "You wanted to talk to me?"

"Yes."

"What's the proposition?"

"Sit down, and we'll talk."

Pinero met the young couple at the door of his inner office.

"Come in, my dears, come in. Sit down. Make yourselves at home. Now tell me, what do you want of Pinero? Surely such young people are not anxious about the final roll call?"

The boy's pleasant young face showed slight confusion. "Well, you see, Dr. Pinero, I'm Ed Hartley and this is my wife, Betty. We're going to have . . . that is, Betty is expecting a baby and, well—"

Pinero smiled benignly. "I understand. You want to know how long you will live in order to make the best possible provision for the youngster. Quite wise. Do you both want readings, or just yourself?"

The girl answered, "Both of us, we think."

Pinero beamed at her. "Quite so. I agree. Your reading presents certain technical difficulties at this time, but I can give you some information now. Now come into my laboratory, my dears, and we'll commence."

He rang for their case histories, then showed them into his workshop. "Mrs. Hartley first, please. If you will go behind that screen and remove your shoes and your outer clothing, please."

He turned away and made some minor adjustments of his apparatus. Ed nodded to his wife, who slipped behind the screen and reappeared almost at once, dressed in a slip. Pinero glanced up.

"This way, my dear. First we must weigh you. There. Now take your place on the stand. This electrode in your mouth. No, Ed, you mustn't touch her while she is in the circuit. It won't take a minute. Remain quiet."

He dove under the machine's hood and the dials sprang into life. Very shortly he came out, with a perturbed look on his face. "Ed, did you touch her?"

"No, doctor." Pinero ducked back again and remained a little longer. When he came out this time, he told the girl to get down and dress. He turned to her husband.

"Ed, make yourself ready."

"What's Betty's reading, doctor?"

"There is a little difficulty. I want to test you first."

When he came out from taking the youth's reading, his face was more troubled than ever. Ed inquired as to his trouble. Pinero shrugged his shoulders and brought a smile to his lips.

"Nothing to concern you, my boy. A little mechanical misadjustment, I think. But I shan't be able to give you two your readings today. I shall need to overhaul my machine. Can you come back tomorrow?"

"Why, I think so. Say, I'm sorry about your machine. I hope it isn't serious."

"It isn't, I'm sure. Will you come back into my office and visit for a bit?"

"Thank you, doctor. You are very kind."

"But, Ed, I've got to meet Ellen."

Pinero turned the full force of his personality on her. "Won't you grant me a few moments, my dear young lady? I am old, and like the sparkle of young folks' company. I get very little of it. Please." He nudged them gently into his office and seated them. Then he ordered lemonade and cookies sent in, offered them cigarettes and lit a cigar.

Forty minutes later Ed listened entranced, while Betty was quite evidently acutely nervous and anxious to leave, as the doctor spun out a story concerning his adventures as a young man in Tierra del Fuego. When the doctor stopped to relight his cigar, she stood up.

"Doctor, we really must leave. Couldn't we hear the rest tomorrow?"

"Tomorrow? There will not be time tomorrow."

"But you haven't time today, either. Your secretary has rung five times."

"Couldn't you spare me just a few more minutes?"

"I really can't today, doctor. I have an appointment. There is someone waiting for me."

"There is no way to induce you?"

"I'm afraid not. Come, Ed."

After they had gone, the doctor stepped to the window and stared out over the city. Presently, he picked out two tiny figures as they left the office building. He watched them hurry to the corner, wait for the lights to change, then start across the street. When they were part way across, there came the scream of a siren. The two little figures hesitated, started back, stopped and turned. Then the car was upon them. As the car slammed to a stop, they showed up from beneath it, no longer two figures, but simply a limp, unorganized heap of clothing.

Presently the doctor turned away from the window. Then he picked up his phone and spoke to his secretary.

"Cancel my appointments for the rest of the day. . . . No. . . . No one. . . . I don't care; cancel them."

Then he sat down in his chair. His cigar went out. Long after dark he held it, still unlighted.

Pinero sat down at his dining table and contemplated the gourmet's luncheon spread before him. He had ordered this meal with particular care, and had come home a little early in order to enjoy it fully.

Somewhat later he let a few drops of fiori d'Alpini roll around his tongue and trickle down his throat. The heavy, fragrant sirup warmed his mouth and reminded him of the little mountain flowers for which it was named. He sighed. It had been a good meal, an exquisite meal and had justified the exotic liqueur.

His musing was interrupted by a disturbance at the front door. The voice of his elderly maidservant was raised in remonstrance. A heavy male voice interrupted her. The commotion moved down the hall and the dining-room door was pushed open.

"Mia Madonna! Non si puo entrare! The master is eating!"

"Never mind, Angela. I have time to see these gentlemen. You may go."

Pinero faced the surly-faced spokesman of the intruders. "You have business with me; yes?"

"You bet we have. Decent people have had enough of your damned nonsense."

"And so?"

The caller did not answer at once. A smaller, dapper individual moved out from behind him and faced Pinero.

"We might as well begin." The chairman of the committee placed a key in the lock box and opened it. "Wenzell, will you help me pick out today's envelopes?" He was interrupted by a touch on his arm.

"Dr. Baird, you are wanted on the telephone."

"Very well. Bring the instrument here."

When it was fetched he placed the receiver to his ear. "Hello. . . . Yes; speaking. . . . What? . . . No, we have heard nothing. . . . Destroyed the machine, you say. . . . Dead! How? . . . No! No statement. None at all. . . . Call me later."

He slammed the instrument down and pushed it from him.

"What's up?"

"Who's dead now?"

Baird held up one hand. "Quiet, gentlemen, please! Pinero was murdered a few moments ago at his home."

"Murdered!"

"That isn't all. About the same time vandals broke into his office and smashed his apparatus."

No one spoke at first. The committee members glanced around at each other. No one seemed anxious to be the first to comment.

Finally one spoke up. "Get it out."

"Get what out?"

"Pinero's envelope. It's in there, too. I've seen it."

Baird located it, and slowly tore it open. He unfolded the single sheet of paper and scanned it.

"Well? Out with it!"

"One thirteen p.m. . . . today."

They took this in silence.

Their dynamic calm was broken by a member across the table from Baird reaching for the lock box. Baird interposed a hand.

"What do you want?"

"My prediction. It's in there—we're all in there."

"Yes, yes."

"We're all in there."

"Let's have them."

Baird placed both hands over the box. He held the eye of the man opposite him, but did not speak. He licked his lips. The corner of his mouth twitched. His hands shook. Still he did not speak. The man opposite relaxed back into his chair.

"You're right, of course," he said.

"Bring me that wastebasket." Baird's voice was low and strained, but steady.

He accepted it and dumped the litter on the rug. He placed the tin basket on the table before him. He tore half a dozen envelopes across, set a match to them, and dropped them in the basket. Then he started tearing a double handful at a time, and fed the fire steadily. The smoke made him cough, and tears ran out of his smarting eyes. Someone got up and opened a window. When Baird was through, he pushed the basket away from him, looked down and spoke.

"I'm afraid I've ruined this table top."

ETHER BREATHER

by Theodore Sturgeon

In the late thirties I was selling stories to a newspaper syndicate—1500-word short-shorts at $5 apiece, and they would buy no more than two a week, on which I lived (if you call that living). My appetite for science fiction and fantasy (and food!) was enormous, and known to my friends. One day one of them slapped down a copy of Unknown, *Vol I No. 1, before me and said, "This is the magazine you ought to be writing for," and suggested that I go and see the editor.*

In fear and trembling I did, and met the awesome John W. Campbell. He bounced the manuscript I brought with me on sight; but then explained exactly why, in just which ways my story was not a story, and what a story had to be to satisfy him. All this was, in itself, quite enough to reduce a tender tyro to a puddle of despair. But along with it were good words about my ability to handle the language and my feeling about people, which is really what fiction is all about. He also urged me to try for his other magazine, Astounding Science Fiction. *In doing so he drew the most succinct distinction between science fiction and fantasy I have yet heard: "For* Astounding," *he said, "I want stories which are logical, possible, and good. For* Unknown *I want stories which are logical and good."*

So I wrote a story for each category and he bought them both. The first one he bought was for Unknown *("A God in a Garden") but the second, "Ether Breather," was the first to appear. It had a sequel, by the way, called "Butyl and the Breather," which appeared a year later. Just how*

87

"possible" the events of the story are, we can't know. *If it
ever happens, it has always been possible.*

It was "The Seashell." It *would* have to be "The Seashell."
I wrote it first as a short story, and it was turned down. Then
I made a novelette out of it, and then a novel. Then a
short short. Then a three-line gag. And it still wouldn't sell.
It got to be a fetish with me, rewriting that "Seashell."
After a while editors got so used to it that they turned it
down on sight. I had enough rejection slips from that num-
ber alone to paper every room in the house of tomorrow.
So when it sold—well, it was like the death of a friend. It
hit me. I hated to see it go.

It was a play by that time, but I hadn't changed it
much. Still the same pastel, froo-froo old "Seashell" story,
about two children who grew up and met each other only
three times as the years went on, and a little seashell that
changed hands each time they met. The plot, if any,
doesn't matter. The dialogue was—well, pastel. Naïve. Un-
sophisticated. Very pretty, and practically salesproof. But
it just happened to ring the bell with an earnest young
reader for Associated Television, Inc., who was looking for
something about that length that could be dubbed "artistic"; something that would not require too much cere-
bration on the part of an audience, so that said audience
could relax and appreciate the new polychrome technique
of television transmission. You know; pastel.

As I leaned back in my old relic of an armchair that
night, and watched the streamlined version of my slow-
moving brainchild, I had to admire the way they put it
over. In spots it was almost good, that "Seashell." Well
suited for the occasion, too. It was a full-hour program
given free to a perfume house by Associated, to try out
the new color transmission as an advertising medium. I
liked the first two acts, if I do say so as shouldn't. It was
at the half-hour mark that I got my first kick on the chin.
It was a two-minute skit for the advertising plug.

A tall and elegant couple were seen standing on marble
steps in an elaborate theater lobby. Says she to he:

"And how do you like the play, Mr. Robinson?"

Says he to she: "It stinks."

Just like that. Like any radio-television listener, I was used to paying little, if any, attention to a plug. That certainly snapped me up in my chair. After all, it was my play, even if it was "The Seashell." They couldn't do that to me.

But the girl smiling archly out of my television set didn't seem to mind. She said sweetly, "I think so, too."

He was looking slushily down into her eyes. He said: "That goes for you, too, my dear. What *is* that perfume you are using?"

"Berbelot's *Doux Rêves*. What do you think of it?"

He said, "You heard what I said about the play."

I didn't wait for the rest of the plug, the station identification, and act three. I headed for my visiphone and dialed Associated. I was burning up. When their pert-faced switchboard girl flashed on my screen I snapped: "Get me Griff. Snap it up!"

"Mr. Griff's line is busy, Mr. Hamilton," she sang to me. "Will you hold the wire, or shall I call you back?"

"None of that, Dorothe," I roared. Dorothe and I had gone to high school together; as a matter of fact I had got her the job with Griff, who was Associated's head script man. "I don't care who's talking to Griff. Cut him off and put me through. He can't do that to me. I'll sue, that's what I'll do. I'll break the company. I'll—"

"Take it easy, Ted," she said. "What's the matter with everyone all of a sudden, anyway? If you must know, the man gabbing with Griff now is old Berbelot himself. Seems he wants to sue Associated, too. What's up?"

By this time I was practically incoherent. "Berbelot, hey? I'll sue him, too. The rat! The dirty— What are you laughing at?"

"He wants to sue you!" she giggled. "And I'll bet Griff will, too, to shut Berbelot up. You know, this might turn out to be really funny!" Before I could swallow that she switched me over to Griff.

As he answered he was wiping his heavy jowls with a handkerchief. "Well?" he asked in a shaken voice.

"What are you, a wise guy?" I bellowed. "What kind of a stunt is that you pulled on the commercial plug on my play? Whose idea was that, anyway? Berbelot's? What the—"

"Now, Hamilton," Griff said easily, "don't excite yourself this way." I could see his hands trembling—evidently old Berbelot had laid it on thick. "Nothing untoward has occurred. You must be mistaken. I assure you—"

"You pompous old sociophagus," I growled, wasting a swell two-dollar word on him, "don't call me a liar. I've been listening to that program and I know what I heard. I'm going to sue you. And Berbelot. And if you try to pass the buck onto the actors in that plug skit, I'll sue them, too. And if you make any more cracks about me being mistaken, I'm going to come up there and feed you your teeth. Then I'll sue you personally as well as Associated."

I dialed out and went back to my television set, fuming. The program was going on as if nothing had happened. As I cooled—and I cool slowly—I began to see that the last half of "The Seashell" was even better than the first. You know, it's poison for a writer to fall in love with his own stuff; but, by golly, sometimes you turn out a piece that really has something. You try to be critical, and you can't be. The Ponta Delgada sequence in "The Seashell" was like that.

The girl was on a cruise and the boy was on a training ship. They met in the Azore Islands. Very touching. The last time they saw each other was before they were in their teens, but in the meantime they had had their dreams. Get the idea of the thing? Very pastel. And they did do it nicely. The shots of Ponta Delgada and the scenery of the Azores were swell. Came the moment, after four minutes of ickey dialogue, when he gazed at her, the light of true, mature love dawning on his young face.

She said shyly, "Well—"

Now, his lines, as written—and I should know!—went:

"Rosalind . . . it *is* you, then, isn't it? Oh, I'm afraid"—he grasps her shoulders—"afraid that it can't be real. So many times I've seen someone who might be you, and it has never been . . . Rosalind, Rosalind, guardian angel, reason for living, beloved . . . beloved—" Clinch.

Now, as I say, it went off as written, up to and including the clinch. But then came the payoff. He took his lips from hers, buried his face in her hair and said clearly: "I hate your — guts." And that "—" was the most per-

fectly enunciated present participle of a four-letter verb
I have ever heard.

Just what happened after that I couldn't tell you. I went
haywire, I guess. I scattered two hundred and twenty
dollars' worth of television set over all three rooms of my
apartment. Next thing I knew I was in a 'press tube, hurtling toward the three-hundred-story skyscraper that housed
Associated Television. Never have I seen one of those
'press cars, forced by compressed air through tubes under
the city, move so slowly, but it might have been my imagination. If I had anything to do with it, there was going to
be one dead script boss up there.

And who should I run into on the 229th floor but old
Berbelot himself. The perfume king had blood in his eye.
Through the haze of anger that surrounded me, I began to
realize that things were about to be very tough on Griff.
And I was quite ready to help out all I could.

Berbelot saw me at the same instant, and seemed to
read my thought. "Come on," he said briefly, and together
we ran the gantlet of secretaries and assistants and burst
into Griff's office.

Griff rose to his feet and tried to look dignified, with
little success. I leaped over his glass desk and pulled the
wings of his stylish open-necked collar together until he
began squeaking.

Berbelot seemed to be enjoying it. "Don't kill him,
Hamilton," he said after a bit. "I want to."

I let the script man go. He sank down to the floor, gasping. He was like a scared kid, in more ways than one. It
was funny.

We let him get his breath. He climbed to his feet, sat
down at his desk, and reached out toward a battery of
push buttons. Berbelot snatched up a Dow-metal paper
knife and hacked viciously at the chubby hand. It retreated.

"Might I ask," said Griff heavily, "the reason for this
unprovoked rowdiness?"

Berbelot cocked an eye at me. "Might he?"

"He might tell us what this monkey business is all
about," I said.

Griff cleared his throat painfully. "I told both you . . .
er . . . gentlemen over the phone that, as far as I know,
there was nothing amiss in our interpretation of your play,

Mr. Hamilton, nor in the commercial section of the broadcast, Mr. Berbelot. After your protests over the wire, I made it a point to see the second half of the broadcast myself. Nothing was wrong. And as this is the first commercial color broadcast, it has been recorded. If you are not satisfied with my statements, you are welcome to see the recording yourselves, immediately."

What else could we want? It occurred to both of us that Griff was really up a tree; that he was telling the truth as far as he knew it, and that he thought we were both screwy. I began to think so myself.

Berbelot said, "Griff, didn't you hear that dialogue near the end, when those two kids were by that sea wall?"

Griff nodded.

"Think back now," Berbelot went on. "What did the boy say to the girl when he put his muzzle into her hair?"

" 'I love you,' " said Griff self-consciously, and blushed. "He said it twice."

Berbelot and I looked at each other. "Let's see that recording," I said.

Well, we did, in Griff's luxurious private projection room. I hope I never have to live through an hour like that again. If it weren't for the fact that Berbelot was seeing the same thing I saw, and feeling the same way about it, I'd have reported to an alienist. Because that program came off Griff's projector positively shimmering with innocuousness. My script was A-1; Berbelot's plugs were right. On that plug that had started everything, where the man and the girl were gabbing in the theater lobby, the dialogue went like this:

"And how do you like the play, Mr. Robinson?"

"Utterly charming . . . and that goes for you, too, my dear. What *is* that perfume you are using?"

"Berbelot's *Doux Rêves*. What do you think of it?"

"You heard what I said about the play."

Well, there you are. And by the recording, Griff had been right about the repetitious three little words in the Azores sequence. I was floored.

After it was over, Berbelot said to Griff: "I think I can speak for Mr. Hamilton when I say that if this is an actual recording, we owe you an apology; also when I say that we do not accept your evidence until we have compiled our own. I recorded that program as it came over my set, as I have recorded all my advertising. We will see you tomorrow, and we will bring that sound film. Coming, Hamilton?"

I nodded and we left, leaving Griff to chew his lip.

I'd like to skip briefly over the last chapter of that evening's nightmare. Berbelot picked up a camera expert on the way, and we had the films developed within an hour after we arrived at the fantastic "house that perfume built." And if I was crazy, so was Berbelot; and if he was, then so was the camera. So help me, that blasted program came out on Berbelot's screen exactly as it had on my set and his. If anyone ever took a long-distance cussing out, it was Griff that night. We figured, of course, that he had planted a phony recording on us, so that we wouldn't sue. He'd do the same thing in court, too. I told Berbelot so. He shook his head.

"No, Hamilton, we can't take it to court. Associated gave me that broadcast, the first color commercial, on condition that I sign away their responsibility for 'incomplete, or inadequate, or otherwise unsatisfactory performance.' They didn't quite trust that new apparatus, you know."

"Well, I'll sue for both of us, then," I said.

"Did they buy all rights?" he asked.

"Yes . . . damn! They got me, too! They have a legal right to do anything they want." I threw my cigarette into the electric fire, and snapped on Berbelot's big television set, turning it to Associated's XZB.

Nothing happened.

"Hey! Your set's on the bum!" I said. Berbelot got up and began fiddling with the dial. I was wrong. There was nothing the matter with the set. It was Associated. All of their stations were off the air—all four of them. We looked at each other.

"Get XZW," said Berbelot. "It's an Associated affiliate, under cover. Maybe we can—"

XZW blared out at us as I spun the dial. A dance program, the new five-beat stuff. Suddenly the announcer stuck his face into the transmitter.

"A bulletin from Iconoscope News Service," he said conversationally. "FCC has clamped down on Associated Television and its stations. They are off the air. The reasons were not given, but it is surmised that it has to do with a little strong language used on the world première of Associated's new color transmission. That is all."

"I expected that," smiled Berbelot. "Wonder how Griff'll alibi himself out of that? If he tries to use that recording of his, I'll most cheerfully turn mine over to the government, and we'll have him for perjury."

"Sorta tough on Associated, isn't it?" I said.

"Not particularly. You know these big corporations. Associated gets millions out of their four networks, but those millions are just a drop in the bucket compared with the other pies they've got their fingers in. That color technique, for instance. Now that they can't use it for a while, how many other outfits will miss the chance of bidding for the method and equipment? They lose some advertising contracts, and they save by not operating. They won't even feel it. I'll bet you'll see color transmission within forty-eight hours over a rival network."

He was right. Two days later Cineradio had a color broadcast scheduled, and all hell broke loose. What they'd done to the Berbelot hour and my "Seashell" was really tame.

The program was sponsored by one of the antigravity industries—I forget which. They'd hired Raouls Stavisk, the composer, to play one of the ancient Gallic operas he'd exhumed. It was a piece called "Carmen" and had been practically forgotten for two centuries. News of it had created quite a stir among music lovers, although personally, I don't go for it. It's too barbaric for me. Too hard to listen to, when you've been hearing five-beat all your life. And those oldtimers had never heard of a quarter tone.

Anyway, it was a big affair, televised right from the huge Citizens' Auditorium. It was more than half full—there were about 130,000 people there. Practically all of the select highbrow music fans from that section of the city. Yes, 130,000 pairs of eyes saw that show in the flesh, and countless millions saw it on their own sets; remember that.

Those that saw it at the Auditorium got their money's worth, from what I hear. They saw the complete opera; saw it go off as scheduled. The coloratura, Maria Jeff, was in perfect voice, and Stavisk's orchestra rendered the ancient tones perfectly. So what?

So, those that saw it at home saw the first half of the program the same as broadcast—of course. But—and get this—they saw Maria Jeff, on a close-up, in the middle of an aria, throw back her head, stop singing, and shout raucously: "The hell with this! Whip it up, boys!"

They heard the orchestra break out of that old two-four music—"Habañera," I think they called it—and slide into a wicked old-time five-beat song about "alco-pill Alice," the girl who didn't believe in eugenics. They saw her step lightly about the stage, shedding her costume—not that I blame her for that; it was supposed to be authentic, and must have been warm. But there was a certain something about the way she did it.

I've never seen or heard of anything like it. First, I thought that it was part of the opera, because from what I learned in school I gather that the ancient people used to go in for things like that. I wouldn't know. But I knew it wasn't opera when old Stavisk himself jumped up on the stage and started dancing with the prima donna. The televisors flashed around to the audience, and there they were, every one of them, dancing in the aisles. And I mean dancing. Wow!

Well, you can imagine the trouble that that caused. Cineradio, Inc., was flabbergasted when they were shut down by FCC like Associated. So were 130,000 people who had seen the opera and thought it was good. Every last one of them denied dancing in the aisles. No one had seen Stavisk jump on the stage. It just didn't make sense.

Cineradio, of course, had a recording. So, it turned out, did FCC. Each recording proved the point of its respective group. That of Cineradio, taken by a sound camera right there in the auditorium, showed a musical program. FCC's, photographed right off a government standard receiver, showed the riot that I and millions of others had seen over the air. It was too much for me. I went out to see Berbelot. The old boy had a lot of sense, and he'd seen the beginning of this crazy business.

He looked pleased when I saw his face on his house televisor. "Hamilton!" he exclaimed. "Come on in! I've been phoning all over the five downtown boroughs for you!" He pressed a button and the foyer door behind me closed. I was whisked up into his rooms. That combination foyer and elevator of his is a nice gadget.

"I guess I don't have to ask you why you came," he said as we shook hands. "Cineradio certainly pulled a boner, hey?"

"Yes and no," I said. "I'm beginning to think that Griff was right when he said that, as far as he knew, the program was on the up and up. But if he was right, what's it all about? How can a program reach the transmitters in perfect shape, and come out of every receiver in the nation like a practical joker's idea of paradise?"

"It can't," said Berbelot. He stroked his chin thoughtfully. "But it did. Three times."

"Three? When—"

"Just now, before you got in. The secretary of state was making a speech over XZM, Consolidated Atomic, you know. XZM grabbed the color equipment from Cineradio as soon as they were blacked out by FCC. Well, the honorable secretary droned on as usual for just twelve and a half minutes. Suddenly he stopped, grinned into the transmitter, and said, 'Say, have you heard the one about the traveling farmer and the salesman's daughter?' "

"I have," I said. "My gosh, don't tell me he spieled it?"

"Right," said Berbelot. "In detail, over the unsullied airwaves. I called up right away, but couldn't get through. XZM's trunk lines were jammed. A very worried-looking switchboard girl hooked up I don't know how many lines together and announced into them: 'If you people are calling up about the secretary's speech, there is nothing wrong with it. Now please get off the lines!' "

"Well," I said, "let's see what we've got. First, the broadcasts leave the studios as scheduled and as written. Shall we accept that?"

"Yes," said Berbelot. "Then, since so far no black-and-white broadcasts have been affected, we'll consider that this strange behavior is limited to the polychrome technique."

"How about the recordings at the studios? They were in polychrome, and they weren't affected."

Berbelot pressed a button, and an automatic serving table rolled out of its niche and stopped in front of each of us. We helped ourselves to smokes and drinks, and the table returned to its place.

"Cineradio's wasn't a television recording, Hamilton. It was a sound camera. As for Associated's . . . I've got it! Griff's recording was transmitted to his recording machines by wire, from the studios! It didn't go out on the air at all!"

"You're right. Then we can assume that the only programs affected are those in polychrome, actually aired. Fine, but where does that get us?"

"Nowhere," admitted Berbelot. "But maybe we can find out. Come with me."

We stepped into an elevator and dropped three floors. "I don't know if you've heard that I'm a television bug," said my host. "Here's my lab. I flatter myself that a more complete one does not exist anywhere."

I wouldn't doubt it. I never in my life saw a layout like that. It was part museum and part workshop. It had in it a copy of a genuine relic of each and every phase of television down through the years, right from the old original scanning-disk sets down to the latest three-dimensional atomic jobs. Over in the corner was an extraordinarily complicated mass of apparatus which I recognized as a polychrome transmitter.

"Nice job, isn't it?" said Berbelot. "It was developed in here, you know, by one of the lads who won the Berbelot scholarship." I hadn't known. I began to have real respect for this astonishing man.

"Just how does it work?" I asked him.

"Hamilton," he said testily, "we have work to do. I would be talking all night if I told you. But the general idea is that the vibrations sent out by this transmitter are all out of phase with each other. Tinting in the receiver is achieved by certain blendings of these out-of-phase vibrations as they leave this rig. The effect is a sort of irregular vibration—a vibration in the electromagnetic waves themselves, resulting in a totally new type of wave which is still receivable in a standard set."

"I see," I lied. "Well, what do you plan to do?"

"I'm going to broadcast from here to my country place up north. It's eight hundred miles away from here, which ought to be sufficient. My signals will be received there and automatically returned to us by wire." He indicated a receiver standing close by. "If there is any difference between what we send and what we get, we can possibly find out just what the trouble is."

"How about FCC?" I asked. "Suppose—it sounds funny to say it—but just suppose that we get the kind of strong talk that came over the air during my 'Seashell' number?"

Barbelot snorted. "That's taken care of. The broadcast will be directional. No receiver can get it but mine."

What a man! He thought of everything. "O.K.," I said. "Let's go."

Berbelot threw a couple of master switches and we sat down in front of the receiver. Lights blazed on, and through a bank of push buttons at his elbow, Berbelot maneuvered the transmitting cells to a point above and behind the receiver, so that we could see and be seen without turning our heads. At a nod from Berbelot I leaned forward and switched on the receiver.

Berbelot glanced at his watch. "If things work out right, it will be between ten and thirty minutes before we get any interference." His voice sounded a little metallic. I realized that it was coming from the receiver as he spoke.

The images cleared on the view-screen as the set warmed up. It gave me an odd sensation. I saw Berbelot and myself sitting side by side—just as if we were sitting in front of a mirror, except that the images were not reversed. I thumbed my nose at myself, and my image returned the compliment.

Berbelot said: "Go easy, boy. If we get the same kind of interference the others got, your image will make something out of that." He chuckled.

"Damn right," said the receiver.

Berbelot and I stared at each other, and back at the screen. Berbelot's face was the same, but mine had a vicious sneer on it. Berbelot calmly checked with his watch. "Eight forty-six," he said. "Less time each broadcast. Pretty soon the interference will start with the broadcast, if this keeps up."

"Not unless you start broadcasting on a regular schedule," said Berbelot's image.

It had apparently dissociated itself completely from Berbelot himself. I was floored.

Berbelot sat beside me, his face frozen. "You see?" he whispered to me. "It takes a minute to catch up with itself. Till it does, it is my image."

"What does it all mean?" I gasped.

"Search me," said the perfume king.

We sat and watched. And so help me, so did our images. They were watching *us!*

Berbelot tried a direct question. "Who are you?" he asked.

"Who do we look like?" said my image; and both laughed uproariously.

Berbelot's image nudged mine. "We've got 'em on the run, hey, pal?" it chortled.

"Stop your nonsense!" said Berbelot sharply. Surprisingly, the merriment died.

"Aw," said my image plaintively. "We don't mean anything by it. Don't get sore. Let's all have fun. *I'm* having fun."

"Why, they're like kids!" I said.

"I think you're right," said Berbelot.

"Look," he said to the images, which sat there expectantly, pouting. "Before we have any fun, I want you to tell me who you are, and how you are coming through the receiver, and how you messed up the three broadcasts before this."

"Did we do wrong?" asked my image innocently. The other one giggled.

"High-spirited sons o' guns, aren't they?" said Berbelot.

"Well, are you going to answer my questions, or *do I turn the transmitter off?*" he asked the images.

They chorused frantically: "We'll tell! We'll tell! Please don't turn it off!"

"What on earth made you think of that?" I whispered to Berbelot.

"A stab in the dark," he returned. "Evidently they like coming through like this and can't do it any other way but on the polychrome wave."

"What do you want to know?" asked Berbelot's image, its lip quivering.

"Who are you?"

"Us? We're . . . I don't know. You don't have a name for us, so how can I tell you?"

"Where are you?"

"Oh, everywhere. We get around."

Berbelot moved his hand impatiently toward the switch.

The images squealed: "Don't! Oh, please don't! This is fun!"

"Fun, is it?" I growled. "Come on, give us the story, or we'll black you out!"

My image said pleadingly: "Please believe us. It's the truth. We're everywhere."

"What do you look like?" I asked. "Show yourselves as you are!"

"We can't," said the other image, "because we don't 'look' like anything. We just . . . are, that's all."

"We don't reflect light," supplemented my image.

Berbelot and I exchanged a puzzled glance. Berbelot said, "Either somebody is taking us for a ride or we've stumbled on something utterly new and unheard-of."

"You certainly have," said Berbelot's image earnestly. "We've known about you for a long time—as you count time—"

"Yes," the other continued. "We knew about you some two hundred of your years ago. We had felt your vibrations for a long time before that, but we never knew just who you were until then."

"Two hundred years—" mused Berbelot. "That was about the time of the first atomic-powered television sets."

"That's right!" said my image eagerly. "It touched our brain currents and we could see and hear. We never could get through to you until recently, though, when you sent us that stupid thing about a seashell."

"None of that, now," I said angrily, while Berbelot chuckled.

"How many of you are there?" he asked them.

"One, and many. We are finite and infinite. We have no size or shape as you know it. We just . . . are."

We just swallowed that without comment. It was a bit big.

"How did you change the programs? How are you changing this one?" Berbelot asked.

"These broadcasts pass directly through our brain currents. Our thoughts change them as they pass. It was impossible before; we were aware, but we could not be heard. This new wave has let us be heard. Its convolutions are in phase with our being."

"How did you happen to pick that particular way of

breaking through?" I asked. "I mean all that wisecracking business."

For the first time one of the images—Berbelot's—looked abashed. "We wanted to be liked. We wanted to come through to you and find you laughing. We knew how. Two hundred years of listening to every single broadcast, public and private, has taught us your language and your emotions and your ways of thought. Did we really do wrong?"

"Looks as if we have walked into a cosmic sense of humor," remarked Berbelot to me.

To his image: "Yes, in a way, you did. You lost three huge companies their broadcasting licenses. You embarrassed exceedingly a man named Griff and a secretary of state. You"—he chuckled—"made my friend here very, very angry. That wasn't quite the right thing to do, now, was it?"

"No," said my image. It actually blushed. "We won't do it any more. We were wrong. We are sorry."

"Aw, skip it," I said. I was embarrassed myself. "Everybody makes mistakes."

"That *is* good of you," said my image on the television screen. "We'd like to do something for you. And you, too, Mr.—"

"Berbelot," said Berbelot. Imagine introducing yourself to a television set!

"You can't do anything for us," I said, "except to stop messing up color televising."

"You really want us to stop, then?" My image turned to Berbelot's. "We have done wrong. We have hurt their feelings and made them angry."

To us: "We will not bother you again. Good-by!"

"Wait a minute!" I yelped, but I was too late. The view-screen showed the same two figures, but they had lost their peculiar life. They were Berbelot and me. Period.

"Now look what you've done," snapped Berbelot.

He began droning into the transmitter: "Calling interrupter on polychrome wave! Can you hear me? Can you hear me? Calling—"

He broke off and looked at me disgustedly. "You dope," he said quietly, and I felt like going off into a corner and bursting into tears.

Well, that's all. The FCC trials reached a "person or

persons unknown" verdict, and color broadcasting became a universal reality. The world has never learned, until now, the real story of that screwy business. Berbelot spent every night for three months trying to contact that ether-intelligence, without success. Can you beat it? It waited two hundred years for a chance to come through to us, and then got its feelings hurt and withdrew!

My fault, of course. That admission doesn't help any. I wish I could do something—

PROOF

by Hal Clement

"Proof" wasn't exactly written; it evolved. About a dozen years before, my attention had been caught by a balloon in the Buck Rogers comic strip in which the speaker was saying of a disappearing space ship, "They're heading for Mars, 47,000,000 miles away. It'll take them twenty days to get there, even if they travel at 100,000 miles an hour." I had never heard of Mars, didn't know anything was that many miles away, and the automobiles of 1930 couldn't quite make the speed mentioned. Naturally, I asked my father what it was all about.

Dad was an accountant, a good one as far as I know, but had never been to college. He couldn't answer little Harry's questions, but knew what to do. Together we hiked down to the Arlington public library, and came back with one book on astronomy and one copy of Jules Verne's "Journey to the Moon." It was an addictive combination, but at first all I could find for my fixes were astronomy books. For some reason, the lurid covers of the science fiction magazines already on the news stands just didn't catch my eye; I wasn't even aware of G-8 and his Battle Aces.

By the time I was ten or eleven a friend of about the same age (whom I haven't heard of, or from, since World War II—are you still around, Roger Hotaling?) had educated me; we used to read Amazing Stories *on the sly, in his cellar. The first one I remember was the October, 1933, issue; the cover illustration was for Stanton A. Coblentz' "Men Without Shadows." It also contained Neil R.*

103

Jones' "Into the Hydrosphere," and it was Professor
Jameson and the Zoromes who can probably be blamed for
the existence of Hal Clement. A year or so later, about
Thanksgiving of 1934, I had for the first time an entire
quarter—twenty-five cents—at my own disposal, and I
bought the December Amazing. It contained another
Professor Jameson story, "The Sunless World." I was
hooked forever.

I was still, it must be remembered, reading real science.
I was also one of those spectacled nuisances who make life
difficult for school teachers by not always accepting what
I was told and sometimes even being right (I have been a
teacher for over thirty years now, and have paid back with
interest the debts I incurred during that period). I had the
same attitude toward science fiction stories; I was always
finding fault with their science, though I never had the
courage to write in to their letter columns.

At first, I simply told the stories—I could do it almost
verbatim in those days—at Boy Scout campfires and similar gatherings. John Campbell's "Who Goes There?," which
I still consider the best science fiction story ever written,
has caused a good many juvenile nightmares out in the
New Hampshire woods. As time went on, I began to take
the liberty of fixing some of the science errors in the
stories; and finally, when I was about seventeen, got the
idea of actually writing one of my very own.

My favorite cousin and I spent much of that last summer
I saw him—he was killed in Italy in 1944, five years later
—trying to write stories against each other. I don't know
how long they were; paper wasn't too easy to come by on
the Canadian farm, and we scribbled in pencil as small as
we could write. I don't know what became of the manuscripts. Certainly we never seriously considered sending
them to anyone for publication.

I entered college that fall, but still told stories to the
Boy Scouts and still read magazines, though for some reason I had come to prefer Astounding to Amazing. I finally
got serious about writing, and produced something of
about 18,000 words which I thought might have a chance
of publication. My mother typed out the pencil-written
item, and I sent it to John Campbell of Astounding, not
really expecting much to happen. This was fortunate, for
not much did—though with the returned story came a

letter from John of the sort which I later learned he called the "circle bounce"—the kind he used when he thought there was some hope for the writer. He was, all things considered, quite encouraging.

I had to type the next effort myself; Mother had gone on strike over my handwriting. As you will see, it still bore the marks of the goggle-eyed classroom nuisance. I had developed by then, and still have, a very specific attitude toward the phrase "of course." Whenever I hear it, I can't help devoting thought to the things which would happen if that particular "of course" happened to be untrue.

Of course, life has to be confined to the temperature range at which matter can be solid and liquid, since after all living things have to have rather complex structures. Of course, therefore, life could not exist in a star.

Of course, I had read Jack Williamson's "Islands of the Sun," and about the days when the planets were floating within the star in their geodesic shells, menaced by the "winged xyli from their worlds of flame . . ."

Of course, I had to give more explanation than Jack did as to how life on the sun—no, in the sun—might be possible. He was the experienced writer who knew when to hold his hand and let the reader guess how certain things might happen; I knew enough to avoid a really detailed attempt at explanation, but lacked the maturity, will power, or what have you of a Jack Williamson (I still do, Master). Therefore, I talked vaguely about neutron structures and a circulatory system of magnetic fields. I sneaked in my professional knowledge—I was majoring in astronomy—and described the white dwarf companion of Sirius as a binary. I had, after all, recently read something in the Astrophysical Journal which offered this as a possible explanation for some discrepancy between theory and observation. After all, if the thing did turn out to be a binary, I'd be famous. Dean Swift had predicted the moons of Mars, hadn't he?

And, as John pointed out in the header when he published the story, "most of the universe is incandescent gas; solid matter is most unusual."

Of course. That was "Proof."

*   *   *

Kron held his huge freighter motionless, feeling forward
for outside contact. The tremendous interplay of magnetic
and electrostatic fields just beyond the city's edge was as
clearly perceptible to his senses as the city itself—a mile-
wide disk ringed with conical field towers, stretching away
behind and to each side. The ship was poised between two
of the towers; immediately behind it was the field from
which Kron had just taken off. The area was covered with
cradles of various forms—cup-shaped receptacles which
held city craft like Kron's own; long, boat-shaped hollows
wherein reposed the cigarlike vessels which plied between
the cities; and towering skeleton frameworks which held
upright the slender double cones that hurtled across the
dark, lifeless regions between stars.

Beyond the landing field was the city proper; the surface of the disk was covered with geometrically shaped
buildings—cones, cylinders, prisms, and hemispheres,
jumbled together.

Kron could "see" all this as easily as a human being in
an airplane can see New York; but no human eyes could
have perceived this city, even if a man could have existed
anywhere near it. The city, buildings and all, glowed a
savage, white heat; and about and beyond it—a part of it,
to human eyes—raged the equally dazzling, incandescent
gases of the solar photosphere.

The freighter was preparing to launch itself into that
fiery ocean; Kron was watching the play of the artificial
reaction fields that supported the city, preparatory to
plunging through them at a safe moment.

There was considerable risk of being flattened against
the edge of the disk if an inauspicious choice was made,
but Kron was an experienced flier, and slipped past the
barrier with a sudden, hurtling acceleration that would
have pulped any body of flesh and bone. The outer fringe
of the field flung the globe sharply downward; then it was
free, and the city was dwindling above them.

Kron and four others remained at their posts; the rest of
the crew of thirty relaxed, their spherical bodies lying
passive in the cuplike rests distributed through the ship,
bathing in the fierce radiance on which those bodies fed,
and which was continually streaming from a three-inch
spheroid at the center of the craft. That an artificial source
of energy should be needed in such an environment may

seem strange, but to these creatures the outer layers of the
Sun were far more inhospitable to life than is the stratosphere of Earth to human beings.

They had evolved far down near the solar core, where
pressures and temperatures were such that matter existed
in the "collapsed" state characteristic of the entire mass of
white dwarf stars. Their bodies were simply constructed:
a matrix of close-packed electrons—really an unimagin-
ably dense electrostatic field, possessing quasi-solid properties—surrounded a core of neutrons, compacted to the ultimate degree. Radiation of sufficient energy, falling on the
"skin," was stabilized, altered to the pattern and structure
of neutrons; the tiny particles of neutronium which re-
sulted were borne along a circulatory system—of magnetic
fields, instead of blood—to the nucleus, where it was
stored.

The race had evolved to the point where no material
appendages were needed. Projected beams and fields of
force were their limbs, powered by the annihilation of
some of their own neutron substance. Their strange senses
gave them awareness not only of electromagnetic radiation,
permitting them to "see" in a more or less normal fashion,
but also of energies still undreamed of by human scientists. Kron, now hundreds of miles below the city, was
still dimly aware of its location, though radio waves, light,
and gamma rays were all hopelessly fogged in the clouds of
free electrons. At his goal, far down in the solar interior,
"seeing" conditions would be worse—anything more than
a few hundred yards distant would be quite indetectable
even to him.

Poised beside Kron, near the center of the spheroidal
Sunship, was another being. Its body was ovoid in shape,
like that of the Solarian, but longer and narrower, while
the ends were tipped with pyramidal structures of neutronium, which projected through the "skin." A second,
fainter static aura outside the principal surface enveloped
the creature; and as the crew relaxed in their cups, a beam
of energy from this envelope impinged on Kron's body.
It carried a meaning, transmitting a clear thought from
one being to the other.

"I still find difficulty in believing my senses," stated the
stranger. "My own worlds revolve about another which is
somewhat similar to this; but such a vast and tenuous at-

mosphere is most unlike conditions at home. Have you ever been away from Sol?"

"Yes," replied Kron, "I was once on the crew of an interstellar projectile. I have never seen your star, however; my acquaintance with it is entirely through hearsay. I am told it consists almost entirely of collapsed matter, like the core of our own; but there is practically no atmosphere. Can this be so? I should think, at the temperature necessary for life, gases would break free of the core and form an envelope."

"They tend to do so, of course," returned the other, "but our surface gravity is immeasurably greater than anything you have here; even your core pull is less, since it is much less dense than our star. Only the fact that our worlds are small, thus causing a rapid diminution of gravity as one leaves them, makes it possible to get a ship away from them at all; atoms, with only their original velocities, remain within a few miles of the surface.

"But you remind me of my purpose on this world—to check certain points of a new theory concerning the possible behavior of aggregations of normal atoms. That was why I arranged a trip on your flier; I have to make density, pressure, temperature, and a dozen other kinds of measurements at a couple of thousand different levels, in your atmosphere. While I'm doing it, would you mind telling me why you make these regular trips—and why, for that matter, you live so far above your natural level? I should think you would find life easier below, since there would be no need to remain in sealed buildings or to expend such a terrific amount of power in supporting your cities?"

Kron's answer was slow.

"We make the journeys to obtain neutronium. It is impossible to convert enough power from the immediate neighborhood of the cities to support them; we must descend periodically for more, even though our converters take so much as to lower the solar temperature considerably for thousands of miles around each city.

"The trips are dangerous—you should have been told that. We carry a crew of thirty, when two would be enough to man this ship, for we must fight, as well as fly. You spoke truly when you said that the lower regions of Sol are our natural home; but for aeons we have not dared to make more than fleeting visits, to steal the power which is life to us.

"Your little worlds have been almost completely subjugated by your people, Sirian; they never had life forms sufficiently powerful to threaten seriously your domination. But Sol, whose core alone is far larger than the Sirius B pair, did develop such creatures. Some are vast, stupid, slow-moving, or immobile; others are semi-intelligent, and rapid movers; all are more than willing to ingest the ready-compacted neutronium of another living being."

Kron's tale was interrupted for a moment, as the Sirian sent a ray probing out through the ship's wall, testing the physical state of the inferno beyond. A record was made, and the Solarian resumed.

"We, according to logical theory, were once just such a race—of small intelligence, seeking the needs of life among a horde of competing organisms. Our greatest enemy was a being much like ourselves in size and power— just slightly superior in both ways. We were somewhat ahead in intelligence, and I suppose we owe them some thanks—without the competition they provided, we should not have been forced to develop our minds to their present level. We learned to cooperate in fighting them, and from that came the discovery that many of us together could handle natural forces that a single individual could not even approach, and survive. The creation of force effects that had no counterpart in nature was the next step; and, with the understanding of them, our science grew.

"The first cities were of neutronium, like those of today, but it was necessary to stabilize the neutrons with fields of energy; at core temperature, as you know, neutronium is a gas. The cities were spherical and much smaller than our present ones. For a long time, we managed to defend them.

"But our enemies evolved, too; not in intelligence, but in power and fecundity. With overspecialization of their physical powers, their mentalities actually degenerated; they became little more than highly organized machines, driven by an age-old enmity toward our race, to seek us out and destroy us. Their new powers at last enabled them to neutralize, by brute force, the fields which held our cities in shape; and then it was that, from necessity, we fled to the wild, inhospitable upper regions of Sol's atmosphere. Many cities were destroyed by the enemy before a means of supporting them was devised; many more fell victims to forces which we generated, without being able to control, in the effort. The dangers of our present-day trips seem trivial beside those our ancestors braved, in spite of the fact that ships not infrequently fail to return from their flights. Does that answer your question?"

The Sirian's reply was hesitant. "I guess it does. You of Sol must have developed far more rapidly than we, under that drive; your science, I know, is superior to ours in certain ways, although it was my race which first developed space flight."

"You had greater opportunities in that line," returned Kron. "Two small stars, less than a diameter apart, circling a larger one at a distance incomparably smaller than the usual interstellar interval, provided perfect ground for experimental flights; between your world and mine, even radiation requires some hundred and thirty rotations to make the journey, and even the nearest other star is almost half as far.

"But enough of this—history is considered by too many to be a dry subject. What brings you on a trip with a power flier? You certainly have not learned anything yet which you could not have been told in the city."

During the conversation, the Sirian had periodically tested the atmosphere beyond the hull. He spoke rather absently, as though concentrating on something other than his words.

"I would not be too sure of that, Solarian. My measurements are of greater delicacy than we have ever before achieved. I am looking for a very special effect, to substantiate or disprove an hypothesis which I have recently advanced—much to the detriment of my prestige. If you are interested, I might explain: laugh afterward if you care to—you will not be the first.

"The theory is simplicity itself. It has occurred to me that matter—ordinary substances like iron and calcium—might actually take on solid form, like neutronium, under the proper conditions. The normal gas, you know, consists of minute particles traveling with considerable speed in all directions. There seems to be no way of telling whether or not these atoms exert appreciable forces on one another; but it seems to me that if they were brought closely enough together, or slowed down sufficiently, some such effects might be detected."

"How, and why?" asked Kron. "If the forces are there, why should they not be detectable under ordinary conditions?"

"Tiny changes in velocity due to mutual attraction or repulsion would scarcely be noticed when the atomic speeds are of the order of hundreds of kilometers per second," returned the Sirian. "The effects I seek to detect are of a different nature. Consider, please. We know the sizes of the various atoms, from their radiations. We also know that under normal conditions, a given mass of any particular gas fills a certain volume. If, however, we surround this gas with an impenetrable container and exert pressure, that volume decreases. We would expect that decrease to be proportional to the pressure, except for an easily determined constant due to the size of the atoms, if no interatomic forces existed; to detect such forces, I am making a complete series of pressure-density tests, more delicate than any heretofore, from the level of your cities down to the neutron core of your world.

"If we could reduce the kinetic energy of the atoms—slow down their motions of translation—the task would probably be simpler; but I see no way to accomplish that. Perhaps, if we could negate nearly all of that energy, the interatomic forces would actually hold the atoms in definite relative positions, approximating the solid state. It was that somewhat injudicious and perhaps too imaginative suggestion which caused my whole idea to be ridiculed on Sirius."

The ship dropped several hundred miles in the few seconds after Kron answered; since gaseous friction is independent of change in density, the high pressures of the regions being penetrated would be no bar to high speed of flight. Unfortunately, the viscosity of a gas does increase directly as the square root of its temperature; and at the lower levels of the Sun, travel would be slow.

"Whether or not our scientists will listen to you, I cannot say," said Kron finally. "Some of them are a rather imaginative crowd, I guess, and none of them will ignore any data you may produce.

"I do not laugh, either. My reason will certainly interest you, as your theory intrigues me. It is the first time anyone has accounted even partly for the things that happened to us on one of my flights."

The other members of the crew shifted slightly on their cradles; a ripple of interest passed through them, for all had heard rumors and vague tales of Kron's time in the space carrier fleets. The Sirian settled himself more comfortably; Kron dimmed the central globe of radiance a trifle, for the outside temperature was now considerably higher, and began the tale.

"This happened toward the end of my career in space. I had made many voyages with the merchant and passenger vessels, had been promoted from the lowest ranks, through many rotations, to the post of independent captain. I had my own cruiser—a special long-period explorer, owned by the Solarian government. She was shaped like our modern interstellar carriers, consisting of two cones, bases together, with the field ring just forward of their meeting point. She was larger than most, being designed to carry fuel for exceptionally long flights.

"Another cruiser, similar in every respect, was under the command of a comrade of mine, named Akro; and the two of us were commissioned to transport a party of scientists and explorers to the then newly discovered Fourth System, which lies, as you know, nearly in the plane of the solar equator, but about half again as distant as Sirius.

"We made good time, averaging nearly half the speed of radiation, and reached the star with a good portion of our hulls still unconsumed. We need not have worried about that, in any case; the star was denser even than the Sirius B twins, and neutronium was very plentiful. I restocked at once, plating my inner walls with the stuff until they had reached their original thickness, although experience indicated that the original supply was ample to carry us back to Sol, to Sirius, or to Procyon B.

"Akro, at the request of the scientists, did not refuel. Life was present on the star, as it seems to be on all stars where the atomic velocities and the density are high enough; and the biologists wanted to bring back specimens. That meant that room would be needed, and if Akro replated his walls to normal thickness, that room would be lacking—as I have mentioned, these were special long-range craft, and a large portion of their volume consisted of available neutronium.

"So it happened that the other ship left the Fourth System with a low, but theoretically sufficient, stock of fuel, and half a dozen compartments filled with specimens of alien life. I kept within detection distance at all times, in case of trouble, for some of those life forms were as dangerous as those of Sol, and like them, all consumed neutronium. They had to be kept well under control to safeguard the very walls of the ship, and it is surprisingly difficult to make a wild beast, surrounded by food, stay on short rations.

"Some of the creatures proved absolutely unmanageable; they had to be destroyed. Others were calmed by lowering the atomic excitation of their compartments, sending them into a stupor; but the scientists were reluctant to try that in most cases, since not all of the beings could stand such treatment.

"So, for nearly four hundred solar rotations, Akro practically fought his vessel across space—fought successfully. He managed on his own power until we were within a few hundred diameters of Sol; but I had to help him with the landing—or try to, for the landing was never made.

"It may seem strange, but there is a large volume of space in the neighborhood of this Sun which is hardly ever traversed. The normal landing orbit arches high over one of the poles of rotation, enters atmosphere almost tangentially somewhere between that pole and the equator, and kills as much as remains of the ship's velocity in the outer atmospheric layers. There is a minimum of magnetic interference that way, since the flier practically coasts along the lines of force of the solar magnetic field.

"As a result, few ships pass through the space near the plane of the solar equator. One or two may have done so before us, and I know of several that searched the region later; but none encountered the thing which we found.

"About the time we would normally have started correcting our orbits for a tangential landing, Akro radiated me the information that he could not possibly control his ship any farther with the power still available to him. His walls were already so thin that radiation loss, ordinarily negligible, was becoming a definite menace to his vessel.

All his remaining energy would have to be employed in keeping the interior of his ship habitable.

"The only thing I could do was to attach our ships together with an attractor beam, and make a nearly perpendicular drop to Sol. We would have to take our chances with magnetic and electrostatic disturbances in the city-supporting fields which cover so much of the near-equatorial zones, and try to graze the nucleus of the Sun instead of its outer atmosphere, so that Akro could replenish his rapidly failing power.

"Akro's hull was radiating quite perceptibly now; it made an easy target for an attractor. We connected without difficulty, and our slightly different linear velocities caused us to revolve slowly about each other, pivoting on the center of mass of our two ships. I cut off my driving fields, and we fell spinning toward Sol.

"I was becoming seriously worried about Akro's chances of survival. The now-alarming energy loss through his almost consumed hull threatened to exhaust his supply long before we reached the core; and we were still more than a hundred diameters out. I could not give him any power; we were revolving about each other at a distance of about one-tenth of a solar diameter. To lessen that distance materially would increase our speed of revolution to a point where the attractor could not overcome centrifugal force; and I had neither power nor time to perform the delicate job of exactly neutralizing our rotary momentum without throwing us entirely off course. All we could do was hope.

"We were somewhere between one hundred and one hundred and fifty diameters out when there occurred the most peculiar phenomenon I have ever encountered. The plane of revolution of our two ships passed near Sol, but was nearly perpendicular to the solar equator; at the time of which I speak, Akro's ship was almost directly between my flier and the Sun. Observations had just shown that we were accelerating Sunward at an unexpectedly high pace, when a call came from Akro.

" 'Kron! I am being pulled away from your attractor! There is a large mass somewhere near, for the pull is gravitational, but it emits no radiation that I can detect. Increase your pull, if you can; I cannot possibly free myself alone.'

"I did what I could, which was very little. Since we did not know the location of the disturbing dark body, it was impossible to tell just what I should do to avoid bringing my own or Akro's vessel too close. I think now that if I had released him immediately he would have swung clear, for the body was not large, I believe. Unfortunately, I did the opposite, and nearly lost my own ship as well. Two of my crew were throwing as much power as they could convert and handle into the attractor, and trying to hold it on the still easily visible hull of Akro's ship; but the motions of the latter were so peculiar that aiming was a difficult task. They held the ship as long as we could see it; but quite suddenly the radiations by means of which we perceived the vessel faded out, and before we could find a band which would get through, the sudden cessation of our centripetal acceleration told us that the beam had slipped from its target.

"We found that electromagnetic radiations of wavelengths in the octave above H-alpha would penetrate the interference, and Akro's hull was leaking energy enough to radiate in that band. When we found him, however, we could scarcely believe our senses; his velocity was now nearly at right angles to his former course, and his hull radiation had become far weaker. What terrific force had caused this acceleration, and what strange field was blanketing the radiation, were questions none of us could answer.

"Strain as we might, not one of us could pick up an erg of radiant energy that might emanate from the thing that had trapped Akro. We could only watch, and endeavor to plot his course relative to our own, at first. Our ships were nearing each other rapidly, and we were attempting to determine the time and distance of closest approach, when we were startled by the impact of a communicator beam. Akro was alive! The beam was weak, very weak, showing what an infinitesimal amount of power he felt he could spare. His words were not encouraging.

" 'Kron! You may as well cut your attractor, if you are still trying to catch me. No power that I dare supply seems to move me perceptibly in any direction from this course. We are badly shocked, for we hit something that felt almost solid. The walls, even, are strained, and may go at any time.'

" 'Can you perceive anything around you?' I returned. 'You seem to us to be alone in space, though something is absorbing most of your radiated energy. There must be energies in the cosmos of which we have never dreamed, simply because they did not affect our senses. What do your scientists say?'

" 'Very little,' was the answer. 'They have made a few tests, but they say that anything they project is absorbed without reradiating anything useful. We seem to be in a sort of energy vacuum—it takes everything and returns nothing.'

"This was the most alarming item yet. Even in free space, we had been doubtful of Akro's chances of survival; now they seemed reduced to the ultimate zero.

"Meanwhile, our ships were rapidly approaching each other. As nearly as my navigators could tell, both vessels were pursuing almost straight lines in space. The lines were nearly perpendicular but did not lie in a common plane; their minimum distance apart was about one one-thousandth of a solar diameter. His velocity seemed nearly constant, while I was accelerating Sunward. It seemed that we would reach the near-intersection point almost simultaneously, which meant that my ship was certain to approach the energy vacuum much too closely. I did not dare to try to pull Akro free with an attractor; it was only too obvious that such an attempt could only end in disaster for both vessels. If he could not free himself, he was lost.

"We could only watch helplessly as the point of light marking the position of Akro's flier swept closer and closer. At first, as I have said, it semed perfectly free in space; but as we looked, the region around it began to radiate feebly. There was nothing recognizable about the vibrations, simply a continuous spectrum, cut off by some interference just below the H-alpha wavelength and, at the other end, some three octaves higher. As the emission grew stronger, the visible region around the stranded ship grew larger, fading into nothingness at the edges. Brighter and broader the patch of radiance grew, as we swept toward it."

That same radiance was seriously inconveniencing Gordon Aller, who was supposed to be surveying for a geological map of northern Australia. He was camped by the

only water hole in many miles, and had stayed up long
after dark preparing his cameras, barometer, soil kit, and
other equipment for the morrow's work.

The arrangement of instruments completed, he did not
at once retire to his blankets. With his back against a
smooth rock, and a short, blackened pipe clenched in his
teeth, he sat for some time, pondering. The object of his
musing does not matter to us; though his eyes were directed heavenward, he was sufficiently accustomed to the
southern sky to render it improbable that he was paying
much attention to its beauties.

However that may be, his gaze was suddenly attracted
to the zenith. He had often seen stars which appeared to
move when near the edge of his field of vision—it is a
common illusion; but this one continued to shift as he
turned his eyes upward.

Not far from Achernar was a brilliant white point, which
brightened as Aller watched it. It was moving slowly
northward, it seemed; but only a moment was needed for
the man to realize that the slowness was illusory. The
thing was slashing almost vertically downward at an
enormous speed, and must strike Earth not far from his
camp.

Aller was not an astronomer and had no idea of astronomical distances or speeds. He may be forgiven for thinking of the object as traveling perhaps as fast as a modern
fighting plane, and first appearing at a height of two or
three miles. The natural conclusion from this belief was
that the crash would occur within a few hundred feet of
the camp. Aller paled; he had seen pictures of the Devil's
Pit in Arizona.

Actually, of course, the meteor first presented itself to
his gaze at a height of some eighty miles, and was then
traveling at a rate of many miles per second relative to
Earth. At that speed, the air presented a practically solid
obstacle to its flight, and the object was forced to a fairly
constant velocity of ten or twelve hundred yards a second
while still nearly ten miles from Earth's surface. It was at
that point that Aller's eyes caught up with, and succeeded
in focusing upon, the celestial vistor.

That first burst of light had been radiated by the frightfully compressed and heated air in front of the thing; as
the original velocity departed, so did the dazzling light.

Aller got a clear view of the meteor at a range of less than five miles, for perhaps ten seconds before the impact. It was still incandescent, radiating a bright cherry-red; this must have been due to the loss from within, for so brief a contact even with such highly heated air could not have warmed the Sunship's neutronium walls a measurable fraction of a degree.

Aller felt the ground tremble as the vessel struck. A geyser of earth, barely visible in the reddish light of the hull, spouted skyward, to fall back seconds later with a long-drawn-out rumble. The man stared at the spot, two miles away, which was still giving off a faint glow. Were "shooting stars" as regularly shaped as that? He had seen a smooth, slender body, more than a hundred feet in length, apparently composed of two cones of unequal length, joined together at the bases. Around the longer cone, not far from the point of juncture, was a thick bulging ring; no further details were visible at the distance from which he had observed. Aller's vague recollections of meteorites, seen in various museums, brought images of irregular, clinkerlike objects before his mind's eye. What, then, could this thing be?

He was not imaginative enough to think for a moment of any possible extraterrestrial source for an aircraft; when it did occur to him that the object was of artificial origin, he though more of some experimental machine produced by one of the more progressive Earth nations.

At the thought, Aller strapped a first-aid kit to his side and set out toward the crater, in the face of the obvious fact that nothing human could possibly have survived such a crash. He stumbled over the uneven terrain for a quarter of a mile and then stopped on a small rise of ground to examine more closely the site of the wreck.

The glow should have died by this time, for Aller had taken all of ten minutes to pick his way those few hundred yards; but the dull-red light ahead had changed to a brilliant orange radiance against which the serrated edges of the pit were clearly silhouetted. No flames were visible; whence came the increasing heat? Aller attempted to get closer, but a wave of frightfully hot air blistered his face and hands and drove him back. He took up a station near his former camp, and watched.

If the hull of the flier had been anywhere near its normal thickness, the tremendous mass of neutronium would have sunk through the hardest of rocks as though they were liquid. There was, however, scarcely more than a paper thickness of the substance at any part of the walls; and an upthrust of adamantine volcanic rock not far beneath the surface of the desert proved thick enough to absorb the Sunship's momentum and to support its still enormous weight. Consequently, the ship was covered only by a thin layer of powdered rock which had fallen back into the crater. The disturbances arising from the now extremely rapid loss of energy from Akro's ship were, as a result, decidedly visible from the surface.

The hull, though thin, was still intact; but its temperature was now far above the melting point of the surrounding rocks. The thin layer of pulverized material above the ship melted and flowed away almost instantly, permitting free radiation to the air above; and so enormous is the specific heat of neutronium that no perceptible lowering of hull temperature occurred.

Aller, from his point of observation, saw the brilliant fan of light that sprang from the pit as the flier's hull was exposed—the vessel itself was invisible to him, since he was only slightly above the level of the crater's mouth. He wondered if the impact of the "meteor" had released some pent-up volcanic energy, and began to doubt, quite justifiably, if he was at a safe distance. His doubts vanished and were replaced by certainty as the edges of the crater began to glow dull red, then bright orange, and slowly subsided out of sight. He began packing the most valuable items of his equipment, while a muted, continuous roaring and occasional heavy thuds from the direction of the pit admonished him to hasten.

When he straightened up, with the seventy-pound pack settled on his shoulders, there was simply a lake of lava where the crater had been. The fiery area spread even as he watched; and without further delay he set off on his own back trail. He could see easily by the light diffused from the inferno behind him; and he made fairly good time, considering his burden and the fact that he had not slept since the preceding night.

The rock beneath Akro's craft was, as we have said, extremely hard. Since there was relatively free escape upward for the constantly liberated energy, this stratum melted very slowly, gradually letting the vessel sink deeper into the earth. What would have happened if Akro's power supply had been greater is problematical; Aller can tell us only that some five hours after the landing, as he was resting for a few moments near the top of a rocky hillock, the phenomenon came to a cataclysmic end.

A quivering of the earth beneath him caused the surveyor to look back toward his erstwhile camp. The lake of lava, which by this time was the better part of a mile in breadth, seemed curiously agitated. Aller, from his rather poor vantage point, could see huge bubbles of pasty lava hump themselves up and burst, releasing brilliant clouds of vapor. Each cloud illuminated earth and sky before cooling to invisibility, so that the effect was somewhat similar to a series of lightning flashes.

For a short time—certainly no longer than a quarter of a minute—Aller was able to watch as the activity increased. Then a particularly violent shock almost flung him from the hilltop, and at nearly the same instant the entire volume of molten rock fountained skyward. For an instant it seemed to hang there, a white, raging pillar of liquid and gas; then it dissolved, giving way before the savage thrust of the suddenly released energy below. A tongue of radiance, of an intensity indescribable in mere words, stabbed upward, into and through the lava, volatilizing instantly. A dozen square miles of desert glowed white, then an almost invisible violet, and disappeared in superheated gas. Around the edges of this region, great gouts of lava and immense fragments of solid rock were hurled to all points of the compass.

Radiation exerts pressure; at the temperature found in the cores of stars, that pressure must be measured in thousands of tons per square inch. It was this thrust, rather than the by no means negligible gas pressure of the boiling lava, which wrought most of the destruction.

Aller saw little of what occurred. When the lava was hurled upward, he had flung an arm across his face to protect his eyes from the glare. That act unquestionably saved his eyesight as the real flash followed; as it was, his body was seared and blistered through his clothing. The second, heavier, shock knocked his feet from under him, and he half crawled, half rolled down to the comparative shelter of the little hill. Even here, gusts of hot air almost cooked him; only the speed with which the phenomenon ended saved his life.

Within minutes, both the temblors and hot winds had ceased; and he crawled painfully to the hilltop again to gaze wonderingly at the five-mile-wide crater, ringed by a pile of tumbled, still-glowing rock fragments.

Far beneath that pit, shards of neutronium, no more able to remain near the surface than the steel pieces of a wrecked ocean vessel can float on water, were sinking through rock and metal to a final resting place at Earth's heart.

"The glow spread as we watched, still giving no clue to the nature of the substance radiating it," continued Kron. "Most of it seemed to originate between us and Akro's ship; Akro himself said that but little energy was being lost on the far side. His messages, during that last brief period as we swept by our point of closest approach, were clear—so clear that we could almost see, as he did, the tenuous light beyond the ever-thinning walls of his ship; the light that represented but a tiny percentage of the energy being sucked from the hull surface.

"We saw, as though with his own senses, the tiny perforation appear near one end of the ship; saw it extend, with the speed of thought, from one end of the hull to the other, permitting the free escape of all the energy in a single instant; and, from our point of vantage, saw the glowing area where the ship had been suddenly brightened, blazing for a moment almost as brightly as a piece of Sun matter.

"In that moment, every one of us saw the identifying frequencies as the heat from Akro's disrupted ship raised the substance which had trapped him to an energy level which permitted atomic radiation. Every one of us recognized the spectra of iron, of calcium, of carbon, and of silicon and a score of the other elements—Sirian, I tell you that that 'trapping field' was *matter*—matter in such a state that it could not radiate, and could offer resistance to other bodies in exactly the fashion of a solid. I thought, and have always thought, that some strange field of force held the atoms in their 'solid' positions; you have convinced me that I was wrong. The 'field' was the sum of the interacting atomic forces which you are trying to detect.

The energy level of that material body was so low that those forces were able to act without interference. The condition you could not conceive of reaching artificially actually exists in nature!"

"You go too fast, Kron," responded the Sirian. "Your first idea is far more likely to be the true one. The idea of unknown radiant or static force fields is easy to grasp; the one you propose in its place defiies common sense. My theories called for some such conditions as you described, granted the one premise of a sufficiently low energy level; but a place in the real Universe so devoid of energy as to absorb that of a well-insulated interstellar flier is utterly inconceivable. I have assumed your tale to be true as to details, though you offer neither witnesses nor records to support it; but I seem to have heard that you have somewhat of a reputation as an entertainer, and you seem quick-witted enough to have woven such a tale on the spot, purely from the ideas I suggested. I compliment you on the tale, Kron; it was entrancing; but I seriously advise you not to make anything more out of it. Shall we leave it at that, my friend?"

"As you will," replied Kron.

LOOPHOLE

by Arthur C. Clarke

The only thing I remember about this story is that it was my first to appear in Astounding—though not the first I sold to John Campbell. (That was "Rescue Party.") However, digging into my records I discover that it was written during 5–7 September 1945, in the closing months of my Air Force career. I was stationed at the time just outside Stratford-on-Avon; the influence of that location will be found in "The Curse."

The first editor I sent it to was Walter H. Gillings, who returned it immediately. He did this with several stories which he said were too good for him, and should go to the American market, though I am not sure if "Loophole" was one of these.

A critic recently referred to "Rescue Party" as a particularly blatant piece of Earth chauvinism; so is "Loophole." However, I don't let this charge worry me unduly— I've smacked down H. sapiens often enough in other stories.

And as, alas, we now know, there are no Martians to apologise to. . . .

From: President
To: Secretary, Council of Scientists.

I have been informed that the inhabitants of Earth have succeeded in releasing atomic energy and have been making experiments with rocket propulsion. This is most seri-

ous. Let me have a full report immediately. And make it
brief this time.

                                        K.K. IV.

From: Secretary, Council of Scientists.
To: President.

The facts are as follows. Some months ago our instruments detected intense neutron emission from Earth, but
an analysis of radio programs gave no explanation at the
time. Three days ago a second emission occurred and soon
afterwards all radio transmissions from Earth announced
that atomic bombs were in use in the current war. The
translators have not completed their interpretation, but it
appears that the bombs are of considerable power. Two
have so far been used. Some details of their construction
have been released, but the elements concerned have not
yet been identified. A fuller report will be forwarded as
soon as possible. For the moment all that is certain is that
the inhabitants of Earth *have* liberated atomic power, so
far only explosively.

Very little is known concerning rocket research on
Earth. Our astronomers have been observing the planet
carefully ever since radio emissions were detected a generation ago. It is certain that long-range rockets of some
kind are in existence on Earth, for there have been numerous references to them in recent military broadcasts. However, no serious attempt has been made to reach interplanetary space. When the war ends, it is expected that
the inhabitants of the planet may carry out research in this
direction. We will pay very careful attention to their
broadcasts and the astronomical watch will be rigorously
enforced.

From what we have inferred of the planet's technology,
it should require about twenty years before Earth develops
atomic rockets capable of crossing space. In view of this,
it would seem that the time has come to set up a base on
the Moon, so that a close scrutiny can be kept on such
experiments when they commence.

                                        Trescon.

(Added in manuscript.)

The war on Earth has now ended, apparently owing to
the intervention of the atomic bomb. This will not affect

the above arguments but it may mean that the inhabitants of Earth can devote themselves to pure research again more quickly than expected. Some broadcasts have already pointed out the application of atomic power in rocket propulsion.

T.

From: President.
To: Chief of Bureau of Extra-Planetary Security.
(C.B.E.P.S.)
You have seen Trescon's minute.

Equip an expedition to the satellite of Earth immediately. It is to keep a close watch on the planet and to report at once if rocket experiments are in progress.

The greatest care must be taken to keep our presence on the Moon a secret. You are personally responsible for this. Report to me at yearly intervals, or more often if necessary.

K.K. IV.

From: President.
To: C.B.E.P.S.
Where is the report on Earth?!!

K.K. IV.

From: C.B.E.P.S.
To: President.
The delay is regretted. It was caused by the breakdown of the ship carrying the report.

There have been no signs of rocket experimenting during the past year, and no reference to it in broadcasts from the planet.

Ranthe.

From: C.B.E.P.S.
To: President.
You will have seen my yearly reports to your respected father on this subject. There have been no developments of interest for the past seven years, but the following message has just been received from our base on the Moon:

Rocket projectile, apparently atomically propelled, left Earth's atmosphere today from Northern land-mass, traveling into space for one quarter diameter of planet before returning under control.

Ranthe.

From: President.
    To: Chief of State.
    Your comments, please.

K. K. V.

From: Chief of State.
To: President.
    This means the end of our traditional policy.
    The only hope of security lies in preventing the Terrestrials from making further advances in this direction. From what we know of them, this will require some overwhelming threat.
    Since its high gravity makes it impossible to land on the planet, our sphere of action is restricted. The problem was discussed nearly a century ago by Anvar, and I agree with his conclusions. We must act *immediately* along those lines.

F.K.S.

From: President.
To: Secretary of State.
    Inform the Council that an emergency meeting is convened for noon tomorrow.

K.K. V.

From: President.
To: C.B.E.P.S.
    Twenty battleships should be sufficient to put Anvar's plan into operation. Fortunately there is no need to arm them—yet. Report progress of construction to me weekly.

K.K. V.

From: C.B.E.P.S.
To: President.
    Nineteen ships are now completed. The twentieth is still delayed owing to hull failure and will not be ready for at least a month.

Ranthe.

From: President.
To: C.B.E.P.S.

Nineteen will be sufficient. I will check the operational plan with you tomorrow. Is the draft of our broadcast ready yet?

K.K. V.

From: C.B.E.P.S.
To: President.

Draft herewith:

People of Earth!

We, the inhabitants of the planet you call Mars, have for many years observed your experiments towards achieving interplanetary travel. *These experiments must cease.* Our study of your race has convinced us that you are not fitted to leave your planet in the present state of your civilization. The ships you now see floating above your cities are capable of destroying them utterly, and will do so unless you discontinue your attempts to cross space.

We have set up an observatory on your Moon and can immediately detect any violation of these orders. If you obey them, we will not interfere with you again. Otherwise, one of your cities will be destroyed every time we observe a rocket leaving the Earth's atmosphere.

By order of the President and Council of Mars.

Ranthe.

From: President.
To: C.B.E.P.S.

I approve. The translation can go ahead.

I shall not be sailing with the fleet, after all. You will report to me in detail immediately on your return.

K.K. V.

From: C.B.E.P.S.
To: President.

I have the honor to report the successful completion of our mission. The voyage to Earth was uneventful: radio messages from the planet indicated that we were detected at a considerable distance and great excitement had been aroused before our arrival. The fleet was dispersed according to plan and I broadcast the ultimatum. We left immediately and no hostile weapons were brought to bear against us.

I shall report in detail within two days.

Ranthe.

From: Secretary, Council of Scientists.
To: President.

The psychologists have completed their report, which is attached herewith.

As might be expected, our demands at first infuriated this stubborn and high-spirited race. The shock to their pride must have been considerable, for they believed themselves to be the only intelligent beings in the Universe.

However, within a few weeks there was a rather unexpected change in the tone of their statements. They had begun to realize that we were intercepting all their radio transmissions, and some messages have been broadcast directly to us. They state that they have agreed to ban all rocket experiments, in accordance with our wishes. This is as unexpected as it is welcome. Even if they are trying to deceive us, we are perfectly safe now that we have established the second station just outside the atmosphere. They cannot possibly develop spaceships without our seeing them or detecting their tube radiation.

The watch on Earth will be continued rigorously, as instructed.

Trescon.

From: C.B.E.P.S.
To: President.

Yes, it is quite true that there have been no further rocket experiments in the last ten years. We certainly did not expect Earth to capitulate so easily!

I agree that the existence of this race now constitutes a permanent threat to our civilization and we are making experiments along the lines you suggest. The problem is a difficult one, owing to the great size of the planet. Explosives would be out of the question, and a radioactive poison of some kind appears to offer the greatest hope of success.

Fortunately, we now have an indefinite time in which to complete this research, and I will report regularly.

Ranthe.

End of Document

From: Lieutenant Commander Henry Forbes, Intelligence Branch, Special Space Corps.

To: Professor S. Maxton, Philological Department, University of Oxford.

Route: Transender II (via Schenectady.)

The above papers, with others, were found in the ruins of what is believed to be the capital Martian city. (Mars Grid KL302895.) The frequent use of the ideograph for "Earth" suggests that they may be of special interest and it is hoped that they can be translated. Other papers will be following shortly.

H. Forbes, Lt/Cdr.

(Added in manuscript.)
Dear Max,

Sorry I've had no time to contact you before. I'll be seeing you as soon as I get back to Earth.

Gosh! Mars *is* in a mess! Our co-ordinates were dead accurate and the bombs materialized right over their cities, just as the Mount Wilson boys predicted.

We're sending a lot of stuff back through the two small machines, but until the big transmitter is materialized we're rather restricted, and, of course, none of us can return. So hurry up with it!

I'm glad we can get to work on rockets again. I may be old-fashioned, but being squirted through space at the speed of light doesn't appeal to me!

Yours in haste,

Henry.

TOMORROW'S CHILDREN

by Poul Anderson

At the age of thirteen, I lived for some months in Silver Spring, Maryland, and found a good friend in a classmate, Neil Waldrop. (He is actually Francis Neil Waldrop, but has always preferred the middle name.) After my family moved to Minnesota, he and I corresponded. It was he who got me hooked on science fiction, by sending me a bunch of magazines. We used to write stories, too, and mail them back and forth for comments. Eventually he abandoned that hobby, but I didn't.

In due course I went to the University of Minnesota, majoring in physics. Neil came out there for about a year, as a pre-medical student, since the place had a particularly good department in an area of special interest to him. Naturally, we spent a lot of time talking. This was in 1946, when the prospect of nuclear war was on everybody's mind. So were the possible mutagenic effects of hard radiation. One day Neil raised the question, "What if such a war spreads so much radioactivity around that every life form on Earth suffers genetic alteration?"

I saw a story in that, wrote it, and showed it to him. He said it was good enough that it should be submitted to Astounding, something I'd never had the nerve to do, apart from one entry in the old "Probability Zero" section. Thus encouraged, I borrowed my mother's typewriter, copied off my scrawled words, and sent them in. The basic idea having been Neil's, it seemed only proper to give him half the by-line; however, the writing was entirely mine.

Months went by. I came back to school from a summer job in the north woods and had well-nigh forgotten the

131

story—until my mother phoned me at the house where I roomed. A letter had come to her address, which I had used, from Street & Smith. Should she open it and read it to me? Oh, my, yes!

And that's how it all began. I had no intention of becoming a full-time writer. When I graduated, though, it was into a recession, jobs were hard to find, and I thought I'd try to support myself by free-lancing while I looked around. The while got longer and longer. . . .

Let me remark here that the premise of "Tomorrow's Children" is incorrect. Mutation from global fallout would not work as described. Still, this had not been established in 1946.

Let me also set straight a false impression held by some people. At least, I have heard a lady writer declare that before John Campbell would okay her first sale to him, she had to give him a notarized statement that it was her own, original work. She believed this was because of her sex. Actually, I had to do the same thing. Every first-time contributor did.

As for Neil, he returned to Maryland and got his M.D. degree, but presently went into neurological research and became quite important in that field. Recently he retired and, when last heard from, was happily devoting himself to other activities, such as astrophotography. I have never told him what Harlan Ellison wrote about F. N. Waldrop in Dangerous Visions. *Should I?*

> On the world's loom
> Weave the Norns doom,
> Nor may they guide it nor change.
> —WAGNER, *Siegfried*

Ten miles up, it hardly showed. Earth was a cloudy green and brown blur, the vast vault of the stratosphere reaching changelessly out to spatial infinities, and beyond the pulsing engine there was silence and serenity no man could ever touch. Looking down, Hugh Drummond could see the Mississippi gleaming like a drawn sword, and its slow curve matched the contours shown on his map. The hills, the sea, the sun and wind and rain, they didn't change. Not in less than a million slow-striding years, and human efforts flickered too briefly in the unending night for that.

Farther down, though, and especially where cities had been— The lone man in the solitary stratojet swore softly, bitterly, and his knuckles whitened on the controls. He was a big man, his gaunt rangy form sprawling awkwardly in the tiny pressure cabin, and he wasn't quite forty. But his dark hair was streaked with gray, in the shabby flying suit his shoulders stooped, and his long homely face was drawn into haggard lines. His eyes were black-rimmed and sunken with weariness, dark and dreadful in their intensity. He'd seen too much, survived too much, until he began to look like most other people of the world. *Heir of the ages,* he thought dully.

Mechanically, he went through the motions of following his course. Natural landmarks were still there, and he had powerful binoculars to help him. But he didn't use them much. They showed too many broad shallow craters, their vitreous smoothness throwing back sunlight in the flat blank glitter of a snake's eye, the ground about them a churned and blasted desolation. And there were the worse regions of—deadness. Twisted dead trees, blowing sand, tumbled skeletons, perhaps at night a baleful blue glow of fluorescence. The bombs had been nightmares, riding in on wings of fire and horror to shake the planet with the death blows of cities. But the radioactive dust was worse than any nightmare.

He passed over villages, even small towns. Some of them were deserted, the blowing colloidal dust, or plague, or economic breakdown making them untenable. Others still seemed to be living a feeble half-life. Especially in the Midwest, there was a pathetic struggle to return to an agricultural system, but the insects and blights—

Drummond shrugged. After nearly two years of this, over the scarred and maimed planet, he should be used to it. The United States had been lucky. Europe, now—

Der Untergang des Abendlandes, he thought grayly. *Spengler foresaw the collapse of a topheavy civilization. He didn't foresee atomic bombs, radioactive-dust bombs, bacteria bombs, blight bombs—the bombs, the senseless inanimate bombs flying like monster insects over the shivering world. So he didn't guess the extent of the collapse.*

Deliberately he pushed the thoughts out of his conscious

mind. He didn't want to dwell on them. He'd lived with them two years, and that was two eternities too long. And anyway, he was nearly home now.

The capital of the United States was below him, and he sent the stratojet slanting down in a long thunderous dive toward the mountains. Not much of a capital, the little town huddled in a valley of the Cascades, but the waters of the Potomac had filled the grave of Washington. Strictly speaking, there was no capital. The officers of the government were scattered over the country, keeping in precarious touch by plane and radio, but Taylor, Oregon, came as close to being the nerve center as any other place.

He gave the signal again on his transmitter, knowing with a faint spine-crawling sensation of the rocket batteries trained on him from the green of those mountains. When one plane could carry the end of a city, all planes were under suspicion. Not that anyone outside was supposed to know that that innocuous little town was important. But you never could tell. The war wasn't officially over. It might never be, with sheer personal survival overriding the urgency of treaties.

A light-beam transmitter gave him a cautious: "O.K. Can you land in the street?"

It was a narrow, dusty track between two wooden rows of houses, but Drummond was a good pilot and this was a good jet. "Yeah," he said. His voice had grown unused to speech.

He cut speed in a spiral descent until he was gliding with only the faintest whisper of wind across his ship. Touching wheels to the street, he slammed on the brake and bounced to a halt.

Silence struck at him like a physical blow. The engine stilled, the sun beating down from a brassy blue sky on the drabness of rude "temporary" houses, the total-seeming desertion beneath the impassive mountains— Home! Hugh Drummond laughed, a short harsh bark with nothing of humor in it, and swung open the cockpit canopy.

There were actually quite a few people, he saw, peering from doorways and side streets. They looked fairly well fed and dressed, many in uniform, they seemed to have purpose and hope. But this, of course, was the capital of the United States of America, the world's most fortunate country.

"Get out—quick!"

The peremptory voice roused Drummond from the introspection into which those lonely months had driven him. He looked down at a gang of men in mechanics' outfits, led by a harassed-looking man in captain's uniform. "Oh—of course," he said slowly. "You want to hide the plane. And, naturally, a regular landing field would give you away."

"Hurry, get out, you infernal idiot! Anyone, *anyone* might come over and see—"

"They wouldn't get unnoticed by an efficient detection system, and you still have that," said Drummond, sliding his booted legs over the cockpit edge. "And anyway, there won't be any more raids. The war's over."

"Wish I could believe that, but who are you to say? Get a move on!"

The grease monkeys hustled the plane down the street. With an odd feeling of loneliness, Drummond watched it go. After all, it had been his home for—how long?

The machine was stopped before a false house whose whole front was swung aside. A concrete ramp led downward, and Drummond could see a cavernous immensity below. Light within it gleamed off silvery rows of aircraft.

"Pretty neat," he admitted. "Not that it matters any more. Probably it never did. Most of the hell came over on robot rockets. Oh, well." He fished his pipe from his jacket. Colonel's insignia glittered briefly as the garment flipped back.

"Oh . . . sorry, sir!" exclaimed the captain. "I didn't know—"

"'S O.K. I've gotten out of the habit of wearing a regular uniform. A lot of places I've been, an American wouldn't be very popular." Drummond stuffed tobacco into his briar, scowling. He hated to think how often he'd had to use the Colt at his hip, or even the machine guns in his plane, to save himself. He inhaled smoke gratefully. It seemed to drown out some of the bitter taste.

"General Robinson said to bring you to him when you arrived, sir," said the captain. "This way, please."

They went down the street, their boots scuffing up little acrid clouds of dust. Drummond looked sharply about him. He'd left very shortly after the two-month Ragnarok which had tapered off when the organization of both sides broke down too far to keep on making and sending the bombs, and maintaining order with famine and disease starting their ghastly ride over the homeland. At that time, the United States was a cityless, anarchic chaos, and he'd had only the briefest of radio exchanges since then, whenever he could get at a long-range set still in working order. They'd made remarkable progress meanwhile. How much, he didn't know, but the mere existence of something like a capital was sufficient proof.

Robinson— His lined face twisted into a frown. He didn't know the man. He'd been expecting to be received by the President, who had sent him and some others out. Unless the others had— No, he was the only one who had been in eastern Europe and western Asia. He was sure of that.

Two sentries guarded the entrance to what was obviously a converted general store. But there were no more stores. There was nothing to put in them. Drummond entered the cool dimness of an antechamber. The clatter of a typewriter, the Wac operating it— He gaped and blinked. That was—impossible! Typewriters, secretaries—hadn't they gone out with the whole world, two years ago? If the Dark Ages had returned to Earth, it didn't seem—*right*— that there should still be typewriters. It didn't fit, didn't—

He grew aware that the captain had opened the inner door for him. As he stepped in, he grew aware how tired he was. His arm weighed a ton as he saluted the man behind the desk.

"At ease, at ease," Robinson's voice was genial. Despite the five stars on his shoulders, he wore no tie or coat, and his round face was smiling. Still, he looked tough and competent underneath. To run things nowadays, he'd have to be.

"Sit down, Colonel Drummond." Robinson gestured to a chair near his and the aviator collapsed into it, shivering. His haunted eyes traversed the office. It was almost well enough outfitted to be a prewar place.

Prewar! A word like a sword, cutting across history with a brutality of murder, hazing everything in the past until it was a vague golden glow through drifting, red-shot black clouds. And—only two years. *Only two years!* Surely sanity was meaningless in a world of such nightmare inversions. Why, he could barely remember Barbara and the kids. Their faces were blotted out in a tide of other visages —starved faces, dead faces, human faces become beast-formed with want and pain and eating throttled hate. His grief was lost in the agony of a world, and in some ways he had become a machine himself.

"You look plenty tired," said Robinson.

"Yeah . . . yes, sir—"

"Skip the formality. I don't go for it. We'll be working pretty close together, can't take time to be diplomatic."

"Uh-huh. I came over the North Pole, you know. Haven't slept since— Rough time. But, if I may ask, you—" Drummond hesitated.

"I? I suppose I'm President. Ex officio, pro tem, or something. Here, you need a drink." Robinson got bottle and glasses from a drawer. The liquor gurgled out in a pungent stream. "Prewar Scotch. Till it gives out I'm laying off this modern hooch. *Gambai.*"

The fiery, smoky brew jolted Drummond to wakefulness. Its glow was pleasant in his empty stomach. He heard Robinson's voice with a surrealistic sharpness:

"Yes, I'm at the head now. My predecessors made the mistake of sticking together, and of traveling a good deal in trying to pull the country back into shape. So I think the sickness got the President, and I know it got several others. Of course, there was no means of holding an election. The armed forces had almost the only organization left, so we had to run things. Berger was in charge, but he shot himself when he learned he'd breathed radiodust. Then the command fell to me. I've been lucky."

"I see." It didn't make much difference. A few dozen more deaths weren't much, when over half the world was gone. "Do you expect to—continue lucky?" A brutally blunt question, maybe, but words weren't bombs.

"I do." Robinson was firm about that. "We've learned by experience, learned a lot. We've scattered the army, broken it into small outposts at key points throughout the country. For quite a while, we stopped travel altogether except for absolute emergencies, and then with elaborate precautions. That smothered the epidemics. The micro-organisms were bred to work in crowded areas, you know. They were almost immune to known medical techniques, but without hosts and carriers they died. I guess natural bacteria ate up most of them. We still take care in traveling, but we're fairly safe now."

"Did any of the others come back? There were a lot like me, sent out to see what really had happened to the world."

"One did, from South America. Their situation is similar to ours, though they lacked our tight organization and have gone further toward anarchy. Nobody else returned but you."

It wasn't surprising. In fact, it was a cause for astonishment that anyone had come back. Drummond had volunteered after the bomb erasing St. Louis had taken his family, not expecting to survive and not caring much whether he did. Maybe that was why he had.

"You can take your time in writing a detailed report," said Robinson, "but in general, how are things over there?"

Drummond shrugged. "The war's over. Burned out. Europe has gone back to savagery. They were caught between America and Asia, and the bombs came both ways. Not many survivors, and they're starving animals. Russia, from what I saw, has managed something like you've done here, though they're worse off than we. Naturally, I couldn't find out much there. I didn't get to India or China, but in Russia I heard rumors— No, the world's gone too far into disintegration to carry on war."

"Then we can come out in the open," said Robinson softly. "We can really start rebuilding. I don't think there'll ever be another war, Drummond. I think the memory of this one will be carved too deeply on the race for us ever to forget."

"Can you shrug it off that easily?"

"No, no, of course not. Our culture hasn't lost its continuity, but it's had a terrific setback. We'll never wholly get over it. But—we're on our way up again."

The general rose, glancing at his watch. "Six o'clock. Come on, Drummond, let's get home."

"Home?"

"Yes, you'll stay with me. Man, you look like the original zombie. You'll need a month or more of sleeping between clean sheets, of home cooking and home atmosphere. My wife will be glad to have you; we see almost no new faces. And as long as we'll work together, I'd like to keep you handy. The shortage of ●ompetent men is terrific."

They went down the street, an aide following. Drummond was again conscious of the weariness aching in every bone and fiber of him. A home—after two years of ghost towns, of shattered chimneys above blood-dappled snow, of flimsy lean-tos housing starvation and death.

"Your plane will be mighty useful, too," said Robinson. "Those atomic-powered craft are scarcer than hens' teeth used to be." He chuckled hollowly, as at a rather grim joke. "Got you through close to two years of flying without needing fuel. Any other trouble?"

"Some, but there were enough spare parts." No need to tell of those frantic hours and days of slaving, of desperate improvisation with hunger and plague stalking him who stayed overlong. He'd had his troubles getting food, too, despite the plentiful supplies he'd started out with. He'd fought for scraps in the winters, beaten off howling maniacs who would have killed him for a bird he'd shot or a dead horse he'd scavenged. He hated that plundering, and would not have cared personally if they'd managed to destroy him. But he had a mission, and the mission was all he'd had left as a focal point for his life, so he'd clung to it with fanatic intensity.

And now the job was over, and he realized he couldn't rest. He didn't dare. Rest would give him time to remember. Maybe he could find surcease in the gigantic work of reconstruction. Maybe.

"Here we are," said Robinson.

Drummond blinked in new amazement. There was a car, camouflaged under brush, with a military chauffeur—*a car!* And in pretty fair shape, too.

"We've got a few oil wells going again, and a small patched-up refinery," explained the general. "It furnishes enough gas and oil for what traffic we have."

They got in the rear seat. The aide sat in front, a rifle ready. The car started down a mountain road.

"Where to?" asked Drummond a little dazedly.

Robinson smiled. "Personally," he said, "I'm almost the only lucky man on Earth. We had a summer cottage on Lake Taylor, a few miles from here. My wife was there when the war came, and stayed, and nobody came along till I brought the head offices here with me. Now I've got a home all to myself."

"Yeah. Yeah, you're lucky," said Drummond. He looked out the window, not seeing the sun-spattered woods. Presently he asked, his voice a little harsh: "How is the country really doing now?"

"For a while it was rough. Damn rough. When the cities went, our transportation, communication, and distribution systems broke down. In fact, our whole economy disintegrated, though not all at once. Then there was the dust and the plagues. People fled, and there was open fighting when overcrowded safe places refused to take in any more refugees. Police went with the cities, and the army couldn't do much patrolling. We were busy fighting the enemy troops that'd flown over the Pole to invade. We still haven't gotten them all. Bands are roaming the country, hungry and desperate outlaws, and there are plenty of Americans who turned to banditry when everything else failed. That's why we have this guard, though so far none have come this way.

"The insect and blight weapons just about wiped out our crops, and that winter everybody starved. We checked the pests with modern methods, though it was touch and go for a while, and next year got some food. Of course, with no distribution as yet, we failed to save a lot of people. And farming is still a tough proposition. We won't really have the bugs licked for a long time. If we had a research center as well equipped as those which produced the things— But we're gaining. We're gaining."

"Distribution—" Drummond rubbed his chin. "How about railroads? Horse-drawn vehicles?"

"We have some railroads going, but the enemy was as careful to dust most of ours as we were to dust theirs. As for horses, they were nearly all eaten that first winter. I know personally of only a dozen. They're on my place; I'm trying to breed enough to be of use, but"—Robinson smiled wryly—"by the time we've raised that many, the factories should have been going quite a spell."

"And so now—?"

"We're over the worst. Except for outlaws, we have the population fairly well controlled. The civilized people are fairly well fed, with some kind of housing. We have machine shops, small factories, and the like going, enough

to keep our transportation and other mechanism 'level.'
Presently we'll be able to expand these, begin actually increasing what we have. In another five years or so, I guess,
we'll be integrated enough to drop martial law and hold a
general election. A big job ahead, but a good one."

The car halted to let a cow lumber over the road, a calf
trotting at her heels. She was gaunt and shaggy, and skit-
tered nervously from the vehicle into the brush.

"Wild," explained Robinson. "Most of the real wild life
was killed off for food in the last two years, but a lot of
farm animals escaped when their owners died or fled, and
have run free ever since. They—" He noticed Drummond's fixed gaze. The pilot was looking at the calf. Its
legs were half the normal length.

"Mutant," said the general. "You find many such animals. Radiation from bombed or dusted areas. There are
even a lot of human abnormal births." He scowled, worry
clouding his eyes. "In fact, that's just about our worst
problem. It—"

The car came out of the woods onto the shore of a
small lake. It was a peaceful scene, the quiet waters like
molten gold in the slanting sunlight, trees ringing the cir-
cumference and all about them the mountains. Under one
huge pine stood a cottage, a woman on the porch.

It was like one summer with Barbara—Drummond
cursed under his breath and followed Robinson toward the
little building. It wasn't, it wasn't, it could never be. Not
ever again. There were soldiers guarding this place from
chance marauders, and— There was an odd-looking flower
at his foot. A daisy, but huge and red and irregularly
formed.

A squirrel chittered from a tree. Drummond saw that
its face was so blunt as to be almost human.

Then he was on the porch, and Robinson was introducing him to "my wife Elaine." She was a nice-looking
young woman with eyes that were sympathetic on Drummond's exhausted face. The aviator tried not to notice
that she was pregnant.

He was led inside, and reveled in a hot bath. Afterward
there was supper, but he was numb with sleep by then,
and hardly noticed it when Robinson put him to bed.

*   *   *

Reaction set in, and for a week or so Drummond went about in a haze, not much good to himself or anyone else. But it was surprising what plenty of food and sleep could do, and one evening Robinson came home to find him scribbling on sheets of paper.

"Arranging my notes and so on," he explained. "I'll write out the complete report in a month, I guess."

"Good. But no hurry." Robinson settled tiredly into an armchair. "The rest of the world will keep. I'd rather you'd just work at this off and on, and join my staff for your main job."

"O.K. Only what'll I do?"

"Everything. Specialization is gone; too few surviving specialists and equipment. I think your chief task will be to head the census bureau."

"Eh?"

Robinson grinned lopsidedly. "You'll *be* the census bureau, except for what few assistants I can spare you." He leaned forward, said earnestly: "And it's one of the most important jobs there is. You'll do for this country what you did for central Eurasia, only in much greater detail. Drummond, we have to *know*."

He took a map from a desk drawer and spread it out. "Look, here's the United States. I've marked regions known to be uninhabitable in red." His fingers traced out the ugly splotches. "Too many of 'em, and doubtless there are others we haven't found yet. Now, the blue X's are army posts." They were sparsely scattered over the land, near the centers of population groupings. "Not enough of those. It's all we can do to control the more or less well-off, orderly people. Bandits, enemy troops, homeless refugees—they're still running wild, skulking in the backwoods and barrens, and raiding whenever they can. And they spread the plague. We won't really have it licked till everybody's settled down, and that'd be hard to enforce. Drummond, we don't even have enough soldiers to start a feudal system for protection. The plague spread like a prairie fire in those concentrations of men.

"We have to *know*. We have to know how many people survived—half the population, a third, a quarter, whatever it is. We have to know where they are, and how they're fixed for supplies, so we can start up an equitable distribution system. We have to find all the small-town shops and labs and libraries still standing, and rescue their priceless contents before looters or the weather beat us to it. We have to locate doctors and engineers and other professional men, and put them to work rebuilding. We have to find the outlaws and round them up. We— I could go on forever. Once we have all that information, we can set up a master plan for redistributing population, agriculture, industry, and the rest most efficiently, for getting the country back under civil authority and police, for opening regular transportation and communication channels—for getting the nation back on its feet."

"I see," nodded Drummond. "Hitherto, just surviving and hanging on to what was left has taken precedence. Now you're in a position to start expanding, *if* you know where and how much to expand."

"Exactly." Robinson rolled a cigarette, grimacing. "Not much tobacco left. What I have is perfectly foul. Lord, that war was crazy!"

"All wars are," said Drummond dispassionately, "but technology advanced to the point of giving us a knife to cut our throats with. Before that, we were just beating our heads against the wall. Robinson, we can't go back to the old ways. We've *got* to start on a new track—a track of sanity."

"Yes. And that brings up—" The other man looked toward the kitchen door. They could hear the cheerful rattle of dishes there, and smell mouth-watering cooking odors. He lowered his voice. "I might as well tell you this now, but don't let Elaine know. She . . . she shouldn't be worried. Drummond, did you see our horses?"

"The other day, yes. The colts—"

"Uh-huh. There've been five colts born of eleven mares in the last year. Two of them were so deformed they died in a week, another in a few months. One of the two left has cloven hoofs and almost no teeth. The last one looks normal—so far. One out of eleven, Drummond."

"Were those horses near a radioactive area?"

"They must have been. They were rounded up wherever found and brought here. The stallion was caught near the site of Portland, I know. But if he were the only one with mutated genes, it would hardly show in the first generation, would it? I understand nearly all mutations are Mendelian recessives. Even if there were one dominant, it

would show in all the colts, but none of these looked
alike."

"Hm-m-m—I don't know much about genetics, but I do
know hard radiation, or rather the secondary charged particles it produces, will cause mutation. Only mutants are
rare, and tend to fall into certain patterns—"

"*Were* rare!" Suddenly Robinson was grim, something
coldly frightened in his eyes. "Haven't you noticed the
animals and plants? They're fewer than formerly, and . . .
well, I've not kept count, but at least half those seen or
killed have something wrong, internally or externally."

Drummond drew heavily on his pipe. He needed something to hang onto, in a new storm of insanity. Very
quietly, he said:

"In my college biology course, they told me the vast
majority of mutations are unfavorable. More ways of not
doing something than of doing it. Radiation might sterilize
an animal, or might produce several degrees of genetic
change. You could have a mutation so violently lethal the
possessor never gets born, or soon dies. You could have all
kinds of more or less handicapping factors, or just random
changes not making much difference one way or the other.
Or in a few cases you might get something actually favorable, but you couldn't really say the possessor is a true
member of the species. And favorable mutations themselves usually involve a price in the partial or total loss
of some other function."

"Right." Robinson nodded heavily. "One of your jobs
on the census will be to try and locate any and all who
know genetics, and send them here. But your real task,
which only you and I and a couple of others must know
about, the job overriding all other considerations, will be
to find the human mutants."

Drummond's throat was dry. "There've been a lot of
them?" he whispered.

"Yes. But we don't know how many or where. We
only know about those people who live near an army post,
or have some other fairly regular intercourse with us,
and they're only a few thousand all told. Among them,
the birth rate has gone down to about half the prewar
ratio. And over half the births they do have are abnormal."

"Over half—"

"Yeah. Of course, the violently different ones soon die, or are put in an institution we've set up in the Alleghenies. But what can we do with viable forms, if their parents still love them? A kid with deformed or missing or abortive organs, twisted internal structure, a tail, or something even worse . . . well, *it'll* have a tough time in life, but it can generally survive. And perpetuate itself—"

"And a normal-looking one might have some unnoticeable quirk, or a characteristic that won't show up for years. Or even a normal one might be carrying recessives, and pass them on— God!" The exclamation was half blasphemy, half prayer. "But how'd it happen? People weren't all near atom-hit areas."

"Maybe not, though a lot of survivors escaped from the outskirts. But there was that first year, with everybody on the move. One could pass near enough to a blasted region to be affected, without knowing it. And that damnable radiodust, blowing on the wind. It's got a long half-life. It'll be active for decades. Then, as in any collapsing culture, promiscuity was common. Still is. Oh, it'd spread itself, all right."

"I still don't see why it spread itself so much. Even here—"

"Well, I don't know why it shows up here. I suppose a lot of the local flora and fauna came in from elsewhere. This place is safe. The nearest dusted region is three hundred miles off, with mountains between. There must be many such islands of comparatively normal conditions. We have to find them too. But elsewhere—"

"Soup's on," announced Elaine, and went from the kitchen to the dining room with a loaded tray.

The men rose. Grayly, Drummond looked at Robinson and said tonelessly: "O.K. I'll get your information for you. We'll map mutation areas and safe areas, we'll check on our population and resources, we'll eventually get all the facts you want. But—what are you going to do then?"

"I wish I knew," said Robinson haggardly. "I wish I knew."

Winter lay heavily on the north, a vast gray sky seeming frozen solid over the rolling white plains. The last three winters had come early and stayed long. Dust, colloidal dust of the bombs, suspended in the atmosphere and cutting down the solar constant by a deadly percent or two. There had even been a few earthquakes, set off in geologically unstable parts of the world by bombs planted right. Half California had been ruined when a sabotage bomb started the San Andreas Fault on a major slip. And that kicked up still more dust.

Fimbulwinter, thought Drummond bleakly. *The doom of the prophecy. But no, we're surviving. Though maybe not as men—*

Most people had gone south, and there overcrowding had made starvation and disease and internecine struggle the normal aspects of life. Those who'd stuck it out up here, and had luck with their pest-ridden crops, were better off.

Drummond's jet slid above the cratered black ruin of the Twin Cities. There was still enough radioactivity to melt the snow, and the pit was like a skull's empty eye socket. The man sighed, but he was becoming calloused to the sight of death. There was so much of it. Only the struggling agony of life mattered any more.

He strained through the sinister twilight, swooping low over the unending fields. Burned-out hulks of farmhouses, bones of ghost towns, sere deadness of dusted land—but he'd heard travelers speak of a fairly powerful community up near the Canadian border, and it was up to him to find it.

A lot of things had been up to him in the last six months. He'd had to work out a means of search, and organize his few, overworked assistants into an efficient staff, and go out on the long hunt.

They hadn't covered the country. That was impossible. Their few planes had gone to areas chosen more or less at random, trying to get a cross section of conditions. They'd penetrated wildernesses of hill and plain and forest, establishing contact with scattered, still demoralized out-dwellers. On the whole, it was more laborious than anything else. Most were pathetically glad to see any symbol of law and order and the paradisical-seeming "old days." Now and then there was danger and trouble, when they encountered wary or sullen or outright hostile groups suspicious of a government they associated with disaster, and once there had even been a pitched battle with roving outlaws. But the work had gone ahead, and now the preliminaries were about over.

Preliminaries— It was a bigger job to find out exactly how matters stood than the entire country was capable of undertaking right now. But Drummond had enough facts for reliable extrapolation. He and his staff had collected most of the essential data and begun correlating it. By questioning, by observation, by seeking and finding, by any means that came to hand they'd filled their notebooks. And in the sketchy outlines of a Chinese drawing, and with the same stark realism, the truth was there.

Just this one more place, and I'll go home, thought Drummond for the—thousandth?—time. His brain was getting into a rut, treading the same terrible circle and finding no way out. *Robinson won't like what I tell him, but there it is.* And darkly, slowly: *Barbara, maybe it was best you and the kids went as you did. Quickly, cleanly, not even knowing it. This isn't much of a world. It'll never be our world again.*

He saw the place he sought, a huddle of buildings near the frozen shores of the Lake of the Woods, and his jet murmured toward the white ground. The stories he'd heard of this town weren't overly encouraging, but he supposed he'd get out all right. The others had his data anyway, so it didn't matter.

By the time he'd landed in the clearing just outside the village, using the jet's skis, most of the inhabitants were there waiting. In the gathering dusk they were a ragged and wild-looking bunch, clumsily dressed in whatever scraps of cloth and leather they had. The bearded, hard-eyed men were armed with clubs and knives and a few guns. As Drummond got out, he was careful to keep his hands away from his own automatics.

"Hello," he said. "I'm friendly."

"Y' better be," growled the big leader. "Who are you, where from, an' why?"

"First," lied Drummond smoothly, "I want to tell you I have another man with a plane who knows where I am. If I'm not back in a certain time, he'll come with bombs. But we don't intend any harm or interference. This is just a sort of social call. I'm Hugh Drummond of the United States Army."

They digested that slowly. Clearly, they weren't friendly

to the government, but they stood in too much awe of aircraft and armament to be openly hostile. The leader spat. "How long you staying?"

·"Just overnight, if you'll put me up. I'll pay for it." He held up a small pouch. "Tobacco."

Their eyes gleamed, and the leader said, "You'll stay with me. Come on."

Drummond gave him the bribe and went with the group. He didn't like to spend such priceless luxuries thus freely, but the job was more important. And the boss seemed thawed a little by the fragrant brown flakes. He was sniffing them greedily.

"Been smoking bark an' grass," he confided. "Terrible."

"Worse than that," agreed Drummond. He turned up his jacket collar and shivered. The wind starting to blow was bitterly cold.

"Just what y' here for?" demanded someone else.

"Well, just to see how things stand. We've got the government started again, and are patching things up. But we have to know where folks are, what they need, and so on."

"Don't want nothing t' do with the gov'ment," muttered a woman. "They brung all this on us."

"Oh, come now. We didn't ask to be attacked." Mentally, Drummond crossed his fingers. He neither knew nor cared who was to blame. Both sides, letting mutual fear and friction mount to hysteria— In fact, he wasn't sure the United States hadn't sent out the first rockets, on orders of some panicky or aggressive officials. Nobody was alive who admitted knowing.

"It's the jedgment o' God, for the sins o' our leaders," persisted the woman. "The plague, the fire-death, all that, ain't it foretold in the Bible? Ain't we living in the last days o' the world?"

"Maybe." Drummond was glad to stop before a long low cabin. Religious argument was touchy at best, and with a lot of people nowadays it was dynamite.

They entered the rudely furnished but fairly comfortable structure. A good many crowded in with them. For all their suspicion, they were curious, and an outsider in an aircraft was a blue-moon event these days.

Drummond's eyes flickered unobtrusively about the

room, noticing details. Three women—that meant a return to concubinage. Only to be expected in a day of few men and strong-arm rule. Ornaments and utensils, tools and weapons of good quality—yes, that confirmed the stories. This wasn't exactly a bandit town, but it had waylaid travelers and raided other places when times were hard, and built up a sort of dominance of the surrounding country. That, too, was common.

There was a dog on the floor nursing a litter. Only three pups, and one of those was bald, one lacked ears, and one had more toes than it should. Among the wide-eyed children present, there were several two years old or less, and with almost no obvious exceptions, they were also different.

Drummond sighed heavily and sat down. In a way, this clinched it. He'd known for a long time, and finding mutation here, as far as any place from atomic destruction, was about the last evidence he needed.

He had to get on friendly terms, or he wouldn't find out much about things like population, food production, and whatever else there was to know. Forcing a smile to stiff lips, he took a flask from his jacket. "Prewar rye," he said. "Who wants a nip?"

"Do we!" The answer barked out in a dozen voices and words. The flask circulated, men pawing and cursing and grabbing to get at it. *Their homebrew must be pretty bad,* thought Drummond wryly.

The chief shouted an order, and one of his women got busy at the primitive stove. "Rustle you a mess o' chow," he said heartily. "An' my name's Sam Buckman."

"Pleased to meet you, Sam." Drummond squeezed the hairy paw hard. He had to show he wasn't a weakling, a conniving city slicker.

"What's it like, outside?" asked someone presently. "We ain't heard for so long—"

"You haven't missed much," said Drummond between bites. The food was pretty good. Briefly, he sketched conditions. "You're better off than most," he finished.

"Yeah. Mebbe so." Sam Buckman scratched his tangled beard. "What I'd give f'r a razor blade—! It ain't easy, though. The first year we weren't no better off 'n anyone else. Me, I'm a farmer, I kept some ears o' corn an' a little wheat an' barley in my pockets all that winter, even though I was starving. A bunch o' hungry refugees plundered my place, but I got away an' drifted up here. Next year I took an empty farm here an' started over."

Drummond doubted that it had been abandoned, but said nothing. Sheer survival outweighed a lot of considerations.

"Others came an' settled here," said the leader reminiscently. "We farm together. We have to; one man couldn't live by hisself, not with the bugs an' blight, an' the crops sproutin' into all new kinds, an' the outlaws aroun'. Not many up here, though we did beat off some enemy troops last winter." He glowed with pride at that, but Drummond wasn't particularly impressed. A handful of freezing starveling conscripts, lost and bewildered in a foreign enemy's land, with no hope of ever getting home, weren't formidable.

"Things getting better, though," said Buckman. "We're heading up." He scowled blackly, and a palpable chill crept into the room. "If 'twern't for the births—"

"Yes—the births. The new babies. Even the stock an' plants." It was an old man speaking, his eyes glazed with near madness. "It's the mark o' the beast. Satan is loose in the world—"

"Shut up!" Huge and bristling with wrath, Buckman launched himself out of his seat and grabbed the oldster by his scrawny throat. "Shut up 'r I'll bash y'r lying head in. Ain't no son o' mine being marked by the devil."

"Or mine—" "Or mine—" The rumble of voices ran about the cabin, sullen and afraid.

"It's God's jedgment, I tell you!" The woman was shrilling again. "The end o' the world is near. Prepare f'r the second coming—"

"An' you shut up too, Mag Schmidt," snarled Buckman. He stood bent over, gnarled arms swinging loose, hands flexing, little eyes darting red and wild about the room. "Shut y'r trap an' keep it shut. I'm still boss here, an' if you don't like it you can get out. I still don't think that gunny-looking brat o' y'rs fell in the lake by accident."

The woman shrank back, lips tight. The room filled with a crackling silence. One of the babies began to cry. It had two heads.

Slowly and heavily, Buckman turned to Drummond, who sat immobile against the wall. "You see?" he asked dully. "You see how it is? Maybe it is the curse o' God. Maybe the world is ending. I dunno. I just know there's few enough babies, an' most o' them deformed. Will it go on? Will all our kids be monsters? Should we . . . kill these an' hope we get some human babies? What is it? What to do?"

Drummond rose. He felt a weight as of centuries on his shoulders, the weariness, blank and absolute, of having seen that smoldering panic and heard that desperate appeal too often, too often.

"Don't kill them," he said. "That's the worst kind of murder, and anyway it'd do no good at all. It comes from the bombs, and you can't stop it. You'll go right on having such children, so you might as well get used to it."

By atomic-powered stratojet it wasn't far from Minnesota to Oregon, and Drummond landed in Taylor about noon the next day. This time there was no hurry to get his machine under cover, and up on the mountain was a raw scar of earth where a new airfield was slowly being built. Men were getting over their terror of the sky. They had another fear to face now, and it was one from which there was no hiding.

Drummond walked slowly down the icy main street to the central office. It was numbingly cold, a still, relentless intensity of frost eating through clothes and flesh and bone. It wasn't much better inside. Heating systems were still poor improvisations.

"You're back!" Robinson met him in the antechamber, suddenly galvanized with eagerness. He had grown thin and nervous, looking ten years older, but impatience blazed from him. "How is it? How is it?"

Drummond held up a bulky notebook. "All here," he said grimly. "All the facts we'll need. Not formally correlated yet, but the picture is simple enough."

Robinson laid an arm on his shoulder and steered him into the office. He felt the general's hand shaking, but he'd sat down and had a drink before business came up again.

"You've done a good job," said the leader warmly. "When the country's organized again, I'll see you get a medal for this. Your men in the other planes aren't in yet."

"No, they'll be gathering data for a long time. The job won't be finished for years. I've only got a general outline here, but it's enough. It's enough." Drummond's eyes were haunted again.

Robinson felt cold at meeting that too-steady gaze. He whispered shakily: "Is it—bad?"

"The worst. Physically, the country's recovering. But biologically, we've reached a crossroads and taken the wrong fork."

"What do you mean? *What do you mean?*"

Drummond let him have it then, straight and hard as a bayonet thrust. "The birth rate's a little over half the pre-war," he said, "and about seventy-five percent of all births are mutant, of which possibly two-thirds are viable and presumably fertile. Of course, that doesn't include late-maturing characteristics, or those undetectable by naked-eye observation, or the mutated recessive genes that must be carried by a lot of otherwise normal zygotes. And it's everywhere. There are no safe places."

"I see," said Robinson after a long time. He nodded, like a man struck a stunning blow and not yet fully aware of it. "I see. The reason—"

"Is obvious."

"Yes. People going through radioactive areas—"

"Why, no. That would only account for a few. But—"

"No matter. The fact's there, and that's enough. We have to decide what to do about it."

"And soon." Drummond's jaw set. "It's wrecking our culture. We at least preserved our historical continuity, but even that's going now. People are going crazy as birth after birth is monstrous. Fear of the unknown, striking at minds still stunned by the war and its immediate aftermath. Frustration of parenthood, perhaps the most basic instinct there is. It's leading to infanticide, desertion, despair, a cancer at the root of society. We've got to act."

"How? How?" Robinson stared numbly at his hands.

"I don't know. You're the leader. Maybe an educational campaign, though that hardly seems practicable. Maybe an acceleration of your program for re-integrating the country. Maybe—I don't know."

Drummond stuffed tobacco into his pipe. He was near the end of what he had, but would rather take a few good smokes than a lot of niggling puffs. "Of course," he said thoughtfully, "it's probably not the end of things. We won't know for a generation or more, but I rather imagine the mutants can grow into society. They'd better, for they'll outnumber the humans. The thing is, if we just let matters drift there's no telling where they'll go. The situation is unprecedented. We may end up in a culture of specialized variations, which would be very bad from an evolutionary standpoint. There may be fighting between mutant types, or with humans. Interbreeding may produce worse freaks, particularly when accumulated recessives start showing up. Robinson, if we want any say at all in what's going to happen in the next few centuries, we have to act quickly. Otherwise it'll snowball out of all control."

"Yes. Yes, we'll have to act fast. And hard." Robinson straightened in his chair. Decision firmed his countenance, but his eyes were staring. "We're mobilized," he said. "We have the men and the weapons and the organization. They won't be able to resist."

The ashy cold of Drummond's emotions stirred, but it was with a horrible wrenching of fear. "What are you getting at?" he snapped.

"Racial death. All mutants and their parents to be sterilized whenever and wherever detected."

"You're crazy!" Drummond sprang from his chair, grabbed Robinson's shoulders across the desk, and shook him. "You . . . why, it's impossible! You'll bring revolt, civil war, final collapse!"

"Not if we go about it right." There were little beads of sweat studding the general's forehead. "I don't like it any better than you, but it's got to be done or the human race is finished. Normal births a minority—" He surged to his feet, gasping. "I've thought a long time about this. Your facts only confirmed my suspicions. This tears it. Can't you see? Evolution has to proceed slowly. Life wasn't meant for such a storm of change. Unless we can save the true human stock, it'll be absorbed and differentiation will continue till humanity is a collection of freaks, probably intersterile. Or . . . there must be a lot of lethal recessives. In a large population, they can accumulate unnoticed till nearly everybody has them, and then start emerging all at once. That'd wipe us out. It's happened before, in rats and other species. If we eliminate mutant stock now, we can still save the race. It won't be cruel. We have sterilization techniques which are quick and painless, not upsetting the

endocrine balance. But it's got to be done." His voice rose
to a raw scream, broke. "It's got to be done!"

Drummond slapped him, hard. He drew a shuddering
breath, sat down, and began to cry, and somehow that
was the most horrible sight of all. "You're crazy," said the
aviator. "You've gone nuts with brooding alone on this the
last six months, without knowing or being able to act.
You've lost all perspective.

"We can't use violence. In the first place, it would break
our tottering, cracked culture irreparably, into a mad-dog
finish fight. We'd not even win it. We're outnumbered, and
we couldn't hold down a continent, eventually a planet.
And remember what we said once, about abandoning the
old savage way of settling things, that never brings a real
settlement at all? We'd throw away a lesson our noses were
rubbed in not three years ago. We'd return to the beast—
to ultimate extinction.

"And anyway," he went on very quietly, "it wouldn't do
a bit of good. Mutants would still be born. The poison is
everywhere. Normal parents will give birth to mutants,
somewhere along the line. We just have to accept that fact,
and live with it. The *new* human race will have to."

"I'm sorry." Robinson raised his face from his hands.
It was a ghastly visage, gone white and old, but there was
calm on it. "I—blew my top. You're right. I've been thinking of this, worrying and wondering, living and breathing
it, lying awake nights, and when I finally sleep I dream of
it. I . . . yes, I see your point. And you're right."

"It's O.K. You've been under a terrific strain. Three
years with never a rest, and the responsibility for a nation,
and now this— Sure, everybody's entitled to be a little
crazy. We'll work out a solution, somehow."

"Yes, of course." Robinson poured out two stiff drinks
and gulped his. He paced restlessly, and his tremendous
ability came back in waves of strength and confidence.
"Let me see— Eugenics, of course. If we work hard, we'll
have the nation tightly organized inside of ten years. Then
. . . well, I don't suppose we can keep the mutants from
interbreeding, but certainly we can pass laws to protect
humans and encourage their propagation. Since radical
mutations would probably be intersterile anyway, and
most mutants handicapped one way or another, a few

generations should see humans completely dominant again."

Drummond scowled. He was worried. It wasn't like Robinson to be unreasonable. Somehow, the man had acquired a mental blind spot where this most ultimate of human problems was concerned. He said slowly, "That won't work either. First, it'd be hard to impose and enforce. Second, we'd be repeating the old *Herrenvolk* notion. Mutants are inferior, mutants must be kept in their place—to enforce that, especially on a majority, you'd need a full-fledged totalitarian state. Third, that wouldn't work either, for the rest of the world, with almost no exceptions, is under no such control and we'll be in no position to take over that control for a long time—generations. Before then, mutants will dominate everywhere over there, and if they resent the way we treat their kind here, we'd better run for cover."

"You assume a lot. How do you know those hundreds or thousands of diverse types will work together? They're less like each other than like humans, even. They could be played off against each other."

"Maybe. But *that* would be going back onto the old road of treachery and violence, the road to Hell. Conversely, if every not-quite-human is called a 'mutant,' like a separate class, he'll think he is, and act accordingly against the lumped-together 'humans.' No, the only way to sanity—to *survival*—is to abandon class prejudice and race hate altogether, and work as individuals. We're all . . . well, Earthlings, and subclassification is deadly. We all have to live together, and might as well make the best of it."

"Yeah . . . yeah, that's right too."

"Anyway, I repeat that all such attempts would be useless. All Earth is infected with mutation. It will be for a long time. The purest human stock will still produce mutants."

"Y-yes, that's true. Our best bet seems to be to find all such stock and withdraw it into the few safe areas left. It'll mean a small human population, but a *human* one."

"I tell you, that's impossible," clipped Drummond. "There is no safe place. Not one."

Robinson stopped pacing and looked at him as at a

physical antagonist. "That so?" he almost growled. "Why?"

Drummond told him, adding incredulously, "Surely you knew that. Your physicists must have measured the amount of it. Your doctors, your engineers, that geneticist I dug up for you. You obviously got a lot of this biological information you've been slinging at me from him. They *must* all have told you the same thing."

Robinson shook his head stubbornly. "It can't be. It's not reasonable. The concentration wouldn't be great enough."

"Why, you poor fool, you need only look around you. The plants, the animals— Haven't there been any births in Taylor?"

"No. This is still a man's town, though women are trickling in and several babies are on the way—" Robinson's face was suddenly twisted with desperation. "Elaine's is due any time now. She's in the hospital here. Don't you see, our other kid died of the plague. This one's all we have. We want him to grow up in a world free of want and fear, a world of peace and sanity where he can play and laugh and become a man, not a beast starving in a cave. You and I are on our way out. We're the old generation, the one that wrecked the world. It's up to us to build it again, and then retire from it to let our children have it. The future's theirs. We've got to make it ready for them."

Sudden insight held Drummond motionless for long seconds. Understanding came, and pity, and an odd gentleness that changed his sunken bony face. "Yes," he murmured, "yes, I see. That's why you're working with all that's in you to build a normal, healthy world. That's why you nearly went crazy when this threat appeared. That . . . that's why you can't, just can't comprehend—"

He took the other man's arm and guided him toward the door. "Come on," he said. "Let's go see how your wife's making out. Maybe we can get her some flowers on the way."

The silent cold bit at them as they went down the street. Snow crackled underfoot. It was already grimy with town smoke and dust, but overhead the sky was incredibly clean and blue. Breath smoked whitely from their mouths and nostrils. The sound of men at work rebuilding drifted faintly between the bulking mountains.

"We couldn't emigrate to another planet, could we?" asked Robinson, and answered himself: "No, we lack the organization and resources to settle them right now. We'll have to make out on Earth. A few safe spots—there *must* be others besides this one—to house the true humans till the mutation period is over. Yes, we can do it."

"There are no safe places," insisted Drummond. "Even if there were, the mutants would still outnumber us. Does your geneticist have any idea how this'll come out, biologically speaking?"

"He doesn't know. His specialty is still largely unknown. He can make an intelligent guess, and that's all."

"Yeah. Anyway, our problem is to learn to live with the mutants, to accept anyone as—Earthling—no matter how he looks, to quit thinking anything was ever settled by violence or connivance, to build a culture of individual sanity. Funny," mused Drummond, "how the impractical virtues, tolerance and sympathy and generosity, have become the fundamental necessities of simple survival. I guess it was always true, but it took the death of half the world and the end of a biological era to make us see that simple little fact. The job's terrific. We've got half a million years of brutality and greed, superstition and prejudice, to lick in a few generations. If we fail, mankind is done. But we've got to try."

They found some flowers, potted in a house, and Robinson bought them with the last of his tobacco. By the time he reached the hospital, he was sweating. The sweat froze on his face as he walked.

The hospital was the town's biggest building, and fairly well equipped. A nurse met them as they entered.

"I was just going to send for you, General Robinson," she said. "The baby's on the way."

"How . . . is she?"

"Fine, so far. Just wait here, please."

Drummond sank into a chair and with haggard eyes watched Robinson's jerky pacing. *The poor guy. Why is it expectant fathers are supposed to be so funny? It's like laughing at a man on the rack. I know, Barbara, I know.*

"They have some anaesthetics," muttered the general. "They . . . Elaine never was very strong."

"She'll be all right." *It's afterward that worries me.*

"Yeah— Yeah— How long, though, how long?"

"Depends. Take it easy." With a wrench, Drummond made a sacrifice to a man he liked. He filled his pipe and handed it over. "Here, you need a smoke."

"Thanks." Robinson puffed raggedly.

The slow minutes passed, and Drummond wondered vaguely what he'd do when—it—happened. It didn't have to happen. But the chances were all against such an easy solution. He was no psychologist. Best just to let things happen as they would.

The waiting broke at last. A doctor came out, seeming an inscrutable high priest in his white garments. Robinson stood before him, motionless.

"You're a brave man," said the doctor. His face, as he removed the mask, was stern and set. "You'll need your courage."

"She—" It was hardly a human sound, that croak.

"Your wife is doing well. But the baby—"

A nurse brought out the little wailing form. It was a boy. But his limbs were rubbery tentacles terminating in boneless digits.

Robinson looked, and something went out of him as he stood there. When he turned, his face was dead.

"You're lucky," said Drummond, and meant it. He'd seen too many other mutants. "After all, if he can use those hands he'll get along all right. He'll even have an advantage in certain types of work. It isn't a deformity, really. If there's nothing else, you've got a good kid."

"*If!* You can't tell with mutants."

"I know. But you've got guts, you and Elaine. You'll see this through, together." Briefly, Drummond felt an utter personal desolation. He went on, perhaps to cover that emptiness:

"I see why you didn't understand the problem. You *wouldn't.* It was a psychological bloc, suppressing a fact you didn't dare face. That boy is really the center of your life. You couldn't think the truth about him, so your subconscious just refused to let you think rationally on that subject at all.

"Now you know. Now you realize there's no safe place, not on all the planet. The tremendous incidence of mutant births in the first generation could have told you that alone. Most such new characteristics are recessive, which means both parents have to have it for it to show in the zygote. But genetic changes are random, except for a tendency to fall into roughly similar patterns. Four-leaved clovers, for instance. Think how vast the total number of such changes must be, to produce so many corresponding changes in a couple of years. Think how many, *many* recessives there must be, existing only in gene patterns till their mates show up. We'll just have to take our chances of something really deadly accumulating. We'd never know till too late."

"The dust—"

"Yeah. The radiodust. It's colloidal, and uncountable other radiocolloids were formed when the bombs went off, and ordinary dirt gets into unstable isotopic forms near the craters. And there are radiogases too, probably. The poison is all over the world by now, spread by wind and air currents. Colloids can be suspended indefinitely in the atmosphere.

"The concentration isn't too high for life, though a physicist told me he'd measured it as being very near the safe limit and there'll probably be a lot of cancer. But it's everywhere. Every breath we draw, every crumb we eat and drop we drink, every clod we walk on, the dust is there. It's in the stratosphere, clear on down to the surface, probably a good distance below. We could only escape by sealing ourselves in air-conditioned vaults and wearing spacesuits whenever we got out, and under present conditions that's impossible.

"Mutations were rare before, because a charged particle has to get pretty close to a gene and be moving fast before its electromagnetic effect causes physico-chemical changes, and then that particular chromosome has to enter into reproduction. Now the charged particles, and the gamma rays producing still more, are everywhere. Even at the comparatively low concentration, the odds favor a given organism having so many cells changed that at least one will give rise to a mutant. There's even a good chance of like recessives meeting in the first generation, as we've seen. Nobody's safe, no place is free."

"The geneticist thinks some true humans will continue."

"A few, probably. After all, the radioactivity isn't too concentrated, and it's burning itself out. But it'll take fifty or a hundred years for the process to drop to insignificance, and by then the pure stock will be way in the minority. And there'll still be all those unmatched recessives, waiting to show up."

"You were right. We should never have created science. It brought the twilight of the race."

"I never said that. The race brought its own destruction, through misuse of science. Our culture was scientific anyway, in all except its psychological basis. It's up to us to take that last and hardest step. If we do, the race may yet survive."

Drummond gave Robinson a push toward the inner door. "You're exhausted, beat up, ready to quit. Go on in and see Elaine. Give her my regards. Then take a long rest before going back to work. I still think you've got a good kid."

Mechanically, the *de facto* President of the United States left the room. Hugh Drummond stared after him a moment, then went out into the street.

THAT ONLY A MOTHER

by Judith Merril

My first science fiction story was published thirty-two years ago in Astounding *(now* Analog*)—a rather unpleasant story called "That Only a Mother," concerned with the effects, on one small ordinary family, of life during a comparatively "clean" atomic war in (what was then) the near future.*

In 1948, a lot of us were very worried about the imminence of that hypothetical war: not just about death and injury, injustice and destruction; and hardly at all about "winning" or "losing"; but mostly about the insidious aftereffects —cancers and leukemias that might follow years later for apparently untouched survivors—and the effects of sterility and mutations on plants, animals, and human beings for generations to come.

In 1946, 1947, 1948, a great deal was being published about these things. One read the Smythe Report *and* No Place to Hide *and the* Bulletin of the Atomic Scientists *and the publications of the World Federalists and the daily newspapers. If one also read the science fiction magazines, the information total was staggering, unarguable, and terrifying.*

There has been very little change in that total in this quarter-century. We have, of course, learned a great deal meanwhile about bacteriological and chemical warfare, both in theory and in practice. But so far as strictly atomic doom is concerned, the most significant differences are that the more powerful bombs and swifter delivery systems which were then predicted have been realized; and that the global holocaust which was then widely anticipated has not occurred.

I think it has not occurred because it took such a short time—perhaps five or six years—for the information that was fully available in 1948 to be disseminated, absorbed, and understood by many people, including small ordinary families, and even heads of governments. I like to think this rapid understanding came at least in part from the fervent dramatizing efforts of science fiction writers.

"Where do you get those crazy ideas?" This is the question sf writers hear most often. Well, for instance:—

"That Only a Mother" dealt with radiation-caused mutation, not in broad statistical terms, or among bomb-victims, but as a side-effect due to casual exposure in one family on the "winning" side. Its specific sources were two: one, a tiny backpage newspaper article saying that the U.S. Army of Occupation in Japan had definitely established that the "rumors" of wide-spread infanticides in the areas of Hiroshima and Nagasaki were unfounded (even in those days some of us automatically read certain kinds of official U.S. releases backwards); the other, a domestic incident which brought sharply home to me how easily a mother (this one, for instance) can fail/refuse to notice a child's imperfections. The result was a story whose horror was rooted in a familiar domestic truism applied to readily-available public information which most people had simply not yet assimilated.

"Where do you get those crazy ideas?" From the same daily experiences and communications, books, newspapers, broadcasts, we all share. It's not the ingredients that are so strange, but the unexpected juxtapositions: the trick of looking at something familiar against an alien background, or examining the new and different against a familiar setting.

Science fiction is not so much prophecy as "probability." If you put this and this and that together in a certain way, here's what might happen. Sometimes the writer hits frighteningly close to what will happen, though not always for the right reasons.

"Realistic" fiction is about things that have happened. "Fantasy" is about things (we are fairly sure) that don't happen. "Science fiction" is about things that could happen.

*   *   *

Margaret reached over to the other side of the bed where Hank should have been. Her hand patted the empty pillow, and then she came altogether awake, wondering that the old habit should remain after so many months. She tried to curl up, cat-style, to hoard her own warmth, found she couldn't do it any more, and climbed out of bed with a pleased awareness of her increasing clumsy bulkiness.

Morning motions were automatic. On the way through the kitchenette, she pressed the button that would start breakfast cooking—the doctor had said to eat as much breakfast as she could—and tore the paper out of the facsimile machine. She folded the long sheet carefully to the "National News" section, and propped it on the bathroom shelf to scan while she brushed her teeth.

No accidents. No direct hits. At least none that had been officially released for publication. *Now, Maggie, don't get started on that. No accidents. No hits. Take the nice newspaper's word for it.*

The three clear chimes from the kitchen announced that breakfast was ready. She set a bright napkin and cheerful colored dishes on the table in a futile attempt to appeal to a faulty morning appetite. Then, when there was nothing more to prepare, she went for the mail, allowing herself the full pleasure of prolonged anticipation, because today there would *surely* be a letter.

There was. There were. Two bills and a worried note from her mother: "Darling, why didn't you write and tell me sooner? I'm thrilled, of course, but, well one hates to mention these things, but are you *certain* the doctor was right? Hank's been around all that uranium or thorium or whatever it is all these years, and I know you say he's a designer, not a technician, and he doesn't get near anything that might be dangerous, but you know he used to, back at Oak Ridge. Don't you think . . . well, of course, I'm just being a foolish old woman, and I don't want you to get upset. You know much more about it than I do, and I'm sure your doctor was right. He *should* know . . ."

Margaret made a face over the excellent coffee, and caught herself refolding the paper to the medical news.

Stop it, Maggie, stop it! The radiologist said Hank's job couldn't have exposed him. And the bombed area we drove past. . . . No, no. Stop it, now! Read the social notes or the recipes, Maggie girl.

A well-known geneticist, in the medical news, said that it was possible to tell with absolute certainty, at five months, whether the child would be normal, or at least whether the mutation was likely to produce anything freakish. The worst cases, at any rate, could be prevented. Minor mutations, of course, displacements in facial features, or changes in brain structure could not be detected. And there had been some cases recently, of normal embryos with atrophied limbs that did not develop beyond the seventh or eighth month. But, the doctor concluded cheerfully, the *worst* cases could now be predicted and prevented.

"Predicted and prevented." We predicted it, didn't we? Hank and the others, they predicted it. But we didn't prevent. We could have stopped it in '46 and '47. Now . . .

Margaret decided against the breakfast. Coffee had been enough for her in the morning for ten years; it would have to do for today. She buttoned herself into the interminable folds of material that, the salesgirl had assured her, was the *only* comfortable thing to wear during the last few months. With a surge of pure pleasure, the letter and newspaper forgotten, she realized she was on the next to the last button. It wouldn't be long now.

The city in the early morning had always been a special kind of excitement for her. Last night it had rained, and the sidewalks were still damp-gray instead of dusty. The air smelled the fresher, to a city-bred woman, for the occasional pungency of acrid factory smoke. She walked the six blocks to work, watching the lights go out in the all-night hamburger joints, where the plate-glass walls were already catching the sun, and the lights go on in the dim interiors of cigar stores and dry-cleaning establishments.

The office was in a new Government building. In the rolovator, on the way up, she felt, as always, like a frankfurter roll in the ascending half of an old-style rotary toasting machine. She abandoned the air-foam cushioning gratefully at the fourteenth floor, and settled down behind her desk, at the rear of a long row of identical desks.

Each morning the pile of papers that greeted her was a little higher. These were, as everyone knew, the decisive months. The war might be won or lost on these calculations as well as any others. The manpower office had switched her here when her old expediter's job got to be too strenuous. The computer was easy to operate, and the work was absorbing, if not as exciting as the old job. But you didn't just stop working these days. Everyone who could do anything at all was needed.

And—she remembered the interview with the psychologist—*I'm probably the unstable type. Wonder what sort of neurosis I'd get sitting home reading that sensational paper . . .*

She plunged into the work without pursuing the thought.

February 18.

Hank darling,

Just a note—from the hospital, no less. I had a dizzy spell at work, and the doctor took it to heart. Blessed if I know what I'll do with myself lying in bed for weeks, just waiting—but Dr. Boyer seems to think it may not be so long.

There are too many newspapers around here. More infanticides all the time, and they can't seem to get a jury to convict any of them. It's the fathers who do it. Lucky thing you're not around, in case—

Oh, darling, that wasn't a very *funny* joke, was it? Write as often as you can, will you? I have too much time to think. But there really isn't anything wrong, and nothing to worry about.

Write often, and remember I love you.

Maggie.

SPECIAL SERVICE TELEGRAM

February 21, 1953
22:04 LK37G

From: Tech. Lieut. H. Marvell
X47–016 GCNY
To: Mrs. H. Marvell
Women's Hospital
New York City

HAD DOCTOR'S GRAM STOP WILL ARRIVE FOUR OH TEN STOP SHORT LEAVE STOP YOU DID IT MAGGIE STOP LOVE HANK

February 25.

Hank dear,

So you didn't see the baby either? You'd think a place this size would at least have visiplates on the incubators, so the fathers could get a look, even if the poor benighted mommas can't. They tell me I won't see her for another week, or maybe more—but of course, mother always warned me if I didn't slow my pace, I'd probably even have my babies too fast. Why must she *always* be right?

Did you meet that battle-ax of a nurse they put on here? I imagine they save her for people who've already had theirs, and don't let her get too near the prospectives —but a woman like that simply shouldn't be allowed in a maternity ward. She's obsessed with mutations, can't seem to talk about anything else. Oh, well, *ours* is all right, even if it was in an unholy hurry.

I'm tired. They warned me not to sit up so soon, but I *had* to write you. All my love, darling,

Maggie.

February 29.

Darling,

I finally got to see her! It's all true, what they say about new babies and the face that only a mother could love— but it's all there, darling, eyes, ears, and noses—no, only one!—all in the right places. We're so *lucky*, Hank.

I'm afraid I've been a rambunctious patient. I kept telling that hatchet-faced female with the mutation mania that I wanted to *see* the baby. Finally the doctor came in to "explain" everything to me, and talked a lot of nonsense, most of which I'm sure no one could have understood, any more than I did. The only thing I got out of it was that she didn't actually *have* to stay in the incubator; they just thought it was "wiser."

I think I got a little hysterical at that point. Guess I was more worried than I was willing to admit, but I threw a small fit about it. The whole business wound up with one of those hushed medical conferences outside the door, and finally the Woman in White said: "Well, we might as well. Maybe it'll work out better that way."

I'd heard about the way doctors and nurses in these places develop a God complex, and believe me it is as true figuratively as it is literally that a mother hasn't got a leg to stand on around here.

I *am* awfully weak, still. I'll write again soon. Love,

Maggie.

March 8.

Dearest Hank,

Well the nurse was wrong if she told you that. She's an idiot anyhow. It's a girl. It's easier to tell with babies than with cats, and *I know*. How about Henrietta?

I'm home again, and busier than a betatron. They got *everything* mixed up at the hospital, and I had to teach myself how to bathe her and do just about everything else. She's getting prettier, too. When can you get a leave, a *real* leave?

Love,

Maggie.

May 26.

Hank dear,

You should see her now—and you shall. I'm sending along a reel of color movie. My mother sent her those nighties with drawstrings all over. I put one on, and right now she looks like a snow-white potato sack with that beautiful, beautiful flower-face blooming on top. Is that *me* talking? Am I a doting mother? But wait till you *see* her!

July 10.

. . . Believe it or not, as you like, but your daughter can talk, and I don't mean baby talk. Alice discovered it—she's a dental assistant in the WACs, you know—and when she heard the baby giving out what I thought was a string of gibberish, she said the kid knew words and sentences, but couldn't say them clearly because she has no teeth yet. I'm taking her to a speech specialist.

September 13.

. . . We have a prodigy for real! Now that all her front teeth are in, her speech is perfectly clear and—a new talent now—she can sing! I mean really carry a tune! At seven months! Darling, my world would be perfect if you could only get home.

November 19.

. . . at last. The little goon was so busy being clever, it took her all this time to learn to crawl. The doctor says development in these cases is always erratic . . .

SPECIAL SERVICE TELEGRAM

December 1, 1953
08:47 LK59F

From: Tech. Lieut. H. Marvell
X47–016 GCNY
   To: Mrs. H. Marvell
Apt. K-17
504 E. 19 St.
N.Y. N.Y.

WEEK'S LEAVE STARTS TOMORROW STOP WILL AIRPORT TEN OH FIVE STOP DON'T MEET ME STOP LOVE LOVE LOVE HANK

Margaret let the water run out of the bathinette until only a few inches were left, and then loosed her hold on the wriggling baby.

"I think it was better when you were retarded, young woman," she informed her daughter happily. "You *can't* crawl in a bathinette, you know."

"Then why can't I go in the bathtub?" Margaret was used to her child's volubility by now, but every now and then it caught her unawares. She swooped the resistant mass of pink flesh into a towel, and began to rub.

"Because you're too little, and your head is very soft, and bathtubs are very hard."

"Oh. Then when can I go in the bathtub?"

"When the outside of your head is as hard as the inside, brainchild." She reached toward a pile of fresh clothing. "I cannot understand," she added, pinning a square of cloth through the nightgown, "why a child of your intelligence can't learn to keep a diaper on the way other babies do. They've been used for centuries, you know, with perfectly satisfactory results."

The child disdained to reply; she had heard it too often. She waited patiently until she had been tucked, clean and sweet-smelling, into a white-painted crib. Then she favored her mother with a smile that inevitably made Margaret think of the first golden edge of the sun bursting into a rosy pre-dawn. She remembered Hank's reaction to the color pictures of his beautiful daughter, and with the thought, realized how late it was.

"Go to sleep, puss. When you wake up, you know, your *Daddy* will be here."

"Why?" asked the four-year-old mind, waging a losing battle to keep the ten-month-old body awake.

Margaret went into the kitchenette and set the timer for the roast. She examined the table, and got her clothes from the closet, new dress, new shoes, new slip, new everything, bought weeks before and saved for the day Hank's telegram came. She stopped to pull a paper from the facsimile, and, with clothes and news, went into the bathroom, and lowered herself gingerly into the steaming luxury of a scented tub.

She glanced through the paper with indifferent interest. Today at least there was no need to read the national news. There was an article by a geneticist. The same geneticist. Mutations, he said, were increasing disproportionately. It was too soon for recessives; even the first mutants, born near Hiroshima and Nagasaki in 1946 and 1947 were not old enough yet to breed. *But my baby's all right.* Apparently, there was some degree of free radiation from atomic explosions causing the trouble. *My baby's fine. Precocious, but normal.* If more attention had been paid to the first Japanese mutations, he said . . .

There was that little notice in the paper in the spring of '47. That was when Hank quit at Oak Ridge. "Only two or three per cent of those guilty of infanticide are being caught and punished in Japan today . . ." *But* MY BABY'S *all right.*

She was dressed, combed, and ready to the last light brush-on of lip paste, when the door chime sounded. She dashed for the door, and heard, for the first time in eighteen months the almost-forgotten sound of a key turning in the lock before the chime had quite died away.

"Hank!"

"Maggie!"

And then there was nothing to say. So many days, so many months, of small news piling up, so many things to tell him, and now she just stood there, staring at a khaki uniform and a stranger's pale face. She traced the features with the finger of memory. The same highbridged nose, wide-set eyes, fine feathery brows; the same long jaw, the hair a little farther back now on the high forehead, the same tilted curve of his mouth. Pale. . . . Of course, he'd been underground all this time. And strange, stranger because of lost familiarity than any newcomer's face could be.

She had time to think all that before his hand reached out to touch her, and spanned the gap of eighteen months. Now, again, there was nothing to say, because there was no need. They were together, and for the moment that was enough.

"Where's the baby?"

"Sleeping. She'll be up any minute."

No urgency. Their voices were as casual as though it were a daily exchange, as though war and separation did not exist. Margaret picked up the coat he'd thrown on the chair near the door, and hung it carefully in the hall closet. She went to check the roast, leaving him to wander through the rooms by himself, remembering and coming back. She found him, finally, standing over the baby's crib.

She couldn't see his face, but she had no need to.

"I think we can wake her just this once." Margaret pulled the covers down, and lifted the white bundle from the bed. Sleepy lids pulled back heavily from smoky brown eyes.

"Hello." Hank's voice was tentative.

"Hello." The baby's assurance was more pronounced.

He had heard about it, of course, but that wasn't the same as hearing it. He turned eagerly to Margaret. "She really can—?"

"Of course she can, darling. But what's more important, she can even do nice normal things like other babies do, even stupid ones. Watch her crawl!" Margaret set the baby on the big bed.

For a moment young Henrietta lay and eyed her parents dubiously.

"Crawl?" she asked.

"That's the idea. Your Daddy is new around here, you know. He wants to see you show off."

"Then put me on my tummy."

"Oh, of course." Margaret obligingly rolled the baby over.

"What's the matter?" Hank's voice was still casual, but an undercurrent in it began to charge the air of the room. "I thought they turned over first."

"This baby," Margaret would not notice the tension, "*this* baby does things when she wants to."

This baby's father watched with softening eyes while the head advanced and the body hunched up, propelling itself across the bed.

"Why the little rascal," he burst into relieved laughter. "She looks like one of those potato-sack racers they used to have on picnics. Got her arms pulled out of the sleeves already." He reached over and grabbed the knot at the bottom of the long nightie.

"I'll do it, darling." Margaret tried to get there first.

"Don't be silly, Maggie. This may be *your* first baby, but *I* had five kid brothers." He laughed her away, and reached with his other hand for the string that closed one sleeve. He opened the sleeve bow, and groped for an arm.

"The way you wriggle," he addressed his child sternly, as his hand touched a moving knob of flesh at the shoulder, "anyone might think you were a worm, using your tummy to crawl on, instead of your hands and feet."

Margaret stood and watched, smiling. "Wait till you hear her sing, darling—"

His right hand traveled down from the shoulder to where he thought an arm would be, traveled down, and straight down, over firm small muscles that writhed in an attempt to move against the pressure of his hand. He let his fingers drift up again to the shoulder. With infinite care, he opened the knot at the bottom of the nightgown. His wife was standing by the bed, saying: "She can do 'Jingle Bells,' and—"

His left hand felt along the soft knitted fabric of the gown, up towards the diaper that folded, flat and smooth, across the bottom end of his child. No wrinkles. No kicking. *No . . .*

"Maggie." He tried to pull his hands from the neat fold in the diaper, from the wriggling body. "Maggie." His throat was dry; words came hard, low and grating. He spoke very slowly, thinking the sound of each word to make himself say it. His head was spinning, but he had to *know* before he let it go. "Maggie, why . . . didn't you . . . tell me?"

"Tell you what, darling?" Margaret's poise was the immemorial patience of woman confronted with man's childish impetuosity. Her sudden laugh sounded fantastically easy and natural in that room; it was all clear to her now. "Is she wet? I didn't know."

She didn't know. His hands, beyond control, ran up and down the soft-skinned baby body, the sinuous, limbless body. *Oh God, dear God*—his head shook and his muscles contracted, in a bitter spasm of hysteria. His fingers tightened on his child— *Oh God, she didn't know . . .*

SCANNERS LIVE IN VAIN

by Cordwainer Smith

*There are first stories and first stories. Most first stories are
just that—first stories, with little to distinguish them, even
if they foreshadow later talent (Quick—what was the title
of James Blish's first? Would we read "Marooned on
Vesta" if it hadn't been written by Isaac Asimov?).*

*Then there are the first stories that are instant classics,
that create reputations overnight. Stanley G. Weinbaum's
"A Martian Odyssey," A. E. van Vogt's "Black Destroyer."
Cordwainer Smith's "Scanners Live in Vain" is one of
these—sort of.*

When the story appeared in William Crawford's Fantasy
Book *in 1950, it was certainly the first known science fiction story by an author nobody had ever heard of, and
whose identity was unknown (and remained so for years
afterwards).*

*In a newspaper interview in the 1960's, illustrated by a
blanked-out head shot of the author, Cordwainer Smith
teased his readers with the bit of information that his real
first science fiction story had been published under his own
name in 1928, when he was 15 years old, and that it was
called "War No. 81-Q." Just locate that story, sf fans were
assured, and they'd learn who he was.*

*Nobody did. Not surprising, since the publication of
"War No. 81-Q" turned out to have been in a high school
newspaper. His widow unearthed it in time for inclusion
in* The Instrumentality of Mankind *(Ballantine, 1979)—
but by then, Smith had been dead for more than a decade,
and everyone already knew his real identity was Dr. Paul*

Myron Anthony Linebarger, soldier, diplomat, and psychological warfare expert.

"War No. 81-Q" wasn't a professional sale, of course; but then, maybe *"Scanners"* wasn't either—Fantasy Book was such a marginal publication that (according to tradition, at any rate) it couldn't afford to pay for stories. Still, *"Scanners"* got enough attention to be anthologized twice within the next few years—by Crawford himself and Frederik Pohl—and those appearances were paid for.

You might wonder why a story this good appeared in such an obscure place to begin with. The answer is, nobody else wanted it! *"Scanners Live in Vain"* was turned down by every major science fiction magazine, according to Genevieve Linebarger (at least one of the editors involved denies this, it is only fair to point out), and was sent to Crawford only as a last resort. At any rate, the story reached print five years *after it was written.*

That was at the Pentagon. Dr. Linebarger, just returned from China—where he had run a psychological warfare operation and other mysterious activities out of Chungking —was sitting in his office with nothing to do. So he decided to write a science fiction story. Just like that. Well, maybe not quite, as we shall see.

Paul Linebarger had a lot of ideas, some of them whimsical. For instance, there was an abandoned shop in his neighborhood called The Little Cranch. Who had owned it, and what it had sold may forever remain a mystery, let alone what "cranch" was supposed to mean. Yet Linebarger was able to take that nonsense word, and make it not only meaningful, but emotionally charged.

That was one of his talents. Who else but Cordwainer Smith would, or could, have invented the scanners or the pinlighters or the underpeople? Of course, there are always some precedents—the scanners and their weird ritual somehow bring to mind the Beast Folk in The Island of Dr. Moreau (and like any good sf writer, Smith had, of course, read H. G. Wells and the other masters). Yet there was something new here.

"Scanners Live in Vain," unlike most sf (and certainly unlike other first stories) of its time, clearly had an entire history, and even an entire mythology behind it. The scanners themselves, fascinating (or even terrifying) as they might be, were only part of it.

So many unexplained *references. Evidently this future was ruled by something called the Instrumentality of Mankind, but what the devil was that supposed to be? What was this business about the Beasts and the Manshonyaggers, "who with mimicry sought to enter the cities and ports of Mankind?" Who were the Unforgiven?*

Yet one could sense that these were no mere nonsense references, background details just thrown in at random to add verisimilitude. They meant *something—Scanner Martel knew* what *they meant, and Cordwainer Smith did too; but neither was telling. It was as if "Scanners Live in Vain" were already part of an ongoing series of stories.*

There's a chance *it was. Genevieve Linebarger (who wasn't married to him at the time, and therefore can't be certain) understands that Paul Linebarger submitted several sf stories to* Amazing *during World War II. (Yes, he was in China at the time, but it is known that he wrote two mainstream novels,* Ria *and* Carola, *while there). If so, they aren't included in the bound volume that includes his other short-story manuscripts (mostly non-sf, and unpublished) from 1937 through 1956. Perhaps they are lost, if they ever existed.*

What could these stories have been? Accounts of the Ancient Wars? Of the origin of the Vomact family (later retold in "Mark Elf" and "The Queen of the Afternoon," the latter completed by Genevieve Linebarger)? It would be interesting to share Cordwainer Smith's earlier conceptions of his future mythology (and there were changes; "The Colonel Came Back from Nothing at All," for example, was never rewritten to conform to several such alterations between when it was written in 1955 and its book publication 14 years later).

Perhaps we'll never know. And then again, perhaps we shall. The Linebarger home has a very messy attic—and there's no telling what might surface there one of these days.

—JOHN J. PIERCE

Martel was angry. He did not even adjust his blood away from anger. He stamped across the room by judgment, not by sight. When he saw the table hit the floor, and could tell by the expression on Luci's face that the table must have made a loud crash, he looked down to see if his leg was broken. It was not. Scanner to the core, he had to scan himself. The action was reflex and automatic. The inventory included his legs, abdomen, chestbox of instruments, hands, arms, face, and back with the mirror. Only then did Martel go back to being angry. He talked with his voice, even though he knew that his wife hated its blare and preferred to have him write.

"I tell you, I must cranch, I have to cranch. It's my worry, isn't it?"

When Luci answered, he saw only a part of her words as he read her lips: "Darling . . . you're my husband . . . right to love you . . . dangerous . . . do it . . . dangerous . . . wait. . . ."

He faced her, but put sound in his voice, letting the blare hurt her again: "I tell you, I'm going to cranch."

Catching her expression, he became rueful and a little tender: "Can't you understand what it means to me? To get out of this horrible prison in my own head? To be a man again—hearing your voice, smelling smoke? To *feel* again—to feel my feet on the ground, to feel the air move against my face? Don't you know what it means?"

Her wide-eyed worrisome concern thrust him back into pure annoyance. He read only a few words as her lips moved: ". . . love you . . . your own good . . . don't you think I want you to be human? . . . your own good . . . too much . . . he said . . . they said. . . ."

When he roared at her, he realized that his voice must be particularly bad. He knew that the sound hurt her no less than did the words: "Do you think I wanted you to marry a Scanner? Didn't I tell you we're almost as low as the habermans? We're dead, I tell you. We've got to be dead to do our work. How can anybody go to the Up-and-Out? Can you dream what raw Space is? I warned you. But you married me. All right, you married a man. Please, darling, let me be a man. Let me hear your voice, let me feel the warmth of being alive, of being human. Let me!"

He saw by her look of stricken assent that he had won the argument. He did not use his voice again. Instead, he pulled his tablet up from where it hung against his chest. He wrote on it, using the pointed fingernail of his right forefinger—the talking nail of a Scanner—in quick clean-cut script: *Pls, drlng, whrs crnching wire?*

She pulled the long gold-sheathed wire out of the pocket of her apron. She let its field sphere fall to the carpeted floor. Swiftly, dutifully, with the deft obedience of a Scanner's wife, she wound the cranching wire around his head, spirally around his neck and chest. She avoided the instruments set in his chest. She even avoided the radiating scars around the instruments, the stigmata of men who had gone Up and into the Out. Mechanically he lifted a foot as she slipped the wire between his feet. She drew the wire taut. She snapped the small plug into the high-burden control next to his heart-reader. She helped him to sit down, arranging his hands for him, pushing his head back into the cup at the top of the chair. She turned then full-face toward him, so that he could read her lips easily. Her expression was composed.

She knelt, scooped up the sphere at the other end of the wire, stood erect calmly, her back to him. He scanned her, and saw nothing in her posture but grief which would have escaped the eye of anyone but a Scanner. She spoke: he could see her chest-muscles moving. She realized that she was not facing him, and turned so that he could see her lips.

"Ready at last?"

He smiled a *yes*.

She turned her back to him again. (Luci could never bear to watch him go under the wire.) She tossed the wire-sphere into the air. It caught in the force-field and hung there. Suddenly it glowed. That was all. All—except for the sudden red stinking roar of coming back to his senses. Coming back, across the wild threshold of pain.

When he awakened, under the wire, he did not feel as though he had just cranched. Even though it was the second cranching within the week, he felt fit. He lay in the chair. His ears drank in the sound of air touching things in the room. He heard Luci breathing in the next room, where she was hanging up the wire to cool. He smelt the thousand and one smells that are in anybody's room: the crisp freshness of the germ-burner, the sour-sweet tang of the humidifier, the odor of the dinner they had just eaten, the smells of clothes, furniture, of people themselves. All these were pure delight. He sang a phrase or two of his favorite song:

> '*Here's to the haberman, Up-and-Out!*
> *Up—oh!—and Out—oh!—Up-and-Out! . . .*'

He heard Luci chuckle in the next room. He gloated over the sounds of her dress as she swished to the doorway.

She gave him her crooked little smile. "You sound all right. Are you all right, really?"

Even with this luxury of senses, he scanned. He took the flashquick inventory which constituted his professional skill. His eyes swept in the news of the instruments. Nothing showed off scale, beyond the nerve compression hanging in the edge of *Danger*. But he could not worry about the nerve-box. That always came through cranching. You couldn't get under the wire without having it show on the nerve-box. Some day the box would go to *Overload* and drop back down to *Dead*. That was the way a haberman ended. But you couldn't have everything. People who went to the Up-and-Out had to pay the price for Space.

Anyhow, he should worry! He was a Scanner. A good one, and he knew it. If he couldn't scan himself, who could? This cranching wasn't too dangerous. Dangerous, but not too dangerous.

Luci put out her hand and ruffled his hair as if she had been reading his thoughts, instead of just following them: "But you know you shouldn't have! You shouldn't!"

"But I did!" He grinned at her.

Her gaiety still forced, she said: "Come on, darling, let's have a good time. I have almost everything there is in the icebox—all your favorite tastes. And I have two new records just full of smells. I tried them out myself, and even I liked them. And you know me—"

"Which?"

"Which what, you old darling?"

He slipped his hand over her shoulders as he limped out of the room. He could never go back to feeling the floor beneath his feet, feeling the air against his face, without being bewildered and clumsy. As if cranching was real, and being a haberman was a bad dream. But he *was* a haberman, and a Scanner. "You know what I meant, Luci

. . . the smells, which you have. Which one did you like, on the record?"

"Well-l-l," said she, judiciously, "there were some lamb chops that were the strangest things—"

He interrupted: "What are lambtchots?"

"Wait till you smell them. Then guess. I'll tell you this much. It's a smell hundreds and hundreds of years old. They found out about it in the old books."

"Is a lambtchot a Beast?"

"I won't tell you. You've got to wait," she laughed, as she helped him sit down and spread his tasting-dishes before him. He wanted to go back over the dinner first, sampling all the pretty things he had eaten, and savoring them this time with his now-living lips and tongue.

When Luci had found the music wire and had thrown its sphere up into the force-field he reminded her of the new smells. She took out the long glass records and set the first one into a transmitter.

"Now sniff!"

A queer, frightening, exciting smell came over the room. It seemed like nothing in this world, nor like anything from the Up-and-Out. Yet it was familiar. His mouth watered. His pulse beat a little faster; he scanned his heart-box. (Faster, sure enough.) But that smell, what was it? In mock perplexity, he grabbed her hands, looked into her eyes and growled:

"Tell me, darling! Tell me, or I'll eat you up!"

"That's just right!"

"What?"

"You're right. It should make you want to eat me. It's meat."

"Meat. Who?"

"Not a person," said she, knowledgeably, "a Beast. A Beast which people used to eat. A lamb was a small sheep —you've seen sheep out in the wild, haven't you?—and a chop is part of its middle—here!" She pointed at her chest.

Martel did not hear her. All his boxes had swung over toward *Alarm*, some to *Danger*. He fought against the roar of his own mind, forcing his body into excess excitement. How easy it was to be a Scanner when you really stood outside your own body, haberman-fashion, and looked back into it with your eyes alone. Then you could manage the body, rule it coldly even in the enduring agony of

Space. But to realize that you *were* a body, that this thing was ruling you, that the mind could kick the flesh and send it roaring off into panic! That was bad.

He tried to remember the days before he had gone into the haberman device, before he had been cut apart for the Up-and-Out. Had he always been subject to the rush of his emotions from his mind to his body, from his body back to his mind, confounding him so that he couldn't scan? But he hadn't been a Scanner then.

He knew what had hit him. Amid the roar of his own pulse, he knew. In the nightmare of the Up-and-Out, that smell had forced its way through to him, while their ship burned off Venus and the habermans fought the collapsing metal with their bare hands. He had scanned then: all were in *Danger*. Chestboxes went up to *Overload* and dropped to *Dead* all around him as he had moved from man to man, shoving the drifting corpses out of his way as he fought to scan each man in turn, to clamp vices on un-noticed broken legs, to snap the sleeping-valve on men whose instruments showed they were hopelessly near *Overload*. With men trying to work and cursing him for a Scanner while he, professional zeal aroused, fought to do his job and keep them alive in the Great Pain of Space, he had smelled that smell. It had fought its way along his rebuilt nerves, past the haberman cuts, past all the safeguards of physical and mental discipline. In the wildest hour of tragedy, he had smelled aloud. He remembered it was like a bad cranching, connected with the fury and nightmare all around him. He had even stopped his work to scan himself, fearful that the First Effect might come, breaking past all haberman cuts and ruining him with the Pain of Space. But he had come through. His own instruments stayed and stayed at *Danger*, without nearing *Overload*. He had done his job, and won a commendation for it. He had even forgotten the burning ship.

All except the smell.

And here the smell was all over again—the smell of meat-with-fire. . . .

Luci looked at him with wifely concern. She obviously thought he had cranched too much, and was about to haberman back. She tried to be cheerful: "You'd better rest, honey."

He whispered to her: "Cut—off—that—smell."

She did not question his word. She cut the transmitter. She even crossed the room and stepped up the room controls until a small breeze flitted across the floor and drove the smells up to the ceiling.

He rose, tired and stiff. (His instruments were normal, except that heart was fast and nerve still hanging on the edge of *Danger*.) He spoke sadly:

"Forgive me, Luci. I suppose I shouldn't have cranched. Not so soon again. But, darling, I have to get out from being a haberman. How can I ever be near you? How can I be a man—not hearing my own voice, not even feeling my own life as it goes through my veins? I love you, darling. Can't I ever be near you?"

Her pride was disciplined and automatic: "But you're a Scanner!"

"I know I'm a Scanner. But so what?"

She went over the words, like a tale told a thousand times to reassure herself: "You are the bravest of the brave, the most skilful of the skilled: All Mankind owes most honor to the Scanner, who unites the Earths of mankind. Scanners are the protectors of the habermans. They are the judges in the Up-and-Out. They make men live in the place where men need desperately to die. They are the most honored of mankind, and even the Chiefs of the Instrumentality are delighted to pay them homage!"

With obstinate sorrow he demurred: "Luci, we've heard that all before. But does it pay us back—"

" 'Scanners work for more than pay. They are the strong guards of mankind.' Don't you remember that?"

"But our lives, Luci. What can you get out of being the wife of a Scanner? Why did you marry me? I'm human only when I cranch. The rest of the time—you know what I am. A machine. A man turned into a machine. A man who has been killed and kept alive for duty. Don't you realize what I miss?"

"Of course, darling, of course—"

He went on: "Don't you think I remember my childhood? Don't you think I remember what it is to be a man and not a haberman? To walk and feel my feet on the ground? To feel a decent clean pain instead of watching my body every minute to see if I'm alive? How will I know if I'm dead? Did you ever think of that, Luci? How will I know if I'm dead?"

She ignored the unreasonableness of his outburst. Pacifyingly, she said: "Sit down, darling. Let me make you some kind of a drink. You're overwrought."

Automatically, he scanned, "No, I'm not! Listen to me. How do you think it feels to be in the Up-and-Out with the crew tied-for-space all around you? How do you think it feels to watch them sleep? How do you think I like scanning, scanning, scanning month after month, when I can feel the Pain of Space beating against every part of my body, trying to get past my haberman blocks? How do you think I like to wake the men when I have to, and have them hate me for it? Have you ever seen habermans fight —strong men fighting, and neither knowing pain, fighting until one touches *Overload?* Do you think about that, Luci?" Triumphantly he added: "Can you blame me if I cranch, and come back to being a man, just two days a month?"

"I'm not blaming you, darling. Let's enjoy your cranch. Sit down now, and have a drink."

He was sitting down, resting his face in his hands, while she fixed the drink, using natural fruits out of bottles in addition to the secure alkaloids. He watched her restlessly and pitied her for marrying a Scanner; and then, though it was unjust, resented having to pity her.

Just as she turned to hand him the drink, they both jumped a little as the phone rang. It should not have rung. They had turned it off. It rang again, obviously on the emergency circuit. Stepping ahead of Luci, Martel strode over to the phone and looked into it. Vomact was looking at him.

The custom of Scanners entitled him to be brusque, even with a Senior Scanner, on certain given occasions. This was one.

Before Vomact could speak, Martel spoke two words into the plate, not caring whether the old man could read lips or not:

"Cranching. Busy."

He cut the switch and went back to Luci.

The phone rang again.

Luci said, gently, "I can find out what it is, darling. Here, take your drink and sit down."

"Leave it alone," said her husband. "No one has a right

to call when I'm cranching. He knows that. He ought to know that."

The phone rang again. In a fury, Martel rose and went to the plate. He cut it back on. Vomact was on the screen. Before Martel could speak, Vomact held up his talking nail in line with his heartbox. Martel reverted to discipline:

"Scanner Martel present and waiting, sir."

The lips moved solemnly: "Top emergency."

"Sir, I am under the wire."

"Top emergency."

"Sir, don't you understand?" Martel mouthed his words, so he could be sure that Vomact followed. "I . . . am . . . under . . . the . . . wire. Unfit . . . for . . . space!"

Vomact repeated: "Top emergency. Report to Central Tie-in."

"But, sir, no emergency like this—"

"Right, Martel. No emergency like this, ever before. Report to Tie-in." With a faint glint of kindliness, Vomact added: "No need to de-cranch. Report as you are."

This time it was Martel whose phone was cut out. The screen went gray.

He turned to Luci. The temper had gone out of his voice. She came to him. She kissed him, and rumpled his hair. All she could say was, "I'm sorry."

She kissed him again, knowing his disappointment. "Take good care of yourself, darling. I'll wait."

He scanned, and slipped into his transparent aircoat. At the window he paused, and waved. She called, "Good luck!" As the air flowed past him he said to himself, "This is the first time I've felt flight in—eleven years. Lord, but it's easy to fly if you can feel yourself live!"

Central Tie-in glowed white and austere far ahead. Martel peered. He saw no glare of incoming ships from the Up-and-Out, no shuddering flare of Space-fire out of control. Everything was quiet, as it should be on an off-duty night.

And yet Vomact had called. He had called an emergency higher than Space. There was no such thing. But Vomact had called it.

When Martel got there, he found about half the Scanners present, two dozen or so of them. He lifted the talking finger. Most of the Scanners were standing face to face, talking in pairs as they read lips. A few of the old, impatient ones were scribbling on their tablets and then thrusting the tablets into other people's faces. All the faces wore the dull dead relaxed look of a haberman. When Martel entered the room, he knew that most of the others laughed in the deep isolated privacy of their own minds, each thinking things it would be useless to express in formal words. It had been a long time since a Scanner showed up at a meeting cranched.

Vomact was not there: probably, thought Martel, he was still on the phone calling others. The light of the phone flashed on and off; the bell rang. Martel felt odd when he realized that, of all those present, he was the only one to hear that loud bell. It made him realize why ordinary people did not like to be around groups of habermans or Scanners. Martel looked around for company.

His friend Chang was there, busy explaining to some old and testy Scanner that he did not know why Vomact had called. Martel looked farther and saw Parizianski. He walked over, threading his way past the others with a dexterity that showed he could feel his feet from the inside, and did not have to watch them. Several of the others stared at him with their dead faces, and tried to smile. But they lacked full muscular control and their faces twisted into horrid masks. (Scanners usually knew better than to show expression on faces which they could no longer govern. Martel added to himself: I swear *I'll* never smile again unless I'm cranched.)

Parizianski gave him the sign of the talking finger. Looking face to face, he spoke:

"You come here cranched?"

Parizianski could not hear his own voice, so the words roared like the words on a broken and screeching phone; Martel was startled, but knew that the inquiry was well meant. No one could be better-natured than the burly Pole.

"Vomact called. Top emergency."

"You told him you were cranched?"

"Yes."

"He still made you come?"

"Yes."

"Then all this—it is not for Space? You could not go Up-and-Out? You are like ordinary men?"

"That's right."

"Then why did he call us?" Some pre-haberman habit made Parizianski wave his arms in inquiry. The hand struck the back of the old man behind them. The slap could be heard throughout the room, but only Martel heard it. Instinctively, he scanned Parizianski and the old Scanner, and they scanned him back. Only then did the old man ask why Martel had scanned him. When Martel explained that he was under the wire, the old man moved swiftly away to pass on the news that there was a cranched Scanner present at the Tie-in.

Even this minor sensation could not keep the attention of most of the Scanners from the worry about the top emergency. One young man, who had scanned his first transit just the year before, dramatically interposed himself between Parizianski and Martel. He dramatically flashed his tablet at them: *Is Vmct mad?*

The older men shook their heads. Martel, remembering that it had not been too long that the young man had been haberman, mitigated the dead solemnity of the denial with a friendly smile. He spoke in a normal voice, saying, "Vomact is the Senior of Scanners. I am sure that he could not go mad. Would he not see it on his boxes first?"

Martel had to repeat the question, speaking slowly and mouthing his words before the young Scanner could understand the comment. The young man tried to make his face smile, and twisted it into a comic mask. But he took up his tablet and scribbled: *Yr rght.*

Chang broke away from his friend and came over, his half-Chinese face gleaming in the warm evening. (It's strange, thought Martel, that more Chinese don't become Scanners. Or not so strange perhaps, if you think that they never fill their quota of habermans. Chinese love good living too much. The ones who do scan are all good ones.) Chang saw that Martel was cranched, and spoke with voice:

"You break precedents. Luci must be angry to lose you?"

"She took it well. Chang, that's strange."

"What?"

"I'm cranched, and I can hear. Your voice sounds all right. How did you learn to talk like—like an ordinary person?"

"I practiced with soundtracks. Funny you noticed it. I think I am the only Scanner in or between the Earths who can pass for an ordinary man. Mirrors and soundtracks. I found out how to act."

"But you don't . . . ?"

"No. I don't feel, or taste, or hear, or smell things, any more than you do. Talking doesn't do me much good. But I notice that it cheers up the people around me."

"It would make a difference in the life of Luci."

Chang nodded sagely. "My father insisted on it. He said, 'You may be proud of being a Scanner. I am sorry you are not a man. Conceal your defects.' So I tried. I wanted to tell the old boy about the Up-and-Out, and what we did here, but it did not matter. He said, 'Airplanes were good enough for Confucius, and they are for me too.' The old humbug! He tries so hard to be a Chinese when he can't even read Old Chinese. But he's got wonderful good sense, and for somebody going on 200 he certainly gets around."

Martel smiled at the thought: "In his airplane?"

Chang smiled back. This discipline of his facial muscles was amazing; a bystander would not think that Chang was a haberman, controlling his eyes, cheeks, and lips by cold intellectual control. The expression had the spontaneity of life. Martel felt a flash of envy for Chang when he looked at the dead cold faces of Parizianski and the others. He knew that he himself looked fine: but why shouldn't he? He was cranched. Turning to Parizianski he said, "Did you see what Chang said about his father? The old boy uses an airplane."

Parizianski made motions with his mouth, but the sounds meant nothing. He took up his tablet and showed it to Martel and Chang: *Bzz Bzz. Ha ha. Gd ol' boy.*

At that moment, Martel heard steps out in the corridor. He could not help looking toward the door. Other eyes followed the direction of his glance.

Vomact came in.

The group shuffled to attention in four parallel lines. They scanned one another. Numerous hands reached across to adjust the electrochemical controls on chestboxes which had begun to load up. One Scanner held out a broken finger which his counter-Scanner had discovered, and submitted it for treatment and splinting.

Vomact had taken out his Staff of Office. The cube at the top flashed red light through the room, the lines re-formed, and all Scanners gave the sign meaning, *Present and ready!*

Vomact countered with the stance signifying, *I am the Senior and take command.*

Talking fingers rose in the counter-gesture, *We concur and commit ourselves.*

Vomact raised his right arm, dropped the wrist as though it were broken, in a queer searching gesture, meaning: *Any men around? Any habermans not tied? All clear for the Scanners?*

Alone of all those present, the cranched Martel heard the queer rustle of feet as they all turned completely around without leaving position, looking sharply at one another and flashing their belt-lights into the dark corners of the great room. When again they faced Vomact, he made a further sign: *All clear. Follow my words.*

Martel noticed that he alone relaxed. The others could not know the meaning of relaxation with the minds blocked off up there in their skulls, connected only with the eyes, and the rest of the body connected with the mind only by controlling nonsensory nerves and the instrument boxes on their chests. Martel realized that, cranched as he was, he had expected to hear Vomact's voice: the Senior had been talking for some time. No sound escaped his lips. (Vomact never bothered with sounds.)

". . . and when the first men to go Up-and-Out went to the moon, what did they find?"

"Nothing," responded the silent chorus of lips.

"Therefore they went farther, to Mars and to Venus. The ships went out year by year, but they did not come back until the Year One of Space. Then did a ship come back with the First Effect. Scanners, I ask you, what is the First Effect?"

"No one knows. No one knows."

"No one will ever know. Too many are the variables. By what do we know the First Effect?"

"By the Great Pain of Space," came the chorus.

"And by what further sign?"

"By the need, oh, the need for death."

Vomact again: "And who stopped the need for death?"

"Henry Haberman conquered the First Effect, in the Year 83 of Space."

"And, Scanners, I ask you, what did he do?"

"He made the habermans."

"How, O Scanners, are habermans made?"

"They are made with the cuts. The brain is cut from the heart, the lungs. The brain is cut from the ears, the nose. The brain is cut from the mouth, the belly. The brain is cut from desire and pain. The brain is cut from the world. Save for the eyes. Save for the control of the living flesh."

"And how, O Scanners, is flesh controlled?"

"By the boxes set in the flesh, the controls set in the chest, the signs made to rule the living body, the signs by which the body lives."

"How does a haberman live and live?"

"The haberman lives by control of the boxes."

"Whence come the habermans?"

Martel felt in the coming response a great roar of broken voices echoing through the room as the Scanners, habermans themselves, put sound behind their mouthings:

"Habermans are the scum of mankind. Habermans are the weak, the cruel, the credulous, and the unfit. Habermans are the sentenced-to-more-than-death. Habermans live in the mind alone. They are killed for Space but they live for Space. They master the ships that connect the earths. They live in the Great Pain while ordinary men sleep in the cold, cold sleep of the transit."

"Brothers and Scanners, I ask you now: are we habermans or are we not?"

"We are habermans in the flesh. We are cut apart, brain and flesh. We are ready to go to the Up-and-Out. All of us have gone through the haberman device."

"We are habermans, then?" Vomact's eyes flashed and glittered as he asked the ritual question.

Again the chorused answer was accompanied by a roar of voices heard only by Martel: "Habermans we are, and more, and more. We are the Chosen who are habermans by our own free will. We are the Agents of the Instrumentality of Mankind."

"What must the others say to us?"

"They must say to us, 'You are the bravest of the brave, the most skilful of the skilled. All mankind owes most

honor to the Scanner, who unites the Earths of Mankind.
Scanners are the protectors of the habermans. They are the
judges in the Up-and-Out. They make men live in the place
where men need desperately to die. They are the most
honored of mankind, and even the Chiefs of the Instrumentality are delighted to pay them homage!' "

Vomact stood more erect: "What is the secret duty of
the Scanner?"

"To keep secret our law, and to destroy the acquirers
thereof."

"How to destroy?"

"Twice to the *Overload,* back and *Dead.*"

"If habermans die, what the duty then?"

The Scanners all compressed their lips for answer.
(Silence was the code.) Martel, who—long familiar with
the code—was a little bored with the proceedings, noticed
that Chang was breathing too heavily; he reached over and
adjusted Chang's lung-control and received the thanks of
Chang's eyes. Vomact observed the interruption and glared
at them both. Martel relaxed, trying to imitate the dead
cold stillness of the others. It was so hard to do, when you
were cranched.

"If others die, what the duty then?" asked Vomact.

"Scanners together inform the Instrumentality. Scanners
together accept the punishment. Scanners together settle
the case."

"And if the punishment be severe?"

"Then no ships go."

"And if Scanners not be honored?"

"Then no ships go."

"And if a Scanner goes unpaid?"

"Then no ships go."

"And if the Others and the Instrumentality are not in
all ways at all times mindful of their proper obligation to
the Scanners?"

"Then no ships go."

"And what, O Scanners, if no ships go?"

"The Earths fall apart. The Wild comes back in. The
Old Machines and the Beasts return."

"What is the first known duty of a Scanner?"

"Not to sleep in the Up-and-Out."

"What is the second duty of a Scanner?"

"To keep forgotten the name of fear."

"What is the third duty of a Scanner?"

"To use the wire of Eustace Cranch only with care, only with moderation." Several pair of eyes looked quickly at Martel before the mouthed chorus went on. "To cranch only at home, only among friends, only for the purpose of remembering, of relaxing, or of begetting."

"What is the word of the Scanner?"

"Faithful, though surrounded by death."

"What is the motto of the Scanner?"

"Awake, though surrounded by silence."

"What is the work of the Scanner?"

"Labor even in the heights of the Up-and-Out, loyalty even in the depths of the Earths."

"How do you know a Scanner?"

"We know ourselves. We are dead, though we live. And we talk with the tablet and the nail."

"What is this code?"

"This code is the friendly ancient wisdom of Scanners, briefly put that we may be mindful and be cheered by our loyalty to one another."

At this point the formula should have run: "We complete the code. Is there work or word for the Scanners?" But Vomact said, and he repeated:

"Top emergency. Top emergency."

They gave him the sign, *Present and ready!*

He said, with every eye straining to follow his lips:

"Some of you know the work of Adam Stone?"

Martel saw lips move, saying: "The Red Asteroid. The Other who lives at the edge of Space."

"Adam Stone has gone to the Instrumentality, claiming success for his work. He says that he has found how to screen out the Pain of Space. He says that the Up-and-Out can be made safe for ordinary men to work in, to stay awake in. He says that there need be no more Scanners."

Belt-lights flashed on all over the room as Scanners sought the right to speak. Vomact nodded to one of the older men. "Scanner Smith will speak."

Smith stepped slowly up into the light, watching his own feet. He turned so that they could see his face. He spoke: "I say that this is a lie. I say that Stone is a liar. I say that the Instrumentality must not be deceived."

He paused. Then, in answer to some question from the audience which most of the others did not see, he said:

"I invoke the secret duty of the Scanners."

Smith raised his right hand for emergency attention:
"I say that Stone must die."

Martel, still cranched, shuddered as he heard the boos,
groans, shouts, squeaks, grunts, and moans which came
from the Scanners, who forgot noise in their excitement
and strove to make their dead bodies talk to one another's
deaf ears. Belt-lights flashed wildly all over the room.
There was a rush for the rostrum and Scanners milled
around at the top, vying for attention until Parizianski—
by sheer bulk—shoved the others aside and down, and
turned to mouth at the group.

"Brother Scanners, I want your eyes."

The people on the floor kept moving, with their numb
bodies jostling one another. Finally Vomact stepped up in
front of Parizianski, faced the others, and said:

"Scanners, be Scanners! Give him your eyes."

Parizianski was not good at public speaking. His lips
moved too fast. He waved his hands, which took the eyes
of the others away from his lips. Nevertheless, Martel was
able to follow most of the message:

". . . can't do this. Stone may have succeeded. If he
has succeeded, it means the end of the Scanners. It means
the end of the habermans, too. None of us will have to
fight in the Up-and-Out. We won't have anybody else going under the wire for a few hours or days of being
human. Everybody will be Other. Nobody will have to
cranch, never again. Men can be men. The habermans can
be killed decently and properly, the way men were killed
in the old days, without anybody keeping them alive. They
won't have to work in the Up-and-Out! There will be no
more Great Pain—think of it! No . . . more . . . Great
. . . Pain! How do we know that Stone is a liar—" Lights
began flashing directly into his eyes. (The rudest insult of
Scanner to Scanner was this.)

Vomact again exercised authority. He stepped in front
of Parizianski and said something which the others could
not see. Parizianski stepped down from the rostrum.
Vomact again spoke:

"I think that some of the Scanners disagree with our
Brother Parizianski. I say that the use of the rostrum be

suspended till we have had a chance for private discussion. In fifteen minutes I will call the meeting back to order."

Martel looked around for Vomact when the Senior had rejoined the group on the floor. Finding the Senior, Martel wrote swift script on his tablet, waiting for a chance to thrust the tablet before the Senior's eyes. He had written: *Am crnchd. Rspctfly requst prmissn lv now, stnd by fr orders.*

Being cranched did strange things to Martel. Most meetings that he attended seemed formal, hearteningly ceremonial, lighting up the dark inward eternities of habermanhood. When he was not cranched, he noticed his body no more than a marble bust notices its marble pedestal. He had stood with them before. He had stood with them effortless hours, while the long-winded ritual broke through the terrible loneliness behind his eyes, and made him feel that the Scanners, though a confraternity of the damned, were nonetheless forever honored by the professional requirements of their mutilation.

This time, it was different. Coming cranched, and in full possession of smell-sound-taste-feeling, he reacted more or less as a normal man would. He saw his friends and colleagues as a lot of cruelly driven ghosts, posturing out the meaningless ritual of their indefensible damnation. What difference did anything make, once you were a haberman? Why all this talk about habermans and Scanners? Habermans were criminals or heretics, and Scanners were gentlemen-volunteers, but they were all in the same fix—except that Scanners were deemed worthy of the short-time return of the cranching wire, while habermans were simply disconnected while the ships lay in port and were left suspended until they should be awakened, in some hour of emergency or trouble, to work out another spell of their damnation. It was a rare haberman that you saw on the street—someone of special merit or bravery, allowed to look at mankind from the terrible prison of his own mechanified body. And yet, what Scanner ever pitied a haberman? What Scanner ever honored a haberman except perfunctorily in the line of duty? What had the Scanners as a guild and a class ever done for the habermans, except to murder them with a twist of the wrist whenever a haberman, too long beside a Scanner, picked up the tricks of the scanning trade and learned how to live at his own will, not the will the Scanners imposed? What could the Others, the ordinary men, know of what went on inside the ships? The Others slept in their cylinders, mercifully unconscious until they woke up on whatever other Earth they had consigned themselves to. What could the Others know of the men who had to stay alive within the ship?

What could any Other know of the Up-and-Out? What Other could look at the biting acid beauty of the stars in open Space? What could they tell of the Great Pain, which started quietly in the marrow, like an ache, and proceeded by the fatigue and nausea of each separate nerve cell, brain cell, touchpoint in the body, until life itself became a terrible aching hunger for silence and for death?

He was a Scanner. All right, he *was* a Scanner. He had been a Scanner from the moment when, wholly normal, he had stood in the sunlight before a Subchief of the Instrumentality, and had sworn:

"I pledge my honor and my life to Mankind. I sacrifice myself willingly for the welfare of Mankind. In accepting the perilous austere honor, I yield all my rights without exception to the Honorable Chiefs of the Instrumentality and to the Honored Confraternity of Scanners."

He had pledged.

He had gone into the haberman device.

He remembered his hell. He had not had such a bad one, even though it had seemed to last a hundred million years, all of them without sleep. He had learned to feel with his eyes. He had learned to see despite the heavy eye-plates set back of his eyeballs to insulate his eyes from the rest of him. He had learned to watch his skin. He still remembered the time he had noticed dampness on his shirt, and had pulled out his scanning mirror only to discover that he had worn a hole in his side by leaning against a vibrating machine. (A thing like that could not happen to him now; he was too adept at reading his own instruments.) He remembered the way that he had gone Up-and-Out, and the way that the Great Pain beat into him, despite the fact that his touch, smell, feeling and hearing were gone for all ordinary purposes. He remembered killing habermans, and keeping others alive, and standing for months beside the Honorable Scanner-Pilot while neither of them slept. He remembered going ashore on Earth Four, and remembered that he had not enjoyed it, and had realized on that day that there was no reward.

Martel stood among the other Scanners. He hated their awkwardness when they moved, their immobility when they stood still. He hated the queer assortment of smells which their bodies yielded unnoticed. He hated the grunts and groans and squawks which they emitted from their deafness. He hated them, and himself.

How could Luci stand him? He had kept his chestbox reading *Danger* for weeks while he courted her, carrying the cranch wire about with him most illegally, and going direct from one cranch to the other without worrying about the fact his indicators all crept up to the edge of *Overload*. He had wooed her without thinking of what would happen if she did say, "Yes." She had.

"And they lived happily ever after." In old books they did, but how could they, in life? He had had eighteen days under the wire in the whole of the past year! Yet she had loved him. She still loved him. He knew it. She fretted about him through the long months that he was in the Up-and-Out. She tried to make home mean something to him even when he was haberman, make food pretty when it could not be tasted, make herself lovable when she could not be kissed—or might as well not, since a haberman body meant no more than furniture. Luci was patient.

And now, Adam Stone! (He let his tablet fade: how could he leave now?)

God bless Adam Stone!

Martel could not help feeling a little sorry for himself. No longer would the high keen call of duty carry him through 200 or so years of the Others' time, two million private eternities of his own. He could slouch and relax. He could forget High Space, and let the Up-and-Out be tended by Others. He could cranch as much as he dared. He could be almost normal—almost—for one year or five years or no years. But at least he could stay with Luci. He could go with her into the Wild, where there were Beasts and Old Machines still roving the dark places. Perhaps he would die in the excitement of the hunt, throwing spears at an ancient manshonyagger as it leapt from its lair, or tossing hot spheres at the tribesmen of the Unforgiven who still roamed the Wild. There was still life to live, still a good normal death to die, not the moving of a needle out in the silence and agony of Space!

He had been walking about restlessly. His ears were attuned to the sounds of normal speech, so that he did not feel like watching the mouthings of his brethren. Now they seemed to have come to a decision. Vomact was moving to the rostrum. Martel looked about for Chang, and went to stand beside him. Chang whispered:

"You're as restless as water in mid-air! What's the matter? De-cranching?"

They both scanned Martel, but the instruments held steady and showed no sign of the cranch giving out.

The great light flared in its call to attention. Again they formed ranks. Vomact thrust his lean old face into the glare, and spoke:

"Scanners and Brothers, I call for a vote." He held himself in the stance which meant: *I am the Senior and take command.*

A belt-light flashed in protest.

It was old Henderson. He moved to the rostrum, spoke to Vomact, and—with Vomact's nod of approval—turned full-face to repeat his question:

"Who speaks for the Scanners Out in Space?"

No belt-light or hand answered.

Henderson and Vomact, face to face, conferred for a few moments. Then Henderson faced them again:

"I yield to the Senior in command. But I do not yield to a Meeting of the Confraternity. There are sixty-eight Scanners, and only forty-seven present, of whom one is cranched and U.D. I have therefore proposed that the Senior in command assume authority only over an Emergency Committee of the Confraternity, not over a Meeting. Is that agreed and understood by the Honorable Scanners?"

Hands rose in assent.

Chang murmured in Martel's ear, "Lot of difference that makes! Who can tell the difference between a meeting and a committee?" Martel agreed with the words, but was even more impressed with the way that Chang, while haberman, could control his own voice.

Vomact resumed chairmanship: "We now vote on the question of Adam Stone.

"First, we can assume that he has not succeeded, and

that his claims are lies. We know that from our practical experiences as Scanners. The Pain of Space is only part of Scanning" (but the essential part, the basis of it all, thought Martel) "and we can rest assured that Stone cannot solve the problem of Space Discipline."

"That tripe again," whispered Chang, unheard save by Martel.

"The Space Discipline of our Confraternity has kept High Space clean of war and dispute. Sixty-eight disciplined men control all High Space. We are removed by our oath and our haberman status from all Earthly passions.

"Therefore, if Adam Stone has conquered the Pain of Space, so that Others can wreck our Confraternity and bring to Space the trouble and ruin which afflicts Earths, I say that Adam Stone is wrong. If Adam Stone succeeds, Scanners live in vain!

"Secondly, if Adam Stone has not conquered the Pain of Space, he will cause great trouble in all the Earths. The Instrumentality and the Subchiefs may not give us as many habermans as we need to operate the ships of Mankind. There will be wild stories, and fewer recruits, and, worst of all, the Discipline of the Confraternity may relax if this kind of nonsensical heresy is spread around.

"Therefore, if Adam Stone has succeeded, he threatens the ruin of the Confraternity and should die.

"I move the death of Adam Stone."

And Vomact made the sign, *The Honorable Scanners are pleased to vote.*

Martel grabbed wildly for his belt-light. Chang, guessing ahead, had his light out and ready; its bright beam, voting *No*, shone straight up at the ceiling. Martel got his light out and threw its beam upward in dissent. Then he looked around. Out of the forty-seven present, he could see only five or six glittering.

Two more lights went on. Vomact stood as erect as a frozen corpse. Vomact's eyes flashed as he stared back and forth over the group, looking for lights. Several more went on. Finally Vomact took the closing stance: *May it please the Scanners to count the vote.*

Three of the old men went up on the rostrum with Vomact. They looked over the room. (Martel thought:

These damned ghosts are voting on the life of a real man, a live man! They have no right to do it. I'll tell the Instrumentality! But he knew that he would not. He thought of Luci and what she might gain by the triumph of Adam Stone: the heartbreaking folly of the vote was then almost too much for Martel to bear.)

All three of the tellers held up their hands in unanimous agreement on the sign of the number: *Fifteen against.*

Vomact dismissed them with a bow of courtesy. He turned and again took the stance: *I am the Senior and take command.*

Marveling at his own daring, Martel flashed his belt-light on. He knew that any one of the bystanders might reach over and twist his heartbox to *Overload* for such an act. He felt Chang's hand reaching to catch him by the aircoat. But he eluded Chang's grasp and ran, faster than a Scanner should, to the platform. As he ran, he wondered what appeal to make. It was no use talking common sense. Not now. It had to be law.

He jumped up on the rostrum beside Vomact, and took the stance: *Scanners, an Illegality!*

He violated good custom while speaking, still in the stance: "A Committee has no right to vote death by a majority vote. It takes two-thirds of a full Meeting."

He felt Vomact's body lunge behind him, felt himself falling from the rostrum, hitting the floor, hurting his knees and his touch-aware hands. He was helped to his feet. He was scanned. Some Scanner he scarcely knew took his instruments and toned him down.

Immediately Martel felt more calm, more detached, and hated himself for feeling so.

He looked up at the rostrum. Vomact maintained the stance signifying: *Order!*

The Scanners adjusted their ranks. The two Scanners next to Martel took his arms. He shouted at them, but they looked away, and cut themselves off from communication altogether.

Vomact spoke again when he saw the room was quiet: "A Scanner came here cranched. Honorable Scanners, I apologize for this. It is not the fault of our great and worthy Scanner and friend, Martel. He came here under orders. I told him not to decranch. I hoped to spare him an unnecessary haberman. We all know how happily Martel is married, and we wish his brave experiment well. I like Martel. I respect his judgment. I wanted him here. I knew you wanted him here. But he is cranched. He is in no mood to share in the lofty business of the Scanners. I therefore propose a solution which will meet all the requirements of fairness. I propose that we rule Scanner Martel out of order for his violation of rules. This violation would be inexcusable if Martel were not cranched.

"But at the same time, in all fairness to Martel, I further propose that we deal with the points raised so improperly by our worthy but disqualified brother."

Vomact gave the sign, *The Honorable Scanners are pleased to vote.* Martel tried to reach his own belt-light; the dead strong hands held him tightly and he struggled in vain. One lone light shone high: Chang's, no doubt.

Vomact thrust his face into the light again: "Having the approval of our worthy Scanners and present company for the general proposal, I now move that this Committee declare itself to have the full authority of a Meeting, and that this Committee further make me responsible for all misdeeds which this Committee may enact, to be held answerable before the next full Meeting, but not before any other authority beyond the closed and secret ranks of Scanners."

Flamboyantly this time, his triumph evident, Vomact assumed the *vote* stance.

Only a few lights shone: far less, patently, than a minority of one-fourth.

Vomact spoke again. The light shone on his high calm forehead, on his dead relaxed cheekbones. His lean cheeks and chin were half-shadowed, save where the lower light picked up and spotlighted his mouth, cruel even in repose. (Vomact was said to be a descendant of some ancient lady who had traversed, in an illegitimate and inexplicable fashion, some hundreds of years of time in a single night. Her name, the Lady Vomact, has passed into legend; but her blood and her archaic lust for mastery lived on in the mute masterful body of her descendant. Martel could believe the old tales as he stared at the rostrum, wondering what untraceable mutation had left the Vomact kin as predators among Mankind.) Calling loudly with the movement of his lips, but still without sound, Vomact appealed:

"The honorable Committee is now pleased to reaffirm

the sentence of death issued against the heretic and enemy, Adam Stone." Again the *vote* stance.

Again Chang's light shone lonely in its isolated protest.

Vomact then made his final move:

"I call for the designation of the Senior Scanner present as the manager of the sentence. I call for authorization to him to appoint executioners, one or many, who shall make evident the will and majesty of Scanners. I ask that I be accountable for the deed, and not for the means. The deed is a noble deed, for the protection of Mankind and for the honor of the Scanners; but of the means it must be said that they are to be the best at hand, and no more. Who knows the true way to kill an Other, here on a crowded and watchful Earth? This is no mere matter of discharging a cylindered sleeper, no mere question of upgrading the needle of a haberman. When people die down here, it is not like the Up-and-Out. They die reluctantly. Killing within the Earth is not our usual business, O brothers and Scanners, as you know well. You must choose me to choose my agent as I see fit. Otherwise the common knowledge will become the common betrayal, whereas if I alone know the responsibility I alone could betray us, and you will not have far to look in case the Instrumentality comes searching." (What about the killer you choose? thought Martel. He too will know unless—unless you silence him forever.)

Vomact went into the stance: *The Honorable Scanners are pleased to vote.*

One light of protest shone; Chang's, again.

Martel imagined that he could see a cruel joyful smile on Vomact's dead face—the smile of a man who knew himself righteous and who found his righteousness upheld and affirmed by militant authority.

Martel tried one last time to come free.

The dead hands held. They were locked like vices until their owners' eyes unlocked them: how else could they hold the piloting month by month?

Martel then shouted: "Honorable Scanners, this is judicial murder."

No ear heard him. He was cranched, and alone.

None the less, he shouted again: "You endanger the Confraternity."

Nothing happened.

The echo of his voice sounded from one end of the room to the other. No head turned. No eyes met his.

Martel realized that, as they paired for talk, the eyes of the Scanners averted him. He saw that no one desired to watch his speech. He knew that behind the cold faces of his friends there lay compassion or amusement. He knew that they knew him to be cranched—absurd, normal, man-like, temporarily no Scanner. But he knew that in this matter the wisdom of Scanners was nothing. He knew that only a cranched Scanner could feel with his very blood the outrage and anger which deliberate murder would provoke among the Others. He knew that the Confraternity endangered itself, and knew that the most ancient prerogative of law was the monopoly of death. Even the ancient nations, in the times of the Wars, before the Beasts, before men went into the Up-and-Out—even the ancients had known this. How did they say it? *Only the state shall kill.* The states were gone but the Instrumentality remained, and the Instrumentality could not pardon things which occurred within the Earths but beyond its authority. Death in Space was the business, the right of the Scanners: how could the Instrumentality enforce its laws in a place where all men who wakened wakened only to die in the Great Pain? Wisely did the Instrumentality leave Space to the Scanners, wisely had the Confraternity not meddled inside the Earths. And now the Confraternity itself was going to step forth as an outlaw band, as a gang of rogues as stupid and reckless as the tribes of the Unforgiven!

Martel knew this because he was cranched. Had he been haberman, he would have thought only with his mind, not with his heart and guts and blood. How could the other Scanners know?

Vomact returned for the last time to the rostrum: *The Committee has met and its will shall be done.* Verbally he added: "Senior among you, I ask your loyalty and your silence."

At that point, the two Scanners let his arms go. Martel rubbed his numb hands, shaking his fingers to get the circulation back into the cold fingertips. With real freedom, he began to think of what he might still do. He scanned himself: the cranching held. He might have a day. Well, he could go even if haberman, but it would be inconvenient, having to talk with finger and tablet. He looked about for Chang. He saw his friend standing patient and immobile in a quiet corner. Martel moved slowly, so as not to attract any more attention to himself than could be helped. He faced Chang, moved until his face was in the light, and then articulated:

"What are we going to do? You're not going to let them kill Adam Stone, are you? Don't you realize what Stone's work will mean to us, if it succeeds? No more Scanners. No more habermans. No more Pain in the Up-and-Out. I tell you, if the others were all cranched, as I am, they would see it in a human way, not with the narrow crazy logic which they used in the Meeting. We've got to stop them. How can we do it? What are we going to do? What does Parizianski think? Who has been chosen?"

"Which question do you want me to answer?"

Martel laughed. (It felt good to laugh, even then; it felt like being a man.) "Will you help me?"

Chang's eyes flashed across Martel's face as Chang answered: "No. No. No."

"You won't help?"

"No."

"Why not, Chang? Why not?"

"I am a Scanner. The vote has been taken. You would do the same if you were not in this unusual condition."

"I'm not in an unusual condition. I'm cranched. That merely means that I see things the way that the Others would. I see the stupidity. The recklessness. The selfishness. It is murder."

"What is murder? Have you not killed? You are not one of the Others. You are a Scanner. You will be sorry for what you are about to do, if you do not watch out."

"But why did you vote against Vomact, then? Didn't you, too, see what Adam Stone means to all of us? Scanners will live in vain. Thank God for that! Can't you see it?"

"No."

"But you talk to me, Chang. You are my friend?"

"I talk to you. I am your friend. Why not?"

"But what are you going to do?"

"Nothing, Martel. Nothing."

"Will you help me?"

"No."

"Not even to save Stone?"

"No."

"Then I will go to Parizianski for help."

"It will do you no good."

"Why not? He's more human than you, right now."

"He will not help you, because he has the job. Vomact
designated him to kill Adam Stone."

Martel stopped speaking in mid-movement. He suddenly
took the stance: *I thank you, brother, and I depart.*

At the window he turned and faced the room. He saw
that Vomact's eyes were upon him. He gave the stance, *I
thank you, brother, and I depart,* and added the flourish
of respect which is shown when Seniors are present. Vomact caught the sign, and Martel could see the cruel lips
move. He thought he saw the words "Take good care of
yourself" but did not wait to inquire. He stepped backward and dropped out the window.

Once below the window and out of sight, he adjusted
his aircoat to a maximum speed. He swam lazily in the
air scanning himself thoroughly, and adjusting his adrenal
intake down. He then made the movement of release, and
felt the cold air rush past his face like running water.

Adam Stone had to be at Chief Downport.

Adam Stone had to be there.

Wouldn't Adam Stone be surprised in the night? Surprised to meet the strangest of beings, the first renegade
among Scanners. (Martel suddenly appreciated that it was
of himself he was thinking. Martel, the Traitor to Scanners! That sounded strange and bad. But what of Martel,
the Loyal to Mankind? Was that no compensation? And, if
he won, he won Luci. If he lost, he lost nothing—an
unconsidered and expendable haberman. It happened to
be himself. But, in contrast to the immense reward, to
Mankind, to the Confraternity, to Luci, what did that
matter?)

Martel thought to himself: "Adam Stone will have two
visitors tonight. Two Scanners, who are the friends of one
another." He hoped that Parizianski was still his friend.

"And the world," he added, "depends on which of us
gets there first."

Multifaceted in their brightness, the lights of Chief
Downport began to shine through the mist ahead. Martel
could see the outer towers of the city and glimpsed the

phosphorescent periphery which kept back the Wild,
whether Beasts, Machines, or the Unforgiven.

Once more Martel invoked the lords of his chance:
"Help me to pass for an Other!"

Within the Downport, Martel had less trouble than he
thought. He draped his aircoat over his shoulder so that it
concealed the instruments. He took up his scanning mirror,
and made up his face from the inside, by adding tone and
animation to his blood and nerves until the muscles of his
face glowed and the skin gave out a healthy sweat. That
way he looked like an ordinary man who had just completed a long night flight.

After straightening out his clothing, and hiding his tablet
within his jacket, he faced the problem of what to do
about the talking finger. If he kept the nail, it would show
him to be a Scanner. He would be respected but he would
be identified. He might be stopped by the guards whom
the Instrumentality had undoubtedly set around the person
of Adam Stone. If he broke the nail— But he couldn't! No
Scanner in the history of the Confraternity had ever willingly broken his nail. That would be Resignation, and
there was no such thing. The only way *out* was in the
Up-and-Out! Martel put his finger to his mouth and bit off
the nail. He looked at the now-queer finger, and sighed to
himself.

He stepped toward the city gate, slipping his hand into
his jacket and running up his muscular strength to four
times normal. He started to scan, and then realized that
his instruments were masked. *Might as well take all the
chances at once,* he thought.

The watcher stopped him with a searching wire. The
sphere thumped suddenly against Martel's chest.

"Are you a man?" said the unseen voice. (Martel knew
that as a Scanner in haberman condition his own field-
charge would have illuminated the sphere.)

"I am a man." Martel knew that the timbre of his voice
had been good; he hoped that it would not be taken for
that of a manshonyagger or a Beast or an Unforgiven one,
who with mimicry sought to enter the cities and ports of
Mankind.

"Name, number, rank, purpose, function, time departed."

"Martel." He had to remember his old number, not Scanner 34. "Sunward 4234, 782nd Year of Space. Rank, rising Subchief." That was no lie, but his substantive rank. "Purpose, personal, and lawful within the limits of this city. No function of the Instrumentality. Departed Chief Outport 2019 hours." Everything now depended on whether he was believed or would be checked against Chief Outport.

The voice was flat and routine: "Time desired within the city."

Martel used the standard phrase: "Your honorable sufferance is requested."

He stood in the cool night air, waiting. Far above him, through a gap in the mist, he could see the poisonous glittering in the sky of Scanners. The stars are my enemies, he thought: I have mastered the stars but they hate me. Ho, that sounds ancient! Like a book. Too much cranching.

The voice returned: "Sunward 4234 dash 782 rising Subchief Martel, enter the lawful gates of the city. Welcome. Do you desire food, raiment, money, or companionship?" The voice had no hospitality in it, just business. This was certainly different from entering a city in a Scanner's role! Then the petty officers came out, and threw their belt-lights in their fretful faces, and mouthed their words with preposterous deference, shouting against the stone deafness of Scanners' ears. So that was the way that a Subchief was treated: matter of fact, but not bad. Not bad.

Martel replied: "I have that which I need, but beg of the city a favor. My friend Adam Stone is here. I desire to see him, on urgent and personal lawful affairs."

The voice replied: "Did you have an appointment with Adam Stone?"

"No."

"The city will find him. What is his number?"

"I have forgotten it."

"You have forgotten it? Is not Adam Stone a Magnate of the Instrumentality? Are you truly his friend?"

"Truly." Martel let a little annoyance creep into his voice. "Watcher, doubt me and call your Subchief."

"No doubt implied. Why do you not know the number? This must go into the record," added the voice.

"We were friends in childhood. He had crossed the—"

Martel started to say "the Up-and-Out" and remembered that the phrase was current only among Scanners. "He has leaped from Earth to Earth, and has just now returned. I knew him well and I seek him out. I have word of his kith. May the Instrumentality protect us!"

"Heard and believed. Adam Stone will be searched."

At a risk, though a slight one, of having the sphere sound an alarm for *non-human*, Martel cut in on his Scanner speaker within his jacket. He saw the trembling needle of light await his words and he started to write on it with his blunt finger. That won't work, he thought, and had a moment's panic until he found his comb, which had a sharp enough tooth to write. He wrote: "Emergency none. Martel Scanner calling Parizianski Scanner."

The needle quivered and the reply glowed and faded out: "Parizianski Scanner on duty and D.C. Calls taken by Scanner Relay."

Martel cut off his speaker.

Parizianski was somewhere around. Could he have crossed the direct way, right over the city wall, setting off the alert, and invoking official business when the petty officers overtook him in mid-air? Scarcely. That meant that a number of other Scanners must have come in with Parizianski, all of them pretending to be in search of a few of the tenuous pleasures which could be enjoyed by a haberman, such as the sight of the newspictures or the viewing of beautiful women in the Pleasure Gallery. Parizianski was around, but he could not have moved privately, because Scanner Central registered him on duty and recorded his movements city by city.

The voice returned. Puzzlement was expressed in it. "Adam Stone is found and awakened. He has asked pardon of the Honorable, and says he knows no Martel. Will you see Adam Stone in the morning? The city will bid you welcome."

Martel ran out of resources. It was hard enough mimicking a man without having to tell lies in the guise of one. Martel could only repeat: "Tell him I am Martel. The husband of Luci."

"It will be done."

Again the silence, and the hostile stars, and the sense that Parizianski was somewhere near and getting nearer; Martel felt his heart beating faster. He stole a glimpse at his chestbox and set his heart down a point. He felt calmer, even though he had not been able to scan with care.

The voice this time was cheerful, as though an annoyance had been settled: "Adam Stone consents to see you. Enter Chief Downport, and welcome."

The little sphere dropped noiselessly to the ground and the wire whispered away into the darkness. A bright arc of narrow light rose from the ground in front of Martel and swept through the city to one of the higher towers—apparently a hostel, which Martel had never entered. Martel plucked his aircoat to his chest for ballast, stepped heel-and-toe on the beam, and felt himself whistle through the air to an entrance window which sprang up before him as suddenly as a devouring mouth.

A tower guard stood in the doorway. "You are awaited, sir. Do you bear weapons, sir?"

"None," said Martel, grateful that he was relying on his own strength.

The guard led him past the check-screen. Martel noticed the quick flight of a warning across the screen as his instruments registered and identified him as a Scanner. But the guard had not noticed it.

The guard stopped at a door. "Adam Stone is armed. He is lawfully armed by authority of the Instrumentality and by the liberty of this city. All those who enter are given warning."

Martel nodded in understanding at the man and went in.

Adam Stone was a short man, stout and benign. His gray hair rose stiffly from a low forehead. His whole face was red and merry-looking. He looked like a jolly guide from the Pleasure Gallery, not like a man who had been at the edge of the Up-and-Out, fighting the Great Pain without haberman protection.

He stared haberman at Martel. His look was puzzled, perhaps a little annoyed, but not hostile.

Martel came to the point. "You do not know me. I lied. My name is Martel, and I mean you no harm. But I lied. I beg the honorable gift of your hospitality. Remain armed. Direct your weapon against me—"

Stone smiled: "I am doing so," and Martel noticed the small wirepoint in Stone's capable plump hand.

"Good. Keep on guard against me. It will give you

confidence in what I shall say. But do, I beg you, give us a screen of privacy. I want no casual lookers. This is a matter of life and death."

"First: whose life and death?" Stone's face remained calm, his voice even.

"Yours, and mine, and the world's."

"You are cryptic, but I agree." Stone called through the doorway: "Privacy, please." There was a sudden hum, and all the little noises of the night quickly vanished from the air of the room.

Said Adam Stone: "Sir, who are you? What brings you here?"

"I am Scanner 34."

"You a Scanner? I don't believe it."

For answer, Martel pulled his jacket open, showing his chestbox. Stone looked up at him, amazed. Martel explained:

"I am cranched. Have you never seen it before?"

"*Not with men.* On animals. Amazing! But—what do you want?"

"The truth. Do you fear me?"

"Not with this," said Stone, grasping the wirepoint. "But I shall tell you the truth."

"Is it true that you have conquered the Great Pain?"

Stone hesitated, seeking words for an answer.

"Quick, can you tell me how you have done it, so that I may believe you?"

"I have loaded the ships with life."

"Life?"

"Life. I don't know what the Great Pain is, but I did find that in the experiments, when I sent out masses of animals or plants, the life in the centre of the mass lived longest. I built ships—small ones, of course—and sent them out with rabbits, with monkeys—"

"Those are Beasts?"

"Yes. With small Beasts. And the Beasts came back unhurt. They came back because the walls of the ships were filled with life. I tried many kinds, and finally found a sort of life which lives in the waters. Oysters. Oyster-beds. The outermost oysters died in the Great Pain. The inner ones lived. The passengers were unhurt."

"But they were Beasts?"

"Not only Beasts. Myself."

"You!"

"I came through Space alone. Through what you call the Up-and-Out, alone. Awake and sleeping. I am unhurt. If you do not believe me, ask your brother Scanners. Come and see my ship in the morning. I will be glad to see you then, along with your brother Scanners. I am going to demonstrate before the Chiefs of the Instrumentality."

Martel repeated his question: "You came here alone?"

Adam Stone grew testy: "Yes, alone. Go back and check your Scanner's register if you do not believe me. You never put me in a bottle to cross Space."

Martel's face was radiant. "I believe you now. It is true. No more Scanners. No more habermans. No more cranching."

Stone looked significantly toward the door.

Martel did not take the hint. "I must tell you that—"

"Sir, tell me in the morning. Go enjoy your cranch. Isn't it supposed to be pleasure? Medically I know it well. But not in practice."

"It is pleasure. It's normality—for a while. But listen. The Scanners have sworn to destroy you, and your work."

"What!"

"They have met and have voted and sworn. You will make Scanners unnecessary, they say. You will bring the ancient wars back to the world, if scanning is lost and the Scanners live in vain!"

Adam Stone was nervous but kept his wits about him: "You're a Scanner. Are you going to kill me—or try?"

"No, you fool. I have betrayed the Confraternity. Call guards the moment I escape. Keep guards around you. I will try to intercept the killer."

Martel saw a blur in the window. Before Stone could turn, the wirepoint was whipped out of his hand. The blur solidified and took form as Parizianski.

Martel recognized what Parizianski was doing: *High speed.*

Without thinking of his cranch, he thrust his hand to his chest, set himself up to *High speed* too. Waves of fire, like the Great Pain, but hotter, flooded over him. He fought to keep his face readable as he stepped in front of Parizianski and gave the sign, *Top emergency.*

Parizianski spoke, while the normally moving body of

Stone stepped away from them as slowly as a drifting cloud; "Get out of my way. I am on a mission."

"I know it. I stop you here and now. Stop. Stop. Stop. Stone is right."

Parizianski's lips were barely readable in the haze of pain which flooded Martel. (He thought: God, God, God of the ancients! Let me hold on! Let me live under Overload just long enough!) Parizianski was saying: "Get out of my way. By order of the Confraternity, get out of my way!" And Parizianski gave the sign, *Help I demand in the name of my duty!*

Martel choked for breath in the syrup-like air. He tried one last time: "Parizianski, friend, friend, my friend. Stop. Stop." (No Scanner had ever murdered Scanner before.)

Parizianski made the sign: *You are unfit for duty, and I will take over.*

Martel thought, For the first time in the world! as he reached over and twisted Parizianski's brainbox up to *Overload.* Parizianski's eyes glittered in terror and understanding. His body began to drift down toward the floor.

Martel had just strength enough to reach his own chestbox. As he faded into haberman or death, he knew not which, he felt his fingers turning on the control of speed, turning down. He tried to speak, to say, "Get a Scanner, I need help, get a Scanner. . . ."

But the darkness rose about him, and the numb silence clasped him.

Martel awakened to see the face of Luci near his own.

He opened his eyes wider, and found that he was hearing—the sound of her happy weeping, the sound of her chest as she caught the air back into her throat.

He spoke weakly: "Still cranched? Alive?"

Another face swam into the blur beside Luci's. It was Adam Stone. His deep voice rang across immensities of space before coming to Martel's hearing. Martel tried to read Stone's lips, but could not make them out. He went back to listening to the voice:

". . . not cranched. Do you understand me? Not cranched!"

Martel tried to say: "But I can hear! I can feel!" The others got his sense if not his words.

Adam Stone spoke again:

"You have gone back through the haberman. I put you back first. I didn't know how it would work in practice, but I had the theory all worked out. You don't think the Instrumentality would waste the Scanners, do you? You go back to normality. We are letting the habermans die as fast as the ships come in. They don't need to live any more. But we are restoring the Scanners. You are the first. Do you understand? You are the first. Take it easy, now."

Adam Stone smiled. Dimly, behind Stone, Martel thought that he saw the face of one of the Chiefs of the Instrumentality. That face, too, smiled at him, and then both faces disappeared upward and away.

Martel tried to lift his head, to scan himself. He could not. Luci stared at him, calming herself, but with an expression of loving perplexity. She said, "My darling husband! You're back again, to stay!"

Still, Martel tried to see his box. Finally he swept his hand across his chest with a clumsy motion. There was nothing there. The instruments were gone. He was back to normality but still alive.

In the deep weak peacefulness of his mind, another troubling thought took shape. He tried to write with his finger, the way that Luci wanted him to, but he had neither pointed fingernail nor Scanner's tablet. He had to use his voice. He summoned up his strength and whispered:

"Scanners?"

"Yes, darling? What is it?"

"Scanners?"

"Scanners. Oh, yes, darling, they're all right. They had to arrest some of them for going into *High speed* and running away. But the Instrumentality caught them all—all those on the ground—and they're happy now. Do you know, darling," she laughed, "some of them didn't want to be restored to normality. But Stone and the Chiefs persuaded them."

"Vomact?"

"He's fine, too. He's staying cranched until he can be restored. Do you know, he has arranged for Scanners to take new jobs. You're all to be Deputy Chiefs for Space. Isn't that nice? But he got himself made Chief for Space. You're all going to be pilots, so that your fraternity and guild can go on. And Chang's getting changed right now. You'll see him soon."

Her face turned sad. She looked at him earnestly and said: "I might as well tell you now. You'll worry otherwise. There has been one accident. Only one. When you and your friend called on Adam Stone, your friend was so happy that he forgot to scan, and he let himself die of *Overload*."

"Called on Stone?"

"Yes. Don't you remember? Your friend."

He still looked surprised, so she said:

"Parizianski."

TIME TRAP

by Charles L. Harness

One morning about thirty-three years ago I awoke with the realization that I was through with all my academic work, I had passed the D.C. bar, I had a baby daughter, and I needed money. (Government salaries in those days— I was a mineral economist with the Bureau of Mines— were not nearly as tidy as they are today.) So, being an avid reader of Astounding *(now* Analog—shucks), *I saw my new spare time as a chance to fulfill a secret ambition of long standing. I would write an sf story and send it in to John Campbell. And so I began. Now, I did not know you were supposed to have the whole story blocked out, at least mentally, before you started to write. So I just simply began and sort of let the story write itself. The murder case in the tale is taken directly from a case I had in criminal law, Jackson v. Commonwealth, 100 Ky. 239 (1896). In the real case the murderer (despite the eloquence of his lawyer and the lack of murderous intent at the time of the actual killing) was sentenced by an unfeeling judge to hang. In "Time Trap" I got him off.*

I wrote the tale at my office desk, after hours. As I type this, I remember distinctly the texture of the government paper, the chewed end of the government pen (a real genuine fountain pen, which used genuine blue-black ink— something that seems to have gone out of style). When it was all done I typed it up on my wife's portable, sent it in to Astounding, *and waited. After a while, word came back. They were overstocked just then, but if I was willing to wait a couple of months, they would buy it. So of course*

213

I waited. And the check did indeed come in. And so, off and on, I've been writing ever since.

The Great Ones themselves never agreed whether the events constituting Troy's cry for help had a beginning. But the warning signal did have an end. The Great Ones saw to that. Those of the Great Ones who claim a beginning for the story date it with the expulsion of the evil Sathanas from the Place of Suns, when he fled, horribly wounded, spiraling evasively inward, through sterechronia without number, until, exhausted, he sank and lay hidden in the crystallizing magma of a tiny new planet at the galactic rim.

General Blade sometimes felt that leading a resistance movement was far exceeding his debt to decent society and that one day soon he would allow his peaceful nature to override his indignant pursuit of justice. Killing a man, even a very bad man, without a trial, went against his grain. He sighed and rapped on the table.

"As a result of Blogshak's misappropriation of funds voted to fight the epidemic," he announced, "the death toll this morning reached over one hundred thousand. Does the Assassination Subcommittee have a recommendation?"

A thin-lipped man rose from the gathering. "The Provinarch ignored our warning," he said rapidly. "This subcommittee, as you all know, some days ago set an arbitrary limit of one hundred thousand deaths. Therefore this subcommittee now recommends that its plan for killing the Provinarch be adopted at once. Tonight is very favorable for our plan, which, incidentally, requires a married couple. We have thoroughly catasynthesized the four bodyguards who will be with him on this shift and have provided irresistible scent and sensory stimuli for the woman. The probability for its success insofar as assassination is concerned is about 78 percent; the probability of escape of our killers is 62 percent. We regard these probabilities as favorable. The Legal Subcommittee will take it from there."

Another man arose. "We have retained Mr. Poole, who is with us tonight." He nodded gravely to a withered little man beside him. "Although Mr. Poole has been a member of the bar but a short time, and although his prelegal life —some seventy years of it—remains a mystery which he does not explain, our catasynthesis laboratory indicates that his legal knowledge is profound. More important, his persuasive powers, tested with a trial group of twelve professional evaluators, sort of a rehearsal for a possible trial, border on hypnosis. He has also suggested an excellent method of disposing of the corpse to render identification difficult. According to Mr. Poole, if the assassinators are caught, the probability of escaping the devitalizing chamber is 53 percent."

"Mr. Chairman!"

General Blade turned toward the new speaker, who stood quietly several rows away. The man seemed to reflect a gray inconspicuousness, relieved only by a gorgeous rosebud in his lapel. Gray suit, gray eyes, graying temples. On closer examination, one detected an edge of flashing blue in the grayness. The eyes no longer seemed softly unobtrusive, but icy, and the firm mouth and jutting chin seemed polished steel. General Blade had observed this phenomenon dozens of times, but he never tired of it.

"You have the floor, Major Troy," he said.

"I, and perhaps other League officers, would like to know more about Mr. Poole," came the quiet, faintly metallic voice. "He is not a member of the League, and yet Legal and Assassination welcome him in their councils. I think we should be provided some assurance that he has no associations with the Provinarch's administration. One traitor could sell the lives of all of us."

The Legal spokesman arose again. "Major Troy's objections are in some degree merited. We don't know who Mr. Poole is. His mind is absolutely impenetrable to telepathic probes. His fingerprint and eye vein patterns are a little obscure. Our attempts at identification"—he laughed sheepishly—"always key out to yourself, major. An obvious impossibility. So far as the world is concerned, Mr. Poole is an old man who might have been born yesterday! All we know of him is his willingness to cooperate with us to the best of his ability—which, I can assure you, is tremendous. The catasynthesizer has established his sympathetic attitude beyond doubt. Don't forget, too, that he could be charged as a principal in this assassination and devitalized himself. On the whole, he is our man. If our killers are caught, we must use him."

Troy turned and studied the little lawyer with narrowing eyes; Poole's face seemed oddly familiar. The old man returned the gaze sardonically, with a faint suggestion of a smile.

"Time is growing short, major," urged the Assassination chairman. "The Poole matter has already received the attention of qualified League investigators. It is not a proper matter for discussion at this time. If you are satisfied with the arrangements, will you and Mrs. Troy please assemble the childless married couples on your list? The men can draw lots from the fish bowl on the side table. The red ball decides." He eyed Troy expectantly.

Still standing, Troy looked down at the woman in the adjacent seat. Her lips were half-parted, her black eyes somber pools as she looked up at her husband.

"Well, Ann?" he telepathed.

Her eyes seemed to look through him and far beyond. "He will make you draw the red ball, Jon," she murmured, trancelike. "Then he will die, and I will die. But Jon Troy will never die. Never die. Never die. Nev——"

"Wake up, Ann!" Troy shook her by the shoulder. To the puzzled faces about them, he explained quickly, "My wife is something of a seeress." He 'pathed again: "Who is *he?*"

Ann Troy brushed the black hair from her brow slowly. "It's all confused. *He* is someone in this room——" She started to get up.

"Sit down, dear," said Troy gently. "If I'm to draw the red ball, I may as well cut this short." He slid past her into the aisle, strode to the side table, and thrust his hand into the hole in the box sitting there.

Every eye was on him.

His hand hit the invisible fish bowl with its dozen-odd plastic balls. Inside the bowl, he touched the little spheres at random while he studied the people in the room. All old friends, except—Poole. That tantalizing face. Poole was now staring like the rest, except that beads of sweat were forming on his forehead.

Troy swirled the balls around the bowl; the muffled clatter was audible throughout the room. He felt his fingers close on one. His hands were perspiring freely. With an effort he forced himself to drop it. He chose another, and looked at Poole. The latter was frowning. Troy could not bring his hand out of the bowl. His right arm seemed partially paralyzed. He dropped the ball and rolled the mass around again. Poole was now smiling. Troy hesitated a moment, then picked a ball from the center of the bowl. It felt slightly moist. He pulled it out, looked at it grimly, and held it up for all to see.

"Just 'path that!" whispered the jail warden reverently to the night custodian.

"You know I can't telepath," said the latter grumpily. "What are they saying?"

"Not a word all night. They seem to be taking a symposium of the best piano concertos since maybe the twentieth century. Was Chopin twentieth or twenty-first? Anyhow, they're up to the twenty-third now, with Darnoval. Troy reproduces the orchestra and his wife does the piano. You'd think she had fifty years to live instead of five minutes."

"Both seem nice people," ruminated the custodian. "If they hadn't killed the Provinarch, maybe they'd have become famous 'pathic musicians. She had a lousy lawyer. She could have got off with ten years' sleep if he'd half tried." He pushed some papers across the desk. "I've had the chamber checked. Want to look over the readings?"

The warden scanned them rapidly. "Potential difference, eight million; drain rate, ninety vital units/minute; estimated period of consciousness, thirty seconds; estimated durance to nonrecovery point, four minutes; estimated durance to legal death, five minutes." He initialed the front sheet. "That's fine. When I was younger they called it the 'vitality drain chamber.' Drain rate was only two v.u./min. Took an hour to drain them to unconsciousness. Pretty hard on the condemned people. Well, I'd better go officiate."

When Jon and Ann Troy finished the Darnoval concerto they were silent for a few moments, exchanging simply a flow of wordless, unfathomable perceptions between their cells. Troy was unable to disguise a steady beat of gloom. "We'll have to go along with Poole's plan," he 'pathed, "though I confess I don't know what his idea is. Take your capsule now."

His mind registered the motor impulses of her medulla as she removed the pill from its concealment under her armpit and swallowed it. Troy then perceived her awareness of her cell door opening, of grim men and women about her. Motion down corridors. Then the room. A clanging of doors. A titanic effort to hold their fading contact. One last despairing communion, loving, tender.

Then nothing.

He was still sitting with his face buried in his hands, when the guards came to take him to his own trial that morning.

"This murder," announced the Peoples' advocate to the twelve evaluators, "this crime of taking the life of our beloved Provinarch Blogshak, this heinous deed—is the most horrible thing that has happened in Niork in my lifetime. The creature charged with this crime"—he pointed an accusing finger at the prisoner's box—"Jon Troy, has been psyched and has been adjudged integrated at a preliminary hearing. Even his attorney"—here bowing ironically to a beady-eyed little man at counsels' table—"waived the defense of nonintegration."

Poole continued to regard the Peoples' advocate with bitter weariness, as though he had gone through this a thousand times and knew every word that each of them was going to say. The prisoner seemed oblivious to the advocate, the twelve evaluators, the judge, and the crowded courtroom. Troy's mind was blanked out. The dozen or so educated telepaths in the room could detect only a deep beat of sadness.

"I shall prove," continued the inexorable advocate, "that this monster engaged our late Provinarch in conversation in a downtown bar, surreptitiously placed a lethal dose of *skon* in the Provinarch's glass, and that Troy and his wife —who, incidentally, paid the extreme penalty herself early this—"

"Objection!" cried Poole, springing to his feet. "The defendant, not his wife, is now on trial."

"Sustained," declared the judge. "The advocate may not imply to the evaluators that the possible guilt of the present defendant is in any way determined by the proven guilt of any past defendant. The evaluators must ignore that implication. Proceed, advocate."

"Thank you, your honor." He turned again to the evaluators' box and scanned them with a critical eye. "I shall prove that the prisoner and the late Mrs. Troy, after poisoning Provinarch Blogshak, carried his corpse into their sedan, and that they proceeded then to a deserted area on the outskirts of the city. Unknown to them, they were pursued by four of the mayor's bodyguards, who, alas, had been lured aside at the bar by Mrs. Troy. Psychometric determinations taken by the police laboratory will be offered to prove it was the prisoners' intention to dismember the corpse and burn it to hinder the work of the police in tracing the crime to him. He had got only as far as severing the head when the guards' ship swooped up and hovered overhead. He tried to run back to his own ship, where his wife was waiting, but the guards blanketed the area with a low-voltage stun."

The advocate paused. He was not getting the reaction in the evaluators he deserved, but he knew the fault was not his. He was puzzled; he would have to conclude quickly.

"Gentlemen," he continued gravely, "for this terrible thing, the Province demands the life of Jon Troy. The monster must enter the chamber tonight." He bowed to the judge and returned to counsels' table.

The judge acknowledged the retirement and turned to Poole. "Does the defense wish to make an opening statement?"

"The defense reiterates its plea of 'not guilty' and makes no other statement," grated the old man.

There was a buzz around the advocates' end of the table. An alert defense with a weak case always opened to the evaluators. Who was this Poole? What did he have? Had they missed a point? The prosecution was committed now. They'd have to start with their witnesses.

The advocate arose. "The prosecution offers as witness Mr. Fonstile."

"Mr. Fonstile!" called the clerk.

A burly, resentful-looking man blundered his way from the benches and walked up to the witness box and was sworn in.

Poole was on his feet. "May it please the court!" he croaked.

The judge eyed him in surprise. "Have you an objection, Mr. Poole?"

"No objection, your honor," rasped the little man, without expression. "I would only like to say that the testimony of this witness, the bartender in the Shawn Hotel, is probably offered by my opponent to prove facts which the defense readily admits, namely, that the witness observed Mrs. Troy entice the four bodyguards of the deceased to another part of the room, that the present defendant surreptitiously placed a powder in the wine of the deceased, that the deceased drank the wine and collapsed, and was carried out of the room by the defendant, followed by his wife." He bowed to the judge and sat down.

The judge was nonplussed. "Mr. Poole, do you understand that you are responsible for the defense of this prisoner, and that he is charged with a capital offense?"

"That is my understanding, your honor."

"Then if prosecution is agreeable, and wishes to elicit no further evidence from the witness, he will be excused."

The advocate looked puzzled, but called the next witness, Dr. Warkon, of the Provincial Police Laboratory. Again Poole was on his feet. This time the whole court eyed him expectantly. Even Troy stared at him in fascination.

"May it please the court," came the now-familiar monotone, "the witness called by the opposition probably expects to testify that the deceased's fingerprints were found on the wineglass in question, that traces of deceased's saliva were identified in the liquid content of the glass and that a certain quantity of *skon* was found in the wine remaining in the glass."

"And one other point, Mr. Poole," added the Peoples' advocate. "Dr. Warkon was going to testify that death from *skon* poisoning normally occurs within thirty seconds, owing to syncope. Does the defense concede that?"

"Yes."

"The witness is then excused," ordered the judge.

The prisoner straightened up. Troy studied his attorney curiously. The mysterious Poole with the tantalizing face, the man so highly recommended by the League, had let Ann go to her death with the merest shadow of a defense. And now he seemed even to state the prosecution's case rather than defend the prisoner.

Nowhere in the courtroom did Troy see a League member. But then, it would be folly for General Blade to attempt his rescue. That would attract unwelcome attention to the League.

He had been abandoned, and was on his own. Many League officers had been killed by Blogshak's men, but rarely in the devitalizing chamber. It was a point of honor to die weapon in hand. His first step would be to seize a blaster from one of the guards, use the judge as a shield, and try to escape through the judge's chambers. He would wait until he was put on the stand. It shouldn't be long, considering how Poole was cutting corners.

The advocate was conferring with his assistants. "What's Poole up to?" one of them asked. "If he is going on this far, why not get him to admit all the facts constituting a prima facie case: Malice, intent to kill, and all that?"

The advocate's eyes gleamed. "I think I know what he's up to now," he exulted. "I believe he's forgotten an elementary theorem of criminal law. He's going to admit everything, then demand we produce Blogshak's corpse. He must know it was stolen from the bodyguards when their ship landed at the port. No corpse, no murder, he'll say. But you don't need a corpse to prove murder. We'll hang him with his own rope!" He arose and addressed the judge.

"May it please the court, the prosecution would like to ask if the defense will admit certain other facts which I stand ready to prove."

The judge frowned. "The prisoner pleaded not guilty. Therefore the court will not permit any admission of the defense to the effect that the prisoner did kill the deceased, unless he wants to change his plea." He looked inquiringly at Poole.

"I understand, your honor," said Poole. "May I hear what facts the learned prosecutor wishes me to accede to?"

For a moment the prosecutor studied his enigmatic antagonist like a master swordsman.

"First, the prisoner administered a lethal dose of *skon* to the deceased with malice aforethought, and with intent to kill. Do you concede that?"

"Yes."

"And that the deceased collapsed within a few seconds

and was carried from the room by the defendant and his wife?"

"We agree to that."

"And that the prisoner carried the body to the city out-skirts and there decapitated it?"

"I have already admitted that."

The twelve evaluators, a selected group of trained experts in the estimation of probabilities, followed this unusual procedure silently.

"Then your honor, the prosecution rests." The advocate felt dizzy, out of his depth. He felt he had done all that was necessary to condemn the prisoner. Yet Poole seemed absolutely confident, almost bored.

"Do you have any witnesses, Mr. Poole," queried the judge.

"I will ask the loan of Dr. Warkon, if the Peoples' advocate will be so kind," replied the little man.

"I'm willing." The advocate was beginning to look harassed. Dr. Warkon was sworn in.

"Dr. Warkon, did not the psychometer show that the prisoner intended to kill Blogshak in the tavern and de-capitate him at the edge of the city?"

"Yes, sir."

"Was, in fact, the deceased dead when he was carried from the hotel?"

"He had enough *skon* in him to have killed forty people."

"Please answer the question."

"Well, I don't know. I presume he was dead. As an expert, looking at all the evidence, I should say he was dead. If he didn't die in the room, he was certainly dead a few seconds later."

"Did you feel his pulse at any time, or make any examination to determine the time of death?"

"Well, no."

Now, thought the advocate, comes the no corpse, no murder. If he tries that, I've got him.

But Poole was not to be pushed.

"Would you say the deceased was dead when the prisoner's ship reached the city limits?"

"Absolutely!"

"When you, as police investigator, examined the scene of the decapitation, what did you find?"

"The place where the corpse had lain was easily identified. Depressions in the sand marked the back, head, arms, and legs. The knife was lying where the prisoner dropped it. Marks of landing gear of the prisoner's ship were about forty feet away. Lots of blood, of course."

"Where was the blood?"

"About four feet away from the head, straight out."

Poole let the statement sink in, then:

"Dr. Warkon, as a doctor of medicine, do you realize the significance of what you have just said?"

The witness gazed at his inquisitor as though hypnotized. "Four feet . . . jugular spurt—" he muttered to no one. He stared in wonder, first at the withered, masklike face before him, then at the advocate, then at the judge. "Your honor, the deceased's heart was still beating when the prisoner first applied the knife. The poison didn't kill him!"

An excited buzz resounded through the courtroom.

Poole turned to the judge. "Your honor, I move for a summary judgment of acquittal."

The advocate sprang to his feet, wordless.

"Mr. Poole," remonstrated the judge, "your behavior this morning has been extraordinary, to say the least. On the bare fact that the prisoner killed with a knife instead of with poison, as the evidence at first indicated, you ask summary acquittal. The court will require an explanation."

"Your honor"—there was a ghost of a smile flitting about the prim, tired mouth—"to be guilty of a crime, a man must intend to commit a crime. There must be a *mens rea,* as the classic expression goes. The act and the intent must coincide. Here they did not. Jon Troy intended to kill the Provinarch in the bar of the Shawn Hotel. He gave him poison, but Blogshak didn't die of it. Certainly up to the time the knife was thrust into Blogshak's throat, Troy may have been guilty of assault and kidnaping, but not murder. If there was any murder, it must have been at the instant he decapitated the deceased. Yet what was his intent on the city outskirts? He wanted to mutilate a corpse. His intent was not to murder, but to mutilate. We have the act, but not the intent—no *mens rea.* Therefore the act was not murder, but simply mutilation of a corpse—a crime punishable by fine or imprisonment, but not death."

Troy's mind was whirling. This incredible, dusty little man had freed him.

"But Troy's a murderer!" shouted the advocate, his face white. "Sophisms can't restore a life!"

"The court does not recognize the advocate!" said the judge harshly. "Cut those remarks from the record," he directed the scanning clerk. "This court is guided by the principles of common law descended from ancient England. The learned counsel for the defense has stated those principles correctly. Homicide is not murder if there is no intent to kill. And mere intent to kill is not murder if the poison doesn't take effect. This is a strange, an unusual case, and it is revolting for me to do what I have to do. I acquit the prisoner."

"Your honor!" cried the advocate. Receiving recognition, he proceeded. "This . . . this felon should not escape completely. He should not be permitted to make a travesty of the law. His own counsel admits he has broken the statutes on kidnaping, assault, and mutilation. The evaluators can at least return a verdict of guilty on those counts."

"I am just as sorry as you are," replied the judge, "but I don't find those counts in the indictment. You should have included them."

"If you release him, your honor, I'll re-arrest him and frame a new indictment."

"This court will not act on it. It is contrary to the constitution of this province for a person to be prosecuted twice on the same charge or on a charge which should have been included in the original indictment. The Peoples' advocate is estopped from taking further action on this case. This is the final ruling of this court." He took a drink of water, wrapped his robes about him, and strode through the rear of the courtroom to his chambers.

Troy and Poole, the saved and the savior, eyed one another with the same speculative look of their first meeting.

Poole opened the door of the 'copter parked outside the Judiciary Building and motioned for Troy to enter. Troy froze in the act of climbing in.

A man inside the cab, with a face like a claw, was pointing a blaster at his chest.

The man was Blogshak!

Two men recognizable as the Provinarch's bodyguards suddenly materialized behind Troy.

"Don't give us any trouble, major," murmured Poole easily. "Better get in."

The moment Troy was pushed into the subterranean suite he sensed Ann was alive—drugged insensate still, but alive, and near. This knowledge suppressed momentarily Blogshak's incredible existence and Poole's betrayal. Concealing his elation, he turned to Poole.

"I should like to see my wife."

Poole motioned silently to one of the guards, who pulled back sliding doors. Beyond a glass panel, which was actually a transparent wall of a tile room, Ann lay on a high white metal bed. A nurse was on the far side of the bed, exchanging glances with Poole. At some unseen signal from him the nurse swabbed Ann's left arm and thrust a syringe into it.

A shadow crossed Troy's face. "What is the nurse doing?"

"In a moment Mrs. Troy will awaken. Whether she stays awake depends on you."

"On me? What do you mean?"

"Major, what you are about to learn can best be demonstrated rather than described. Sharg, the rabbit!"

The beetle-browed man opened a large enamel pan on the table. A white rabbit eased its way out, wrinkling its nose gingerly. Sharg lifted a cleaver from the table. There was a flash of metal, a spurt of blood, and the rabbit's head fell to the floor. Sharg picked it up by the ears and held it up expectantly. The eyes were glazed almost shut. The rabbit's body lay limp in the pan. At a word from Poole, Sharg carefully replaced the severed head, pressing it gently to the bloody neck stub. Within seconds the nose twitched, the eyes blinked, and the ears perked up. The animal shook itself vigorously, scratched once or twice at the bloody ring around its neck, then began nibbling at a head of lettuce in the pan.

Troy's mind was racing. The facts were falling in line. All at once everything made sense. With knowledge came utmost wariness. The next move was up to Poole, who was examining with keen eyes the effect of his demonstration on Troy.

"Major, I don't know how much you have surmised, but at least you cannot help realizing that life, even highly organized vertebrate life, is resistant to death in your presence."

Troy folded his arms but volunteered nothing. He was finally getting a glimpse of the vast and secret power supporting the Provinarch's tyranny, long suspected by the League but never verified.

"You could not be expected to discover this marvelous property in yourself except by the wildest chance," continued Poole. "As a matter of fact, our staff discovered it only when Blogshak and his hysterical guards reported to us, after your little escapade. But we have been on the lookout for your type for years. Several mutants with this characteristic have been predicted by our probability geneticists for this century, but you are the first known to us—really perhaps the only one in existence. One is all we need.

"As a second and final test of your power, we decided to try the effect of your aura on a person in the devitalizing chamber. For that reason we permitted Mrs. Troy to be condemned, when we could easily have prevented it. As you now know, your power sustained your wife's life against a strong drain of potential. At my instruction she drugged herself in her cell simply to satisfy the doctor who checked her pulse and reflexes afterwards. When the staff—my employers—examined her here, they were convinced that you had the mutation they were looking for, and we put the finishing touches on our plans to save you from the chamber."

Granting I have some strange biotic influence, thought Troy, still, something's wrong. He says his bunch became interested in me *after* my attempt on Blogshak. *But Poole was at the assassination meeting! What is his independent interest?*

Poole studied him curiously. "I doubt that you realize what tremendous efforts have been made to insure your presence here. For the past two weeks the staff has hired several thousand persons to undermine the critical faculties of the four possible judges and nine hundred evaluators who might have heard your case. Judge Gallon, for example, was not in an analytical mood this morning because we saw to it that he won the Province Chess Cham-

pionship with his Inner Gambit—a prize he has sought for
thirty years. But if he had fooled us and given your case
to the evaluators, we were fairly certain of a favorable
decision. You noticed how they were not concentrating
on the advocate's opening statement? They couldn't; they
were too full of the incredible good fortune they had
encountered the previous week. Sommers had been promoted to a full professorship at the Provincial University.
Gunnard's obviously faulty thesis on space strains had been
accepted by the *Steric Quarterly*—after we bought the
magazine. But why go on? Still, if the improbable had occurred, and you had been declared guilty by the evaluators,
we would simply have spirited you away from the courtroom. With a few unavoidable exceptions, every spectator
in the room was a trained staff agent, ready to use his
weapons—though in the presence of your aura, I doubt
they could have hurt anyone.

"Troy, the staff had to get you here, but we preferred
to do it quietly. Now, why are you here? I'll tell you. Your
aura, we think, will keep—" Poole hesitated. "Your aura
will keep . . . *it* . . . from dying during an approaching
crisis in its life stream."

"It? What is this 'it'? And what makes you so sure I'll
stay?"

"The staff has not authorized me to tell you more concerning the nature of the entity you are to protect. Suffice
to say that It is a living, sentient being. And I think you'll
stay, because the hypo just given Mrs. Troy was pure
skon."

Troy had already surmised as much. The move was perfect. If he stayed near her, Ann, though steeped in the
deadliest known poison, would not die. But why had they
been so sure he would not stay willingly, without Ann as
hostage? He 'pathed the thought to Poole, who curtly refused to answer.

"Now, major, I'm going to turn this wing of the City
Building over to you. For your information, your aura is
effective for a certain distance within the building, but just
how far I'm not going to tell you. However, you are not
permitted to leave your apartment at all. The staff has
demoted the Provinarch, and he's now the corporal of
your bodyguard. He would be exceedingly embarrassed if

you succeeded in leaving. Meals will be brought to you regularly. The cinematic and micro library is well stocked on your favorite subjects. Special concessions may even be made as to things you want in town. But you can never touch your wife again. That pane of glass will always be between you. A psychic receptor tuned to your personality integration is fixed within Mrs. Troy's room. If you break the glass panel, or in any other way attempt to enter the room, the receptor will automatically actuate a bomb mechanism imbedded beneath Mrs. Troy's cerebellum. She would be blown to little bits—each of them alive as long as you were around. It grieves us to be crude, but the situation requires some such safeguard."

"When will my wife recover consciousness?"

"Within an hour or so. But what's your hurry? You'll be here longer than you think."

The little lawyer seemed lost in thought for a moment. Then he signaled Blogshak and the guards, and the four left. Blogshak favored Troy with a venomous scowl as he closed and locked the door.

There was complete and utter silence. Even the rabbit sat quietly on the table, blinking its eyes at Troy.

Left alone, the man surveyed the room, his perceptions palping every square foot rapidly but carefully. He found nothing unusual. He debated whether to explore the wing further or to wait until Ann awakened. He decided on the latter course. The nurse had left. They were together, with just a sheet of glass between. He explored Ann's room mentally, found nothing.

Then he walked to the center table and picked up the rabbit. There was the merest suggestion of a cicatrix encircling the neck.

Wonderful, but frightful, thought Troy. Who, what, am I?

He put the rabbit back in the box, pulled a comfortable armchair against the wall opposite the glass panel, where he had a clear view of Ann's room, and began a methodical attempt to rationalize the events of the day.

He was jolted from his reverie by an urgent 'pathic call from Ann. After a flurry of tender perceptions each unlocked his mind to the other.

Poole had planted an incredible message in Ann's ESP lobe.

"Jon," she warned, "it's coded to the Dar— . . . I mean, it's coded to the notes and frequencies of our last concerto, in the death house. You'll have to synchronize. I'll start."

How did Poole know we were familiar with the concerto? thought Troy.

"Think on this carefully, Jon Troy, and guard it well," urged Poole's message. "I cannot risk my identity, but I am your friend. It—the Outcast—has shaped the destinies of vertebrate life on earth for millions of years, for two purposes. One is a peculiar kind of food. The other is . . . you. You have been brought here to preserve an evil life. But I urge you, develop your latent powers and destroy that life!

"Jon Troy, the evil this entity has wreaked upon the earth, entirely through his human agents thus far, is incalculable. It will grow even worse. You thought a subelectronic virus caused the hundred thousand deaths which launched you on your assassination junket. Not so! The monster in the earth directly beneath you simply drained them of vital force, in their homes, on the street, in the theater, anywhere and everywhere. Your puny League has been fighting the Outcast for a generation without the faintest conception of the real enemy. If you have any love for humanity, search Blogshak's mind today. The staff physicians will be in this wing of the building today, too. Probe them. This evening, if I am still alive, I shall explain more, in person, free from Blogshak's crew."

"You have been wondering about the nature of the being whose life you are protecting," said Poole in a low voice, as he looked about the room. "As you learned when you searched the minds of the physicians this morning, he is nothing human. I believe him to have been wounded in a battle with his own kind, and that he has lain in his present pit for millions of years, possibly since pre-Cambrian times. He probably has extraordinary powers even in his weakened state, but to my knowledge he has never used them."

"Why not?" asked Troy.

"He must be afraid of attracting the unwelcome attention of those who look for him. But he has maintained his life somehow. The waste products of his organic metabolism are fed into our sewers daily. He has a group of physicians and physicists—a curious mixture!—who keep in repair his three-dimensional neural cortex and run a huge administrative organization designed for his protection."

"Seems harmless enough, so far," said Troy.

"He's harmless except for one venomous habit. I thought I told you about it in the message I left with Ann. You must have verified it if you probed Blogshak thoroughly."

"But I couldn't understand such near-cannibalism in so advanced—"

"Certainly not cannibalism! Do we think of ourselves as cannibals when we eat steaks? Still, that's my main objection to him. His vitality must be maintained by the absorption of other vitalities, preferably as high up the evolutionary scale as possible. Our thousands of deaths monthly can be traced to his frantic hunger for vital fluid. The devitalizing department, which Blogshak used to run, is the largest section of the staff."

"But what about the people who attend him? Does he snap up any of them?"

"He hasn't yet. They all have a pact with him. Help him, and he helps them. Every one of his band dies old, rich, evil, and envied by their ignorant neighbors. He gives them everything they want. Sometimes they forget, like Blogshak, that society can stand just so much of their evil."

"Assuming all you say is true—how does it concern my own problem, getting Ann out of here and notifying the League?"

Poole shook his head dubiously. "You probably have some tentative plans to hypnotize Blogshak and make him turn off the screen. But no one on the staff understands the screen. None of them can turn it off, because none of them turned it on. The chief surgeon believes it to be a direct, focused emanation from a radiator made long ago and known now only to the Outcast. But don't think of escaping just yet. You can strike a tremendous, fatal blow without leaving this room!"

"This afternoon," Poole continued with growing nervousness, "there culminates a project initiated by the Outcast millennia ago. Just ninety years ago the staff began the blueprints of a surgical operation on the Outcast on a scale which would dwarf the erection of the Mechanical Integrator. Indeed, you won't be surprised to learn that the Integrator, capable of planar sterechronic analysis, was but a preliminary practice project, a rehearsal for the main event."

"Go on," said Troy absently. His sensitive hearing detected heavy breathing from beyond the door.

"To perform this colossal surgery, the staff must disconnect for a few seconds all of the essential neural trunks. When this is done, but for your aura, the Outcast would forever after remain a mass of senseless protoplasm and electronic equipment. With your aura, they can make the most dangerous repairs in perfect safety. When the last neural is down, you simply suppress your aura and the Outcast is dead. Then you could force your way out. From then on, the earth could go its merry way unhampered. Your League would eventually gain ascendancy and—"

"What about Ann?" asked Troy curtly. "Wouldn't she die along with the Outcast?"

"Didn't both of you take an oath to sacrifice each other before you'd injure the League or abandon an assignment?"

"That's a nice legal point," replied Troy, watching the corridor door behind Poole open a quarter of an inch. "I met Ann three years ago in a madhouse, where I had hidden away after a League assignment. She wasn't mad, but the stupid overseer didn't know it. She had the ability to project herself to other probability worlds. I married her to obtain a warning instrument of extreme delicacy and accuracy. Until that night in the death house, I'd have abided by League rules and abandoned her if necessary. But no longer. Any plan which includes her death is out. Suffering humanity can go climb a tree."

Poole's voice was dry and cracking. "I presumed you'd say that. You leave me no recourse. After I tell you who I am you will be willing to turn off your aura even at the cost of Ann's life. I am your . . . agh—"

A knife whistled through the open door and sank in Poole's neck. Blogshak and Sharg rushed in. Each man carried an ax.

"You dirty traitor!" screamed Blogshak. His ax crashed through the skull of the little old man even as Troy sprang forward. Sharg caught Troy under the chin with his ax handle. For some minutes afterward Troy was dimly aware of chopping, chopping, chopping.

Troy's aching jaw finally awoke him. He was lying on the sofa, where his keepers had evidently placed him. There was an undefinable raw odor about the room.

The carpet had been changed.

Troy's stomach muscles tensed. What had this done to Ann? He was unable to catch her ESP lobe. Probably out wandering through the past, or future.

While he tried to touch her mind, there was a knock on the door, and Blogshak entered with a man dressed in surgeon's white.

"Our operation apparently was a success, despite your little mishap," 'pathed the latter to Troy. "The next thirty years will tell us definitely whether we did this correctly. I'm afraid you'll have to stick around until then. I understand you're great chums with the Provinarch—ex-Provinarch, should I say? I'm sure he'll entertain you. I'm sorry about Poole. Poor fellow! Muffed his opportunities. Might have risen very high on the staff. But everything works out for the best, doesn't it?"

Troy glared at him wordlessly.

"Once we're out of here," 'pathed Troy in music code that afternoon, "we'll get General Blade to drop a plute fission on this building. It all revolves around the bomb under your cerebellum. If we can deactivate either the screen or the bomb, we're out. It's child's play to scatter Blogshak's bunch."

"If I had a razor," replied Ann, "I could cut the thing out. I can feel it under my neck muscles."

"Don't talk nonsense. What can you give me on Poole?"

"He definitely forced you to choose the red ball at the League meeting. Also, he knew he was going to be killed in your room. That made him nervous."

"Did he *know* he was going to be killed, or simply anticipate the possibility?"

"He knew. *He had seen it before!*"

Troy began pacing restlessly up and down before the glass panel, but never looking at Ann, who lay quietly in bed apparently reading a book. The nurse sat in a chair at the foot of Ann's bed, arms folded, implacably staring at her ward.

"Puzzling, very puzzling," mused Troy. "Any idea what he was going to tell me about my aura?"

"No."

"Anything on his identity?"

"I don't know—I had a feeling that I . . . we— No, it's all too vague. I noticed just one thing for certain."

"What was that?" asked Troy. He stopped pacing and appeared to be examining titles on the bookshelves.

"He was wearing your rosebud!"

"But that's crazy! I had it on all day. You must have been mistaken."

"You know I can't make errors on such matters."

"That's so." Troy resuming his pacing. "Yet, I refuse to accept the proposition that both of us were wearing my rosebud at the same instant. Well, never mind. While we're figuring a way to deactivate your bomb, we'd also better give a little thought to solving my aura.

"The solution is known—we have to assume that our unfortunate friend knew it. Great Galaxy! What our League biologists wouldn't give for a chance at this! We must change our whole concept of living matter. Have you ever heard of the immortal heart created by Alexis Carrel?" he asked abruptly.

"No."

"At some time during the Second Renaissance, early twentieth century, I believe, Dr. Carrel removed a bit of heart tissue from an embryo chick and put it in a nutrient solution. The tissue began to expand and contract rhythmically. Every two days the nutrient solution was renewed and excess growth cut away. Despite the catastrophe that had overwhelmed the chick—as a chick—the individual tissue lived on independently because the requirements of its cells were met. This section of heart tissue beat for nearly three centuries, until it was finally lost in the Second Atomic War."

"Are you suggesting that the king's men can put Humpty Dumpty together again if due care has been taken to nourish each part?"

"It's a possibility. Don't forget the skills developed by the Muscovites in grafting skin, ears, corneas, and so on."

"But that's a long process—it takes weeks."

"Then let's try another line. Consider this: The amoeba lives in a fluid medium. He bumps into his food, which is generally bacteria or bits of decaying protein, flows around it, digests it at leisure, excretes his waste matter, and moves on. Now go on up the evolutionary scale past the coelenterates and flatworms, until we reach the first truly three-dimensional animals—the coelomates. The flatworm had to be flat because he had no blood vessels. His food simply soaked into him. But cousin roundworm, one of the coelomates, grew plump and solid, because his blood vessels fed his specialized interior cells, which would otherwise have no access to food.

"Now consider a specialized cell—say a nice long muscle cell in the rabbit's neck. It can't run around in stagnant water looking for a meal. It has to have its breakfast brought to it, and its excrement carried out by special messenger, or it soon dies."

Troy picked a book from the shelf and leafed through it idly.

Ann wondered mutely whether her nurse had been weaned on a lemon.

"This messenger," continued Troy, "is the blood. It eventually reaches the muscle cell by means of a capillary —a minute blood vessel about the size of a red corpuscle. The blood in the capillary gives the cell everything it needs and absorbs the cell waste-matter. The muscle cell needs a continuously fresh supply of oxygen, sugar, amino-acids, fats, vitamins, sodium, calcium, and potassium salts, hormones, water, and maybe other things. It gets these from the hemoglobin and plasma, and it sheds carbon dioxide, ammonium compounds, and so on. Our cell can store up a little food within its own boundaries to tide it over for a number of hours. But oxygen it must have, every instant."

"You're just making the problem worse," interposed Ann. "If you prove that blood must circulate oxygen continuously to preserve life, you'll have yourself out on a limb. If you'll excuse the term, the rabbit's circulation was decisively cut off."

"That's the poser," agreed Troy. "The blood didn't circulate, but the cells didn't die. And think of this a moment: Blood is normally alkaline, with a pH of 7.4. When it absorbs carbon dioxide as a cell excretion, blood becomes acid, and this steps up respiration to void the excess carbon dioxide, via the lungs. But so far as I could see, the rabbit didn't even sigh after he got his head back. There was certainly no heavy breathing."

"I'll have to take your word for it; I was out cold."

"Yes, I know." Troy began pacing the room again. "It isn't feasible to suppose the rabbit's plasma was buffered to an unusual degree. That would mean an added concentration of sodium bicarbonate and an increased solids content. The cellular water would dialyze into the blood and kill the creature by simple dehydration."

"Maybe he had unusual reserves of hemoglobin," suggested Ann. "That would take care of your oxygen problem."

Troy rubbed his chin. "I doubt it. There are about five million red cells in a cubic millimeter of blood. If there are very many more, the cells would oxidize muscle tissue at a tremendous rate, and the blood would grow hot, literally cooking the brain. Our rabbit would die of a raging fever. Hemoglobin dissolves about fifty times as much oxygen as plasma, so it doesn't take much hemoglobin to start an internal conflagration."

"Yet the secret must lie in the hemoglobin. You just admitted that the cells could get along for long periods with only oxygen," persisted Ann.

"It's worth thinking about. We must learn more about the chemistry of the cell. You take it easy for a few days while I go through Poole's library."

"Could I do otherwise?" murmured Ann.

". . . thus the effect of confinement varies from person to person. The claustrophobe deteriorates rapidly, but the agoraphobe mellows, and may find excuses to avoid the escape attempt. The person of high mental and physical attainments can avoid atrophy by directing his every thought to the destruction of the confining force. In this case, the increment in mental prowess is 3.1 times the logarithm of the duration of confinement measured in years. The intelligent and determined prisoner can escape if he lives long enough."—J. and A. T., An Introduction to Prison Escape, 4th Edition, League Publishers, p. 14.

In 1811, Avogadro, in answer to the confusing problems of combining chemical weights, invented the molecule. In 1902, Einstein resolved an endless array of incompatible facts by suggesting a mass-energy relation. Three centuries later, in the tenth year of his imprisonment, Jon Troy was driven in near-despair to a similar stand. In one sure step of dazzling intuition, he hypothesized the viton.

"The secret goes back to our old talks on cell preservation," he explained with ill-concealed excitement to Ann. "The cell can live for hours without proteins and salts, because it has means of storing these nutrients from past meals. But oxygen it must have. The hemoglobin takes up molecular oxygen in the lung capillaries, ozonizes it, and, since hemin is easily reduced, the red cells give up oxygen to the muscle cells that need it, in return for carbon dioxide. After it takes up the carbon dioxide, hemin turns purple and enters the vein system on the way back to the lungs, and we can forget it.

"Now, what is hemin? We can break it down into etiopyrophorin, which, like chlorophyll, contains four pyrrole groups. The secret of chlorophyll has been known for years. Under a photon catalyst of extremely short wave length, such as ultraviolet light, chlorophyll seizes molecule after molecule of carbon dioxide and synthesizes starches and sugars, giving off oxygen. Hemin, with its etiopyrophorin, works quite similarly, except that it doesn't need ultraviolet light. Now—"

"But animal cell metabolism works the other way," objected Ann. "Our cells take up oxygen and excrete carbon dioxide."

"It depends which cells you are talking about," reminded Troy. "The red corpuscle takes up carbon dioxide just as its plant cousin, chlorophyll, does, and they both excrete oxygen. Oxygen is just as much an excrement of the red cell as carbon dioxide is of the muscle cell."

"That's true," admitted Ann.

"And that's where the viton comes in," continued Troy. "It preserves the status quo of cell chemistry. Suppose that an oxygen atom has just been taken up by an amino acid molecule within the cell protoplasm. The amino acid immediately becomes unstable, and starts to spit out carbon dioxide. In the red corpuscle, a mass of hemin stands by to seize the carbon dioxide and offer more oxygen. But the exchange never takes place. Just as the amino acid and the hemin reach toward one another, their electronic attractions are suddenly neutralized by a bolt of pure energy

from me: The viton! Again and again the cells try to exchange, with the same result. They can't die from lack of
oxygen, because their individual molecules never attain an
oxygen deficit. The viton gives a very close approach to
immortality!"

"But *we* seem to be getting older. Perhaps your vitons
don't reach every cell?"

"Probably not," admitted Troy. "They must stream
radially from some central point within me, and of course
they would decrease in concentration according to the
inverse square law of light. Even so, they would keep
enough cells alive to preserve life as a whole. In the case
of the rabbit, after the cut cell surfaces were rejoined,
there were still enough of them alive to start the business
of living again. One might suppose, too, that the viton
accelerates the reestablishment of cell boundaries in the
damaged areas. That would be particularly important with
the nerve cells."

"All right," said Ann. "You've got the viton. What are
you going to do with it?"

"That's another puzzler. First, what part of my body
does it come from? There must be some sort of a globular
discharge area fed by a relatively small but impenetrable
duct. If we suppose a muscle controlling the duct—"

"What you need is an old Geiger-Müller," suggested
Ann. "Locate your discharge globe first, then the blind
spot on it caused by the duct entry. The muscle has to be
at that point."

"I wonder—" mused Troy. "We have a burnt-out
cinema projection bulb around here somewhere. The
vacuum ought to be just about soft enough by now to
ionize readily. The severed filament can be the two elec-
tron poles." He laughed mirthlessly: "I don't know why I
should be in a hurry. I won't be able to turn off the viton
stream even if I should discover the duct-muscle."

Weeks later, Troy found his viton sphere, just below
the cerebral frontal lobe. The duct led somewhere into the
pineal region. Very gingerly he investigated the duct environment. A small but dense muscle mass surrounded the
entry of the duct to the bulk of radiation.

On the morning of the first day of the thirty-first year
of their imprisonment, a few minutes before the nurse
was due with the *skon* hypo, Ann 'pathed to Troy that she

thought the screen was down. A joint search of the glass panel affirmed this.

Ann was stunned, like a caged canary that suddenly notices the door is open—she fears to stay, yet is afraid to fly away.

"Get your clothes on, dear," urged Troy. "Quickly now! If we don't contact the League in the next ten minutes, we never shall."

She dressed like an automaton.

Troy picked the lock on the corridor door noiselessly, with a key he had long ago made for this day, and opened the portal a quarter of an inch. The corridor seemed empty for its whole half-mile length. There was a preternatural pall of silence hanging over everything. Ordinarily, someone was always stirring about the corridor at this hour. He peered closely at the guard's cubicle down the hall. His eyes were not what they once were, and old Blogshak had never permitted him to be fitted with contacts.

He sucked in his breath sharply. The door of the cubicle was open, and two bodies were visible on the floor. One of the bodies had been a guard. The green of his uniform was plainly visible. The other corpse had white hair and a face like a wrinkled, arthritic claw. It was Blogshak.

Two mental processes occurred within Troy. To the cold, objective Troy, the thought occurred that the viton flow was ineffective beyond one hundred yards. Troy the human being wondered why the Outcast had not immediately remedied this weak point in the guard system. Heart pounding, he stepped back within the suite. He seized a chair, warned Ann out of the way, and hurled it through the glass panel. Ann stepped gingerly through the jagged gap. He held her for a moment in his arms. Her hair was a pure white, her face furrowed. Her body seemed weak and infirm. But it was Ann. Her eyes were shut and she seemed to be floating through time and space.

"No time for a trance now!" He shook her harshly, pulling her out of the room and down the corridor. He looked for a stair. There was none.

"We'll have to chance an autovator!" he panted, thinking he should have taken some sort of bludgeon with him. If several of the staff should come down with the 'vator, he doubted his ability to hypnotize them all.

He was greatly relieved when he saw an empty 'vator

already on the subterranean floor. He leaped in, pulling
Ann behind him, and pushed the button to close the door.
The door closed quietly, and he pushed the button for the
first floor.

"We'll try the street floor first," he said, breathing heavily. "Don't look around when we leave the 'vator. Just
chatter quietly and act as though we owned the place."

The street floor was empty.

An icy thought began to grow in Troy's mind. He
stepped into a neighboring 'vator, carrying Ann with him
almost bodily, closed the door, and pressed the last button. Ann was mentally out, but was trying to tell him
something. Her thoughts were vague, unfocused.

If they were pursued, wouldn't the pursuer assume they
had left the building? He hoped so.

A malicious laughter seemed to follow them up the
shaft.

He gulped air frantically to ease the roar in his ears.
Ann had sunk into a semi-stupor. He eased her to the floor.
The 'vator continued to climb. It was now in the two
hundreds. Minutes later it stopped gently at the top floor,
the door opened, and Troy managed to pull Ann out into
a little plaza.

They were nearly a mile above the city.

The penthouse roof of the City Building was really a
miniature country club, with a small golf course, swimming pool, and club house for informal administrative
functions. A cold wind now blew across the closely cut
green. The swimming pool was empty. Troy shivered as
he dragged Ann near the dangerously low guard rail and
looked over the city in the early morning sunlight.

As far as he could see, nothing was moving. There
were no cars gliding at any of the authorized traffic levels,
no 'copters or transocean ships in the skies.

For the first time, Troy's mind sagged, and he felt like
the old man he was.

As he stared, gradually understanding, yet half-unbeliev-
ing, the rosebud in his lapel began to speak.

*Mai-kel condensed the thin waste of cosmic gas into
several suns and peered again down into the sterechron.
There could be no mistake—there was a standing wave
of recurrent time emanating from the tiny planet. The
Great One made himself small and approached the little*

world with cautious curiosity. Sathanas had been badly wounded, but it was hard to believe his integration had deteriorated to the point of permitting oscillation in time. And no intelligent life capable of time travel was scheduled for this galaxy. Who, then? Mai-kel synchronized himself with the oscillation so that the events constituting it seemed to move at their normal pace. His excitement multiplied as he followed the cycle.

It would be safest, of course, to volatilize the whole planet. But then, that courageous mite, that microscopic human being who had created the time trap, would be lost. Extirpation was indicated—a clean, fast incision done at just the right point of the cycle.

Mai-kel called his brothers.

Troy suppressed an impulse of revulsion. Instead of tearing the flower from his coat, he pulled it out gently and held it at arm's length, where he could watch the petals join and part again, in perfect mimicry of the human mouth.

"Yes, little man. I am what you call the Outcast. There are no other little men to bring my message to you, so I take this means of—"

"You mean you devitalized every man, woman, and child in the province . . . in the whole world?" croaked Troy.

"Yes. Within the past few months, my appetite has been astonishingly good, and I have succeeded in storing within my neurals enough vital fluid to carry me into the next sterechron. There I can do the same, and continue my journey. There's an excellent little planet waiting for me, just bursting with genial bipedal life. I can almost feel their vital fluid within me, now. And I'm taking you along, of course, in case I meet some . . . old friends. We'll leave now."

"Jon! Jon!" cried Ann, from behind him. She was standing, but weaving dizzily. Troy was at her side in an instant. "Even *he* doesn't know who Poole is!"

"Too late for any negative information now, dear," said Troy dully.

"But it isn't negative. If *he* doesn't know, then he won't stop you from going back." Her voice broke off in a wild cackle.

Troy looked at her in sad wonder.

"Jon," she went on feverishly, "your vitons help preserve the status quo of cells by preventing chemical
change, but that is only part of the reason they preserve
life. Each viton must also contain a quantum of time flow,
which dissolves the vital fluid of the cell and reprecipitates
it into the next instant. This is the only hypothesis which
explains the preservation of the giant neurals of the Outcast. There was no chemical change going on in them
which required stabilization, but something had to keep
the vital fluid alive. Now, if you close the duct suddenly,
the impact of unreleased vitons will send you back through
time in your present body, as an old man. Don't you understand about Poole, now, Jon? You will go back thirty
years through time, establish yourself in the confidence of
both the League and the staff, attend the assassination
conference, make young Troy choose the red ball again,
defend him at the trial, and then you will die in that horrible room again. You have no choice about doing this,
because it has already happened! Good-bye, darling! You
are Poole!"

There was an abrupt swish. Ann had leaped over the
guard rail into space.

A gurgle of horror died in Troy's throat. Still clutching
the now silent rose in his hand, he jammed the viton muscle with all his will power. There was a sickening shock,
then a flutter of passing days and nights. As he fell through
time, cold fingers seemed to snatch frantically at him. But
he knew he was safe.

As he spiraled inward, Troy-Poole blinked his eyes in-
voluntarily, as though reluctant to abandon a languorous
escape from reality. He was like a dreamer awakened by
having his bedclothes blown off in an icy gale.

He slowly realized that this was not the first time he
had suddenly been bludgeoned into reality. Every seventy
years the cycle began for him once more. He knew now
that seventy years ago he had completed another identical
circle in time. And the lifetime before that, and the one
prior. There was no beginning and no ending. The only
reality was this brief lucid interval between cycles, waiting
for the loose ends of time to cement. He had the choice at
this instant to vary the life stream, to fall far beyond
Troy's era, if he liked, and thus to end this existence as

the despairing toy of time. What had he accomplished? Nothing, except retain, at the cost of almost unbearable monotony and pain, a weapon pointed at the heart of the Outcast, a weapon he could never persuade the young Troy to use, on account of Ann. Troy old had no influence over Troy young. Poole could never persuade Troy.

Peering down through the hoary wastes of time he perceived how he had hoped to set up a cycle in the time stream, a standing wave noticeable to the entities who searched for the Outcast. Surely with their incredible intellects and perceptions this discrepancy in the ordered universe would not go unnoticed. He had hoped that this trap in the time flow would hold the Outcast until relief came. But as his memory returned he realized that he had gradually given up hope. Somehow he had gone on from a sense of duty to the race from which he had sprung. From the depths of his aura-fed nervous system he had always found the will to try again. But now his nervous exhaustion, increasing from cycle to cycle by infinitesimal amounts, seemed overpowering.

A curious thought occurred to him. There must have been, at one time, a Troy without a Poole to guide—or entangle—him. There must have been a beginning—some prototype Troy who selected the red ball by pure accident, and who was informed by a prototype staff of his tremendous power. After that, it was easy to assume that the first Troy "went back" as the prototype Poole to scheme against the life of the Outcast.

But searching down time, Troy-Poole now found only the old combination of Troy and Poole he knew so well. Hundreds, thousands, millions of them, each preceding the other. As far back as he could sense, there was always a Poole hovering over a Troy. Now he would become the next Poole, enmesh the next Troy in the web of time, and go his own way to bloody death. He could not even plan a comfortable suicide. No, to maintain perfect oscillation of the time trap, all Pooles must always die in the same manner as the first Poole. There must be no invariance. He suppressed a twinge of impatience at the lack of foresight in the prototype Poole.

"Just this once more," he promised himself wearily, "then I'm through. Next time I'll keep on falling."

* * *

General Blade sometimes felt that leading a resistance movement was far exceeding his debt to decent society and that one day soon he would allow his peaceful nature to override his indignant pursuit of justice. Killing a man, even a very bad man, without a trial, went against his grain. He sighed and rapped on the table.

"As a result of Blogshak's misappropriation of funds to fight the epidemic," he announced, "the death toll this morning reached over one hundred thousand. Does the Assassination Subcommittee have a recommendation?"

A thin-lipped man rose from the gathering. "The Provinarch ignored our warning," he said rapidly. "This subcommittee, as you all know, some days ago set an arbitrary limit of one hundred thousand deaths. Therefore this subcommittee now recommends that its plan for killing the Provinarch be adopted at once. Tonight is very favorable for our—"

A man entered the room quietly and handed General Blade an envelope. The latter read it quickly, then stood up. "I beg your pardon, but I must break in," he announced. "Information I have just received may change our plans completely. This report from our intelligence service is so incredible that I won't read it to you. Let's verify it over the video."

He switched on the instrument. The beam of a local newscasting agency was focused tridimensionally before the group. It showed a huge pit or excavation which appeared to move as the scanning newscaster moved. The news comments were heard in snatches. "No explosion . . . no sign of any force . . . just complete disappearance. An hour ago the City Building was the largest structure in . . . now nothing but a gaping hole a mile deep . . . the Provinarch and his entire council were believed in conference . . . no trace—"

General Blade turned an uncomprehending face to the committee. "Gentlemen, I move that we adjourn this session pending an investigation."

Jon Troy and Ann left through the secret alleyway. As he buttoned his topcoat against the chill night air, he sensed that they were being followed. "Oh, hello?"

"I beg your pardon, Major Troy, and yours, madam. My name is Poole, Legal Subcommittee. You don't know me—yet, but I feel that I know you both very well. Your textbook on prison escape has inspired and sustained me many times in the past. I was just admiring your boutonniere, major. It seems so lifelike for an artificial rosebud. I wonder if you could tell me where I might buy one?"

Troy laughed metallically. "It's not artificial. I've worn it for weeks, but it's a real flower, from my own garden. It just won't die."

"Extraordinary," murmured Poole, fingering the red blossom in his own lapel. "Could we run in here for a cocktail? Bartender Fonstile will fix us something special, and we can discuss a certain matter you really ought to know about."

The doorman of the Shawn Hotel bowed to the three as they went inside.

DEFENSE MECHANISM

by Katherine MacLean

I wrote fiction because the effect of stories on my own mind had convinced me that fiction carried growth and knowledge with the impact and conviction of direct experience.

Admiring and almost worshipping science fiction writers and Campbell's Astounding *for the sweep and magnificence of ideas and adventures, I had wanted to write for the magazine, but was afraid to submit a story.*

But then my college trapped me into a year without employment by holding up my graduation in Economics while they demanded two more terms of volleyball. With the time forced on me, at last I sat down and considered writing.

I wanted to write the best. Stories of human potential and human power and mutation had always given me more of a thrill of vicarious power and achievement and the glory of an evolutionary future than had stories of great and powerful machines at the command of underdeveloped, button-pushing shut-ins. Making a plot of personal development of superhuman powers, I wanted to put it as close to the present and as near to immediate fact as I could, so I outlined a story of a young man developing telepathy as a personal power. Then I spent weeks in the library reading ESP cases, trying to work out the methods of developing the skill.

The dice throwing and card guessing methods did not seem to be the right road, for those methods were boring, and the best results came not from boredom but from intense emotional involvement. The association of ESP with emotion was puzzling and seemed to indicate it was a primitive skill rather than a newly-developing, newly-evolving part of the higher intellect.

But if mind reading was a primitive skill, why did not all animals have it, and why did we not have it?

Abandoning Rhine and Wateley Carrington I picked up the more flashy case reports of spontaneous ESP events. Most seemed to be miraculous rescues, and the apparently usual event of relatives seeing a person appear as if alive to give a last smile when he has died suddenly in a foreign country.

Cases of that sort were often too well attested to be doubted, but they were puzzling because the skill of projecting one's image to a distant relative at the moment of one's death is not a skill one develops by a lifetime of practice. The skill of telepathically calling for help from one's friends when trapped under a fallen log in the forest seemed to appear without practice, yet be fully skilled, as if it had been practiced and perfected.

A skill does not appear fully developed without practice. A person born blind does not instantly see when given lenses by an operation. He must pass through a long period when he cannot tell his house from a fire engine. Yet we have the documented ESP experiences of a mother who sees her son crashing in a plane and lying in the snow moaning, when the authorities assured her he was safe at a training camp in Georgia. She saw it in perfect focus with accurate details, and she was right. He had "thumbed" a ride on an army supply plane, which had crashed in mountains and snow.

How could this mother have picked up this vision of her son solely by the intensity of maternal concern, without previous practice?

I chewed over the problem for months, while starting and working on longer and more complex stories, then tried to explain to a friend why I could not understand telepathy enough to write a story about it.

I said, "It's like the cripples in a hospital who suddenly run down the stairs when the hospital is on fire. It's too sudden."

"But they aren't really crippled. It's all psychological," she said.

A great light began to dawn. "Yes," I agreed. "Like hysterical blindness. In World War I the soldiers had to see their buddies blown up, and corpses lying there, and they went permanently blind even for twenty years, maybe because they did not even want to confront memory images. But I read one man was suddenly able to see when he heard his grandchild crying, drowning in the pond. He rescued her. Maybe we can all see into each other's minds and don't want to confront it. Except when we have to. Except in emergencies."

"Why would we be afraid of reading minds?" she demanded. "I'd like to."

"Maybe everybody has bad memories, maybe we don't want to confront all that. Maybe people in bad trouble broadcast loudest. Pain, dentists, worry . . ." I got up. "Wow! I've got it!"

Later I wondered, "But when do we practice for our skill, and why don't we remember practicing?" And I thought, "We don't remember being babies. We could all have had mind reading then."

The article was coming along smoothly, words flowing from the typewriter in pleasant simple sequence, swinging to their predetermined conclusion like a good tune. Ted typed contentedly, adding pages to the stack at his elbow.

A thought, a subtle modification of the logic of the article began to glow in his mind, but he brushed it aside impatiently. This was to be a short article, and there was no room for subtlety. His articles sold, not for depth, but for an oddly individual quirk that he could give to commonplaces.

While he typed a little faster, faintly in the echoes of his thought the theme began to elaborate itself richly with correlations, modifying qualifications, and humorous parenthetical remarks. An eddy of especially interesting conclusions tried to insert itself into the main stream of his thoughts. Furiously he typed along the dissolving thread of his argument.

"Shut up," he snarled. "Can't I have any privacy around here?"

The answer was not a remark, it was merely a concept; two electro-chemical calculators pictured with the larger in use as a control mech, taking a dangerously high inflow, and controlling it with high resistance and blocs, while the smaller one lay empty and unblocked, its unresistant circuits ramifying any impulses received along the easy channels of pure calculation. Ted recognized the diagram from his amateur concepts of radio and psychology.

"All right. So I'm doing it myself. So you can't help it!" He grinned grudgingly. "Answering back at your age!"

Under the impact of a directed thought the small circuits of the idea came in strongly, scorching their reception and rapport diagram into his mind in flashing repetitions, bright as small lightning strokes. Then it spread and the small other brain flashed into brightness, reporting and repeating from every center. Ted even received a brief kinesthetic sensation of lying down, before it was all cut off in a hard bark of thought that came back in exact echo of his own irritation.

"Tune down!" it ordered furiously. "You're blasting in too loud and jamming everything up! What do you want, an idiot child?"

Ted blanketed down desperately, cutting off all thoughts, relaxing every muscle; but the angry thoughts continued coming in strongly a moment before fading.

"Even when I take a nap," they said, "he starts thinking at me! Can't I get any peace and privacy around here?"

Ted grinned. The kid's last remark sounded like something a little better than an attitude echo. It would be hard to tell when the kid's mind grew past a mere selective echoing of outside thoughts and became true personality, but that last remark was a convincing counterfeit of a sincere kick in the shin. Conditioned reactions can be efficient.

All the luminescent streaks of thought faded and merged with the calm meaningless ebb and flow of waves in the small sleeping mind. Ted moved quietly into the next room and looked down into the blue-and-white crib. The kid lay sleeping, his thumb in his mouth and his chubby face innocent of thought. Junior—Jake.

It was an odd stroke of luck that Jake was born with this particular talent. Because of it they would have to spend the winter in Connecticut, away from the mental blare of crowded places. Because of it Ted was doing free lance in the kitchen, instead of minor editing behind a New York desk. The winter countryside was wide and windswept, as it had been in Ted's own childhood, and the warm contacts with the stolid personalities of animals through Jake's mind were already a pleasure. Old acquaint-ances—Ted stopped himself skeptically. He was no tele-path. He decided that it reminded him of Ernest Thomp-son Seton's animal biographies, and went back to typing, dismissing the question.

It was pleasant to eavesdrop on things through Jake, as long as the subject was not close enough to the article to interfere with it.

Five small boys let out of kindergarten came trooping by on the road, chattering and throwing pebbles. Their thoughts came in jumbled together in distracting cross cur-rents, but Ted stopped typing for a moment, smiling, wait-ing for Jake to show his latest trick. Babies are hypersensi-tive to conditioning. The burnt hand learns to yank back from fire, the unresisting mind learns automatically to evade too many clashing echoes of other minds.

Abruptly the discordant jumble of small boy thoughts and sensations delicately untangled into five compart-mented strands of thoughts, then one strand of little boy thoughts shoved the others out, monopolizing and flowing easily through the blank baby mind, as a dream flows by without awareness, leaving no imprint of memory, fading as the children passed over the hill. Ted resumed typing, smiling. Jake had done the trick a shade faster than he had yesterday. He was learning reflexes easily enough to dem-onstrate normal intelligence. At least he was to be more than a gifted moron.

A half hour later, Jake had grown tired of sleeping and was standing up in his crib, shouting and shaking the bars. Martha hurried in with a double armload of groceries.

"Does he want something?"

"Nope. Just exercising his lungs." Ted stubbed out his cigarette and tapped the finished stack of manuscript con-tentedly. "Got something here for you to proofread."

"Dinner first," she said cheerfully, unpacking food from the bags. "Better move the typewriter and give us some elbow room."

Sunlight came in the windows and shone on the yellow table top, and glinted on her dark hair as she opened packages.

"What's the local gossip?" he asked, clearing off the table. "Anything new?"

"Meat's going up again," she said, unwrapping peas and fillets of mackerel. "Mrs. Watkin's boy, Tom, is back from the clinic. He can see fine now, she says."

He put water on to boil and began greasing a skillet while she rolled the fillets in cracker crumbs. "If I'd had to run a flame thrower during the war, I'd have worked up a nice case of hysteric blindness myself," he said. "I call that a legitimate defense mechanism. Sometimes it's better to be blind."

"But not all the time," Martha protested, putting baby food in the double boiler. In five minutes lunch was cooking.

"Whaaaa—" wailed Jake.

Martha went into the baby's room, and brought him out, cuddling him and crooning. "What do you want, Lovekins? Baby just wants to be cuddled, doesn't baby."

"Yes," said Ted.

She looked up, startled, and her expression changed, became withdrawn and troubled, her dark eyes clouded in difficult thought.

Concerned, he asked: "What is it, Honey?"

"Ted, you shouldn't—" She struggled with words. "I know, it is handy to know what he wants, whenever he cries. It's handy having you tell me, but I don't— It isn't right somehow. It isn't *right*."

Jake waved an arm and squeaked randomly. He looked unhappy. Ted took him and laughed, making an effort to sound confident and persuasive. It would be impossible to raise the kid in a healthy way if Martha began to feel he was a freak. "Why isn't it right? It's normal enough. Look at E. S. P. Everybody has that according to Rhine."

"E. S. P. is different," she protested feebly, but Jake chortled and Ted knew he had her. He grinned, bouncing Jake up and down in his arms.

"Sure it's different," he said cheerfully. "E. S. P. is queer. E. S. P. comes in those weird accidental little flashes that contradict time and space. With clairvoyance you can see through walls, and read pages from a closed book in France. E. S. P., when it comes, is so ghastly precise it seems like tips from old Omniscience himself. It's enough to drive a logical man insane, trying to explain it. It's illogical, incredible, and random. But what Jake has is limited telepathy. It is starting out fuzzy and muddled and developing towards accuracy by plenty of trial and error—like sight, or any other normal sense. You don't mind communicating by English, so why mind communicating by telepathy?"

She smiled wanly. "But he doesn't weigh much, Ted. He's not growing as fast as it says he should in the baby book."

"That's all right. I didn't really start growing myself until I was about two. My parents thought I was sickly."

"And look at you now." She smiled genuinely. "All right, you win. But when does he start talking English? I'd like to understand him, too. After all, I'm his mother."

"Maybe this year, maybe next year," Ted said teasingly. "I didn't start talking until I was three."

"You mean that you don't want him to learn," she told him indignantly, and then smiled coaxingly at Jake. "You'll learn English soon for Mommy, won't you, Lovekins?"

Ted laughed annoyingly. "Try coaxing him next month or the month after. Right now he's not listening to all these thoughts. He's just collecting associations and reflexes. His cortex might organize impressions on a logic pattern he picked up from me, but it doesn't know what it is doing any more than this fist knows that it is in his mouth. That right, bud?" There was no demanding thought behind the question, but instead, very delicately, Ted introspected to the small world of impression and sensation that flickered in what seemed a dreaming corner of his own mind. Right then it was a fragmentary world of green and brown that murmured with the wind.

"He's out eating grass with the rabbit," Ted told her.

Not answering, Martha started putting out plates. "I like animal stories for children," she said determinedly. "Rabbits are nicer than people."

Putting Jake in his pen, Ted began to help. He kissed the back of her neck in passing. "Some people are nicer than rabbits."

Wind rustled tall grass and tangled vines where the rabbit snuffled and nibbled among the sun-dried herbs, moving on habit, ignoring the abstract meaningless contact of minds, with no thought but deep comfort.

Then for a while Jake's stomach became aware that lunch was coming, and the vivid business of crying and being fed drowned the gentler distant neural flow of the rabbit.

Ted ate with enjoyment, toying with an idea fantastic enough to keep him grinning, as Martha anxiously spooned food into Jake's mouth. She caught him grinning and indignantly began justifying herself. "But he only gained four pounds, Ted. I have to make sure he eats something."

"Only!" he grinned. "At that rate he'd be thirty feet high by the time he reaches college."

"So would any baby." But she smiled at the idea, and gave Jake his next spoonful still smiling. Ted did not tell his real thought, that if Jake's abilities kept growing in a straight-line growth curve, by the time he was old enough to vote he would be God; but he laughed again, and was rewarded by an answering smile from both of them.

The idea was impossible, of course. Ted knew enough biology to know that there could be no sudden smooth jumps in evolution. Smooth changes had to be worked out gradually through generations of trial and selection. Sudden changes were not smooth, they crippled and destroyed. Mutants were usually monstrosities.

Jake was no sickly freak, so it was certain that he would not turn out very different from his parents. He could be only a little better. But the contrary idea had tickled Ted and he laughed again. "Boom food," he told Martha. "Remember those straight-line growth curves in the story?"

Martha remembered, smiling, "Redfern's dream—sweet little man, dreaming about a growth curve that went straight up." She chuckled, and fed Jake more spoonfuls of strained spinach, saying, "Open wide. Eat your boom food, darling. Don't you want to grow up like King Kong?"

Ted watched vaguely, toying now with a feeling that these months of his life had happened before, somewhere. He had felt it before, but now it came back with a sense of expectancy, as if something were going to happen.

It was while drying the dishes that Ted began to feel sick. Somewhere in the far distance at the back of his mind a tiny phantom of terror cried and danced and gibbered. He glimpsed it close in a flash that entered and was cut off abruptly in a vanishing fragment of delirium. It had something to do with a tangle of brambles in a field, and it was urgent.

Jake grimaced, his face wrinkled as if ready either to smile or cry. Carefully Ted hung up the dish towel and went out the back door, picking up a billet of wood as he passed the wood-pile. He could hear Jake whimpering, beginning to wail.

"Where to?" Martha asked, coming out the back door.

"Dunno," Ted answered. "Gotta go rescue Jake's rabbit. It's in trouble."

Feeling numb, he went across the fields through an outgrowth of small trees, climbed a fence into a field of deep grass and thorny tangles of raspberry vines, and started across.

A few hundred feet into the field there was a hunter sitting on an outcrop of rock, smoking, with a successful bag of two rabbits dangling near him. He turned an inquiring face to Ted.

"It can't understand being upside down with its legs tied." Moving with shaky urgency he took his penknife and cut the small animal's pulsing throat, then threw the wet knife out of his hand into the grass. The rabbit kicked once more, staring still at the tangled vines of refuge. Then its nearsighted baby eyes lost their glazed bright stare and became meaningless.

"Sorry," the hunter said. He was a quiet-looking man with a sagging, middle-aged face.

"That's all right," Ted replied, "but be a little more careful next time, will you? You're out of season anyhow." He looked up from the grass to smile stiffly at the hunter. It was difficult. There was a crowded feeling in his head, like a coming headache, or a stuffy cold. It was difficult to breathe, difficult to think.

It occurred to Ted then to wonder why Jake had never put him in touch with the mind of an adult. After a frozen stoppage of thought he laboriously started the wheels again and realized that something had put him in touch with the mind of the hunter, and that was what was wrong. His stomach began to rise. In another minute he would retch.

Ted stepped forward and swung the billet of wood in a clumsy sidewise sweep. The hunter's rifle went off and missed as the middle-aged man tumbled face first into the grass.

Wind rustled the long grass and stirred the leafless branches of trees. Ted could hear and think again, standing still and breathing in deep, shuddering breaths of air to clean his lungs. Briefly he planned what to do. He would call the sheriff and say that a hunter hunting out of season had shot at him and he had been forced to knock the man out. The sheriff would take the man away, out of thought range.

Before he started back to telephone he looked again at the peaceful, simple scene of field and trees and sky. It was safe to let himself think now. He took a deep breath and let himself think. The memory of horror came into clarity.

The hunter had been psychotic.

Thinking back, Ted recognized parts of it, like faces glimpsed in writhing smoke. The evil symbols of psychiatry, the bloody poetry of the Golden Bough, that had been the law of mankind in the five hundred thousand lost years before history. Torture and sacrifice, lust and death, a mechanism in perfect balance, a short circuit of conditioning through a glowing channel of symbols, an irreversible and perfect integration of traumas. It is easy to go mad, but it is not easy to go sane.

"Shut up!" Ted had been screaming inside his mind as he struck. "Shut up."

It had stopped. It had shut up. The symbols were fading without having found root in his mind. The sheriff would take the man away out of thought reach, and there would be no danger. It had stopped.

The burned hand avoids the fire. Something else had stopped. Ted's mind was queerly silent, queerly calm and empty, as he walked home across the winter fields, wondering how it had happened at all, kicking himself with humor for a suggestible fool, not yet missing—Jake.

And Jake lay awake in his pen, waving his rattle in random motions, and crowing "glaglagla gla—" in a motor sensory cycle, closed and locked against outside thoughts.

He would be a normal baby, as Ted had been, and as Ted's father before him.

And as all mankind was "normal."

ANGEL'S EGG

by Edgar Pangborn

I'm somewhat baffled by the request to say something about "how this story came to be written." It's the sort of question Edgar would never answer, except to say: Well, it happened. And how can anyone presume to answer such a query for someone who is no longer here to speak for himself?

Edgar had published a number of mystery stories in the "pulp" magazines during the years before the war, mostly under the pen-name "Neil Ryder," but he considered them pot-boilers, and spoke of that work as "learning to write by writing." So although "Angel's Egg" was not his first published work, it was his first fantasy. He was forty-one when he wrote it, and had been writing more or less steadily for about thirty-four years. No, that's not a misprint. At the ages of seven and eight, approximately, we began a furious competition in the creation of other worlds and high adventure, filling I don't know how many big heavy "ledger" notebooks with ecstatic scribbling. This sort of thing is a hereditary disease, leading to a life-long addiction, quite incurable. Sooner or later, wiv a little bit of luck—and if you can do it as well as Edgar did—it breaks into print. In this case luck had a distinguished name: "Angel's Egg" was originally rescued from the bottomless mire of the slush pile by Ted Sturgeon. And here it is.

—MARY PANGBORN

*   *   *

255

LETTER OF RECORD, BLAINE TO MC CARRAN, DATED AUGUST
10, 1951.

Mr. Cleveland McCarran
Federal Bureau of Investigation
Washington, D.C.

Dear Sir:

In compliance with your request I enclose herewith a
transcript of the pertinent sections of the journal of Dr.
David Bannerman, deceased. The original document is
being held at this office until proper disposition can be
determined.

Our investigation has shown no connection between Dr.
Bannerman and any organization, subversive or otherwise.
So far as we can learn, he was exactly what he seemed,
an inoffensive summer resident, retired, with a small independent income—a recluse to some extent, but well
spoken of by local tradesmen and other neighbors. A connection between Dr. Bannerman and the type of activity
that concerns your department would seem most unlikely.

The following information is summarized from the
earlier parts of Dr. Bannerman's journal, and tallies with
the results of our own limited inquiry. He was born in
1898 at Springfield, Massachusetts, attended public school
there, and was graduated from Harvard College in 1922,
his studies having been interrupted by two years' military
service. He was wounded in action in Argonne, receiving a
spinal injury. He earned a doctorate in biology in 1926.
Delayed aftereffects of his war injury necessitated hospital-
ization, 1927–28. From 1929 to 1948 he taught elementary
sciences in a private school in Boston. He published two
textbooks in introductory biology, 1929 and 1937. In 1948
he retired from teaching: a pension and a modest income
from textbook royalties evidently made this possible. Aside
from the spinal deformity, which caused him to walk with
a stoop, his health is said to have been fair. Autopsy findings suggested that the spinal condition must have given
him considerable pain; he is not known to have mentioned
this to anyone, not even to his physician, Dr. Lester Morse.
There is no evidence whatever of drug addiction or alco-
holism.

At one point early in his journal Dr. Bannerman describes himself as "a naturalist of the puttering type—I would rather sit on a log than write monographs: it pays off better." Dr. Morse, and others who knew Dr. Bannerman personally, tell me that this conveys a hint of his personality.

I am not qualified to comment on the material of this journal, except to say I have no evidence to support (or to contradict) Dr. Bannerman's statements. The journal has been studied only by my immediate superiors, by Dr. Morse, and by myself. I take it for granted you will hold the matter in strictest confidence.

With the journal I am also enclosing a statement by Dr. Morse, written at my request for our records and for your information. You will note that he says, with some qualifications, that "death was not inconsistent with an embolism." He has signed a death certificate on that basis. You will recall from my letter of August 5 that it was Dr. Morse who discovered Dr. Bannerman's body. Because he was a close personal friend of the deceased, Dr. Morse did not feel able to perform the autopsy himself. It was done by a Dr. Stephen Clyde of this city, and was virtually negative as regards cause of death, neither confirming nor contradicting Dr. Morse's original tentative diagnosis. If you wish to read the autopsy report in full I shall be glad to forward a copy.

Dr. Morse tells me that so far as he knows Dr. Bannerman had no near relatives. He never married. For the last twelve summers he occupied a small cottage on a back road about twenty-five miles from this city, and had few visitors. The neighbor, Steele, mentioned in the journal is a farmer, age 68, of good character, who tells me he "never got really acquainted with Dr. Bannerman."

At this office we feel that unless new information comes to light, further active investigation is hardly justified.

Respectfully yours,
Garrison Blaine
Capt., State Police
Augusta, Me.

Encl: Extract from Journal of David Bannerman, dec'd.
Statement by Lester Morse, M.D.

LIBRARIAN'S NOTE: The following document, originally attached as an unofficial "rider" to the foregoing letter, was donated to this institution in 1994 through the courtesy of Mrs. Helen McCarran, widow of the martyred first President of the World Federation. Other personal and state papers of President McCarran, many of them dating from the early period when he was employed by the FBI, are accessible to public view at the Institute of World History, Copenhagen.

PERSONAL NOTE, BLAINE TO MC CARRAN, DATED AUGUST 10, 1951

Dear Cleve:

Guess I didn't make it clear in my other letter that that bastard Clyde was responsible for my having to drag you into this. He is something to handle with tongs. Happened thusly— When he came in to heave the autopsy report at me, he was already having pups just because it was so completely negative (he does have certain types of honesty), and he caught sight of a page or two of the journal on my desk. Doc Morse was with me at the time. I fear we both got upstage with him (Clyde has that effect, and we were both in a State of Mind anyway), so right away the old drip thinks he smells something subversive. Belongs to the atomize-'em-NOW-WOW-WOW school of thought—nuf sed? He went into a grand whuff-whuff about referring to Higher Authority, and I knew that meant your hive, so I wanted to get ahead of the letter I knew he'd write. I suppose his literary effort couldn't be just sort of quietly transferred to File 13, otherwise known as the Appropriate Receptacle?

He can say what he likes about my character, if any, but even I never supposed he'd take a sideswipe at his professional colleague. Doc Morse is the best of the best and would not dream of suppressing any evidence important to us, as you say Clyde's letter hints. What Doc did do was to tell Clyde, pleasantly, in the privacy of my office, to go take a flying this-and-that at the moon. I only wish I'd thought of the expression myself. So Clyde rushes off to tell teacher. See what I mean about the tongs? However (knock on wood) I don't think Clyde saw enough of the journal to get any notion of what it's all about.

As for that journal, damn it, Cleve, I don't know. If you have any ideas I want them, of course. I'm afraid I believe in angels, myself. But when I think of the effect on local opinion if the story ever gets out—brother! Here was this old Bannerman living alone with a female angel and they wuzn't even common-law married. Aw, gee. . . . And the flood of phone calls from other crackpots anxious to explain it all to me. Experts in the care and feeding of angels. Methods of angel-proofing. Angels right outside the window a minute ago. Make Angels a Profitable Enterprise in Your Spare Time!!!

When do I see you? You said you might have a week clear in October. If we could get together maybe we could make sense where there is none. I hear the cider promises to be good this year. Try and make it. My best to Ginny and the other young fry, and Helen of course.

> Respeckfully yourn,
> Garry

P.S. If you do see any angels down your way, and they aren't willing to wait for a Republican Administration, by all means have them investigated by the Senate—then we'll *know* we're all nuts.

> G.

EXTRACT FROM JOURNAL OF DAVID BANNERMAN, JUNE 1-JULY 29, 1951

June 1

It must have been at least three weeks ago when we had that flying saucer flurry. Observers the other side of Katahdin saw it come down this side; observers this side saw it come down the other. Size anywhere from six inches to sixty feet in diameter (or was it cigar-shaped?) and speed whatever you please. Seem to recall that witnesses agreed on a rosy-pink light. There was the inevitable gobbledegookery of official explanation designed to leave everyone impressed, soothed, and disappointed. I paid scant attention to the excitement and less to the explanations—naturally, I thought it was just a flying saucer. But now Camilla has hatched out an angel.

It would have to be Camilla. Perhaps I haven't mentioned my hens enough. In the last day or two it has
dawned on me that this journal may be of importance to
other eyes than mine, not merely a lonely man's plaything
to blunt the edge of mortality: an angel in the house makes
a difference. I had better show consideration for possible
readers.

I have eight hens, all yearlings except Camilla: this is
her third spring. I boarded her two winters at my neighbor
Steele's farm when I closed this shack and shuffled my
chilly bones off to Florida, because even as a pullet she
had a manner which overbore me. I could never have eaten
Camilla: if she had looked at the ax with that same expression of rancid disapproval (and she would), I should
have felt I was beheading a favorite aunt. Her only concession to sentiment is the annual rush of maternity to the
brain—normal, for a case-hardened White Plymouth Rock.

This year she stole a nest successfully in a tangle of
blackberry. By the time I located it, I estimated I was
about two weeks too late. I had to outwit her by watching
from a window—she is far too acute to be openly trailed
from feeding ground to nest. When I had bled and pruned
my way to her hideout she was sitting on nine eggs and
hating my guts. They could not be fertile, since I keep no
rooster, and I was about to rob her when I saw the ninth
egg was nothing of hers. It was a deep blue and transparent, with flecks of inner light that made me think of
the first stars in a clear evening. It was the same size as
Camilla's own. There was an embryo, but I could make
nothing of it. I returned the egg to Camilla's bare and
fevered breastbone and went back to the house for a long,
cool drink.

That was ten days ago. I know I ought to have kept a
record; I examined the blue egg every day, watching how
some nameless life grew within it. The angel has been out
of the shell three days now. This is the first time I have
felt equal to facing pen and ink.

I have been experiencing a sort of mental lassitude unfamiliar to me. Wrong word: not so much lassitude as a
preoccupation, with no sure clue to what it is that pre-
occupies me. By reputation I am a scientist of sorts. Right
now I have no impulse to look for data; I want to sit quiet
and let truth come to a relaxed mind if it will. Could be

merely a part of growing older, but I doubt that. The broken pieces of the wonderful blue shell are on my desk. I have been peering at them—into them—for the last ten minutes or more. Can't call it study: my thought wanders into their blue, learning nothing I can retain in words. It does not convey much to say I have gone into a vision of open sky—and of peace, if such a thing there be.

The angel chipped the shell deftly in two parts. This was evidently done with the aid of small horny outgrowths on her elbows; these growths were sloughed off on the second day. I wish I had seen her break the shell, but when I visited the blackberry tangle three days ago she was already out. She poked her exquisite head through Camilla's neck feathers, smiled sleepily, and snuggled back into darkness to finish drying off. So what could I do, more than save the broken shell and wriggle my clumsy self out of there? I had removed Camilla's own eggs the day before—Camilla was only moderately annoyed. I was nervous about disposing of them, even though they were obviously Camilla's, but no harm was done. I cracked each one to be sure. Very frankly rotten eggs and nothing more.

In the evening of that day I thought of rats and weasels, as I should have done earlier. I prepared a box in the kitchen and brought the two in, the angel quiet in my closed hand. They are there now. I think they are comfortable.

Three days after hatching, the angel is the length of my forefinger, say three inches tall, with about the relative proportions of a six-year-old girl. Except for head, hands, and probably the soles of her feet, she is clothed in down the color of ivory; what can be seen of her skin is a glowing pink—I do mean glowing, like the inside of certain sea shells. Just above the small of her back are two stubs which I take to be infantile wings. They do not suggest an extra pair of specialized forelimbs. I think they are wholly differentiated organs; perhaps they will be like the wings on an insect. Somehow, I never thought of angels buzzing. Maybe she won't. I know very little about angels. At present the stubs are covered with some dull tissue, no doubt a protective sheath to be discarded when the membranes (if they are membranes) are ready to grow. Between the stubs is a not very prominent ridge—special musculature, I suppose. Otherwise her shape is quite human, even to a pair of minuscule mammalian buttons just visible under the down; how that can make sense in an egg-laying organism is beyond my comprehension. (Just for the record, so is a Corot landscape; so is Schubert's *Unfinished;* so is the flight of a hummingbird, or the other-world of frost on a window pane.) The down on her head has grown visibly in three days and is of different quality from the body down—later it may resemble human hair, as a diamond resembles a chunk of granite. . . .

A curious thing has happened. I went to Camilla's box after writing that. Judy* was already lying in front of it, unexcited. The angel's head was out from under the feathers, and I thought—with more verbal distinctness than such thoughts commonly take, "So here I am, a naturalist of middle years and cold sober, observing a three-inch oviparous mammal with down and wings." The thing is— she giggled. Now, it might have been only amusement at my appearance, which to her must be enormously gross and comic. But another thought formed unspoken: "I am no longer lonely." And her face (hardly bigger than a dime) immediately changed from laughter to a brooding and friendly thoughtfulness.

Judy and Camilla are old friends. Judy seems untroubled by the angel. I have no worries about leaving them alone together. I must sleep.

June 3

I made no entry last night. The angel was talking to me, and when that was finished I drowsed off immediately on a cot that I have moved into the kitchen so as to be near them.

I had never been strongly impressed by the evidence for extrasensory perception. It is fortunate my mind was able to accept the novelty, since to the angel it is clearly a matter of course. Her tiny mouth is most expressive but moves only for that reason and for eating—not for speech. Probably she could speak to her own kind if she wished, but I dare say the sound would be outside the range of my hearing as well as my understanding.

---

* Dr. Bannerman's dog, mentioned often earlier in the journal. A nine-year-old English setter. According to an entry of May 15, 1951, she was then beginning to go blind.
                                                                —BLAINE.

Last night after I brought the cot in and was about to finish my puttering bachelor supper, she climbed to the edge of the box and pointed, first at herself and then at the top of the kitchen table. Afraid to let my vast hand take hold of her, I held it out flat and she sat in my palm. Camilla was inclined to fuss, but the angel looked over her shoulder and Camilla subsided, watchful but no longer alarmed.

The table top is porcelain, and the angel shivered. I folded a towel and spread a silk handkerchief on top of that; the angel sat on this arrangement with apparent comfort, near my face. I was not even bewildered. Possibly she had already instructed me to blank out my mind. At any rate, I did so, without conscious effort to that end.

She reached me first with visual imagery. How can I make it plain that this had nothing in common with my sleeping dreams? There was no weight of symbolism from my littered past; no discoverable connection with any of yesterday's commonplace; indeed, no actual involvement of my personality at all. I saw. I was moving vision, though without eyes or other flesh. And while my mind saw, it also knew where my flesh was, slumped at the kitchen table. If anyone had entered the kitchen, if there had been a noise of alarm out in the henhouse, I should have known it.

There was a valley such as I have not seen (and never will) on Earth. I have seen many beautiful places on this planet—some of them were even tranquil. Once I took a slow steamer to New Zealand and had the Pacific as a plaything for many days. I can hardly say how I knew this was not Earth. The grass of the valley was an earthly green; a river below me was a blue-and-silver thread under familiar-seeming sunlight; there were trees much like pine and maple, and maybe that is what they were. But it was not Earth. I was aware of mountains heaped to strange heights on either side of the valley—snow, rose, amber, gold. Perhaps the amber tint was unlike any mountain color I have noticed in this world at midday.

Or I may have known it was not Earth simply because her mind—dwelling within some unimaginable brain smaller than the tip of my little finger—told me so.

I watched two inhabitants of that world come flying, to rest in the field of sunny grass where my bodiless vision had brought me. Adult forms, such as my angel would

surely be when she had her growth, except that both of
these were male and one of them was dark-skinned. The
latter was also old, with a thousand-wrinkled face, knowing and full of tranquility; the other was flushed and lively
with youth; both were beautiful. The down of the brown-
skinned old one was reddish-tawny; the other's was ivory
with hints of orange. Their wings were true membranes,
with more variety of subtle iridescence than I have seen
even in the wings of a dragonfly; I could not say that any
color was dominant, for each motion brought a ripple of
change. These two sat at their ease on the grass. I realized
that they were talking to each other, though their lips did
not move in speech more than once or twice. They would
nod, smile, now and then illustrate something with twinkling hands.

A huge rabbit lolloped past them. I knew (thanks to my
own angel's efforts, I suppose) that this animal was of the
same size as our common wild ones. Later, a blue-green
snake three times the size of the angels came flowing
through the grass; the old one reached out to stroke its
head carelessly, and I think he did it without interrupting
whatever he was saying.

Another creature came, in leisured leaps. He was monstrous, yet I felt no alarm in the angels or in myself. Imagine a being built somewhat like a kangaroo up to the
head, about eight feet tall, and katydid-green. Really, the
thick balancing tail and enormous legs were the only
kangaroo-like features about him: the body above the
massive thighs was not dwarfed but thick and square; the
arms and hands were quite humanoid: the head was round,
manlike except for its face—there was only a single nostril
and his mouth was set in the vertical; the eyes were large
and mild. I received an impression of high intelligence and
natural gentleness. In one of his manlike hands two tools
so familiar and ordinary that I knew my body by the
kitchen table had laughed in startled recognition. But, after
all, a garden spade and rake are basic. Once invented—I
expect we did it ourselves in the Neolithic Age—there is
little reason why they should change much down the
millennia.

This farmer halted by the angels, and the three con-
versed a while. The big head nodded agreeably. I believe
the young angel made a joke; certainly the convulsions in

the huge green face made me think of laughter. Then this amiable monster turned up the grass in a patch a few yards square, broke the sod and raked the surface smooth, just as any competent gardener might do—except that he moved with the relaxed smoothness of a being whose strength far exceeds the requirements of his task. . . .

I was back in my kitchen with everyday eyes. My angel was exploring the table. I had a loaf of bread there and a dish of strawberries and cream. She was trying a bread crumb; seemed to like it fairly well. I offered the strawberries; she broke off one of the seeds and nibbled it but didn't care so much for the pulp. I held up the great spoon with sugary cream; she steadied it with both hands to try some. I think she liked it. It had been most stupid of me not to realize that she would be hungry. I brought wine from the cupboard; she watched inquiringly, so I put a couple of drops on the handle of a spoon. This really pleased her: she chuckled and patted her tiny stomach, though I'm afraid it wasn't awfully good sherry. I brought some crumbs of cake, but she indicated that she was full, came close to my face, and motioned me to lower my head.

She reached towards me until she could press both hands against my forehead—I felt it only enough to know her hands were there—and she stood so a long time, trying to tell me something.

It was difficult. Pictures come through with relative ease, but now she was transmitting an abstraction of a complex kind: my clumsy brain really suffered in the effort to receive. Something did come across. I have only the crudest way of passing it on. Imagine an equilateral triangle; place the following words one at each corner—"recruiting," "collecting," "saving." The meaning she wanted to convey ought to be near the center of the triangle.

I had also the sense that her message provided a partial explanation of her errand in this lovable and damnable world.

She looked weary when she stood away from me. I put out my palm and she climbed into it, to be carried back to the nest.

She did not talk to me tonight, nor eat, but she gave a reason, coming out from Camilla's feathers long enough to turn her back and show me the wing stubs. The protec-

tive sheaths have dropped off; the wings are rapidly growing. They are probably damp and weak. She was quite
tired and went back into the warm darkness almost at
once.

Camilla must be exhausted, too. I don't think she has
been off the nest more than twice since I brought them
into the house.

June 4

Today she can fly.

I learned it in the afternoon, when I was fiddling about
in the garden and Judy was loafing in the sunshine she
loves. Something apart from sight and sound called me to
hurry back to the house. I saw my angel through the
screen door before I opened it. One of her feet had caught
in a hideous loop of loose wire at a break in the mesh. Her
first tug of alarm must have tightened the loop so that her
hands were not strong enough to force it open.

Fortunately I was able to cut the wire with a pair of
shears before I lost my head; then she could free her foot
without injury. Camilla had been frantic, rushing around
fluffed up, but—here's an odd thing—perfectly silent. None
of the recognized chicken noises of dismay: if an ordinary
chick had been in trouble she would have raised the roof.

The angel flew to me and hovered, pressing her hands on
my forehead. The message was clear at once: "No harm
done." She flew down to tell Camilla the same thing.

Yes, in the same way. I saw Camilla standing near my
feet with her neck out and head low, and the angel put a
hand on either side of her scraggy comb. Camilla relaxed,
clucked in the normal way, and spread her wings for a
shelter. The angel went under it, but only to oblige Camilla, I think—at least, she stuck her head through the
wing feathers and winked.

She must have seen something else, then, for she came
out and flew back to me and touched a finger to my cheek,
looked at the finger, saw it was wet, put it in her mouth,
made a face and laughed at me.

We went outdoors into the sun (Camilla, too), and the
angel gave me an exhibition of what flying ought to be.
Not even Schubert can speak of joy as her first free flying
did. At one moment she would be hanging in front of my
eyes, radiant and delighted; the next instant she would be

a dot of color against a cloud. Try to imagine something that would make a hummingbird seem a bit dull and sluggish.

They do hum. Softer than a hummingbird, louder than a dragonfly.

Something like the sound of hawk-moths—*Heinmaris thisbe,* for instance: the one I used to call Hummingbird Moth when I was a child.

I was frightened, naturally. Frightened first at what might happen to her, but that was unnecessary; I don't think she would be in danger from any savage animal except possibly Man. I saw a Cooper's hawk slant down the visible ray toward the swirl of color where she was dancing by herself; presently she was drawing iridescent rings around him; then, while he soared in smaller circles, I could not see her, but (maybe she felt my fright) she was again in front of me, pressing my forehead in the now familiar way. I knew she was amused and caught the idea that the hawk was a "lazy character." Not quite the way I'd describe *Accipiter Cooperi,* but it's all in the point of view. I believe she had been riding his back, no doubt with her speaking hands on his terrible head.

And later I was frightened by the thought that she might not want to return to me. Can I compete with sunlight and open sky? The passage of that terror through me brought her back swiftly, and her hands said with great clarity: "Don't ever be afraid of anything—it isn't necessary for you."

Once this afternoon I was saddened by the realization that old Judy can take little part in what goes on now. I can well remember Judy running like the wind. The angel must have heard this thought in me, for she stood a long time beside Judy's drowsy head, while Judy's tail thumped cheerfully on the warm grass. . . .

In the evening the angel made a heavy meal on two or three cake crumbs and another drop of sherry, and we had what was almost a sustained conversation. I will write it in that form this time, rather than grope for anything more exact. I asked her, "How far away is your home?"

"My home is here."

"Thank God!—but I meant, the place your people came from."

"Ten light-years."

"The images you showed me—that quiet valley—that is ten light-years away?"

"Yes. But that was my father talking to you, through me. He was grown when the journey began. He is two hundred and forty years old—our years, thirty-two days longer than yours."

Mainly I was conscious of a flood of relief: I had feared, on the basis of terrestrial biology, that her explosively rapid growth after hatching must foretell a brief life. But it's all right—she can outlive me, and by a few hundred years, at that. "Your father is here now, on this planet—shall I see him?"

She took her hands away—listening, I believe. The answer was: "No. He is sorry. He is ill and cannot live long. I am to see him in a few days, when I fly a little better. He taught me for twenty years after I was born."

"I don't understand. I thought—"

"Later, friend. My father is grateful for your kindness to me."

I don't know what I thought about that. I felt no faintest trace of condescension in the message. "And he was showing me things he had seen with his own eyes, ten light-years away?"

"Yes." Then she wanted me to rest a while; I am sure she knows what a huge effort it is for my primitive brain to function in this way. But before she ended the conversation by humming down to her nest she gave me this, and I received it with such clarity that I cannot be mistaken: "He says that only fifty million years ago it was a jungle there, just as Terra is now."

June 8

When I woke four days ago the angel was having breakfast, and little Camilla was dead. The angel watched me rub sleep out of my eyes, watched me discover Camilla, and then flew to me. I received this: "Does it make you unhappy?"

"I don't know exactly." You can get fond of a hen, especially a cantankerous and homely old one whose personality has a lot in common with your own.

"She was old. She wanted a flock of chicks, and I couldn't stay with her. So I—" Something obscure here: probably my mind was trying too hard to grasp it—". . .

so I saved her life." I could make nothing else out of it. She said "saved."

Camilla's death looked natural, except that I should have expected the death contractions to muss the straw, and that hadn't happened. Maybe the angel had arranged the old lady's body for decorum, though I don't see how her muscular strength would have been equal to it—Camilla weighed at least seven pounds.

As I was burying her at the edge of the garden and the angel was humming over my head, I recalled a thing which, when it happened, I had dismissed as a dream. Merely a moonlight image of the angel standing in the nest box with her hands on Camilla's head, then pressing her mouth gently on Camilla's throat, just before the hen's head sank down out of my line of vision. Probably I actually waked and saw it happen. I am somehow unconcerned—even, as I think more about it, pleased. . . .

After the burial the angel's hands said, "Sit on the grass and we'll talk. . . . Question me. I'll tell you what I can. My father asks you to write it down."

So that is what we have been doing for the last four days, I have been going to school, a slow but willing pupil. Rather than enter anything in this journal (for in the evenings I was exhausted), I made notes as best I could. The angel has gone now to see her father and will not return until morning. I shall try to make a readable version of my notes.

Since she had invited questions, I began with something which had been bothering me, as a would-be naturalist, exceedingly. I couldn't see how creatures no larger than the adults I had observed could lay eggs as large as Camilla's. Nor could I understand why, if they were hatched in an almost adult condition and able to eat a varied diet, she had any use for that ridiculous, lovely, and apparently functional pair of breasts. When the angel grasped my difficulty she exploded with laughter—her kind, which buzzed her all over the garden and caused her to fluff my hair on the wing and pinch my ear lobe. She lit on a rhubarb leaf and gave a delectably naughty representation of herself as a hen laying an egg, including the cackle. She got me to bumbling helplessly—my kind of laughter—and it was some time before we could quiet down. Then she did her best to explain.

They are true mammals, and the young—not more than two or at most three in a lifetime averaging two hundred and fifty years—are delivered in very much the human way. The baby is nursed—human fashion—until his brain begins to respond a little to their unspoken language; that takes three to four weeks. Then he is placed in an altogether different medium. She could not describe that clearly, because there was very little in my educational storehouse to help me grasp it. It is some gaseous medium that arrests bodily growth for an almost indefinite period, while mental growth continues. It took them, she says, about seven thousand years to perfect this technique after they first hit on the idea: they are never in a hurry. The infant remains under this delicate and precise control for anywhere from fifteen to thirty years, the period depending not only on his mental vigor but also on the type of lifework he tentatively elects as soon as his brain is knowing enough to make a choice. During this period his mind is guided with unwavering patience by teachers who—

It seems those teachers know their business. This was peculiarly difficult for me to assimilate, although the fact came through clearly enough. In their world, the profession of teacher is more highly honored than any other—can such a thing be possible?—and so difficult to enter that only the strongest minds dare attempt it. (I had to rest a while after absorbing that.) An aspirant must spend fifty years (not including the period of infantile education) in merely getting ready to begin, and the acquisition of factual knowledge, while not understressed, takes only a small portion of those fifty years. Then—if he's good enugh—he can take a small part in the elementary instruction of a few babies, and if he does well on that basis for another thirty or forty years, he is considered a fair beginner. . . . Once upon a time I lurched around stuffy classrooms trying to insert a few predigested facts (I wonder how many of them *were* facts?) into the minds of bored and preoccupied adolescents, some of whom may have liked me moderately well. I was even able to shake hands and be nice while their terribly well-meaning parents explained to me how they ought to be educated. So much of our human effort goes down the drain of futility, I sometimes wonder how we ever got as far as the

Bronze Age. Somehow we did, though, and a short way beyond.

After that preliminary stage of an angel's education is finished, the baby is transferred to more ordinary surroundings, and his bodily growth completes itself in a very short time. Wings grow abruptly (as I have seen), and he reaches a maximum height of six inches (our measure). Only then does he enter on that lifetime of two hundred and fifty years, for not until then does his body begin to age. My angel has been a living personality for many years but will not celebrate her first birthday for almost a year. I like to think of that.

At about the same time that they learned the principles of interplanetary travel (approximately twelve million years ago) these people also learned how, by use of a slightly different method, growth could be arrested at any point short of full maturity. At first the knowledge served no purpose except in the control of illnesses which still occasionally struck them at that time. But when the long periods of time required for space travel were considered, the advantages became obvious.

So it happens that my angel was born ten light-years away. She was trained by her father and many others in the wisdom of seventy million years (that, she tells me, is the approximate sum of their *recorded* history), and then she was safely sealed and cherished in what my superamoebic brain regarded as a blue egg. Education did not proceed at that time; her mind went to sleep with the rest of her. When Camilla's temperature made her wake and grow again, she remembered what to do with the little horny bumps provided for her elbows. And came out— into this planet, God help her.

I wondered why her father should have chosen any combination so unreliable as an old hen and a human being. Surely he must have had plenty of excellent ways to bring the shell to the right temperature. Her answer should have satisfied me immensely, but I am still compelled to wonder about it. "Camilla was a nice hen, and my father studied your mind while you were asleep. It was a bad landing, and much was broken—no such landing was ever made before after so long a journey: forty years. Only four other grownups could come with my father. Three

of them died en route and he is very ill. And there were
nine other children to care for."

Yes, I knew she'd said that an angel thought I was good
enough to be trusted with his daughter. If it upsets me, all
I need do is look at her and then in the mirror. As for the
explanation, I can only conclude there must be more that
I am not ready to understand. I was worried about those
nine others, but she assured me they were all well, and I
sensed that I ought not to ask more about them at
present. . . .

Their planet, she says, is closely similar to this. A trifle
larger, moving in a somewhat longer orbit around a sun
like ours. Two gleaming moons, smaller than ours—their
orbits are such that two-moon nights come rarely. They
are magic, and she will ask her father to show me one, if
he can. Their year is thirty-two days longer than ours;
because of a slower rotation, their day has twenty-six of
our hours. Their atmosphere is mainly nitrogen and oxygen in the proportions familiar to us; slightly richer in
some of the rare gases. The climate is now what we should
call tropical and subtropical, but they have known glacial
rigors like those in our world's past. There are only two
great continental land masses, and many thousands of
large islands.

Their total population is only five billion. . . .

Most of the forms of life we know have parallels there
—some quite exact parallels: rabbits, deer, mice, cats. The
cats have been bred to an even higher intelligence than
they possess on our Earth; it is possible, she says, to have
a good deal of intellectual intercourse with their cats, who
learned several million years ago that when they kill, it
must be done with lightning precision and without torture.
The cats had some difficulty grasping the possibility of
pain in other organisms, but once that educational hurdle
was passed, development was easy. Nowadays many of
the cats are popular storytellers; about forty million years
ago they were still occasionally needed as a special police
force, and served the angels with real heroism.

It seems my angel wants to become a student of animal
life here on Earth. I, a teacher!—but bless her heart for
the notion, anyhow. We sat and traded animals for a
couple of hours last night. I found it restful, after the
mental struggle to grasp more difficult matters. Judy was

something new to her. They have several luscious monsters on that planet but, in her view, so have we. She told me of a blue sea snake fifty feet long (relatively harmless) that bellows cow-like and comes into the tidal marshes to lay black eggs; so I gave her a whale. She offered a bat-winged, day-flying ball of mammalian fluff as big as my head and weighing under an ounce; I matched her with a marmoset. She tried me with a small-sized pink bronto-saur (very rare), but I was ready with the duck-billed platypus, and that caused us to exchange some pretty smart remarks about mammalian eggs; she bounced. All trivial in a way; also, the happiest evening in my fifty-three tangled years of life.

She was a trifle hesitant to explain these kangaroo-like people, until she was sure I really wanted to know. It seems they are about the nearest parallel to human life on that planet; not a near parallel, of course, as she was care-ful to explain. Agreeable and always friendly souls (though they weren't always so, I'm sure) and of a somewhat more alert intelligence than we possess. Manual workers, mainly, because they prefer it nowadays, but some of them are excellent mathematicians. The first practical spaceship was invented by a group of them, with some assistance. . . .

Names offer difficulties. Because of the nature of the angelic language, they have scant use for them except for the purpose of written record, and writing naturally plays little part in their daily lives—no occasion to write a letter when a thousand miles is no obstacle to the speech of your mind. An angel's formal name is about as important to him as, say, my Social Security number is to me. She has not told me hers, because the phonetics on which their written language is based have no parallel in my mind. As we would speak a friend's name, an angel will project the friend's image to his friend's receiving mind. More pleasant and more intimate, I think—although it was a shock to me at first to glimpse my own ugly mug in my mind's eye. Stories are occasionally written, if there is something in them that should be preserved precisely as it was in the first telling; but in their world the true storyteller has a more important place than the printer—he offers one of the best of their quieter pleasures: a good one can hold his audience for a week and never tire them.

"What is this 'angel' in your mind when you think of me?"

"A being men have imagined for centuries, when they thought of themselves as they might like to be and not as they are."

I did not try too painfully hard to learn much about the principles of space travel. The most my brain could take in of her explanation was something like: "Rocket—then phototropism." Now, that makes scant sense. So far as I know, phototropism—movement toward light—is an organic phenomenon. One thinks of it as a response of protoplasm, in some plants and animal organisms (most of them simple), to the stimulus of light; certainly not as a force capable of moving inorganic matter. I think that whatever may be the principle she was describing, this word "phototropism" was merely the nearest thing to it in my reservoir of language. Not even the angels can create understanding out of blank ignorance. At least I have learned not to set neat limits to the possible.

(There was a time when I did, though. I can see myself, not so many years back, like a homunculus squatting at the foot of Mt. McKinley, throwing together two handfuls of mud and shouting, "Look at the big mountain *I* made!")

And if I did know the physical principles which brought them here, and could write them in terms accessible to technicians resembling myself, I would not do it.

Here is a thing I am afraid no reader of this journal will believe: These people, as I have written, learned their method of space travel some twelve million years ago. But this is the first time they have ever used it to convey them to another planet. The heavens are rich in worlds, she tells me; on many of them there is life, often on very primitive levels. No external force prevented her people from going forth, colonizing, conquering, as far as they pleased. They could have populated a Galaxy. They did not, and for this reason: they believed they were not ready. More precisely: *Not good enough.*

Only some fifty million years ago, by her account, did they learn (as we may learn eventually) that intelligence without goodness is worse than high explosive in the hands of a baboon. For beings advanced beyond the level of Pithecanthropus, intelligence is a cheap commodity—not too hard to develop, hellishly easy to use for unconsidered ends. Whereas goodness is not to be achieved without unending effort of the hardest kind, within the self, whether the self be man or angel.

It is clear even to me that the conquest of evil is only one step, not the most important. For goodness, so she tried to tell me, is an altogether positive quality; the part of living nature that swarms with such monstrosities as cruelty, meanness, bitterness, greed, is not to be filled by a vacuum when these horrors are eliminated. When you clear away a poisonous gas, you try to fill the whole room with clean air. Kindness, for only one example: one who can define kindness only as the absence of cruelty has surely not begun to understand the nature of either.

They do not aim at perfection, these angels: only at the attainable. . . . That time fifty million years ago was evidently one of great suffering and confusion. War and all its attendant plagues. They passed through many centuries while advances in technology merely worsened their condition and increased the peril of self-annihilation. They came through that, in time. War was at length so far outgrown that its recurrence was impossible, and the development of wholly rational beings could begin. Then they were ready to start growing up, through millennia of self-searching, self-discipline, seeking to derive the simple from the complex, discovering how to use knowledge and not be used by it. Even then, of course, they slipped back often enough. There were what she refers to as "eras of fatigue." In their dimmer past, they had had many dark ages, lost civilizations, hopeful beginnings ending in dust. Earlier still, they had come out of the slime, as we did.

But their period of deepest uncertainty and sternest self-appraisal did not come until twelve million years ago, when they knew a Universe could be theirs for the taking and knew they were not yet good enough.

They are in no more hurry than the stars. She tried to convey something tentatively, at this point, which was really beyond both of us. It had to do with time (not as I understand time) being perhaps the most essential attribute of God (not as I was ever able to understand that word). Seeing my mental exhaustion, she gave up the effort and later told me that the conception was extremely difficult for her, too—not only, I gathered, because of her youth and relative ignorance. There was also a hint that her father might not have wished her to bring my brain up to a hurdle like that one. . . .

Of course, they explored. Their little spaceships were roaming the ether before there was anything like Man on this earth—roaming and listening, observing, recording; never entering nor taking part in the life of any home but their own. For five million years they even forbade themselves to go beyond their own Solar System, though it would have been easy to do so. And in the following seven million years, although they traveled to incredible distances, the same stern restraint was in force. It was altogether unrelated to what we should call fear—that, I think, is as extinct in them as hate. There was so much to do at home!—I wish I could imagine it. They mapped the heavens and played in their own sunlight.

Naturally, I cannot tell you what goodness is. I know only, moderately well, what it seems to mean to us human beings. It appears that the best of us can, with enormous difficulty, achieve a manner of life in which goodness is reasonably dominant, by a not too precarious balance, for the greater part of the time. Often, wise men have indicated they hope for nothing better than that in our present condition. We are, in other words, a fraction alive; the rest is in the dark. Dante was a bitter masochist, Beethoven a frantic and miserable snob, Shakespeare wrote potboilers. And Christ said, "My Father, if it be possible, let this cup pass from me."

But give us fifty million years—I am no pessimist. After all, I've watched one-celled organisms on the slide and listened to Brahms' Fourth. Night before last I said to the angel, "In spite of everything, you and I are kindred."

She granted me agreement.

June 9

She was lying on my pillow this morning so that I could see her when I waked.

Her father has died, and she was with him when it happened. There was again that thought-impression that I could interpret only to mean that his life had been "saved." I was still sleep-bound when my mind asked, "What will you do?"

"Stay with you, if you wish it, for the rest of your life."

Now, the last part of the message was clouded, but I am

familiar with that—it seems to mean there is some further element that eludes me. I could not be mistaken about the part I did receive. It gives me amazing speculations. After all, I am only fifty-three; I might live for another thirty or forty years. . . .

She was preoccupied this morning, but whatever she felt about her father's death that might be paralleled by sadness in a human being was hidden from me. She did say her father was sorry he had not been able to show me a two-moon night.

One adult, then, remains in this world. Except to say that he is two hundred years old and full of knowledge, and that he endured the long journey without serious ill effects, she has told me little about him. And there are ten children, including herself.

Something was sparkling at her throat. When she was aware of my interest in it she took it off, and I fetched a magnifying glass. A necklace; under the glass, much like our finest human workmanship, if your imagination can reduce it to the proper scale. The stones appeared similar to the jewels we know: diamonds, sapphires, rubies, emeralds, the diamonds snapping out every color under heaven; but there were two or three very dark-purple stones unlike anything I know—not amethysts, I am sure. The necklace was strung on something more slender than cobweb, and the design of the joining clasp was too delicate for my glass to help me. The necklace had been her mother's, she told me; as she put it back around her throat I thought I saw the same shy pride that any human girl might feel in displaying a new pretty.

She wanted to show me other things she had brought, and flew to the table where she had left a sort of satchel an inch and a half long—quite a load for her to fly with, but the translucent substance is so light that when she rested the satchel on my finger I scarcely felt it. She arranged a few articles happily for my inspection, and I put the glass to work again. One was a jeweled comb; she ran it through the down on her chest and legs to show me its use. There was a set of tools too small for the glass to interpret; I learned later they were a sewing kit. A book, and some writing instrument much like a metal pencil: imagine a book and pencil that could be used comfortably by hands hardly bigger than the paws of a mouse—that is the best I can do. The book, I understand, is a blank record for her use as needed.

And finally, when I was fully awake and dressed and we had finished breakfast, she reached in the bottom of the satchel for a parcel (heavy for her) and made me understand it was a gift for me. "My father made it for you, but I put in the stone myself, last night." She unwrapped it. A ring, precisely the size for my little finger.

I broke down, rather. She understood that, and sat on my shoulder petting my ear lobe till I had command of myself.

I have no idea what the jewel is. It shifts with the light from purple to jade-green to amber. The metal resembles platinum in appearance except for a tinge of rose at certain angles of light. . . . When I stare into the stone, I think I see—never mind that now. I am not ready to write it down, and perhaps never will be; anyway, I must be sure.

We improved our housekeeping later in the morning. I showed her over the house. It isn't much—Cape Codder, two rooms up and two down. Every corner interested her, and when she found a shoe box in the bedroom closet, she asked for it. At her direction, I have arranged it on a chest near my bed and near the window, which will be always open; she says the mosquitoes will not bother me, and I don't doubt her. I unearthed a white silk scarf for the bottom of the box; after asking my permission (as if I could want to refuse her anything!) she got her sewing kit and snipped off a piece of the scarf several inches square, folded it on itself several times, and sewed it into a narrow pillow an inch long. So now she had a proper bed and a room of her own. I wish I had something less coarse than silk, but she insists it's nice.

We have not talked very much today. In the afternoon she flew out for an hour's play in the cloud country; when she returned she let me know that she needed a long sleep. She is still sleeping, I think; I am writing this downstairs, fearing the light might disturb her.

Is it possible I can have thirty or forty years in her company? I wonder how teachable my mind still is. I seem to be able to assimilate new facts as well as I ever could; this ungainly carcass should be durable, with reasonable care. Of course, facts without a synthetic imagination are no better than scattered bricks; but perhaps my imagination—

I don't know.

Judy wants out. I shall turn in when she comes back. I wonder if poor Judy's life could be—the word is certainly "saved." I must ask.

Last night when I stopped writing I did go to bed but I was restless, refusing sleep. At some time in the small hours—there was light from a single room—she flew over to me. The tensions dissolved like an illness, and my mind was able to respond with a certain calm.

I made plain (what I am sure she already knew) that I would never willingly part company with her, and then she gave me to understand that there are two alternatives for the remainder of my life. The choice, she says, is altogether mine, and I must take time to be sure of my decision.

I can live out my natural span, whatever it proves to be, and she will not leave me for long at any time. She will be there to counsel, teach, help me in anything good I care to undertake. She says she would enjoy this; for some reason she is, as we'd say in our language, fond of me. We'd have fun.

Lord, the books I could write! I fumble for words now, in the usual human way: whatever I put on paper is a miserable fraction of the potential; the words themselves are rarely the right ones. But under her guidance—

I could take a fair part in shaking the world. With words alone. I could preach to my own people. Before long, I would be heard.

I could study and explore. What small nibblings we have made at the sum of available knowledge! Suppose I brought in one leaf from outdoors, or one common little bug—in a few hours of studying it with her I'd know more of my own specialty than a flood of the best textbooks could tell me.

She has also let me know that when she and those who came with her have learned a little more about the human picture, it should be possible to improve my health greatly, and probably my life expectancy. I don't imagine my back could ever straighten, but she thinks the pain might be cleared away, possibly without drugs. I could have a clearer mind, in a body that would neither fail nor torment me.

Then there is the other alternative.

It seems they have developed a technique by means of which any unresisting living subject whose brain is capable of memory at all can experience a total recall. It is a by-product, I understand, of their silent speech, and a very recent one. They have practiced it for only a few thousand years, and since their own understanding of the phenomenon is very incomplete, they classify it among their experimental techniques. In a general way, it may somewhat resemble that reliving of the past that psychoanalysis can sometimes bring about in a limited way for therapeutic purposes; but you must imagine that sort of thing tremendously magnified and clarified, capable of including every detail that has ever registered on the subject's brain; and the end result is very different. The purpose is not therapeutic, as we would understand it: quite the opposite. The end result is death. Whatever is recalled by this process is transmitted to the receiving mind, which can retain it and record any or all of it if such a record is desired; but to the subject who recalls it, it is a flowing away, without return. Thus it is not a true "remembering" but a giving. The mind is swept clear, naked of all its past, and, along with memory, life withdraws also. Very quietly. At the end, I suppose it must be like standing without resistance in the engulfment of a flood time, until finally the waters close over.

That, it seems, is how Camilla's life was "saved." Now, when I finally grasped that, I laughed, and the angel of course caught my joke. I was thinking about my neighbor Steele, who boarded the old lady for me in his henhouse for a couple of winters. Somewhere safe in the angelic records there must be a hen's-eye image of the patch in the seat of Steele's pants. Well—good. And, naturally, Camilla's view of me, too: not too unkind, I hope—she couldn't help the expression on her rigid little face, and I don't believe it ever meant anything.

At the other end of the scale is the saved life of my angel's father. Recall can be a long process, she says, depending on the intricacy and richness of the mind recalling; and in all but the last stages it can be halted at will. Her father's recall was begun when they were still far out in space and he knew that he could not long survive the journey. When that journey ended, the recall had progressed so far that very little actual memory remained to

him of his life on that other planet. He had what must be
called a "deductive memory"; from the material of the
years not yet given away, he could reconstruct what must
have been; and I assume the other adult who survived the
passage must have been able to shelter him from errors
that loss of memory might involve. This, I infer, is why he
could not show me a two-moon night. I forgot to ask her
whether the images he did send me were from actual or
deductive memory. Deductive, I think, for there was a
certain dimness about them not present when my angel
gives me a picture of something seen with her own eyes.

Jade-green eyes, by the way—were you wondering?

In the same fashion, my own life could be saved. Every
aspect of existence that I even touched, that ever touched
me, could be transmitted to some perfect record. The
nature of the written record is beyond me, but I have no
doubt of its relative perfection. Nothing important, good
or bad, would be lost. And they need a knowledge of
humanity, if they are to carry out whatever it is they have
in mind.

It would be difficult, she tells me, and sometimes painful. Most of the effort would be hers, but some of it would
have to be mine. In her period of infantile education, she
elected what we should call zoology as her lifework; for
that reason she was given intensive theoretical training in
this technique. Right now, I guess she knows more than
anyone else on this planet not only about what makes a
hen tick but about how it feels to be a hen. Though a
beginner, she is in all essentials already an expert. She
can help me, she thinks (if I choose this alternative)—at
any rate, ease me over the toughest spots, soothe away
resistance, keep my courage from too much flagging.

For it seems that this process of recall is painful to an
advanced intellect (she, without condescension, calls us
very advanced) because, while all pretense and self-
delusion are stripped away, there remains conscience, still
functioning by whatever standards of good and bad the individual has developed in his lifetime. Our present knowledge of our own motives is such a pathetically small beginning!—hardly stronger than an infant's first effort to
focus his eyes. I am merely wondering how much of my
life (if I choose this way) will seem to me altogether
hideous. Certainly plenty of the "good deeds" that I still

cherish in memory like so many well-behaved cherubs will turn up with the leering aspect of greed or petty vanity or worse.

Not that I am a bad man, in any reasonable sense of the term; not a bit of it. I respect myself; no occasion to grovel and beat my chest; I'm not ashamed to stand comparison with any other fair sample of the species. But there you are: I *am* human, and under the aspect of eternity so far, plus this afternoon's newspaper, that is a rather serious thing.

Without real knowledge, I think of this total recall as something like a passage down a corridor of myriad images —now dark, now brilliant; now pleasant, now horrible— guided by no certainty except an awareness of the open blind door at the end of it. It could have its pleasing moments and its consolations. I don't see how it could ever approximate the delight and satisfaction of living a few more years in this world with the angel lighting on my shoulder when she wishes, and talking to me.

I had to ask her of how great value such a record would be to them. Very great. Obvious enough—they can be of little use to us, by their standards, until they understand us; and they came here to be of use to us as well as to themselves. And understanding us, to them, means knowing us inside out with a completeness such as our most dedicated and laborious scholars could never imagine. I remember those twelve million years: they will not touch us until they are certain no harm will come of it. On our tortured planet, however, there is a time factor. They know that well enough, of course. . . . Recall cannot begin unless the subject is willing or unresisting; to them, that has to mean willing, for any being with intellect enough to make a considered choice. Now, I wonder how many they could find who would be honestly willing to make that uneasy journey into death, for no reward except an assurance that they were serving their own kind and the angels?

More to the point, I wonder if I would be able to achieve such willingness myself, even with her help?

When this had been explained to me, she urged me again to make no hasty decision. And she pointed out to me what my thoughts were already groping at—why not both alternatives, within a reasonable limit of time? Why couldn't I have ten or fifteen years or more with her and then undertake the total recall—perhaps not until my physical powers had started toward senility? I thought that over.

This morning I had almost decided to choose that most welcome and comforting solution. Then the mailman brought my daily paper. Not that I needed any such reminder.

In the afternoon I asked her if she knew whether, in the present state of human technology, it would be possible for our folly to actually destroy this planet. She did not know, for certain. Three of the other children have gone away to different parts of the world, to learn what they can about that. But she had to tell me that such a thing has happened before, elsewhere in the heavens. I guess I won't write a letter to the papers advancing an explanation for the occasional appearance of a nova among the stars. Doubtless others have hit on the same hypothesis without the aid of angels.

And that is not all I must consider. I could die by accident or sudden disease before I had begun to give my life.

Only now, at this very late moment, rubbing my sweaty forehead and gazing into the lights of that wonderful ring, have I been able to put together some obvious facts in the required synthesis.

I don't know, of course, what forms their assistance to us will take. I suspect human beings won't see or hear much of the angels for a long time to come. Now and then disastrous decisions may be altered, and those who believe themselves wholly responsible won't quite know why their minds worked that way. Here and there, maybe an influential mind will be rather strangely nudged into a better course. Something like that. There may be sudden new discoveries and inventions of kinds that will tend to neutralize the menace of our nastiest playthings. But whatever the angels decide to do, the record and analysis of my not too atypical life will be an aid: it could even be the small weight deciding the balance between triumph and failure. That is fact one.

Two: my angel and her brothers and sisters, for all their amazing level of advancement, are of perishable protoplasm, even as I am. Therefore, if this ball of earth becomes a ball of flame, they also will be destroyed. Even if they have the means to use their spaceship again or to build another, it might easily happen that they would not learn their danger in time to escape. And for all I know, this could be tomorrow. Or tonight.

So there can no longer be any doubt as to my choice, and I will tell her when she wakes.

July 9

Tonight* there is no recall—I am to rest a while. I see it is almost a month since I last wrote in this journal. My total recall began three weeks ago, and I have already been able to give away the first twenty-eight years of my life.

Since I no longer require normal sleep, the recall begins at night, as soon as the lights begin to go out over there in the village and there is little danger of interruption. Daytimes, I putter about in my usual fashion. I have sold Steele my hens, and Judy's life was saved a week ago; that practically winds up my affairs, except that I want to write a codicil to my will. I might as well do that now, right here in this journal, instead of bothering my lawyer. It should be legal.

> TO WHOM IT MAY CONCERN: I hereby bequeath to my friend Lester Morse, M.D., of Augusta, Maine, the ring which will be found at my death on the fifth finger of my left hand; and I would urge Dr. Morse to retain this ring in his private possession at all times, and to make provision for its disposal, in the event of his own death, to some person in whose character he places the utmost faith.
>
> (Signed) David Bannerman†

Tonight she has gone away for a while, and I am to rest and do as I please until she returns. I shall spend the time filling in some blanks in this record, but I am afraid it

---

* At this point Dr. Bannerman's handwriting alters curiously. From here on he used a soft pencil instead of a pen, and the script shows signs of haste. In spite of this, however, it is actually much clearer, steadier, and easier to read than the earlier entries in his normal hand.   —BLAINE.

† In spite of superficial changes in the handwriting, this signature has been certified genuine by an expert graphologist.
                                                    —BLAINE.

will be a spotty job, unsatisfactory to any readers who are subject to the blessed old itch for facts. Mainly because there is so much I no longer care about. It is troublesome to try to decide what things would be considered important by interested strangers.

Except for the lack of any desire for sleep, and a bodily weariness that is not at all unpleasant, I notice no physical effects thus far. I have no faintest recollection of anything that happened earlier than my twenty-eighth birthday. My deductive memory seems rather efficient, and I am sure I could reconstruct most of the story if it were worth the bother: this afternoon I grubbed around among some old letters of that period, but they weren't very interesting. My knowledge of English is unaffected; I can still read scientific German and some French, because I had occasion to use those languages fairly often after I was twenty-eight. The scraps of Latin dating from high school are quite gone. So are algebra and all but the simplest propositions of high-school geometry: I never needed 'em. I can remember thinking of my mother after twenty-eight, but do not know whether the image this provides really resembles her; my father died when I was thirty-one, so I remember him as a sick old man. I believe I had a younger brother, but he must have died in childhood.*

Judy's passing was tranquil—pleasant for her, I think. It took the better part of a day. We went out to an abandoned field I know, and she lay in the sunshine with the angel sitting by her, while I dug a grave and then rambled off after wild raspberries. Toward evening the angel came and told me it was finished. And most interesting, she said. I don't see how there can have been anything distressing about it for Judy; after all, what hurts us worst is to have our favorite self-deceptions stripped away.

As the angel has explained it to me, her people, their cats, those kangaroo-folk, Man, and just possibly the cats on our planet (she hasn't met them yet) are the only animals she knows who are introspective enough to develop self-delusion and related pretenses. I suggested she might find something of the sort, at least in rudimentary

---

* Dr. Bannerman's mother died in 1918 of influenza. His brother (three years older, not younger) died of pneumonia, 1906.   —BLAINE.

form, among some of the other primates. She was immensely interested and wanted to learn everything I could tell her about monkeys and apes. It seems that long ago on the other planet there used to be clumsy, winged creatures resembling the angels to about the degree that the large anthropoids resemble us. They became extinct some forty million years ago, in spite of enlightened efforts to keep their kind alive. Their birth rate became insufficient for replacement, as if some necessary spark had simply flickered out; almost as if nature, or whatever name you prefer for the unknown, had with gentle finality written them off. . . .

I have not found the recall painful, at least not in retrospect. There must have been sharp moments, mercifully forgotten, along with their causes, as if the process had gone on under anesthesia. Certainly there were plenty of incidents in my first twenty-eight years that I should not care to offer to the understanding of any but the angels. Quite often I must have been mean, selfish, base in any number of ways, if only to judge by the record since twenty-eight. Those old letters touch on a few of these things. To me, they now matter only as material for a record which is safely out of my hands.

However, to any persons I may have harmed, I wish to say this: you were hurt by aspects of my humanity which may not, in a few million years, be quite so common among us all. Against these darker elements I struggled, in my human fashion, as you do yourselves. The effort is not wasted.

It was a week after I told the angel my decision before she was prepared to start the recall. During that week she searched my present mind more closely than I should have imagined was possible: she had to be sure. During that week of hard questions I dare say she learned more about my kind than has ever gone on record even in a physician's office; I hope she did. To any psychiatrist who might question that, I offer a naturalist's suggestion: it is easy to imagine, after some laborious time, that we have noticed everything a given patch of ground can show us; but alter the viewpoint only a little—dig down a foot with a spade, say, or climb a tree branch and look downward—it's a whole new world.

When the angel was not exploring me in this fashion,

she took pains to make me glimpse the satisfactions and million rewarding experiences I might have if I chose the other way. I see how necessary that was; at the time it seemed almost cruel. She had to do it, for my own sake, and I am glad that I was somehow able to stand fast to my original choice. So was she, in the end; she has even said she loves me for it. What that troubling word means to her is not within my mind: I am satisfied to take it in the human sense.

Some evening during that week—I think it was June 12 —Lester dropped around for sherry and chess. Hadn't seen him in quite a while, and haven't since. There is a moderate polio scare this summer, and it keeps him on the jump. The angel retired behind some books on an upper shelf—I'm afraid it was dusty—and had fun with our chess. She had a fair view of your bald spot, Lester; later she remarked that she liked your looks, and can't you do something about that weight? She suggested an odd expedient, which I believe has occurred to your medical self from time to time—eating less.

Maybe she shouldn't have done what she did with those chess games. Nothing more than my usual blundering happened until after my first ten moves; by that time I suppose she had absorbed the principles and she took over, slightly. I was not fully aware of it until I saw Lester looking like a boiled duck: I had imagined my astonishing moves were the result of my own damn cleverness.

Seriously, Lester, think back to that evening. You've played in stiff amateur tournaments; you know your own abilities and you know mine. Ask yourself whether I could have done anything like that without help. I tell you again, I didn't study the game in the interval when you weren't there. I've never had a chess book in the library, and if I had, no amount of study would take me into your class. Haven't that sort of mentality—just your humble sparring partner, and I've enjoyed it on that basis, as you might enjoy watching a prima-donna surgeon pull off some miracle you wouldn't dream of attempting yourself. Even if your game had been way below par that evening (I don't think it was), I could never have pinned your ears back three times running, without help. That evening you were a long way out of *your* class, that's all.

I couldn't tell you anything about it at the time—she

was clear on that point—so I could only bumble and preen myself and leave you mystified. But she wants me to write anything I choose in this journal, and somehow, Lester, I think you may find the next few decades pretty interesting. You're still young—some ten years younger than I. I think you'll see many things that I do wish I myself might see come to pass—or I would so wish if I were not convinced that my choice was the right one.

Most of those new events will not be spectacular, I'd guess. Many of the turns to a better way will hardly be recognized at the time for what they are, by you or anyone else. Obviously, our nature being what it is, we shall not jump into heaven overnight. To hope for that would be as absurd as it is to imagine that any formula, ideology, theory of social pattern, can bring us into Utopia. As I see it, Lester—and I think your consulting room would have told you the same even if your own intuition were not enough—there is only one battle of importance: Armageddon. And Armageddon field is within each self, world without end.

At the moment I believe I am the happiest man who ever lived.

July 20

All but the last ten years now given away. The physical fatigue (still pleasant) is quite overwhelming. I am not troubled by the weeds in my garden patch—merely a different sort of flowers where I had planned something else. An hour ago she brought me the seed of a blown dandelion, to show me how lovely it was—I don't suppose I had ever noticed. I hope whoever takes over this place will bring it back to farming: they say the ten acres below the house used to be good potato land—nice early ground.

It is delightful to sit in the sun, as if I were old.

After thumbing over earlier entries in this journal, I see I have often felt quite bitter toward my own kind. I deduce that I must have been a lonely man—much of the loneliness self-imposed. A great part of my bitterness must have been no more than one ugly by-product of a life spent too much apart. Some of it doubtless came from objective causes, yet I don't believe I ever had more cause than any moderately intelligent man who would like to see his world a pleasanter place than it ever has been. My angel tells me that the pain in my back is due to an injury received in some early stage of the world war that still goes on. That could have soured me, perhaps. It's all right—it's all in the record.

She is racing with a hummingbird—holding back, I think, to give the ball of green fluff a break.

Another note for you, Lester. I have already indicated that my ring is to be yours. I don't want to tell you what I have discovered of its properties, for fear it might not give you the same pleasure and interest that it has given me. Of course, like any spot of shifting light and color, it is an aid to self-hypnosis. It is much, much more than that, but—find out for yourself, at some time when you are a little protected from everyday distractions. I know it can't harm you, because I know its source.

By the way, I wish you would convey to my publishers my request that they either discontinue manufacture of my *Introductory Biology* or else bring out a new edition revised in accordance with some notes you will find in the top left drawer of my library desk. I glanced through that book after my angel assured me that I wrote it, and I was amazed. However, I'm afraid my notes are messy (I call them mine by a poetic license), and they may be too advanced for the present day—though the revision is mainly a matter of leaving out certain generalities that ain't so. Use your best judgment: it's a very minor textbook, and the thing isn't too important. A last wriggle of my personal vanity.

July 27

I have seen a two-moon night.

It was given to me by that other grownup, at the end of a wonderful visit, when he and six of those nine other children came to see me. It was last night, I think—yes, must have been. First there was a murmur of wings above the house; my angel flew in, laughing; then they were here, all about me. Full of gaiety and colored fire, showing off in every way they knew would please me. Each one had something graceful and friendly to say to me. One brought me a moving image of the St. Lawrence seen at morning from half a mile up—clouds—eagles; now, how could he know that would delight me so much? And each one thanked me for what I had done.

But it's been so easy!

And at the end the old one—his skin is quite brown, and his down is white and gray—gave the remembered image of a two-moon night. He saw it some sixty years ago.

I have not even considered making an effort to describe it—my fingers will not hold this pencil much longer to-night. Oh—soaring buildings of white and amber, untroubled countryside, silver on curling rivers, a glimpse of open sea; a moon rising in clarity, another setting in a wreath of cloud, between them a wide wandering of unfamiliar stars; and here and there the angels, worthy after fifty million years to live in such a night. No, I cannot describe anything like that. But, you human kindred of mine, I can do something better. I can tell you that this two-moon night, glorious as it was, was no more beautiful than a night under a single moon on this ancient and familiar Earth might be—if you will imagine that the rubbish of human evil has been cleared away and that our own people have started at last on the greatest of all explorations.

July 29

Nothing now remains to give away but the memory of the time that has passed since the angel came. I am to rest as long as I wish, write whatever I want to. Then I shall get myself over to the bed and lie down as if for sleep. She tells me that I can keep my eyes open: she will close them for me when I no longer see her.

I remain convinced that our human case is hopeful. I feel sure that in only a few thousand years we may be able to perform some of the simpler preparatory tasks, such as casting out evil and loving our neighbors. And if that should prove to be so, who can doubt that in another fifty million years we might well be only a little lower than the angels?

LIBRARIAN'S NOTE: As is generally known, the original of the Bannerman Journal is said to have been in the possession of Dr. Lester Morse at the time of the latter's disappearance in 1964, and that disappearance has remained an unsolved mystery to the present day. McCarran is known to have visited Captain Garrison Blaine in October, 1951, but no record remains of that visit. Captain Blaine appears to have been a bachelor who lived alone. He was killed in line of duty, December, 1951. McCarran is believed not to have written about nor discussed the Bannerman affair with anyone else. It is almost certain that he himself removed the extract and related papers from the files (unofficially, it would seem!) when he severed his connection with the FBI in 1957; at any rate, they were found among his effects after his assassination and were released to the public, considerably later, by Mrs. McCarran.

The following memorandum was originally attached to the extract from the Bannerman Journal; it carries the McCarran initialing.

Aug. 11, 1951

The original letter of complaint written by Stephen Clyde, M.D., and mentioned in the accompanying letter of Captain Blaine, has unfortunately been lost, owing perhaps to an error in filing.

Personnel presumed responsible have been instructed not to allow such error to be repeated except if, as, and/or when necessary.

C. McC.

On the margin of this memorandum there was a penciled notation, later erased. The imprint is sufficient to show the unmistakable McCarran script. The notation read in part as follows: *Far be it from a McC. to lose his job except if, as, and/or*—the rest is undecipherable, except for a terminal word which is regrettably unparliamentary.

STATEMENT BY LESTER MORSE, M.D., DATED AUGUST 9, 1951

On the afternoon of July 30, 1951, acting on what I am obliged to describe as an unexpected impulse, I drove out to the country for the purpose of calling on my friend Dr. David Bannerman. I had not seen him nor had word from him since the evening of June 12 of this year.

I entered, as was my custom, without knocking. After calling to him and hearing no response, I went upstairs to his bedroom and found him dead. From superficial indications I judged that death must have taken place during the previous night. He was lying on his bed on his left side, comfortably disposed as if for sleep but fully dressed, with a fresh shirt and clean summer slacks. His eyes and mouth were closed, and there was no trace of the disorder to be expected at even the easiest natural death. Because of these signs I assumed, as soon as I had determined the absence of breath and heartbeat and noted the chill of the body, that some neighbor must have found him already, performed these simple rites out of respect for him, and probably notified a local physician or other responsible person. I therefore waited (Dr. Bannerman had no telephone), expecting that someone would soon call.

Dr. Bannerman's journal was on a table near his bed, open to that page on which he has written a codicil to his will. I read that part. Later, while I was waiting for others to come, I read the remainder of the journal, as I believe he wished me to do. The ring he mentions was on the fifth finger of his left hand, and it is now in my possession. When writing that codicil Dr. Bannerman must have overlooked or forgotten the fact that in his formal will, written some months earlier, he had appointed me executor. If there are legal technicalities involved, I shall be pleased to cooperate fully with the proper authorities.

The ring, however, will remain in my keeping, since that was Dr. Bannerman's expressed wish, and I am not prepared to offer it for examination or discussion under any circumstances.

The notes for a revision of one of his textbooks were in his desk, as noted in the journal. They are by no means "messy"; nor are they particularly revolutionary except insofar as he wished to rephrase, as theory or hypothesis, certain statements that I would have supposed could be regarded as axiomatic. This is not my field, and I am not competent to judge. I shall take up the matter with his publishers at the earliest opportunity.*

So far as I can determine, and bearing in mind the results of the autopsy performed by Stephen Clyde, M.D., the death of Dr. David Bannerman was not inconsistent with the presence of an embolism of some type not distinguishable post mortem. I have so stated on the certificate

---

* LIBRARIAN'S NOTE: But it seems he never did. No new edition of *Introductory Biology* was ever brought out, and the textbook has been out of print since 1952.

of death. It would seem to be not in the public interest to leave such questions in doubt. I am compelled to add one other item of medical opinion for what it may be worth:

I am not a psychiatrist, but, owing to the demands of general practice, I have found it advisable to keep as up to date as possible with current findings and opinion in this branch of medicine. Dr. Bannerman possessed, in my opinion, emotional and intellectual stability to a better degree than anyone else of comparable intelligence in the entire field of my acquaintance, personal and professional. If it is suggested that he was suffering from a hallucinatory psychosis, I can only say that it must have been of a type quite outside my experience and not described, so far as I know, anywhere in the literature of psychopathology.

Dr. Bannerman's house, on the afternoon of July 30, was in good order. Near the open, unscreened window of his bedroom there was a coverless shoe box with a folded silk scarf in the bottom. I found no pillow such as Dr. Bannerman describes in the journal, but observed that a small section had been cut from the scarf. In this box, and near it, there was a peculiar fragrance, faint, aromatic, and very sweet, such as I have never encountered before and therefore cannot describe.

It may or may not have any bearing on the case that, while I remained in this house that afternoon, I felt no sense of grief or personal loss, although Dr. Bannerman had been a loved and honored friend for a number of years. I merely had, and have, a conviction that after the completion of some very great undertaking, he had found peace.

COME ON, WAGON!

by Zenna Henderson

My first serious, sustained effort to write fantasy and science fiction stories coincided with the advent of The Magazine of Fantasy and Science Fiction.

At that time, Tony Boucher and Frances McComas were the editors. At least they were the ones who wrote to me and poked and prodded and suggested me and, finally, helped me acquire an agent and launch my first book, too. That was Pilgrimage: The Book of The People.

I have to speak of them as "they" because I never thought of them as separate people. Their letters were so alike that I couldn't tell which one of them had written to me without looking at the signature first. I met one of them, 'way back in the late '50s in Tucson, but to this day I couldn't swear which one it was. And neither one of them was ever fully convinced that most of my bad spelling was lousy typing.

When the magazine first began, I liked it. It was new to the field and so was I, so I decided to try it. I sent them several stories that they—sensibly—rejected, but always with a note, not a printed form letter.

Then came "Come On, Wagon!"

The manuscript was returned to me and I opened it with that sinking feeling. But, instead of rejecting it, they suggested that I amplify my theme and come up with a longer story.

Which I did. And sent it back in. And it was accepted. For One Hundred Dollars! (on publication)

I nearly died of the wonder of it. No check I'll ever

295

receive will be of greater value. Not only was it half of my teacher take-home pay for a month, but now I was an Author!

I bought a Smith-Corona portable typewriter, and had almost ten dollars left. I used that typewriter for all my stories until the 1960s. It's still being used in Mexico by friends of the family.

The reasons why I started writing are prosaic and run-of-the-mill, even the fact that I wanted to write and insisted on writing, even when it was only for my own astonishment. The reasons I gravitated to fantasy and science fiction are just as prosaic.

I couldn't write domestic difficulty stories, because I couldn't stand to read them, so that cut out all the confessions and women's magazines.

I didn't have enough to say about any subject to be able to produce a novel.

I couldn't write children's stories. I could tell them, to my classes, but not write them.

And I was bored to the bones by most of the science fiction I was reading then. Themes repeated themselves. Plots became rows of ditto marks. Dialogue was so predictable that if a word was missing I went back to see why. So I decided to try writing something I'd like to read.

I had to face the fact that I didn't have sufficient technical knowledge to be able to write successful technical stories; but, I reasoned, no matter what the technology, there are always people who do not understand what's going on scientifically, even though they are acted upon by whatever is going on. That doesn't invalidate the technology nor erase the people. The two co-exist—and intersect just enough sometimes to make a possible story.

Moving a step farther away from my areas of ignorance, there was fantasy, where I could always intersect the ordinary world with whatever world I wanted to create, subject to a few restrictions if I wanted to be published.

The theme I used in "Come On, Wagon!" is much simpler than its explanation.

What if we find some actions impossible just because we think they are impossible? And then systematically bring up our children with the same limitations by systematically telling them that this, that and the other is impossible? What if we really could control the inanimate much more simply if we were only convinced that we could?

I have returned to this same theme many times since, perhaps because in the increasingly complex world, it sounds so much simpler and quieter. Perhaps because I wish that mankind had gone the route of The People and developed their God-given Gifts and Persuasions instead of going the way of gadgets and gizmos and—Things.

Not that I think that any given generation could suddenly believe to the point that they could overcome all the previous pressures to disbelieve.

I only wish it could be so.

I don't like kids—never have. They're too uncanny. For one thing, there's no bottom to their eyes. They haven't learned to pull down their mental curtains the way adults have. For another thing, there's so much they don't know. And not knowing things makes them know lots of other things grownups can't know. That sounds confusing and it is. But look at it this way. Every time you teach a kid something, you teach him a hundred things that are impossible because that one thing is so. By the time we grow up, our world is so hedged around by impossibilities that it's a wonder we ever try anything new.

Anyway, I don't like kids, so I guess it's just as well that I've stayed a bachelor.

Now take Thaddeus. I don't like Thaddeus. Oh, he's a fine kid, smarter than most—he's my nephew—but he's too young. I'll start liking him one of these days when he's ten or eleven. No, that's still too young. I guess when his voice starts cracking and he begins to slick his hair down, I'll get to liking him fine. Adolescence ends lots more than it begins.

The first time I ever really got acquainted with Thaddeus was the Christmas he was three. He was a solemn little fellow, hardly a smile out of him all day, even with the avalanche of everything to thrill a kid. Starting first thing Christmas Day, he made me feel uneasy. He stood still in the middle of the excited squealing bunch of kids that crowded around the Christmas tree in the front room at the folks' place. He was holding a big rubber ball with both hands and looking at the tree with his eyes wide with wonder. I was sitting right by him in the big chair and I said, "How do you like it, Thaddeus?"

He turned his big solemn eyes to me, and for a long time, all I could see was the deep, deep reflections in his eyes of the glitter and glory of the tree and a special shiningness that originated far back in his own eyes. Then he blinked slowly and said solemnly, "Fine."

Then the mob of kids swept him away as they all charged forward to claim their Grampa-gift from under the tree. When the crowd finally dissolved and scattered all over the place with their play-toys, there was Thaddeus squatting solemnly by the little red wagon that had fallen to him. He was examining it intently, inch by inch, but only with his eyes. His hands were pressed between his knees and his chest as he squatted.

"Well, Thaddeus." His mother's voice was a little provoked. "Go play with your wagon. Don't you like it?"

Thaddeus turned his face up to her in that blind, unseeing way little children have.

"Sure," he said, and standing up, tried to take the wagon in his arms.

"Oh for pity sakes," his mother laughed. "You don't carry a wagon, Thaddeus." And aside to us, "Sometimes I wonder. Do you suppose he's got all his buttons?"

"Now, Jean." Our brother Clyde leaned back in his chair. "Don't heckle the kid. Go on, Thaddeus. Take the wagon outside."

So what does Thaddeus do but start for the door, saying over his shoulder, "Come on, Wagon."

Clyde laughed. "It's not that easy, Punkin-Yaller, you've gotta have pull to get along in this world."

So Jean showed Thaddeus how and he pulled the wagon outdoors, looking down at the handle in a puzzled way, absorbing this latest rule for acting like a big boy.

Jean was embarrassed the way parents are when their kids act normal around other people.

"Honest. You'd think he never saw a wagon before."

"He never did," I said idly. "Not his own, anyway." And had the feeling that I had said something profound, but wasn't quite sure what.

The whole deal would have gone completely out of my

mind if it hadn't been for one more little incident. I was out by the barn waiting for Dad. Mom was making him change his pants before he demonstrated his new tractor for me. I saw Thaddeus loading rocks into his little red wagon. Beyond the rock pile, I could see that he had started a playhouse or ranch of some kind, laying the rocks out to make rooms or corrals or whatever. He finished loading the wagon and picked up another rock that took both arms to carry, then he looked down at the wagon.

"Come on, Wagon." And he walked over to his play place.

And the wagon went with him, trundling along over the uneven ground, following at his heels like a puppy.

I blinked and inventoried rapidly the Christmas cheer I had imbibed. It wasn't enough for an explanation. I felt a kind of cold grue creep over me.

Then Thaddeus emptied the wagon and the two of them went back for more rocks. He was just going to pull the same thing again when a big boy-cousin came by and laughed at him.

"Hey, Thaddeus, how you going to pull your wagon with both hands full? It won't go unless you pull it."

"Oh," said Thaddeus and looked off after the cousin who was headed for the back porch and some pie.

So Thaddeus dropped the big rock he had in his arms and looked at the wagon. After struggling with some profound thinking, he picked the rock up again and hooked a little finger over the handle of the wagon.

"Come on, Wagon," he said, and they trundled off together, the handle of the wagon still slanting back over the load while Thaddeus grunted along by it with his heavy armload.

I was glad Dad came just then, hooking the last strap of his striped overalls. We started into the barn together. I looked back at Thaddeus. He apparently figured he'd need his little finger on the next load, so he was squatting by the wagon, absorbed with a piece of flimsy red Christmas string. He had twisted one end around his wrist and was intent on tying the other to the handle of the little red wagon.

It wasn't so much that I avoided Thaddeus after that. It isn't hard for grownups to keep from mingling with kids. After all, they do live in two different worlds. Anyway, I didn't have much to do with Thaddeus for several years after that Christmas. There was the matter of a side trip to the South Pacific where even I learned that there are some grown-up impossibilities that are not always absolute. Then there was a hitch in the hospital where I waited for my legs to put themselves together again. I was luckier than most of the guys. The folks wrote often and regularly and kept me posted on all the home talk. Nothing spectacular, nothing special, just the old familiar stuff that makes home, home and folks, folks.

I hadn't thought of Thaddeus in a long time. I hadn't been around kids much and unless you deal with them, you soon forget them. But I remembered him plenty when I got the letter from Dad about Jean's new baby. The kid was a couple of weeks overdue and when it did come— a girl—Jean's husband, Bert, was out at the farm checking with Dad on a land deal he had cooking. The baby came so quickly that Jean couldn't even make it to the hospital and when Mom called Bert, he and Dad headed for town together, but fast.

"Derned if I didn't have to hold my hair on," wrote Dad. "I don't think we hit the ground but twice all the way to town. Dern near overshot the gate when we finally tore up the hill to their house. Thaddeus was playing out front and we dang near ran him down. Smashed his trike to flinders. I saw the handle bars sticking out from under the front wheel when I followed Bert in. Then I got to thinking that he'd get a flat parking on all that metal so I went out to move the car. Lucky I did. Bert musta forgot to set the brakes. Derned if that car wasn't headed straight for Thaddeus. He was walking right in front of it. Even had his hand on the bumper and the dern thing rolling right after him. I yelled and hit out for the car. But by the time I got there, it had stopped and Thaddeus was squatting by his wrecked trike. What do you suppose the little cuss said? 'Old car broke my trike. I made him get off.'

"Can you beat it? Kids get the dernedest ideas. Lucky it wasn't much down hill, though. He'd have been hurt sure."

I lay with the letter on my chest and felt cold. Dad had forgotten that they "tore up the hill" and that the car must have rolled up the slope to get off Thaddeus' trike.

That night I woke up the ward yelling, "Come on, Wagon!"

It was some months later when I saw Thaddeus again. He and half a dozen other nephews—and the one persistent niece—were in a tearing hurry to be somewhere else and nearly mobbed Dad and me on the front porch as they boiled out of the house with mouths and hands full of cookies. They all stopped long enough to give me the once-over and fire a machine gun volley with my crutches, then they disappeared down the land on their bikes, heads low, rear ends high, and every one of them being bombers at the tops of their voices.

I only had time enough to notice that Thaddeus had lanked out and was just one of the kids as he grinned engagingly at me with the two-tooth gap in his front teeth.

"Did you ever notice anything odd about Thaddeus?" I pulled out the makin's.

"Thaddeus?" Dad glanced up at me from firing up his battered old corncob pipe. "Not particularly. Why?"

"Oh, nothing." I ran my tongue along the paper and rolled the cigarette shut. "He just always seemed kinda different."

"Well, he's always been kinda slow about some things. Not that he's dumb. Once he catches on, he's as smart as anyone, but he's sure pulled some funny ones."

"Give me a fer-instance," I said, wondering if he'd remember the trike deal.

"Well, coupla years ago at a wienie roast he was toting something around wrapped in a paper napkin. Jean saw him put it in his pocket and she thought it was probably a dead frog or a beetle or something like that, so she made him fork it over. She unfolded the napkin and derned if there wasn't a big live coal in it. Dern thing flamed right up in her hand. Thaddeus bellered like a bull calf. Said he wanted to take it home cause it was pretty. How he 'ever carried it around that long without setting himself afire is what got me."

"That's Thaddeus," I said, "odd."

"Yeah." Dad was firing his pipe again, flicking the burned match down, to join the dozen or so others by the porch railing. "I guess you might call him odd. But he'll outgrow it. He hasn't pulled anything like that in a long time."

"They do outgrow it," I said. "Thank God." And I think it was a real prayer. I *don't* like kids. "By the way, where's Clyde?"

"Down in the East Pasture, plowing. Say, that tractor I got that last Christmas you were here is a bear cat. It's lasted me all this time and I've never had to do a lick of work on it. Clyde's using it today."

"When you get a good tractor you got a good one," I said. "Guess I'll go down and see the old son-of-a-gun— Clyde, I mean. Haven't seen him in a coon's age." I gathered up my crutches.

Dad scrambled to his feet. "Better let me run you down in the pickup. I've gotta go over to Jesperson's anyway."

"Okay," I said. "Won't be long till I can throw these things away." So we piled in the pickup and headed for the East Pasture.

We were ambushed at the pump corner by the kids and were killed variously by P-38s, atomic bombs, ackack, and the Lone Ranger's six-guns. Then we lowered our hands which had been raised all this time and Dad reached out and collared the nearest nephew.

"Come along, Punkin-Yaller. That blasted Holstein has busted out again. You get her out of the alfalfa and see if you can find where she got through this time."

"Aw, gee whiz!" The kid—and of course it was Thaddeus—climbed into the back of the pickup. "That dern cow."

We started up with a jerk and I turned half around in the seat to look back at Thaddeus.

"Remember your little red wagon?" I yelled over the clatter.

"Red wagon?" Thaddeus yelled back. His face lighted. "Red wagon?"

I could tell he had remembered and then, as plainly as the drawing of a shade, his eyes went shadowy and he yelled, "Yeah, kinda." And turned around to wave violently at the unnoticing kids behind us.

So, I thought, he is outgrowing it. Then spent the rest of the short drive trying to figure just what it was he was outgrowing.

Dad dumped Thaddeus out at the alfalfa field and took me on across the canal and let me out by the pasture gate.

"I'll be back in about an hour if you want to wait. Might as well ride home."

"I might start back afoot," I said. "It'd feel good to stretch my legs again."

"I'll keep a look out for you on my way back." And he rattled away in the ever present cloud of dust.

I had trouble managing the gate. It's one of those wire affairs that open by slipping a loop off the end post and lifting the bottom of it out of another loop. This one was taut and hard to handle. I just got it opened when Clyde turned the far corner and started back toward me, the plow behind the tractor curling up red-brown ribbons in its wake. It was the last go-round to complete the field.

I yelled, "Hi!" and waved a crutch at him.

He yelled, "Hi!" back at me. What came next was too fast and too far away for me to be sure what actually happened. All I remember was a snort and roar and the tractor bucked and bowed. There was a short yell from Clyde and the shriek of wires pulling loose from a fence post followed by a choking smothering silence.

Next thing I knew, I was panting halfway to the tractor, my crutches sinking exasperatingly into the soft plowed earth. A nightmare year later I knelt by the stalled tractor and called, "Hey, Clyde!"

Clyde looked up at me, a half grin, half grimace on his muddy face.

"Hi. Get this thing off me, will you. I need that leg." Then his eyes turned up white and he passed out.

The tractor had toppled him from the seat and then run over top of him, turning into the fence and coming to rest with one huge wheel half burying his leg in the soft dirt and pinning him against a fence post. The far wheel was on the edge of the irrigation ditch that bordered the field just beyond the fence. The huge bulk of the machine was balanced on the raw edge of nothing and it looked like a breath would send it on over—then God have mercy on Clyde. It didn't help much to notice that the red-brown dirt was steadily becoming redder around the imprisoned leg.

I knelt there paralyzed with panic. There was nothing I could do. I didn't dare to try to start the tractor. If I touched it, it might go over. Dad was gone for an hour. I couldn't make it by foot to the house in time.

Then all at once out of nowhere I heard a startled "Gee whiz!" and there was Thaddeus standing goggle-eyed on the ditch bank.

Something exploded with a flash of light inside my head and I whispered to myself, *Now take it easy. Don't scare the kid, don't startle him.*

"Gee whiz!" said Thaddeus again. "What happened?"

I took a deep breath. "Old Tractor ran over Uncle Clyde. Make it get off."

Thaddeus didn't seem to hear me. He was intent on taking in the whole shebang.

"Thaddeus," I said, "make Tractor get off."

Thaddeus looked at me with that blind, unseeing stare he used to have. I prayed silently, *Don't let him be too old. O God, don't let him be too old.* And Thaddeus jumped across the ditch. He climbed gingerly through the barb-wire fence and squatted down by the tractor, his hands caught between his chest and knees. He bent his head forward and I stared urgently at the soft vulnerable nape of his neck. Then he turned his blind eyes to me again.

"Tractor doesn't want to."

I felt a yell ball up in my throat, but I caught it in time. *Don't scare the kid,* I thought. *Don't scare him.*

"Make Tractor get off anyway," I said as matter-of-factly as I could manage. "He's hurting Uncle Clyde."

Thaddeus turned and looked at Clyde.

"He isn't hollering."

"He can't. He's unconscious." Sweat was making my palms slippery.

"Oh." Thaddeus examined Clyde's quiet face curiously. "I never saw anybody unconscious before."

"Thaddeus." My voice was sharp. "Make—Tractor—get —off."

Maybe I talked too loud. Maybe I used the wrong words, but Thaddeus looked up at me and I saw the shutters close in his eyes. They looked up at me, blue and shallow and bright.

"You mean start the tractor?" His voice was brisk as he stood up. "Gee whiz! Grampa told us kids to leave the tractor alone. It's dangerous for kids. I don't know whether I know how—"

"That's not what I meant," I snapped, my voice whetted on the edge of my despair. "Make it get off Uncle Clyde. He's dying."

"But I can't! You can't just make a tractor do something. You gotta run it." His face was twisting with approaching tears.

"You could if you wanted to," I argued, knowing how useless it was. "Uncle Clyde will die if you don't."

"But I can't! I don't know how! Honest I don't." Thaddeus scrubbed one bare foot in the plowed dirt, sniffing miserably.

I knelt beside Clyde and slipped my hand inside his dirt-smeared shirt. I pulled my hand out and rubbed the stained palm against my thigh. "Never mind," I said bluntly, "it doesn't matter now. He's dead."

Thaddeus started to bawl, not from grief but bewilderment. He knew I was put out with him and he didn't know why. He crooked his arm over his eyes and leaned against a fence post, sobbing noisily. I shifted myself over in the dark furrow until my shadow sheltered Clyde's quiet face from the hot afternoon sun. I clasped my hands palm to palm between my knees and waited for Dad.

I knew as well as anything that *once* Thaddeus could have helped. Why couldn't he then, when the need was so urgent? Well, maybe he really *had* outgrown his strangeness. Or it might be that he actually couldn't do anything just because Clyde and I were grownups. Maybe if it had been another kid—

Sometimes my mind gets cold trying to figure it out. Especially when I get the answer that kids and grownups live in two worlds so alien and separate that the gap can't be bridged even to save a life. Whatever the answer is— I still don't like kids.

WALK TO THE WORLD

by Algis Budrys

"Walk to the World" was written before I had ever sold any fiction. I think I was about 20, perhaps 19. In 1951, I was taking writing classes at Columbia University, and never submitted this piece, so I think it dates from 1950. It was written in Great Neck, Long Island, after a long, wandering walk on a foggy midnight, and I remember the walk well.

In those days of apprenticeship, my only method for producing a story was to sense a mood which told me I was about to produce a story. My conscious function then was to get away from all other thoughts; take my body someplace where no one would speak to it, and throw my consciousness in Neutral. After a suitable amount of time, my subconscious would give me back my body, for the sole first purpose of getting to my typewriter immediately and setting down the story without pause.

Some time around seven A.M. I discovered that I had written the last paragraph, which struck me as a totally unexpected and perfectly apt summation of the story. My shoulders ached and my eyes were gritty. My stomach was on the verge of outright nausea. Good preparation for the next sixteen hours, which would be spent working a double shift as a short-order cook. Voilà, the Muse!

Whenever it rained on week-ends, my father would stand in front of the big window in the living room and face the wheat fields as they danced and rippled. He would look at the wheat, and beyond it at the mountains, with the big ashtray slowly filling beside him. His feet would carry him in a sort of shuffling dance, back and forth, and his hips would swing as though he were walking down the long road that ran through the fields to the mountains, and over and through the mountains to the city.

Those were the two things everybody noticed about my father: the way he loved to walk, and the way he smoked. He would set himself on the road, a pack of cigarettes in both pockets of the faded TSN jumper with the frayed sleeves, and he would stride along with the swaying hill man's gait he had learned on Earth, until one pack of cigarettes was gone. Then he would turn around and come home.

I guess people wondered about him. During the week he would be working out in the fields like our neighbors, but even then he would stop the tractor on top of a rise, sometimes, and stand up with one leg thrown around the gear levers to steady him, and look at the road going out to the mountains. He would put one of the expensive Earthside cigarettes between his lips and light a match one-handed, touching it to the cigarette without looking. Then he would sit down in the saddle again, and the converter would go *Whee!* for a minute, until he remembered to put the motor in gear, and then the tractor would roll down the other side of the rise with the cultivator combing the earth behind it.

"John," he said to me once, when Mom was in the kitchen and we were sitting in the living room, "don't you ever wonder where the world is?"

"The world's right here, isn't it, Dad?" I said, wondering what he meant. "We're on it. It's the fourth planet from Wolf, and people have been on it for a hundred years."

He shook his head slowly, crossing his lean legs as he reached for a cigarette in his shirt pocket. "The world used to be here, son, when the first men came here, when the grass grew where the wheat grows now, when the wind rolled over this hill instead of splitting to go around the house. Before that, the world was on Centaurus, and before that—before Columbus—the world was America, and before that it was anywhere that wasn't plowed and tended."

He lit the cigarette and leaned back in the comfortable chair that surrounded him with foam and cloth. "But none of those places are the world now. They've become places like New York and Risley, New Jersey, and Leyport and Rogersville, Simbala and Kenton's Landing, and all of them are called Home. Home is a familiar place, son. Home is where the hearth is, Home is where you hang your hat. Home is where every wide space between the boards on the floor has a memory of a lost pin to be dug out, where every loose hinge on a door brings back the feel of a knob to be lifted before it can be turned. Home is where the cooking tastes just right." He stopped, and I could hear Mom washing the dishes.

"But when a place becomes Home, it stops being the world. Son, have you ever felt you'd like to go out and see the world?"

I thought about that for a minute. "You mean, the world is always somewhere else?"

"Something like that. The world is where the cracks in the floorboards are just places where dust gathers, places where the doors stick, where you have to put salt in your food, or put an extra piece of ice in your drink. You can see the world, John. You can ride the big ships, like I did, and find the world. You can see the new people, and hear the new voices. You can wear the strange clothes and live in the strange houses, and for a while you are seeing the world."

I remember the picture that hung from a nail in the attic, a picture of a young man in a black and silver uniform, proud in his black boots and lieutenant's stripes, with little crinkles at the corners of his eyes that were crows' feet now.

"And then, one day, you reach out in the dark for the light switch, and you find it without fumbling. You lift your feet so you won't trip over the place where the carpet has curled up at one edge," he went on. "Your friends come in from the big ships, looking for a good time, and you guide them to it. You tell them which drinks are the good drinks, and which prices are the right prices. When two people pass by in the street, murmuring exotic words, glamorous words, in the lilting, singing language of the strange world, and your friends ask you, eyes glittering with intrigue, what mystery they were discussing, you can tell them they were talking about the price of socks." My father sighed. "As soon after that as you can, you leave your new home, and you seek the world anew."

"You mean, you can see the world, but you can't live in it without its becoming Home."

"Not for very long, son."

My mother came out of the kitchen, drying her hands. "How's your homework coming along, Johnnie?" she asked. I wanted to stay and talk to my father about the world, but she looked at me as if she knew I hadn't even started my history term paper, so I went upstairs and began working on it.

On sunny week-ends, or even when it was just not raining, my father would get up very early in the morning and put on his jumper. He would eat breakfast alone in the kitchen, and then he would go to the cabinet where the cartons of cigarettes were kept, and fill his pockets. He would go out of the house, closing the door hard to wake me, and walk down the road. I sometimes went to the window and watched him. He would look straight ahead of him, ignoring the wheat, swinging his arms, a cigarette in one hand leaving jagged curves of smoke in the air beside him.

At supper time he would be back with dust on his shoes, his hair rumpled. He would hang up the jumper, wash his hands, and sit down to eat. Sometimes my mother would tease him, and he would grin and tease her back, but sometimes she was very quiet, and then he would be quiet too.

Once, when he was gone, my mother saw me standing in front of the window, smoking a cigarette, one of the local brands my father wouldn't touch. She came over to me and put an arm around me. "He likes to walk, doesn't he, Johnnie?" she said.

"He sure does," I answered, grinning.

"How about you, Johnnie? Do you like to walk, too?" For the first time I can remember, my mother's voice was anxious when she spoke to me.

"Shucks, Maw, I'm jest a little ol' country boy. Why should I want to go out and see the world?"

She shook her head. "You're Jack Gallery's son. Lieutenant John Gallery, Terrestrial Space Navy, Retired. And I retired him, Johnnie." She smiled, remembering.

"The first time I saw him, he was walking. He was striding up the path to the Port Director's office on Centaurus, his cap way back on his head, his heels hitting the ground hard, and he was coming off the ends of his toes, driving himself forward. His uniform was just a day too long unpressed, and the trim was cracked and blackened.

"I was looking out of the window, instead of transcribing a new set of directives like I should have been. I thought to myself, 'I wonder what's eating him!' The impatience trailed behind him and around him so thickly you could almost see it.

"In a few minutes, he was standing over my desk in the outer office.

" 'Would you tell the Port Director that Lieutenant Gallery of the *Anzio* would like to see him.'

" 'You're the captain of this vessel?'

" 'I am.'

" 'What do you wish to see the Port Director about?' I asked, although I knew the answer.

" 'I want to submit a written request for review of a Condition of Vessel report,' he answered, and took a manila envelope from under his arm. His big knuckles were red and white, and there was a smudge of grease under one eye that gave him a glowering look.

" 'Well, maybe I could give it to him,' I said. The *Anzio* had been red-lined the day before, and ordered to stand down until a new auxiliary drive could be fitted. Not even Jack Gallery could do anything about that.

"I guess he knew I was going to file his request and forget it, because he shook his head. 'I'll give it to him myself,' he said.

" 'Uh-huh. Look, Lieutenant, if you want to put yourself in a high sling, that's your business, and I'll tell the Director you're here, but I transcribed that order myself, and I know the decision's airtight. Nobody, and that includes Jack Gallery, is going to bust in on the Port Director of a very busy station and convince him otherwise.'

"I saw him start to simmer down, so I said very gently, 'And Lieutenant—there's grease on your face. I don't think he'd like that on top of your second best uniform.'

"So he never got to see the Port Director, but he did take me out often enough to give me an excuse to go to him almost every day when they brought him back to the Base Hospital a year later. He got the Medal of Honor for that wound of his, and the world it won for the Union.

"When he married me, he retired. He acted just like he did the time they red-lined his ship, but I finally convinced him.

"And that's the way your father is," my mother finished with a sigh. She squeezed my hand.

"So that's why you don't want me to take any long hikes," I said; I'd been wondering.

"I didn't say that, Johnnie, I never said that." Her deep eyes were turned away from me. Then she let go of my hand and walked quickly into the kitchen.

I stood at the window, looking past the wheat at the mountains, and far off, just at the big rise the road makes before it dips down into the valley below our house, I saw my father, the faded jumper black against the yellow dust, walking.

"I've taken you up to the mountaintop, John. Now I'm going to show you the world," my father said.

The road fell away from us, blacktopped now, and went into the city.

"That's Sky City," my father said, although he knew I knew that. "The road runs into Sky and becomes a street. The street leads to the spaceport."

I could see the flat white concrete plain on the other side of the buildings.

"The big ships leave the spaceport and go to the stars. Most of them go Home, but some of them go out to find a world." He stopped to light a cigarette. The wind pushed the jumper against his back and fluttered its open front. The match flared against his thumb, and he muttered, very softly, "Damn!"

"The ships go farther every day to find the world," my father continued, "for wherever men go, they build their houses and lay their streets, or they learn the strange languages, or they conquer the beings of these worlds, and the world becomes Home."

"So this road leads to the world," I said, watching a

ship, all black and gold, sunlit, threading its way into the sky.

"You can walk toward the mountains from our house," my father replied. "And stand here looking at Sky and the spaceport, and watch the ships going out. And that way, the road leads to the world." His eyes, too, were on the ship as it pushed through a cloud and broke out above it. "But, when you turn around, finally, and you see the road kinking through the wheat, then this road leads to Home." He coughed a little and threw the cigarette away. "Time to be getting back," he said.

We walked down the road, my father and I, his strides long and effortless, mine as long, but not as free and swinging. He had that walk from his father, he told me once, and I saw the old man, thin-bodied, in wash-bleached denims, crossing the pine-topped hills. That was the only way I pictured my grandfather, a picture of a man traveling over the top of the hills.

It wasn't long after that the purring, catlike car came over the mountains and to our house, bending the wheat away from the black and silver fenders. A uniformed man drove the car, and another man rode in the back, looking at the fields and the house. He was about as old as my father, with the same lines at the eyes, but he wore a vice-admiral's uniform on sagging shoulders and tightly over his stomach. My father met him and took him into the house while the driver cramped his car into a circle and went back over the mountains.

"Hello, Bill," my father said. He shook the admiral's hand warmly, but his eyes, warm too, had something strange in them. "What's brought you out here?"

"No hurry about that, Jack," the admiral said, and I thought his voice was too accustomed to giving orders, but I liked him nevertheless. "How's Marion? And your son? Lord, he's a man!" He shook my hand, and looked at my father. "He looks like you," he said, and I liked him even more, but still I was not sure if I always would.

My mother came into the room, and for a moment, when she saw the admiral, she hesitated at the threshold and looked at my father too rapidly for him to feel. But then she walked quickly across the room and took the admiral's hand. "Bill! How are you? And you used to swear they'd Summary Court you before you got too old to make snap decisions!"

"Luck, I guess, Marion. And how're you?"

"Oh, fine," she said, and then she asked the same question my father had, in her own way. "Don't tell me they're giving you a week-end in the country along with the simply fabulous pay you must be drawing."

"You might say I was combining business with pleasure," he answered. "This is a beautiful house you have."

"Built it ourselves," my father said, and I could see that he and my mother knew their old friend well enough not to press him.

That was the way they spent the afternoon. Father showed him the land, and mother cooked supper. The admiral looked at everything, admiring the crop, enthusiastically praising the swimming in the valley stream, chuckling over the antics of the pups in the yard. Mother kept rattling pots in the kitchen, opening cabinets, closing drawers, thumbing the recipe book, busily. As I watched her and helped set the table, I saw she was keeping herself far too busy, even with a supper guest.

"Mom," I said, "do you think Dad'll be taking an extra long walk?"

"Getting pretty smart, aren't you?" she said, looking up from a low cabinet. She straightened up, sighing. "He's getting pretty old for hiking, isn't he?"

"It's hard to say."

"It is, isn't it, Johnny? Very hard." She said it so that it meant what it actually said. She went busily back to the stove.

Supper was a quiet meal. Every time either my mother, my father, or the admiral would raise their heads, I could see the uncertain looks in their eyes. Finally it was over, and we went into the living room. The admiral sat down facing the three of us.

"Jack, Marion, I've known you both for a long time, and there's no sense beating around," he said. Both mother and father sat quietly in their chairs, but they were quiet in different ways. "We used to think, back on Centaurus, that nothing would ever stop Jack Gallery." He said it matter of factly, and I had never been so proud of my father before.

"Well, nothing ever did," he went on. "You could have stayed in the service, Jack. That wound wasn't anything big. When you retired, you were still the champ."

And now you need the champ again, I thought. Somewhere, something needs to be done.

I think my mother would have said something, but my father put out his hand and touched hers.

"What I'm going to tell you is a military secret, Jack. You'll be going back to school soon, Young Jack. Remember not to talk about it."

Nobody had ever called me that before.

"You know how we operate, Jack. The Union centers on Earth, and we send our ships in toward the center of the galaxy, fanning out so that we're gradually biting a chunk out of the galactic rim and making it ours." He leaned forward a bit. "Well, somebody else has the same idea."

"No!" my father exclaimed, and the look on his face was eagerness. "I used to tell you that'd happen someday." The admiral nodded. My mother looked at my father, but I don't understand how I could know that, because her face was in a shadow.

"They're a little farther in than we are, and their ships seem to be slower, or else they're not hustling like we are. Anyway, the damnedest thing happened. One of our ships grounded on a planet two days after they landed. Can you imagine that? Our ships buzzing around for months in that sector, and theirs doing the same thing, and not noticing each other?"

"Sounds like they've got an entirely different type of drive," my father said, "If that's true, then their whole concept of electronics must be different. Are they humanoid?"

"Human, or so close to it the difference isn't apparent. And about that drive—You always were a jump ahead of me, weren't you?—you're right, and about their science, too."

"Okay then, what's your problem? We've got all kinds of contact teams primed for just this situation," my father said.

"They won't talk to us."

"Hostile?"

"Hostile! They haven't even got sidearms on those ships. It's been something like a thousand years since they had a war, and that, from the little they tell us, was more of a ritualistic affair with fixed combat areas, umpires, and a predetermined armistice date."

"Are you kidding?"

"I wish I was. Anytime somebody makes a pass at them, they just go away and leave him alone. They figure space is plenty big enough for everybody." The admiral gripped the arms of his chair in frustration. "All of which is a fine and dandy way to live, but they're figuring to do just that to us. Turn around and go home."

"What on Earth for? Somebody accidentally fire something in their direction?"

"Not even that. Trouble is, their ships are privately operated. If one of them decides the grass is greener on the other side of the galaxy, he just packs and takes off with the wife and kids and anybody else that feels like tagging along. They go where they please, just drifting around until they find a likely looking world, and then they settle on it, if the natives don't mind. If there's room, he sends out a call for anybody else that's interested, they set up a trading colony, and after two or three hundred years the world's assimilated into their federation."

"Well, look, if this is just one tribe, or whatever, maybe their government's not as huffy as they are. Not that I see why they shouldn't be friendlier themselves. Maybe they just feel they can't speak for the whole federation," my father said, puzzled.

"With humans, you could say that, but not with these cookies. Each and every one of them's a member of their government. What they've got, actually, is a perfectly coordinated anarchy, if you can imagine such a thing. They've got some kind of instantaneous communication, and every one of them carries a personal transceiver. Yeah —powered for interstellar distances. Everybody knows what everybody else is doing, and the system works fine, for them." The admiral's jaws clamped together. "So naturally, being so lily pure and untrammeled, they refuse to have anything to do with anything as inherently aggressive as a military organization."

"Did you explain to them that our economic and social structure won't let it be handled any other way?"

"I did. They want to know what we want with all that territory, then. Am I supposed to explain the paradoxes of human motives to these holier-than-thous?"

I didn't have time to consider the paradoxes of military thinking, because I realized, finally, what the admiral wanted. So did my father, and my mother must have guessed long before.

"You want me to talk to them?" my father asked quietly. My mother didn't say anything.

"I'm not trying to say please, Jack. You're the man for the job. If Jack Gallery can't explain it, it can't be done. If we don't find *some* common ground, we'll lose them, and if we lose them, two thirds of our frontier is blocked off. We may not be little lambs of God, but we can't blast our way through them, and that's the only way they'll let us do it."

Oh, give yourself fifty years, admiral, I thought. Let fifty years of respect for the rights of another civilization hold you back. Let the pressure build up, and then see if you won't cut those peaceful strangers to ribbons. The world lies beyond them, admiral, and wherever men go, the places they reach become home, so that the world is always somewhere else, and must be reached.

"What happens if I say no?" my father asked, still in an even voice. There was a sound from my mother's chair, the sound people make when they start to speak and then think better of it.

"We find somebody else that isn't as good," the admiral said.

"There's no sense telling you I don't know there's a lot to hold you back," the admiral said, and I hated him. "Think it over and let me know tomorrow."

My father took his eyes from the mountains. "Sure, Bill. I'll let you know."

Tell him now, I thought. Why not, why waste the Admiral's time, why hold back human progress? Tell him you'll go out and look at this whole set of new worlds he's offering you on a silver platter. You'll do it tomorrow anyhow. But all that time I was shouting inside, I was hoping he wouldn't.

My mother got up from the chair. How does a woman get up, what is it she does, that tells everyone in sight that there is something special, something dramatic, in this arising? The admiral's eyes locked on her, and my father's, too.

She walked into the kitchen. I heard her open the cabinet, and when she came back the jumper was over her arm and the half-case of Earthside cigarettes was held out in front of her.

"Here," she said. My father got up, his face half surprised, but half grateful, too. They stood together, the cigarettes and the jumper on the floor between them, and they didn't speak.

The admiral got to his feet. "You don't have to be that quick about it, Marion," he said, but his voice was relieved.

"Shut up," my mother said. "You got in a jam and you reached back in the files and pulled out the right folder. Well, he's yours. But I don't think he'll perform the way you'd like him to. He'll solve it all for you, all right, but it won't be the way you and Jack Gallery solved things twenty years ago."

"Marion! Don't take that attitude. You're just upset," the admiral said. My mother looked at him, and he dropped his eyes. My father didn't say anything. He put on the jumper and took the cigarettes out to the porch. The admiral went outside when my father came back in to say goodbye.

My mother and I watched the growling car escape from our yard.

"He'll be back in a few months," I said.

"Yes, he'll be back," my mother answered me. "Ten years ago, I wouldn't have let him go. Ten years ago he was still like the admiral. He wanted to see the world."

Father had never told her about the search for the world, because she knew how he felt without needing words from him, but it surprised me to hear her using his exact phrase.

"The men of Earth go out," my mother said, "and they seek the world. The world must be new, unknown, an adventure, a thing to be discovered and conquered. But they come home, Johnnie, like he always came home from the mountains."

"But when you turn around, finally, this road leads to Home," my father had told me and I understood, at last, that sometimes you walk to the mountains and the world just for the sake of being able to turn around and come home.

"The admiral—did you notice how he talked, Johnnie? Either we push through them, or we stop dead. Remember?" my mother asked. "But Jack and I were thinking about the thing the admiral never considered." She put an arm around my waist and held me strongly. "We can join them, Johnnie. They aren't very different from us, for they search for the world too. And we will go out to their worlds, and they will come to ours, for the world is anywhere, John, where you haven't been."

I thought of my father, talking to the strangers. They would understand each other, I thought.

I kissed my mother, and looked at our home, which was warm and comfortable. How foolish, I thought, to go out to the world, if you will always come Home again.

"I'll never walk to the mountains, Mom," I said, struck by my revelation, but Mother looked at me with eyes wiser than mine.

BEYOND LIES THE WUB

by Philip K. Dick

The idea I wanted to get down on paper had to do with the definition of "human." The dramatic way I trapped the idea was to present ourselves, the literal humans, and then an alien life form that exhibits the deeper traits that I associate with humanity: not a biped with an enlarged cortex—a forked raddish that thinks, to paraphrase the old saying—but an organism that is human in terms of its soul.

I'm sorry if the word "soul" offends you, but I can think of no other term. Certainly, when I wrote the story "Beyond Lies the Wub" back in my youth in politically-active Berkeley, I myself would never have thought of the crucial ingredient in the wub as being a soul; I was a fireball radical and atheist, and religion was totally foreign to me. However, even in those days (I was about twenty-two years old) I was casting about in an effort to contrast the truly human from what I was later to call the "android or reflex machine" that looks human but is not—the subject of the speech I gave in Vancouver in 1972, twenty years after "Beyond Lies the Wub" was published. The germ of the idea behind the speech lies in this my first published story. It has to do with empathy, or, as it was called in earlier times, caritas or agape.

In this story, empathy (on the part of the wub, who looks like a big pig and has the feelings of a man) becomes an actual weapon for survival. Empathy is defined as the ability to put yourself in someone else's place. The wub does this even better than we ordinarily suppose could be done: its spiritual capacity is its literal salvation. The wub was my idea of a higher life form; it was then and it is now. On the other hand, Captain Franco (the name is deliberately based on General Franco of Spain, which is my concession in the story to political considerations) looks on other creatures in terms of sheer utility; they are objects to him, and he pays the ultimate price for this total failure of empathy. So I show empathy possessing a survival value; in terms of inter-species competition, empathy gives you the edge. Not a bad idea for a very early story by a very young person!

I liked the blurbs that Planet Stories printed for "Beyond Lies the Wub." On the title page of the magazine they wrote:

> Many men talk like philosophers and live like fools, proclaimed the slovenly wub, after death.

And ahead of the story proper they wrote:

> The slovenly wub might well have said: Many men talk like philosophers and live like fools.

Reader reaction to the story was excellent, and Jack O'Sullivan, editor of Planet, wrote to tell me that in his opinion it was a very fine little story—whereupon he paid me something like fifteen dollars. It was my introduction to pulp payment rates.

Just a week ago while going through my closet I came across an ancient pulp magazine with ragged edges, its cover missing, its pages yellow . . . wondering what it was I picked it up—and found that this ancient remnant, this artifact from another epoch, was indeed the July, 1952 issue of Planet Stories with my first published story in it. Profound emotions touched me as I gazed down at the illustration for "wub"; it is a superb little illo, done by Vestal, and under it is written, " 'The wub, sir,' Peterson said. 'It spoke!' " Well, here we are in the eighties, twenty-eight years later, and the gentle wub still speaks. May he always speak . . . and may other humans always listen.

*   *   *

They had almost finished with the loading. Outside stood the Optus, his arms folded, his face sunk in gloom. Captain Franco walked leisurely down the gangplank, grinning.

"What's the matter?" he said. "You're getting paid for all this."

The Optus said nothing. He turned away, collecting his robes. The Captain put his boot on the hem of the robe.

"Just a minute. Don't go off. I'm not finished."

"Oh?" The Optus turned with dignity. "I am going back to the village." He looked toward the animals and birds being driven up the gangplank into the spaceship. "I must organize new hunts."

Franco lit a cigarette. "Why not? You people can go out into the veldt and track it all down again. But when we run halfway between Mars and Earth—"

The Optus went off, wordless. Franco joined the first mate at the bottom of the gangplank.

"How's it coming?" he said. He looked at his watch. "We got a good bargain here."

The mate glanced at him sourly. "How do you explain that?"

"What's the matter with you? We need it more than they do."

"I'll see you later, Captain." The mate threaded his way up the plank, between the long-legged Martian gobirds, into the ship. Franco watched him disappear. He was just starting up after him, up the plank toward the port, when he saw *it*.

"My God!" He stood staring, his hands on his hips. Peterson was walking along the path, his face red, leading *it* by a string.

"I'm sorry, Captain," he said, tugging at the string. Franco walked toward him.

"What is it?"

The wub stood sagging, its great body settling slowly. It was sitting down, its eyes half shut. A few flies buzzed about its flank, and it switched its tail.

It sat. There was silence.

"It's a wub," Peterson said. "I got it from a native for fifty cents. He said it was a very unusual animal. Very respected."

"This?" Franco poked the great sloping side of the wub. "It's a pig! A huge dirty pig!"

"Yes, sir, it's a pig. The natives call it a wub."

"A huge pig. It must weigh four hundred pounds." Franco grabbed a tuft of the rough hair. The wub gasped. Its eyes opened, small and moist. Then its great mouth twitched.

A tear rolled down the wub's cheek and splashed on the ground.

"Maybe it's good to eat," Peterson said nervously.

"We'll soon find out," Franco said.

The wub survived the takeoff, sound asleep in the hold of the ship. When they were out in space and everything was running smoothly, Captain Franco bade his men fetch the wub upstairs so that he might perceive what manner of beast it was.

The wub grunted and wheezed, squeezing up the passageway.

"Come on," Jones grated, pulling at the rope. The wub twisted, rubbing its skin off on the smooth chrome walls. It burst into the anteroom, tumbling down in a heap. The men leaped up.

"Good Lord," French said. "What is it?"

"Peterson says it's a wub," Jones said. "It belongs to him." He kicked at the wub. The wub stood up unsteadily, panting.

"What's the matter with it?" French came over. "Is it going to be sick?"

They watched. The wub rolled its eyes mournfully. It gazed around at the men.

"I think it's thirsty," Peterson said. He went to get some water. French shook his head.

"No wonder we had so much trouble taking off. I had to reset all my ballast calculations."

Peterson came back with the water. The wub began to lap gratefully, splashing the men.

Captain Franco appeared at the door.

"Let's have a look at it." He advanced, squinting critically. "You got this for fifty cents?"

"Yes, sir," Peterson said. "It eats almost anything. I fed it on grain and it liked that. And then potatoes, and mash, and scraps from the table, and milk. It seems to enjoy eating. After it eats it lies down and goes to sleep."

"I see," Captain Franco said. "Now, as to its taste.

That's the real question. I doubt if there's much point in fattening it up any more. It seems fat enough to me already. Where's the cook? I want him here. I want to find out—"

The wub stopped lapping and looked up at the Captain.

"Really, Captain," the wub said. "I suggest we talk of other matters."

The room was silent.

"What was that?" Franco said. "Just now."

"The wub, sir," Peterson said. "It spoke."

They all looked at the wub.

"What did it say? What did it say?"

"It suggested we talk about other things."

Franco walked toward the wub. He went all around it, examining it from every side. Then he came back over and stood with the men.

"I wonder if there's a native inside it," he said thoughtfully. "Maybe we should open it up and have a look."

"Oh, goodness!" the wub cried. "Is that all you people can think of, killing and cutting?"

Franco clenched his fists. "Come out of there! Whoever you are, come out!"

Nothing stirred. The men stood together, their faces blank, staring at the wub. The wub swished its tail. It belched suddenly.

"I beg your pardon," the wub said.

"I don't think there's anyone in there," Jones said in a low voice. They all looked at each other.

The cook came in.

"You wanted me, Captain?" he said. "What's this thing?"

"This is a wub," Franco said. "It's to be eaten. Will you measure it and figure out—"

"I think we should have a talk," the wub said. "I'd like to discuss this with you, Captain, if I might. I can see that you and I do not agree on some basic issues."

The Captain took a long time to answer. The wub waited goodnaturedly, licking the water from its jowls.

"Come into my office," the Captain said at last. He turned and walked out of the room. The wub rose and padded after him. The men watched it go out. They heard it climbing the stairs.

"I wonder what the outcome will be," the cook said.

"Well, I'll be in the kitchen. Let me know as soon as you hear."

"Sure," Jones said. "Sure."

The wub eased itself down in the corner with a sigh. "You must forgive me," it said. "I'm afraid I'm addicted to various forms of relaxation. When one is as large as I—"

The Captain nodded impatiently. He sat down at his desk and folded his hands.

"All right," he said. "Let's get started. You're a wub? Is that correct?"

The wub shrugged. "I suppose so. That's what they call us, the natives, I mean. We have our own term."

"And you speak English? You've been in contact with Earthmen before?"

"No."

"Then how do you do it?"

"Speak English? Am I speaking English? I'm not conscious of speaking anything in particular. I examined your mind—"

"My mind?"

"I studied the contents, especially the semantic warehouse, as I refer to it—"

"I see," the Captain said. "Telepathy. Of course."

"We are a very old race," the wub said. "Very old and very ponderous. It is difficult for us to move around. You can appreciate that anything so slow and heavy would be at the mercy of more agile forms of life. There was no use in our relying on physical defenses. How could we win? Too heavy to run, too soft to fight, too good-natured to hunt for game—"

"How do you live?"

"Plants. Vegetables. We can eat almost anything. We're very catholic. Tolerant, eclectic, catholic. We live and let live. That's how we've gotten along."

The wub eyed the Captain.

"And that's why I so violently objected to this business about having me boiled. I could see the image in your mind—most of me in the frozen-food locker, some of me in the kettle, a bit for your pet cat—"

"So you read minds?" the Captain said. "How interesting. Anything else? I mean, what else can you do along those lines?"

"A few odds and ends," the wub said absently, staring around the room. "A nice apartment you have here, Captain. You keep it quite neat. I respect life forms that are tidy. Some Martian birds are quite tidy. They throw things out of their nests and sweep them—"

"Indeed." The Captain nodded. "But to get back to the problem—"

"Quite so. You spoke of dining on me. The taste, I am told, is good. A little fatty, but tender. But how can any lasting contact be established between your people and mine if you resort to such barbaric attitudes? Eat me? Rather you should discuss questions with me, philosophy, the arts—"

The Captain stood up. "Philosophy. It might interest you to know that we will be hard put to find something to eat for the next month. An unfortunate spoilage—"

"I know." The wub nodded. "But wouldn't it be more in accord with your principles of democracy if we all drew straws, or something along that line? After all, democracy is to protect the minority from such infringements. Now, if each of us casts one vote—"

The Captain walked to the door.

"Nuts to you," he said. He opened the door. He opened his mouth.

He stood frozen, his mouth wide, his eyes staring, his fingers still on the knob.

The wub watched him. Presently it padded out of the room, edging past the Captain. It went down the hall, deep in meditation.

The room was quiet.

"So you see," the wub said, "we have a common myth. Your mind contains many familiar myth symbols. Ishtar, Odysseus—"

Peterson sat silently, staring at the floor. He shifted in his chair.

"Go on," he said. "Please go on."

"I find in your Odysseus a figure common to the mythology of most self-conscious races. As I interpret it, Odysseus wanders as an individual aware of himself as such. This is the idea of separation, of separation from family and country. The process of individuation."

"But Odysseus returns to his home." Peterson looked

out the port window, at the stars, endless stars, burning intently in the empty universe. "Finally he goes home."

"As must all creatures. The moment of separation is a temporary period, a brief journey of the soul. It begins, it ends. The wanderer returns to land and race . . ."

The door opened. The wub stopped, turning its great head.

Captain Franco came into the room, the men behind him. They hesitated at the door.

"Are you all right?" French said.

"Do you mean me?" Peterson said, surprised. "Why me?"

Franco lowered his gun. "Come over here," he said to Peterson. "Get up and come here."

There was silence.

"Go ahead," the wub said. "It doesn't matter."

Peterson stood up. "What for?"

"It's an order."

Peterson walked to the door. French caught his arm. "What's going on?" Peterson wrenched loose. "What's the matter with you?"

Captain Franco moved toward the wub. The wub looked up from where it lay in the corner, pressed against the wall.

"It is interesting," the wub said, "that you are obsessed with the idea of eating me. I wonder why."

"Get up," Franco said.

"If you wish." The wub rose, grunting. "Be patient. It is difficult for me." It stood, gasping, its tongue lolling foolishly.

"Shoot it now," French said.

"For God's sake!" Peterson exclaimed. Jones turned to him quickly, his eyes gray with fear.

"You didn't see him—like a statue, standing there, his mouth open. If we hadn't come down, he'd still be there."

"Who? The Captain?" Peterson stared around. "But he's all right now."

They looked at the wub, standing in the middle of the room, its great chest rising and falling.

"Come on," Franco said. "Out of the way."

The men pulled aside toward the door.

"You are quite afraid, aren't you?" the wub said. "Have

I done anything to you? I am against the idea of hurting. All I have done is try to protect myself. Can you expect me to rush eagerly to my death? I am a sensible being like yourselves. I was curious to see your ship, learn about you. I suggested to the native—"

The gun jerked.

"See," Franco said. "I thought so."

The wub settled down, panting. It put its paw out, pulling its tail around it.

"It is very warm," the wub said. "I understand that we are close to the jets. Atomic power. You have done many wonderful things with it—technically. Apparently your scientific hierarchy is not equipped to solve moral, ethical—"

Franco turned to the men, crowding behind him, wide-eyed, silent.

"I'll do it. You can watch."

French nodded. "Try to hit the brain. It's no good for eating. Don't hit the chest. If the rib cage shatters, we'll have to pick bones out."

"Listen," Peterson said, licking his lips. "Has it done anything? What harm has it done? I'm asking you. And anyhow, it's still mine. You have no right to shoot it. It doesn't belong to you."

Franco raised his gun.

"I'm going out," Jones said, his face white and sick. "I don't want to see it."

"Me, too," French said. The men straggled out, murmuring. Peterson lingered at the door.

"It was talking to me about myths," he said. "It wouldn't hurt anyone."

He went outside.

Franco walked toward the wub. The wub looked up slowly. It swallowed.

"A very foolish thing," it said. "I am sorry that you want to do it. There was a parable that your Savior related—"

It stopped, staring at the gun.

"Can you look me in the eye and do it?" the wub said. "Can you do that?"

The Captain gazed down. "I can look you in the eye," he said. "Back on the farm we had hogs, dirty razorback hogs. I can do it."

Staring down at the wub, into the gleaming, moist eyes, he pressed the trigger.

The taste was excellent.

They sat glumly around the table, some of them hardly eating at all. The only one who seemed to be enjoying himself was Captain Franco.

"More?" he said, looking around. "More? And some wine, perhaps."

"Not me," French said. "I think I'll go back to the chart room."

"Me, too." Jones stood up, pushing his chair back. "I'll see you later."

The Captain watched them go. Some of the others excused themselves.

"What do you suppose the matter is?" the Captain said. He turned to Peterson. Peterson sat staring down at his plate, at the potatoes, the green peas, and at the thick slab of tender, warm meat.

He opened his mouth. No sound came.

The Captain put his hand on Peterson's shoulder.

"It is only organic matter, now," he said. "The life essence is gone." He ate, spooning up the gravy with some bread. "I, myself, love to eat. It is one of the greatest things that a living creature can enjoy. Eating, resting, meditation, discussing things."

Peterson nodded. Two more men got up and went out. The Captain drank some water and sighed.

"Well," he said. "I must say that this was a very enjoyable meal. All the reports I had heard were quite true—the taste of wub. Very fine. But I was prevented from enjoying this in times past."

He dabbed at his lips with his napkin and leaned back in his chair. Peterson stared dejectedly at the table.

The Captain watched him intently. He leaned over.

"Come, come," he said. "Cheer up! Let's discuss things."

He smiled.

"As I was saying before I was interrupted, the role of Odysseus in the myths—"

Peterson jerked up, staring.

"To go on," the Captain said. "Odysseus, as I understand him—"

MY BOY FRIEND'S NAME IS JELLO

by Avram Davidson

This harmless trifle does not require many words. Although it was my first Science Fiction or Fantasy story to be printed, it was neither the first written nor the first submitted. I don't remember what was, but the first one written which eventually sold was "The Montevarde Camera" (1943), rejected by Anthony Boucher for F&SF the first time around, c. 1950, and subsequently accepted by F&SF in c. 1960, seventeen years later (and after some rewriting suggested by Tony's successor, Robert P. Mills). Tony Boucher had rejected a few other stories before accepting this one, and several years later he accepted a couple of them. It was not, he said, that he now thought they were better, it was that better stories had gotten harder to get.

I don't recall when I first observed the resemblance of the designs chalked on sidewalks to Etruscan thunder (or whatever) charts, but I think it was in the late 1940s. And when I observed my then-little cousins, Judith and Miriam Greenwald, chanting the Boy Friend song, all seemed to fit into place. And I wrote the story. Boucher bought a story a year for a few years, this was during the SF Boom of the early 50s, but no one told me about the Boom, and if Tony didn't buy the stories I wrote I didn't send them elsewhere. By the time I learned of the Boom, it had busted. Story of my life.

Another version of The Song has Nello and Monticello instead of Jello and Cincinello. (Child's Ballads does not list either.) Eventually John Christopher wrote me from Guernsey that he had just heard it there, with the words and twenty black toes (*an image which made him, he said, shudder*): *it had taken 25 years to cross the Oceans, / And the wild waste of seas.* Sir Thomas Browne has asked, *Who knows what song the Sirens sang? Could this have been it?*

Fashion, nothing but fashion. Virus X having in the medical zodiac its course half i-run, the physician (I refuse to say "doctor" and, indeed, am tempted to use the more correct "apothecary")—the physician, I say, tells me I have Virus Y. No doubt in the Navy it would still be called Catarrhal Fever. They say that hardly anyone had appendicitis until Edward VII came down with it a few weeks before his coronation, and thus made it fashionable. He (the medical man) is dosing me with injections of some stuff that comes in vials. A few centuries ago he would have used herbal clysters. . . . Where did I read that old remedy for the quinsy ("putrescent sore throat," says my dictionary)? *Take seven weeds from seven meads and seven nails from seven steeds.* Oh dear, how my mind runs on. I must be feverish. An ague, no doubt.

Well, rather an ague than a pox. A pox is something one wishes on editors . . . strange breed, editors. The females all have names like Lulu Annabelle Smith or Minnie Lundquist Bloom, and the males have little horns growing out of their brows. They must all be Quakers, I suppose, for their letters invariably begin, "Dear Richard Roe" or "Dear John Doe," as if the word *mister* were a Vanity . . . when they write at all, that is; and meanwhile Goodwife Moos calls weekly for the rent. If I ever have a son (than which nothing is more unlikely) who shows the slightest inclination of becoming a writer, I shall instantly prentice him to a fishmonger or a Master Chimney Sweep. Don't write about Sex, the editors say, and don't write about Religion, or about History. If, however, you *do* write about History, be sure to add Religion and Sex. If one sends in a story about a celibate atheist, however, do you think they'll buy it?

In front of the house two little girls are playing one of those clap-handie games. Right hand, left hand, cross hands on bosom, left hand, right hand . . . it makes one dizzy to watch. And singing the while:

> My *boy* friend's *name* is *Je*llo,
> He *comes* from *Cin*cin*ello*,
> With a *pim*ple on his *nose*
> And *three* fat toes;
> And *that's* the *way* my *story* goes!

There is a pleasing surrealist quality to this which intrigues me. In general I find little girls enchanting. What a shame they grow up to be *big* girls and make our lives as miserable as we allow them, and oft-times more. Silly, nasty-minded critics, trying to make poor Dodgson a monster of abnormality, simply because he loved Alice and was capable of following her into Wonderland. I suppose they would have preferred him to have taken a country curacy and become another Pastor Quiverful. A perfectly normal and perfectly horrible existence, and one which would have left us all still on *this* side of the looking glass.

Whatever was in those vials doesn't seem to be helping me. I suppose old Dover's famous Powders hadn't the slightest fatal effect on the germs, bacteria, or virus (viri?), but at least they gave one a good old sweat (ipecac) and a mild, non-habit-forming jag (opium). But they're old-fashioned now, and so there we go again, round and round, one's train of thought like a Japanese waltzing mouse. I used to know a Japanese who—now, stop that. Distract yourself. Talk to the little girls. . . .

Well, that was a pleasant interlude. We discussed (quite gravely, for I never condescend to children) the inconveniences of being sick, the unpleasantness of the heat; we agreed that a good rain would cool things off. Then their attention began to falter, and I lay back again. Miss Thurl may be in soon. Mrs. Moos (perfect name, she lacks only the antlers) said, whilst bringing in the bowl of slops which the medicine man allows me for victuals, said, My Sister Is Coming Along Later And She's Going To Fix You Up Some Nice Flowers. Miss Thurl, I do believe, spends most of her time fixing flowers. Weekends she joins a con-fraternity of over-grown campfire girls and boys who go on hiking trips, comes back sunburned and sweating and carrying specimen samples of plant and lesser animal life.

However, I must say for Miss Thurl that she is quiet. Her brother-in-law, the bull-Moos, would be in here all the time if I suffered it. He puts stupid quotations in other people's mouths. He will talk about the weather and I will not utter a word, then he will say, Well, It's Like You Say, It's Not The Heat But The Humidity.

Thinking of which, I notice a drop in the heat, and I see it is raining. That should cool things off. How pleasant. A pity that it is washing away the marks of the little girls' last game. They played this one on the sidewalk, with chalked-out patterns and bits of stone and broken glass. They chanted and hopped back and forth across the chalk-marks and shoved the bits of stone and glass—or were they potshards—"potsie" from potshard, perhaps? I shall write a monograph, should I ever desire a Ph.D. I will compare the chalkmarks with Toltec emblems and masons' marks and the signs which Hindoo holy men smear on themselves with wood ashes and perfumed cow dung. All this passes for erudition.

I feel terrible, despite the cool rain. Perhaps without it, I should feel worse.

Miss Thurl was just here. A huge bowl of blossoms, arranged on the table across the room. Intricately arranged, I should say; but she put some extra touches to it, humming to herself. Something ever so faintly reminiscent about that tune, and vaguely disturbing. Then she made one of her rare remarks. She said that I needed a wife to take care of me. My blood ran cold. An icy sweat (to quote Catullus, that wretched Priapist), bedewed my limbs. I moaned. Miss Thurl at once departed, murmuring something about a cup of tea. If I weren't so weak I'd knot my bedsheets together and escape. But I am terribly feeble.

It's unmanly to weep. . . .

Back she came, literally poured the tea down my throat. A curious taste it had. Sassafrass? Bergamot? Mandrake root? It is impossible to say how old Miss Thurl is. She wears her hair parted in the center and looped back. Ageless . . . ageless . . .

I thank whatever gods may be that Mr. Ahyellow came in just then. The other boarder (upstairs), a greengrocer, decent fellow, a bit short-tempered. He wished me soon well. He complained he had his own troubles, foot troubles. . . . I scarcely listened, just chattered, hoping the

Thurl would get her hence. . . . Toes . . . something about his toes. Swollen, three of them, quite painful. A bell tinkled in my brain. I asked him how he spelt his name. A-j-e-l-l-o. Curious, I never thought of that. Now, I wonder what he could have done to offend the little girls? Chased them from in front of his store, perhaps. There is a distinct reddish spot on his nose. By tomorrow he will have an American Beauty of a pimple.

Fortunately he and Miss Thurl went out together. I must think this through. I must remain cool. Aroint thee, thou mist of fever. This much is obvious: There are sorcerers about. Sorceresses, I mean. The little ones made rain. And they laid a minor curse on poor Ajello. The elder one has struck me in the very vitals, however. If I had a cow it would doubtless be dry by this time. Should I struggle? Should I submit? Who knows what lies behind those moss-colored eyes, what thoughts inside the skull covered by those heavy tresses? Life with Mr. and Mr. Moos is—even by itself—too frightful to contemplate. Why doesn't she lay her traps for Ajello? Why should I be selected as the milk-white victim for the Hymeneal sacrifice? Useless to question. Few men have escaped once the female cast the runes upon them. And the allopath has nothing in his little black bag, either, which can cure.

Blessed association of words! Allopath—Homeopath—homoios, the like, the same, pathos, feeling, suffering—similia similibus curantur—

The little girls are playing beneath my window once more, clapping hands and singing. Something about a boy friend named Tony, who eats macaroni, has a great big knife and a pretty little wife, and will always lead a happy life . . . that must be the butcher opposite; he's always kind to the children. . . . Strength, strength! The work of a moment to get two coins from my wallet and throw them down. What little girl could resist picking up a dime which fell in front of her? "Cross my palm with silver, pretty gentleman!"—eh? And now to tell them my tale . . .

I feel better already. I don't think I'll see Miss Thurl again for a while. She opened the door, the front door, and when the children had sung the new verse she slammed the door shut quite viciously.

It's too bad about Ajello, but every man for himself.

Listen to them singing away, bless their little hearts! I love little girls. Such sweet, innocent voices.

> My *boy* friend will *soon* be *heal*thy.
> He *shall* be *very* *weal*thy.
> No *wo*man shall *har*ry
> Or *seek* to *mar*ry;
> *Two* and two is *four*, and *one* to *carry!*

It will be pleasant to be wealthy, I hope. I must ask Ajello where Cincinello is.

T

by Brian W. Aldiss

My experience may not be particularly uncommon. When one begins to write, one is not clear exactly what one writes about. The anecdote's the thing. But there are significant reasons why one tells one kind of story, laughs at one kind of joke, in preference to another.

You become aware with practice that there are only a few themes to which you respond with your best—because most deeply felt—endeavors. As it happens, I began writing in the target area where I operate most tellingly, about a living creature being cruelly mistreated, so that its nature is wrenched out of true. In the background runs a parallel theme, the richness of life cheek-by-jowl with an ever-present sterility. Does T suffer, and will a whole planet live or die?

So I was delighted when "T" was accepted for publication. It was my first story to be taken by a science fiction magazine, in this case Nebula, *edited by Peter Hamilton. Nothing is more maddening than when, thirsty for glory, you have to sit and wait for your little masterpiece to appear in print, and the world to change in consequence. I had to wait for three years. Never was debut so delayed.*

By that time, another magazine had taken another story (not so good a story, to my mind) and it was published in Science Fantasy *some months before "T" came out. By then, the world had changed. (How it changed! I recklessly threw up my job, ruined my marriage, lost my children, and sold up my house. If I was going to be a writer, I was going to act like one. . . .)*

I have said that "T" illustrates a theme on which I feel deeply. The obvious now occurs to me, that the story is a preliminary skirmish for my first sf novel, Non-Stop, *which was published in the U.S.A. by a man who, because he cared one hundred percent less about my novel than I did, arbitrarily re-christened it* Starship. *In* Non-Stop *also one finds beings imprisoned in an interstellar ship, traveling to destinations unknown to the crew. Oh well, it's a metaphor for life, I suppose. Just as life itself must be a metaphor for something or other.*

According to my file card, "T" was written in January 1953. What were you doing in January 1953, dear reader? Were you born? I was living on small wages and a lot of hope. The world has changed again, and greatly, since then. I can't say I have.

By the time T was ten years old, his machine was already on the fringes of his galaxy. T was not his name—the laboratory never considered christening him—but it was the symbol on the hull of his machine and it will suffice for a name. And again, it was not his machine; rather, he belonged to it. He could not claim the honorable role of pilot, nor even the humbler one of passenger; he was a chattel whose seconds of utility lay two hundred years ahead.

He waited like a maggot in an apple at the center of the machine as it fled through space and time. He never moved; the impulse to move did not present itself to him, nor would he have been able to obey if it had. T had been created legless—his single limb was an arm, and the machine hemmed him in on all sides.

The machine nourished him by means of pipes which fed a thin stream of vitamins and proteins into his body. It circulated his blood by a tiny motor that throbbed in the starboard bulkhead like a heart. It removed his waste products by a steady syphoning process. It produced his supply of oxygen. It regulated T so that he neither grew nor wasted. It saw that he would be alive in two hundred years.

T had one reciprocal duty. His ears were filled perpetually with an even droning note, and before his lidless eyes there was a screen on which a red band traveled forever down a fixed green line. The drone represented (although not to T) a direction through space, while the red band indicated (although not to T) a direction in time. Occasionally, perhaps only once a decade, the drone changed pitch or the band faltered from its green line. These variations registered in T's consciousness as acute discomforts, and accordingly he would adjust one of the two small wheels by his hand, until conditions returned to normal and the even tenor of monotony was resumed.

Although T was aware of his own life, loneliness was one of the innumerable concepts that his creators had arranged he should never sense. He lay passive, in an artificial contentment. His time was divided not by night or day, or by waking or sleeping, or by feeding periods, but by silence or speaking. Part of the machine spoke to him at intervals, giving him short monologues on duty and reward, and instructions as to the working of a simple apparatus that would be required two centuries ahead. The speaker presented T with a carefully distorted picture of his environs. It made no reference to the inter-galactic night outside, nor to the fast backward seepage of time. The idea of motion was not a factor with which to trouble an entombed thing like T. But it did refer to the Koax, and in reverent terms, speaking also—but in words filled with loathing—of that inevitable enemy of the Koax, Man. The machine informed T that he would be responsible for the complete destruction of Man.

Although T was utterly alone, the machine which carried him had company on its flight. Eleven other identical machines—each occupied by beings similar to T—bored through the continuum. This continuum was empty and lightless and stood in the same relationship to the universe proper as a fold on a silk dress stands to the dress: when the sides of the fold touch, a funnel is formed by the surface of the material inside the surface of the dress. Or you may liken it to the negativity of the square root of minus two, which has a positive value. It was a vacuum inside a vacuum. The machines were undetectable, piercing the dark like light itself and sinking through the hovering millenia like stones.

The twelve machines were built for an emergency by a non-human race so ancient that they had abandoned the construction of other machinery aeons ago. They had progressed beyond the need of material assistance—beyond the need of corporal bodies—beyond the need at last of planets with which to associate their tenuous egos. They had come finally, in their splendid maturity, to call themselves only by the name of their galaxy, Koax. In that safe island of several million stars, they moved and had their being, and brooded over the coming end of the universe.

While they brooded, another race grew to seniority in a galaxy far beyond the meaning of distance. The new race, unlike the Koax, was extravert and warlike; it tumbled out among the stars like an explosion, and its name was Man. There came a time when this race, spreading from one infinitesimal planetary body, had multiplied, and filled its own galaxy. For a while it paused as if to catch its breath —the jump between the stars is nothing to the gulf between the great star cities—and then the time/space equations were formulated: Man strode to the nearest galaxy armed with the greatest of all weapons, Stasis. The temporal mass/energy relationship that regulates the functioning of the universe, they found, might be upset in certain of the more sparsely starred galaxies by impeding their orbital revolution, causing, virtually, a fixation of the temporal factor—Stasis—whereby everything affected ceases to continue along the universal timeflow and ceases thereupon to exist. But Man had no need to use this devastating weapon; as on its bi-product, the Stasis drive, he swept from one galaxy to another, he found no rival, nor any ally. He seemed destined to be sole occupant of the universe. The innumerable planets revealed only that life was an accident. And then the Koax were reached.

The Koax were aware of Man before he knew of their existence, and their immaterial substance cringed to think that soon it would be torn through by the thundering drives of the Supreme Fleet.

They acted quickly. Materializing onto a black dwarf, a group of their finest minds prepared to combat the invader with every power possible. They had some useful abilities, of which being able to alter the course of suns was not the least. And so nova after nova flared into the middle of the Supreme Fleet. But Man came invincibly on, driving into the Koax like a cataclysm. From a small frightened tribe a few hundred strong, roaming a hostile earth, he had swelled into an unquenchable multitude, ruling the stars. As the Koax wiped out more and more ships, it was decided that their home must be eliminated by Stasis, and ponderous preparations were begun. The forces of Man gathered themselves for a massive final blow.

Unfortunately, a Fleet Library Ship was captured intact by the Koax, and from it something of the long tangled history of Man was discovered. There was even a plan of the Solar System as it had been when Man first knew it. The Koax heard for the first time of Sol and its attendants. Sol at this period, far across the universe, was a faintly radiating smudge with a diameter twice the size of the planetary system that had long ago girdled it. As it had expanded into old age, the planets had one by one been swallowed into its bulk; now even Pluto was gone to feed the dying fires.

The Koax finally developed a plan that would rid them entirely of their foes. Since they were unable to cope in the present with the inexhaustible resources of Man, they evolved in their devious fashion a method of dealing with him in the far past, when he wasn't even there. They built a dozen machines that would slip through time and space and annihilate Earth before Man appeared upon it; the missiles would strike, it was determined, during the Silurian age and reduce the planet to its component atoms. So T was born.

"We will have them," one of the greatest Koax announced in triumph when the matter was thrashed out. "Unless these ancient Earth records lie, and there is no reason why they should do, Sol originally supported nine planets, before its degenerate stage set in. Working inwards, in the logical order, these were—I have the names here, thanks to Man's sentimentality—Pluto, Neptune, Uranus, Saturn, Jupiter, Mars, Earth, Venus and Mercury. Earth, you see, is the seventh planet in, or the third that was drawn into Sol in its decline. That is our target gentlemen, a speck remote in time and space. See that your calculations are accurate—that seventh planet *must* be destroyed."

There was no error. The seventh planet was destroyed. Man never had any chance of detecting and blasting T and his eleven dark companions, for he had never discovered the alien continuum in which they traveled.

The faint possibility of interception varied inversely with the distance the machines covered, for as they neared Man's first galaxy, time was rolled back to when he had first spiraled tentatively up to the Milky Way. The machines bore in and back. It was growing early.

The Koax by now was a young race without the secret of deep space travel, dwindling away across the other side of the universe. Man himself had only a few old-type fluid fuel ships patrolling half a hundred systems. T still lay in his fixed position, waiting, waiting. His two centuries of existence—the long wait—were almost ended. Somewhere in his cold brain was a knowledge that the climax lay close now.

Not all of his few companions were as fortunate, for the machines, perfect when they set out, developed flaws over the long journey (the two hundred years of travel represented a distance in space/time of some ninety-five hundred million light years). The Koax were natural mathematical philosophers, but they had long ago given up being mechanics—otherwise they would have devised relay systems to manage the job that T had to do. The nutrition feed in one machine slowly developed an increasing rate of supply, and the being died not so much from overeating as from growing pains—which were very painful indeed as he swelled against a steel bulkhead and finally sealed off the air vents with his own bulging flesh. In another machine, a transistor failed, shorting the temporal drive; it broke through into real space and buried itself in an M-type variable sun. In a third, the guide system came adrift and the missile hurtled on at an increasing acceleration until it burned itself out and fried its occupant. In a fourth, the occupant went quietly and unpredictably mad, and pulled a little lever that was not then due to be pulled for another hundred years. His machine erupted into fiery radioactive particles and destroyed two other machines.

When the Solar System was only a few light years away, the remaining machines switched off their main drive and appeared in normal space/time. Only three of them had completed the journey, T and two others.

They found themselves in a galaxy now devoid of life. Only the great stars shone on their new planets, fresh, comparatively speaking, from the womb of creation. Man had long before sunk back into the primaeval mud, and the suns and planets were nameless again. Over Earth, the mists of the early Silurian age hovered, and in the shallows of its waters molluscs and trilobites were the main expression of life. The placid seas of Mars were also alive with half-sentient things.

Meanwhile, T concentrated on the seventh planet. He had performed the few simple movements necessary to switch his machine back into the normal universe; now all that was left for him to do was to watch a small pressure dial. When the machine entered the atmospheric fringes of the seventh planet, the tiny hand on the pressure dial would begin to climb. When it reached a clearly indicated line on the dial, T would turn a small wheel (this would release the dampers—but T needed to know the How, not the Why). Then two more gauges would begin to register. When they both attained the same reading, T had to pull down the little lever. The speaker had explained all this to him regularly. What it did not explain was what happened after the lever was down, but T knew very well that then Man would be destroyed, and that that would be good.

The seventh planet swung into position ahead of the blunt bows of T's machine, and grew in apparent magnitude. It was a young world, with a future about to be wiped forever off the slate of probability. As T entered its atmosphere, the hand began to climb the pressure dial. For the first time in his existence, something like excitement stirred in the fluid of T's brain. He neither saw nor cared for the panorama spreading below him, for the machine had not been constructed with ports. The dim instrument dials were all his eyes had ever rested on. He behaved exactly as the Koax had intended. When the hand reached top, he turned the damper wheel, and his other two gauges started to creep. By now he was plunging down through the stratosphere of the seventh planet. The load was planned to explode before impact, for as the Koax had no details about the planet's composition they had made certain that it went off before the machine struck and T was killed. The safety factor had been well devised. T pulled his last little lever twenty miles up. In the holocaust that immediately followed, he went out in a sullen joy.

T was highly successful. The seventh planet was utterly obliterated.

The other two machines did less brilliantly. One missed the Solar System entirely and went on into the depths of space, a speck with a patiently dying burden. The other was much nearer target. It swung in close to T and hit the sixth planet. Unfortunately, it detonated too high, and that planet, instead of being obliterated, was pounded into chunks of rock that took up erratic orbits between the orbits of the massive fifth planet and the eighth, which was a small body encircled by two tiny moons. The ninth planet, of course, was quite unharmed, it rolled serenely on, accompanied by its pale satellite and carrying its load of elementary life forms.

The Koax achieved what they had set out to do. They had calculated for the seventh planet and hit it, annihilating it utterly. But that success, of course, was already recorded on the only chart they had to go by, as they should have realized. So while the sixth was accidentally shattered, the seventh disappeared—Pluto, Neptune, Uranus, Saturn, Jupiter, the Asteroid planet, T's planet, Mars, Earth, Venus, Mercury—the seventh disappeared without trace.

On the ninth planet, the molluscs moved gently in the bright, filtering sunlight.

PRIMA BELLADONNA

by J. G. Ballard

Prima Belladonna is not only the first short story I wrote, but in many ways the best. The idea that I reached my peak with my first published story, and then went into a long decline, has a certain appeal to my sense of irony, and in a sense tallies exactly with the spirit of this story and the others collected under the title "Vermilion Sands." For the chief characteristic of this desert resort, not abandoned but forever out of season, is that everything is over. Its past lies behind it, and nothing that can happen in the future will substantially change it again. It has come to terms with its past, and now lies there on its deck-chair beside a drained swimming-pool, somewhere in the middle of this endless afternoon. It's against this background that chimeras stir, fancies take flight.

I always felt very much at home in Vermilion Sands, and over the past twenty-five years have made a number of return trips to it. In fact, if I had to make a guess I would say that Vermilion Sands is what the future will be like, a place where work will be the ultimate play, and play the ultimate work. It's a place where nothing happens but everything is possible, and where the contents of the psyche pass freely through the barrier of the skull and take up residence at the bottom of the garden, to be cared for in that off-hand way in which the hero of "Prima Belladonna" cares for his singing flowers. And of course, nothing is so likely to attract the attention of the nearest off-duty witch than a well-stocked psychic garden.

Where is Vermilion Sands? Somewhere, I suppose be-

*tween Palm Springs, Juan Les Pins, and Ipanema Beach.
Vermilion Sands is very much a beach resort, but needless
to say there is no sea. The beach extends continuously, in
all directions, merging with the beaches of its neighboring
resorts, extensions of the afternoon minds of its inhabitants.*

*I look forward more and more to going back to Ver-
milion Sands, and this time staying forever.*

I first met Jane Ciracylides during the Recess, that world
slump of boredom, lethargy, and high summer which carried us all so blissfully through ten unforgettable years, and
I suppose that may have had a lot to do with what went
on between us. Certainly I can't believe I could make myself as ridiculous now, but then again, it might have been
just Jane herself.

Whatever else they said about her, everyone had to
agree she was a beautiful girl, even if her genetic background was a little mixed. The gossips at Vermilion Sands
soon decided there was a good deal of mutant in her, because she had a rich patina-golden skin and what looked
like insects for eyes, but that didn't bother either myself or
any of my friends, one or two of whom, like Tony Miles
and Harry Devine, have never since been quite the same
to their wives.

We spent most of our time in those days on the balcony
of my apartment off Beach Drive, drinking beer—we always kept a useful supply stacked in the refrigerator of
my music shop on the street level—yarning in a desultory
way and playing i-Go, a sort of decelerated chess which
was popular then. None of the others ever did any work;
Harry was an architect and Tony Miles sometimes sold a
few ceramics to the tourists, but I usually put a couple of
hours in at the shop each morning, getting off the foreign
orders and turning the beer.

One particularly hot lazy day I'd just finished wrapping
up a delicate soprano mimosa wanted by the Hamburg
Oratorio Society when Harry phoned down from the balcony.

"Parker's Choro-Flora?" he said. "You're guilty of overproduction. Come up here. Tony and I have something beautiful to show you."

When I went up I found them grinning happily like two dogs who had just discovered an interesting tree.

"Well?" I asked. "Where is it?"

Tony tilted his head slightly. "Over there."

I looked up and down the street, and across the face of the apartment house opposite.

"Careful," he warned me. "Don't gape at her."

I slid into one of the wicker chairs and craned my head around cautiously.

"Fourth floor," Harry elaborated slowly, out of the side of his mouth. "One left from the balcony opposite. Happy now?"

"Dreaming," I told him, taking a long slow focus on her. "I wonder what else she can do?"

Harry and Tony sighed thankfully. "Well?" Tony asked.

"She's out of my league," I said. "But you two shouldn't have any trouble. Go over and tell her how much she needs you."

Harry groaned. "Don't you realize, this one is poetic, emergent, something straight out of the primal apocalyptic sea. She's probably divine."

The woman was strolling around the lounge, rearranging the furniture, wearing almost nothing except a large metallic hat. Even in shadow the sinuous lines of her thighs and shoulders gleamed gold and burning. She was a walking galaxy of light. Vermilion Sands had never seen anything like her.

"The approach has got to be equivocal," Harry continued, gazing into his beer. "Shy, almost mystical. Nothing urgent or grabbing."

The woman stooped down to unpack a suitcase and the metal vanes of her hat fluttered over her face. She saw us staring at her, looked around for a moment and lowered the blinds.

We sat back and looked thoughtfully at each other, like three triumvirs deciding how to divide an empire, not saying too much, and one eye watching for any chance of a double-deal.

Five minutes later the singing started.

At first I thought it was one of the azalea trios in trouble with an alkaline pH, but the frequencies were too high.

They were almost out of the audible range, a thin tremolo quaver which came out of nowhere and rose up the back of the skull.

Harry and Tony frowned at me.

"Your livestock's unhappy about something," Tony told me. "Can you quieten it down?"

"It's not the plants," I told him. "Can't be."

The sound mounted in intensity, scraping the edges off my occipital bones. I was about to go down to the shop when Harry and Tony leapt out of their chairs and dived back against the wall.

"Steve, look out!" Tony yelled at me. He pointed wildly at the table I was leaning on, picked up a chair and smashed it down on the glass top.

I stood up and brushed the fragments out of my hair. "What the hell's the matter?"

Tony was looking down at the tangle of wickerwork tied around the metal struts of the table. Harry came forward and took my arm gingerly.

"That was close. You all right?"

"It's gone," Tony said flatly. He looked carefully over the balcony floor and down over the rail into the street. "What was it?" I asked.

Harry peered at me closely. "Didn't you see it? It was about three inches from you. Emperor scorpion, big as a lobster." He sat down weakly on a beer crate. "Must have been a sonic one. The noise has gone now."

After they'd left I cleared up the mess and had a quiet beer to myself. I could have sworn nothing had got on to the table.

On the balcony opposite, wearing a gown of ionized fiber, the golden woman was watching me.

I found out who she was the next morning. Tony and Harry were down at the beach with their wives, probably enlarging on the scorpion, and I was in the shop tuning up a Khan-Arachnid orchid with the UV lamp. It was a difficult bloom, with a normal full range of twenty-four octaves, but unless it got a lot of exercise it tended to relapse into neurotic minor-key transpositions which were the devil to break. And as the senior bloom in the shop it naturally affected all the others. Invariably when I opened the shop in the mornings, it sounded like a madhouse, but as soon

as I'd fed the Arachnid and straightened out one or two
pH gradients the rest promptly took their cues from it
and dimmed down quietly in their control tanks, two-time,
three-four, the multi-tones, all in perfect harmony.

There were only about a dozen true Arachnids in cap-
tivity; most of the others were either mutes or grafts from
dicot stems, and I was lucky to have mine at all. I'd bought
the place five years earlier from an old half-deaf man
called Sayers, and the day before he left he moved a lot
of rogue stock out to the garbage disposal scoop behind the
apartment block. Reclaiming some of the tanks I'd come
across the Arachnid, thriving on a diet of algae and perished rubber tubing.

Why Sayers had wanted to throw it away I had never
discovered. Before he came to Vermilion Sands he'd been
a curator at the Kew Conservatoire where the first choro-
flora had been bred, and had worked under the Director,
Dr. Mandel. As a young botanist of twenty-five Mandel
had discovered the prime Arachnid in the Guiana forest.
The orchid took its name from the Khan-Arachnid spider
which pollinated the flower, simultaneously laying its own
eggs in the fleshy ovule, guided, or as Mandel always
insisted, actually mesmerized to it by the vibrations which
the orchid's calyx emitted at pollination time. The first
Arachnid orchids beamed out only a few random frequencies, but by cross-breeding and maintaining them
artificially at the pollination stage Mandel had produced a
strain that spanned a maximum of twenty-four octaves.

Not that he had ever been able to hear them. At the
climax of his life's work Mandel, like Beethoven, was stone
deaf, but apparently by merely looking at a blossom he
could listen to its music. Strangely though, after he went
deaf he never looked at an Arachnid.

That morning I could almost understand why. The
orchid was in a vicious mood. First it refused to feed, and
I had to coax it along in a fluoraldehyde flush, and then it
started going ultra-sonic, which meant complaints from
all the dog owners in the area. Finally it tried to fracture
the tank by resonating.

The whole place was in uproar, and I was almost re-
signed to shutting them down and waking them all by hand
individually—a backbreaking job with eighty tanks in the
shop—when everything suddenly died away to a murmur.

I looked round and saw the golden-skinned woman walk in.

"Good morning," I said. "They must like you."

She laughed pleasantly. "Hello. Weren't they behaving?"

Under the black beachrobe her skin was a softer, more mellow gold, and it was her eyes that held me. I could just see them under the wide-brimmed hat. Insect legs wavered delicately around two points of purple light.

She walked over to a bank of mixed ferns and stood looking at them. The ferns reached out toward her and trebled eagerly in their liquid fluted voices.

"Aren't they sweet?" she said, stroking the fronds gently. "They need so much affection."

Her voice was low in the register, a breath of cool sand pouring, with a lilt that gave it music.

"I've just come to Vermilion Sands," she said, "and my apartment seems awfully quiet. Perhaps if I had a flower, one would be enough, I shouldn't feel so lonely."

I couldn't take my eyes off her.

"Yes," I agreed, brisk and businesslike. "What about something colorful? This Sumatra Samphire, say? It's a pedigree mezzo-soprano from the same follicle as the Bayreuth Festival Prima Belladonna."

"No," she said. "It looks rather cruel."

"Or this Louisiana Lute Lily? If you thin out its SO_2 it'll play some beautiful madrigals. I'll show you how to do it."

She wasn't listening to me. Slowly, her hands raised in front of her breasts so that she almost seemed to be praying, she moved toward the display counter on which the Arachnid stood.

"How beautiful it is," she said, gazing at the rich yellow and purple leaves hanging from the scarlet-ribbed vibro-calyx.

I followed her across the floor and switched on the Arachnid's audio so that she could hear it. Immediately the plant came to life. The leaves stiffened and filled with colour and the calyx inflated, its ribs sprung tautly. A few sharp disconnected notes spat out.

"Beautiful, but evil," I said.

"Evil?" she repeated. "No, proud." She stepped closer to the orchid and looked down into its malevolent head.

The Arachnid quivered and the spines on its stem arched and flexed menacingly.

"Careful," I warned her. "It's sensitive to the faintest respiratory sounds."

"Quiet," she said, waving me back. "I think it wants to sing."

"Those are only key fragments," I told her. "It doesn't perform. I use it as a frequency—"

"Listen!" She held my arm and squeezed it tightly.

A low, rhythmic fusion of melody had been coming from the plants around the shop, and mounting above them I heard a single stronger voice calling out, at first a thin high-pitched reed of sound that began to pulse and deepen and finally swelled into full baritone, raising the other plants in chorus about itself.

I had never heard the Arachnid sing before. I was listening to it open-eared when I felt a glow of heat burn against my arm. I turned and saw the woman staring intently at the plant, her skin aflame, the insects in her eyes writhing insanely. The Arachnid stretched out toward her, calyx erect, leaves like blood-red sabres.

I stepped around her quickly and switched off the argon feed. The Arachnid sank to a whimper, and around us there was a nightmarish babel of broken notes and voices toppling from high C's and L's into discord. A faint whispering of leaves moved over the silence.

The woman gripped the edge of the tank and gathered herself. Her skin dimmed and the insects in her eyes slowed to a delicate wavering.

"Why did you turn it off?" she asked heavily.

"I'm sorry," I said. "But I've got ten thousand dollars' worth of stock here and that sort of twelve-tone emotional storm can blow a lot of valves. Most of these plants aren't equipped for grand opera."

She watched the Arachnid as the gas drained out of its calyx. One by one its leaves buckled and lost their color.

"How much is it?" she asked me, opening her bag.

"It's not for sale," I said. "Frankly I've no idea how it picked up those bars—"

"Will a thousand dollars be enough?" she asked, her eyes fixed on me steadily.

"I can't," I told her. "I'd never be able to tune the others without it. Anyway," I added, trying to smile, "that Arachnid would be dead in ten minutes if you took it out of its vivarium. All these cylinders and leads would look a little odd inside your lounge."

"Yes, of course," she agreed, suddenly smiling back at me. "I was stupid." She gave the orchid a last backward glance and strolled away across the floor to the long Tchaikovsky section popular with the tourists.

"*Pathétique*," she read off a label at random. "I'll take this."

I wrapped up the scabia and slipped the instructional booklet into the crate, keeping my eye on her all the time.

"Don't look so alarmed," she said with amusement. "I've never heard anything like that before."

I wasn't alarmed. It was that thirty years at Vermilion Sands had narrowed my horizons.

"How long are you staying at Vermilion Sands?" I asked her.

"I open at the Casino tonight," she said. She told me her name was Jane Ciracylides and that she was a speciality singer.

"Why don't you look in?" she asked, her eyes fluttering mischievously. "I come on at eleven. You may find it interesting."

I did. The next morning Vermilion Sands hummed. Jane created a sensation. After her performance three hundred people swore they'd seen everything from a choir of angels taking the vocal in the music of the spheres to Alexander's Ragtime Band. As for myself, perhaps I'd listened to too many flowers, but at least I knew where the scorpion on the balcony had come from.

Tony Miles had heard Sophie Tucker singing the "St. Louis Blues," and Harry, the elder Bach conducting the B Minor Mass.

They came around to the shop and argued over their respective performances while I wrestled with the flowers.

"Amazing," Tony exclaimed. "How does she do it? Tell me."

"The Heidelberg score," Harry ecstased. "Sublime, absolute." He looked irritably at the flowers. "Can't you keep these things quiet? They're making one hell of a row."

They were, and I had a shrewd idea why. The Arachnid was completely out of control, and by the time I'd clamped it down in a weak saline it had blown out over three hundred dollars' worth of shrubs.

"The performance at the Casino last night was nothing on the one she gave here yesterday," I told them. *The Ring of the Niebelungs* played by Stan Kenton. That Arachnid went insane. I'm sure it wanted to kill her."

Harry watched the plant convulsing its leaves in rigid spasmic movements.

"If you ask me it's in an advanced state of rut. Why should it want to kill her?"

"Her voice must have overtones that irritate its calyx. None of the other plants minded. They cooed like turtle doves when she touched them."

Tony shivered happily.

Light dazzled in the street outside.

I handed Tony the broom. "Here, lover, brace yourself on that. Miss Ciracylides is dying to meet you."

Jane came into the shop, wearing a flame yellow cocktail skirt and another of her hats.

I introduced her to Harry and Tony.

"The flowers seem very quiet this morning," she said. "What's the matter with them?"

"I'm cleaning out the tanks," I told her. "By the way, we all want to congratulate you on last night. How does it feel to be able to name your fiftieth city?"

She smiled shyly and sauntered away around the shop. As I knew she would, she stopped by the Arachnid and leveled her eyes at it.

I wanted to see what she'd say, but Harry and Tony were all around her, and soon got her up to my apartment, where they had a hilarious morning playing the fool and raiding my Scotch.

"What about coming out with us after the show tonight?" Tony asked her. "We can go dancing at the Flamingo."

"But you're both married," Jane protested. "Aren't you worried about your reputations?"

"Oh, we'll bring the girls," Harry said airily. "And Steve here can come along and hold your coat."

We played i-Go together. Jane said she'd never played the game before, but she had no difficulty picking up the rules, and when she started sweeping the board with us I knew she was cheating. Admittedly it isn't every day that you get a chance to play i-Go with a golden-skinned woman with insects for eyes, but never the less I was annoyed. Harry and Tony, of course, didn't mind.

"She's charming," Harry said, after she'd left. "Who cares? It's a stupid game anyway."

"I care," I said. "She cheats."

The next three or four days at the shop were an audio-vegetative armageddon. Jane came in every morning to look at the Arachnid, and her presence was more than the flower could bear. Unfortunately I couldn't starve the plants below their thresholds. They needed exercise and they had to have the Arachnid to lead them. But instead of running through its harmonic scales the orchid only screeched and whined. It wasn't the noise, which only a couple of dozen people complained about, but the damage being done to their vibratory chords that worried me. Those in the seventeenth century catalogues stood up well to the strain, and the moderns were immune, but the Romantics burst their calyxes by the score. By the third day after Jane's arrival I'd lost two hundred dollars' worth of Beethoven and more Mendelssohn and Schubert than I could bear to think about.

Jane seemed oblivious to the trouble she was causing me.

"What's wrong with them all?" she asked, surveying the chaos of gas cylinders and drip feeds spread across the floor.

"I don't think they like you," I told her. "At least the Arachnid doesn't. Your voice may move men to strange and wonderful visions, but it throws that orchid into acute melancholia."

"Nonsense," she said, laughing at me. "Give it to me and I'll show you how to look after it."

"Are Tony and Harry keeping you happy?" I asked her. I was annoyed that I couldn't go down to the beach with them and instead had to spend my time draining tanks and titrating up norm solutions, none of which ever worked.

"They're very amusing," she said. "We play i-Go and I sing for them. But I wish you could come out more often."

After another two weeks I had to give up. I decided to close the plants down until Jane had left Vermilion Sands.

I knew it would take me three months to rescore the stock, but I had no alternative.

The next day I received a large order for mixed coloratura herbaceous from the Santiago Garden Choir. They wanted delivery in three weeks.

"I'm sorry," Jane said, when she heard I wouldn't be able to fill the order. "You must wish that I'd never come to Vermilion Sands."

She stared thoughtfully into one of the darkened tanks.

"Couldn't I score them for you?" she suggested.

"No thanks," I said, laughing. "I've had enough of that already."

"Don't be silly, of course I could."

I shook my head.

Tony and Harry told me I was crazy.

"Her voice has a wide enough range," Tony said. "You admit it yourself."

"What have you got against her?" Harry asked. "That she cheats at i-Go?"

"It's nothing to do with that," I said. "And her voice has a wider range than you think."

We played i-Go at Jane's apartment. Jane won ten dollars from each of us.

"I am lucky," she said, very pleased with herself. "I never seem to lose." She counted up the bills and put them away carefully in her bag, her golden skin glowing.

Then Santiago sent me a repeat query.

I found Jane down among the cafés, holding off a siege of admirers.

"Have you given in yet?" she asked me, smiling at the young men.

"I don't know what you're doing to me," I said, "but anything is worth trying."

Back at the shop I raised a bank of perennials past their thresholds. Jane helped me attach the gas and fluid lines.

"We'll try these first," I said. "Frequencies 543–785. Here's the score."

Jane took off her hat and began to ascend the scale, her voice clear and pure. At first the Columbine hesitated and Jane went down again and drew them along with her. They went up a couple of octaves together and then the plants stumbled and went off at a tangent of stepped chords.

"Try K sharp," I said. I fed a little chlorous acid into the tank and the Columbine followed her up eagerly, the infra-calyxes warbling delicate variations on the treble clef.

"Perfect," I said.

It took us only four hours to fill the order.

"You're better than the Arachnid," I congratulated her. "How would you like a job? I'll fit you out with a large cool tank and all the chlorine you can breathe."

"Careful," she told me. "I may say yes. Why don't we rescore a few more of them while we're about it?"

"You're tired," I said. "Let's go and have a drink."

"Let me try the Arachnid," she suggested. "That would be more of a challenge."

Her eyes never left the flower. I wondered what they'd do if I left them together. Try to sing each other to death?

"No," I said. "Tomorrow perhaps."

We sat on the balcony together, glasses at our elbows, and talked the afternoon away.

She told me little about herself, but I gathered that her father had been a mining engineer in Peru and her mother a dancer at a Lima vu-tavern. They'd wandered from deposit to deposit, the father digging his concessions, the mother signing on at the nearest bordello to pay the rent.

"She only sang, of course," Jane added. "Until my father came." She blew bubbles into her glass. "So you think I give them what they want at the Casino. By the way, what do you see?"

"I'm afraid I'm your one failure," I said. "Nothing. Except you."

She dropped her eyes. "That sometimes happens," she said. "I'm glad this time."

A million suns pounded inside me. Until then I'd been reserving judgment on myself.

Harry and Tony were polite, if disappointed.

"I can't believe it," Harry said sadly. "I won't. How did you do it?"

"That mystical left-handed approach, of course," I told him. "All ancient seas and dark wells."

"What's she like?" Tony asked eagerly. "I mean, does she burn or just tingle?"

*   *   *

Jane sang at the Casino every night from eleven to three, but apart from that I suppose we were always together. Sometimes in the late afternoons we'd drive out along the beach to the Scented Desert and sit alone by one of the pools, watching the sun fall away behind the reefs and hills, lulling ourselves on the rose-sick air. When the wind began to blow cool across the sand we'd slip down into the water, bathe ourselves, and drive back to town, filling the streets and café terraces with jasmine and musk-rose and helianthemum.

On other evenings we'd go down to one of the quiet bars at Lagoon West, and have supper out on the flats, and Jane would tease the waiters and sing honeybirds and angelcakes to the children who came in across the sand to watch her.

I realize now that I must have achieved a certain notoriety along the beach, but I didn't mind giving the old women—and beside Jane they all seemed to be old women —something to talk about. During the Recess no one cared very much about anything, and for that reason I never questioned myself too closely over my affair with Jane Ciracylides. As I sat on the balcony with her looking out over the cool early evenings or felt her body glowing beside me in the darkness I allowed myself few anxieties.

Absurdly, the only disagreement I ever had with her was over her cheating.

I remember that I once taxed her with it.

"Do you know you've taken over five hundred dollars from me, Jane? You're still doing it. Even now!"

She laughed impishly. "Do I cheat? I'll let you win one day."

"But why do you?" I insisted.

"It's more fun to cheat," she said. "Otherwise it's so boring."

"Where will you go when you leave Vermilion Sands?" I asked her.

She looked at me in surprise. "Why do you say that? I don't think I shall ever leave."

"Don't tease me, Jane. You're a child of another world than this."

"My father came from Peru," she reminded me.

"But you didn't get your voice from him," I said.

"I wish I could have heard your mother sing. Had she a better voice than yours, Jane?"

"She thought so. My father couldn't stand either of us."

That was the evening I last saw Jane. We'd changed, and in the half an hour before she left for the Casino we sat on the balcony and I listened to her voice, like a spectral fountain, pour its luminous notes into the air. The music remained with me even after she'd gone, hanging faintly in the darkness around her chair.

I felt curiously sleepy, almost sick on the air she'd left behind, and at 11:30, when I knew she'd be appearing on stage at the Casino, I went out for a walk along the beach.

As I left the elevator I heard music coming from the shop.

At first I thought I'd left one of the audio switches on, but I knew the voice only too well.

The windows of the shop had been shuttered, so I got in through the passage which led from the garage court-yard around at the back of the apartment house.

The lights had been turned out, but a brilliant glow filled the shop, throwing a golden fire on to the tanks along the counters. Across the ceiling liquid colors danced in reflection.

The music I had heard before, but only in overture.

The Arachnid had grown to three times its size. It towered nine feet high out of the shattered lid of the control tank, leaves tumid and inflamed, its calyx as large as a bucket, raging insanely.

Arched forward into it, her head thrown back, was Jane.

I ran over to her, my eyes filling with light, and grabbed her arm, trying to pull her away from it.

"Jane!" I shouted over the noise. "Get down!"

She flung my hand away. In her eyes, fleetingly, was a look of shame.

While I was sitting on the stairs in the entrance Tony and Harry drove up.

"Where's Jane?" Harry asked. "Has anything happened to her? We were down at the Casino." They both turned toward the music. "What the hell's going on?"

Tony peered at me suspiciously. "Steve, anything wrong?"

Harry dropped the bouquet he was carrying and started toward the rear entrance.

"Harry!" I shouted after him. "Get back!"

Tony held my shoulder. "Is Jane in there?"

I caught them as they opened the door into the shop.

"Good God!" Harry yelled. "Let go of me, you fool!" He struggled to get away from me. "Steve, it's trying to kill her!"

I jammed the door shut and held them back.

I never saw Jane again. The three of us waited in my apartment. When the music died away we went down and found the shop in darkness. The Arachnid had shrunk to its normal size.

The next day it died.

Where Jane went to I don't know. Not long afterward the Recess ended, and the big government schemes came along and started up all the clocks and kept us too busy working off the lost time to worry about a few bruised petals. Harry told me that Jane had been seen on her way through Red Beach, and I heard recently that someone very like her was doing the nightclubs this side out of Pernambuco.

So if any of you around here keep a choro-florist's, and have a Khan-Arachnid orchid, look out for a golden-skinned woman with insects for eyes. Perhaps she'll play i-Go with you, and I'm sorry to have to say it; but she'll always cheat.

APRIL IN PARIS

by Ursula K. Le Guin

This is the first story I ever got paid for; the second story I ever got published; and maybe the thirtieth or fortieth story I wrote. I had been writing poetry and fiction ever since my brother Ted, tired of having an illiterate five-year-old sister around, taught me to read. At about twenty I began sending things off to publishers. Some of the poetry got printed, but I didn't get systematic about sending out the fiction till I was getting on to thirty. It kept systematically coming back.

"April in Paris" was the first "genre" piece—recognizably fantasy or science fiction—that I had written since 1942, when I wrote an Origin-of-Life-on-Earth story for Astounding, which for some inconceivable reason rejected it (I never did synch with John Campbell). At age twelve I was very pleased to get a genuine printed rejection slip, but by age thirty-two I was very pleased to get a check. "Professionalism" is no virtue; a professional is simply one who gets paid for doing what an amateur does for love. But in a money economy, the fact of being paid means your work is going to be circulated, is going to be read; it's the means to communication, which is the artist's goal. Cele Goldsmith Lalli, who bought this story in 1962, was as enterprising and perceptive an editor as the science fiction magazines have ever had, and I am grateful to her for opening the door to me.

* * *

Professor Barry Pennywither sat in a cold, shadowy garret and stared at the table in front of him, on which lay a book and a breadcrust. The bread had been his dinner, the book had been his lifework. Both were dry. Dr. Pennywither sighed, and then shivered. Though the lower-floor apartments of the old house were quite elegant, the heat was turned off on April 1st, come what may; it was now April 2nd, and sleeting. If Dr. Pennywither raised his head a little he could see from his window the two square towers of Notre Dame de Paris, vague and soaring in the dusk, almost near enough to touch: for the Island of Saint-Louis, where he lived, is like a little barge being towed downstream behind the Island of the City, where Notre Dame stands. But he did not raise his head. He was too cold.

The great towers sank into darkness. Dr. Pennywither sank into gloom. He stared with loathing at his book. It had won him a year in Paris—publish or perish, said the Dean of Faculties, and he had published, and been rewarded with a year's leave from teaching, without pay. Munson College could not afford to pay unteaching teachers. So on his scraped-up savings he had come back to Paris, to live again as a student in a garret, to read fifteenth-century manuscripts at the Library, to see the chestnuts flower along the avenues. But it hadn't worked. He was forty, too old for lonely garrets. The sleet would blight the budding chestnut flowers. And he was sick of his work. Who cared about his theory, the Pennywither Theory, concerning the mysterious disappearance of the poet François Villon in 1463? Nobody. For after all his Theory about poor Villon, the greatest juvenile delinquent of all time, was only a theory and could never be proved, not across the gulf of five hundred years. Nothing could be proved. And besides, what did it matter if Villon died on Montfaucon gallows or (as Pennywither thought) in a Lyons brothel on the way to Italy? Nobody cared. Nobody else loved Villon enough. Nobody loved Dr. Pennywither, either; not even Dr. Pennywither. Why should he? An unsocial, unmarried, underpaid pedant, sitting here alone in an unheated attic in an unrestored tenement trying to write another unreadable book. "I'm unrealistic," he said aloud with another sigh and another shiver. He got up and took the blanket off his bed, wrapped himself in it, sat down thus bundled at the table, and tried to light a Gauloise

Bleue. His lighter snapped vainly. He sighed once more, got up, fetched a can of vile-smelling French lighter fluid, sat down, rewrapped his cocoon, filled the lighter, and snapped it. The fluid had spilled around a good bit. The lighter lit, so did Dr. Pennywither, from the wrists down. "Oh hell!" he cried, blue flames leaping from his knuckles, and jumped up batting his arms wildly, shouting "Hell!" and raging against Destiny. Nothing ever went right. What was the use? It was then 8:12 on the night of April 2nd, 1961.

A man sat hunched at a table in a cold, high room. Through the window behind him the two square towers of Notre Dame loomed in the Spring dusk. In front of him on the table lay a hunk of cheese and a huge, iron-latched, handwritten book. The book was called (in Latin) *On the Primacy of the Element Fire over the Other Three Elements*. Its author stared at it with loathing. Nearby on a small iron stove a small alembic simmered. Jehan Lenoir mechanically inched his chair nearer the stove now and then, for warmth, but his thoughts were on deeper problems. "Hell!" he said finally (in Late Mediaeval French), slammed the book shut, and got up. What if his theory was wrong? What if water were the primal element? How could you prove these things? There must be some way— some method—so that one could be sure, absolutely sure, of one single fact! But each fact led into others, a monstrous tangle, and the Authorities conflicted, and anyway no one would read his book, not even the wretched pedants at the Sorbonne. They smelled heresy. What was the use? What good this life spent in poverty and alone, when he had learned nothing, merely guessed and theorized? He strode about the garret, raging, and then stood still. "All right!" he said to Destiny. "Very good! You've given me nothing, so I'll take what I want!" He went to one of the stacks of books that covered most of the floor-space, yanked out a bottom volume (scarring the leather and bruising his knuckles when the overlying folios avalanched), slapped it on the table and began to study one page of it. Then, still with a set cold look of rebellion, he got things ready: sulfur, silver, chalk. . . . Though the room was dusty and littered, his little workbench was neatly and handily arranged. He was soon ready. Then he paused. "This is ridiculous," he muttered, glancing out the window into the darkness where now one could only guess at the two square towers. A watchman passed below calling out the hour, eight o'clock of a cold clear night. It was so still he could hear the lapping of the Seine. He shrugged, frowned, took up the chalk and drew a neat pentagram on the floor near his table, then took up the book and began to read in a clear but self-conscious voice: "Haere, haere, audi me . . ." It was a long spell, and mostly nonsense. His voice sank. He stood bored and embarrassed. He hurried through the last words, shut the book, and then fell backwards against the door, gap-mouthed, staring at the enormous, shapeless figure that stood within the pentagram, lit only by the blue flicker of its waving, fiery claws.

Barry Pennywither finally got control of himself and put out the fire by burying his hands in the folds of the blanket wrapped around him. Unburned but upset, he sat down again. He looked at his book. Then he stared at it. It was no longer thin and gray and titled *The Last Years of Villon: an Investigation of Possibilities*. It was thick and brown and titled *Incantatoria Magna*. On his table? A priceless manuscript dating from 1407 of which the only extant undamaged copy was in the Ambrosian Library in Milan? He lookly slowly around. His mouth dropped slowly open. He observed a stove, a chemist's workbench, two or three dozen heaps of unbelievable leatherbound books, the window, the door. His window, his door. But crouching against his door was a little creature, black and shapeless, from which came a dry rattling sound.

Barry Pennywither was not a very brave man, but he was rational. He thought he had lost his mind, and so he said quite steadily, "Are you the Devil?"

The creature shuddered and rattled.

Experimentally, with a glance at invisible Notre Dame, the professor made the sign of the Cross.

At this the creature twitched; not a flinch, a twitch. Then it said something, feebly, but in perfectly good English—no, in perfectly good French—no, in rather odd French: "Mais vous estes de Dieu," it said.

Barry got up and peered at it. "Who are you?" he demanded, and it lifted up a quite human face and answered meekly, "Jehan Lenoir."

"What are you doing in my room?"

There was a pause. Lenoir got up from his knees and stood straight, all five foot two of him. "This is *my* room," he said at last, though very politely.

Barry looked around at the books and alembics. There was another pause. "Then how did I get here?"

"I brought you."

"Are you a doctor?"

Lenoir nodded, with pride. His whole air had changed. "Yes, I'm a doctor," he said. "Yes, I brought you here. If Nature will yield me no knowledge, then I can conquer Nature herself, I can work a miracle! To the Devil with science, then. I was a scientist—" he glared at Barry. "No longer! They call me a fool, a heretic, well by God I'm worse! I'm a sorcerer, a black magician, Jehan the Black! Magic works, does it? Then science is a waste of time. Ha!" he said, but he did not really look triumphant. "I wish it hadn't worked," he said more quietly, pacing up and down between folios.

"So do I," said the guest.

"Who are you?" Lenoir looked up challengingly at Barry, though there was nearly a foot difference in their heights.

"Barry A. Pennywither, I'm a professor of French at Munson College, Indiana, on leave in Paris to pursue my studies of Late Mediaeval Fr—" He stopped. He had just realized what kind of accent Lenoir had. "What year is this? What century? Please, Dr. Lenoir—" The Frenchman looked confused. The meanings of words change, as well as their pronunciations. "Who rules this country?" Barry shouted.

Lenoir gave a shrug, a French shrug (some things never change), "Louis is king," he said. "Louis the Eleventh. The dirty old spider."

They stood staring at each other like wooden Indians for some time. Lenoir spoke first. "Then you're a man?"

"Yes. Look, Lenoir, I think you—your spell—you must have muffed it a bit."

"Evidently," said the alchemist. "Are you French?"

"No."

"Are you English?" Lenoir glared. "Are you a filthy Goddam?"

"No. No. I'm from America. I'm from the—from your

future. From the twentieth century A.D." Barry blushed. It sounded silly, and he was a modest man. But he knew this was no illusion. The room he stood in, his room, was new. Not five centuries old. Unswept, but new. And the copy of Albertus Magnus by his knee was new, bound in soft supple calfskin, the gold lettering gleaming. And there stood Lenoir in his black gown, not in costume, at home. . . .

"Please sit down, sir," Lenoir was saying. And he added, with the fine though absent courtesy of the poor scholar, "Are you tired from the journey? I have bread and cheese, if you'll honor me by sharing it."

They sat at the table munching bread and cheese. At first Lenoir tried to explain why he had tried black magic. "I was fed up," he said. "Fed up! I've slaved in solitude since I was twenty, for what? For knowledge. To learn some of Nature's secrets. They are not to be learned." He drove his knife half an inch into the table, and Barry jumped. Lenoir was a thin little fellow, but evidently a passionate one. It was a fine face, though pale and lean: intelligent, alert, vivid. Barry was reminded of the face of a famous atomic physicist, seen in newspaper pictures up until 1953. Somehow this likeness prompted him to say, "Some are, Lenoir; we've learned a good bit, here and there. . . ."

"What?" said the alchemist, skeptical but curious.

"Well, I'm no scientist—"

"Can you make gold?" He grinned as he asked.

"No, I don't think so, but they do make diamonds."

"How?"

"Carbon—coal, you know—under great heat and pressure, I believe. Coal and diamond are both carbon, you know, the same element."

"Element?"

"Now as I say, I'm no—"

"Which is the primal element?" Lenoir shouted, his eyes fiery, the knife poised in his hand.

"There are about a hundred elements," Barry said coldly, hiding his alarm.

Two hours later, having squeezed out of Barry every dribble of the remnants of his college chemistry course, Lenoir rushed out into the night and reappeared shortly with a bottle. "O my master," he cried, "to think I offered you only bread and cheese!" It was a pleasant burgundy, vintage 1477, a good year. After they had drunk a glass together Lenoir said, "If somehow I could repay you . . ."

"You can. Do you know the name of the poet François Villon?"

"Yes," Lenoir said with some surprise, "but he wrote only French trash, you know, not in Latin."

"Do you know how or when he died?"

"Oh, yes; hanged at Montfaucon here in '64 or '65, with a crew of no-goods like himself. Why?"

Two hours later the bottle was dry, their throats were dry, and the watchman had called three o'clock of a cold clear morning. "Jehan, I'm worn out," Barry said, "you'd better send me back." The alchemist was too polite, too grateful, and perhaps also too tired to argue. Barry stood stiffly inside the pentagram, a tall bony figure muffled in a brown blanket, smoking a Gauloise Bleue. "Adieu," Lenoir said sadly. "Au revoir," Barry replied. Lenoir began to read the spell backwards. The candle flickered, his voice softened. "Me audi, haere, haere," he read, sighed, and looked up. The pentagram was empty. The candle flickered. "But I learned so little!" Lenoir cried out to the empty room. Then he beat the open book with his fists and said, "And a friend like that—a real friend—" He smoked one of the cigarettes Barry had left him—he had taken to tobacco at once. He slept, sitting at his table, for a couple of hours. When he woke he brooded a while, relit his candle, smoked the other cigarette, then opened the *Incantatoria* and began to read aloud: "Haere, haere . . ."

"Oh, thank God," Barry said, stepping quickly out of the pentagram and grasping Lenoir's hand. "Listen, I got back there—this room, this same room, Jehan! but old, horribly old, and empty, you weren't there—I thought, my God, what have I done? I'd sell my soul to get back there, to him—What can I do with what I've learned? Who'll believe it? How can I prove it? And who the devil could I tell it to anyhow? Who cares? I couldn't sleep, I sat and cried for an hour—"

"Will you stay?"

"Yes. Look, I brought these—in case you did invoke me." Sheepishly he exhibited eight packs of Gauloises, several books, and a gold watch. "It might fetch a price," he explained. "I knew paper francs wouldn't do much good."

At sight of the printed books Lenoir's eyes gleamed with curiosity, but he stood still. "My friend," he said, "you said you'd sell your soul . . . you know . . . so would I. Yet we haven't. How—after all—how did this happen? That we're both men. No devils. No pacts in blood. Two men who've lived in this room . . ."

"I don't know," said Barry. "We'll think that out later. Can I stay with you, Jehan?"

"Consider this your home," Lenoir said with a gracious gesture around the room, the stacks of books, the alembics, the candle growing pale. Outside the window, gray on gray, rose up the two great towers of Notre Dame. It was the dawn of April 3rd.

After breakfast (bread crusts and cheese rinds) they went out and climbed the south tower. The cathedral looked the same as always, though cleaner than in 1961, but the view was rather a shock to Barry. He looked down upon a little town. Two small islands covered with houses; on the right bank more houses crowded inside a fortified wall; on the left bank a few streets twisting around the college; and that was all. Pigeons chortled on the sun-warmed stone between gargoyles. Lenoir, who had seen the view before, was carving the date (in Roman numerals) on a parapet. "Let's celebrate," he said. "Let's go out into the country. I haven't been out of the city for two years. Let's go clear over there—" he pointed to a misty green hill on which a few huts and a windmill were just visible—"to Montmartre, eh? There are some good bars there, I'm told."

Their life soon settled into an easy routine. At first Barry was a little nervous in the crowded streets, but, in a spare black gown of Lenoir's, he was not noticed as outlandish except for his height. He was probably the tallest man in fifteenth-century France. Living standards were low and lice were unavoidable, but Barry had never valued comfort much; the only thing he really missed was coffee at breakfast. When they had bought a bed and a razor—Barry had forgotten his—and introduced him to the landlord as M. Barrie, a cousin of Lenoir's from the Auvergne, their housekeeping arrangements were complete. Barry's watch brought a tremendous price, four gold pieces, enough to live on for a year. They sold it as a wondrous new timepiece from Illyria, and the buyer, a Court cham-

berlain looking for a nice present to give the king, looked
at the inscription—Hamilton Bros., New Haven, 1881—
and nodded sagely. Unfortunately he was shut up in one
of King Louis's cages for naughty courtiers at Tours before he had presented his gift, and the watch may still be
there behind some brick in the ruins of Plessis; but this
did not affect the two scholars. Mornings they wandered
about sightseeing the Bastille and the churches, or visiting
various minor poets in whom Barry was interested; after
lunch they discussed electricity, the atomic theory, physi-
ology, and other matters in which Lenoir was interested,
and performed minor chemical and anatomical experiments, usually unsuccessfully; after supper they merely
talked. Endless, easy talks that ranged over the centuries
but always ended here, in the shadowy room with its window open to the Spring night, in their friendship. After
two weeks they might have known each other all their
lives. They were perfectly happy. They knew they would
do nothing with what they had learned from each other.
In 1961 how could Barry ever prove his knowledge of old
Paris, in 1482 how could Lenoir ever prove the validity of
the scientific method? It did not bother them. They had
never really expected to be listened to. They had merely
wanted to learn.

So they were happy for the first time in their lives; so
happy, in fact, that certain desires always before subjugated to the desire for knowledge, began to awaken. "I
don't suppose," Barry said one night across the table, "that
you ever thought much about marrying?"

"Well, no," his friend answered, doubtfully. "That is,
I'm in minor orders . . . and it seemed irrelevant. . . ."

"And expensive. Besides, in my time, no self-respecting
woman would want to share my kind of life. American
women are so damned poised and efficient and glamorous,
terrifying creatures. . . ."

"And women here are little and dark, like beetles, with
bad teeth," Lenoir said morosely.

They said no more about women that night. But the next
night they did; and the next; and on the next, celebrating
the successful dissection of the main nervous system of a
pregnant frog, they drank two bottles of Montrachet '74
and got soused. "Let's invoke a woman, Jehan," Barry said
in a lascivious bass, grinning like a gargoyle.

"What if I raised a devil this time?"

"Is there really much difference?"

They laughed wildly, and drew a pentagram. "Haere, haere," Lenoir began; when he got the hiccups, Barry took over. He read the last words. There was a rush of cold, marshy-smelling air, and in the pentagram stood a wild-eyed being with long black hair, stark naked, screaming.

"Woman, by God," said Barry.

"Is it?"

It was. "Here, take my cloak," Barry said, for the poor thing now stood gawping and shivering. He put the cloak over her shoulders. Mechanically she pulled it round her, muttering, "Gratias ago, domine."

"Latin!" Lenoir shouted. "A woman speaking Latin?" It took him longer to get over that shock than it did Bota to get over hers. She was, it seemed, a slave in the house-hold of the Sub-Prefect of North Gaul, who lived on the smaller island of the muddy island town called Lutetia. She spoke Latin with a thick Celtic brogue, and did not even know who was emperor in Rome in her day. A real bar-barian, Lenoir said with scorn. So she was, an ignorant, taciturn, humble barbarian with tangled hair, white skin, and clear gray eyes. She had been waked from a sound sleep. When they convinced her that she was not dreaming, she evidently assumed that this was some prank of her foreign and all-powerful master the Sub-Prefect, and ac-cepted the situation without further question. "Am I to serve you, my masters?" she inquired timidly but without sullenness, looking from one to the other.

"Not me," Lenoir growled, and added in French to Barry, "Go on; I'll sleep in the store-room." He departed.

Bota looked up at Barry. No Gauls, and few Romans, were so magnificently tall; no Gauls and no Romans ever spoke so kindly. "Your lamp" (it was a candle, but she had never seen a candle) "is nearly burnt out," she said. "Shall I blow it out?"

For an additional two sols a year the landlord let them use the store-room as a second bedroom, and Lenoir now slept alone again in the main room of the garret. He ob-served his friend's idyll with a brooding, unjealous interest. The professor and the slave-girl loved each other with de-light and tenderness. Their pleasure overlapped Lenoir in waves of protective joy. Bota had led a brutal life, treated always as a woman but never as a human. In one short week she bloomed, she came alive, evincing beneath her gentle passiveness a cheerful, clever nature. "You're turning out a regular Parisienne," he heard Barry accuse her one night (the attic walls were thin). She replied, "If you knew what it is for me not to be always defending myself, always afraid, always alone . . ."

Lenoir sat up on his cot and brooded. About midnight, when all was quiet, he rose and noiselessly prepared the pinches of sulfur and silver, drew the pentagram, opened the book. Very softly he read the spell. His face was apprehensive.

In the pentagram appeared a small white dog. It cowered and hung its tail, then came shyly forward, sniffed Lenoir's hand, looked up at him with liquid eyes and gave a modest, pleading whine. A lost puppy. . . . Lenoir stroked it. It licked his hands and jumped all over him, wild with relief. On its white leather collar was a silver plaque engraved, "Jolie. Dupont, 36 rue de Seine, Paris VIe."

Jolie went to sleep, after gnawing a crust, curled up under Lenoir's chair. And the alchemist opened the book again and read, still softly, but this time without self-consciousness, without fear, knowing what would happen.

Emerging from his store-room-bedroom-honeymoon in the morning, Barry stopped short in the doorway. Lenoir was sitting up in bed, petting a white puppy, and deep in conversation with the person sitting on the foot of the bed, a tall red-haired woman dressed in silver. The puppy barked. Lenoir said, "Good morning!" The woman smiled wondrously.

"Jumping Jesus," Barry muttered (in English). Then he said, "Good morning. When are you from?" The effect was Rita Hayworth, sublimated—Hayworth plus the Mona Lisa, perhaps?

"From Altair, about seven thousand years from now," she said, smiling still more wondrously. Her French accent was worse than that of a football-scholarship freshman. "I'm an archaeologist. I was excavating the ruins of Paris III. I'm sorry I speak the language so badly; of course we know it only from inscriptions."

"From Altair? The star? But you're human—I think—"

"Our planet was colonized from Earth about four thousand years ago—that is, three thousand years from now." She laughed, most wondrously, and glanced at Lenoir. "Jehan explained it all to me, but I still get confused."

"It was a dangerous thing to try it again, Jehan!" Barry accused him. "We've been awfully lucky, you know."

"No," said the Frenchman. "Not lucky."

"But after all it's black magic you're playing with— Listen—I don't know your name, madame."

"Kislk," she said.

"Listen, Kislk," Barry said without even a stumble, "your science must be fantastically advanced—is there any magic? Does it exist? Can the laws of Nature really be broken, as we seem to be doing?"

"I've never seen nor heard of an authenticated case of magic."

"Then what goes on?" Barry roared. "Why does that stupid old spell work for Jehan, for us, that one spell, and here, nowhere else, for nobody else, in five—no, eight—no, fifteen thousand years of recorded history? Why? Why? And where did that damn puppy come from?"

"The puppy was lost," Lenoir said, his dark face grave. "Somewhere near this house, on the Ile Saint-Louis."

"And I was sorting potsherds," Kislk said, also gravely, "in a house-site, Island 2, Pit 4, Section D. A lovely Spring day, and I hated it. Loathed it. The day, the work, the people around me." Again she looked at the gaunt little alchemist, a long, quiet look. "I tried to explain it to Jehan last night. We have improved the race, you see. We're all very tall, healthy, and beautiful. No fillings in our teeth. All skulls from Early America have fillings in the teeth. . . . Some of us are brown, some white, some gold-skinned. But all beautiful, and healthy, and well-adjusted, and aggressive, and successful. Our professions and degree of success are preplanned for us in the State Pre-School Homes. But there's an occasional genetic flaw. Me, for instance. I was trained as an archaeologist because the Teachers saw that I really didn't like people, live people. People bored me. All like me on the outside, all alien to me on the inside. When everything's alike, which place is home? . . . But now I've seen an unhygienic room with insufficient heating. Now I've seen a cathedral not in ruins. Now I've met a living man who's shorter than me, with bad teeth and a short temper. Now I'm home, I'm where I can be myself, I'm no longer alone!"

"Alone," Lenoir said gently to Barry. "Loneliness, eh? Loneliness is the spell, loneliness is stronger. . . . Really it doesn't seem unnatural."

Bota was peering round the doorway, her face flushed between the black tangles of her hair. She smiled shyly and said a polite Latin good-morning to the newcomer.

"Kislk doesn't know Latin," Lenoir said with immense satisfaction. "We must teach Bota some French. French is the language of love, anyway, eh? Come along, let's go out and buy some bread. I'm hungry."

Kislk hid her silver tunic under the useful and anonymous cloak, while Lenoir pulled on his moth-eaten black gown. Bota combed her hair, while Barry thoughtfully scratched a louse-bite on his neck. Then they set forth to get breakfast. The alchemist and the interstellar archaeologist went first, speaking French; the Gaulish slave and the professor from Indiana followed, speaking Latin, and holding hands. The narrow streets were crowded, bright with sunshine. Above them Notre Dame reared its two square towers against the sky. Beside them the Seine rippled softly. It was April in Paris, and on the banks of the river the chestnuts were in bloom.